REVENGE?
REDEMPTION?
OR JUST FOR CONVENIENCE?

by Randy Harris

DORRANCE
PUBLISHING CO
EST. 1920
PITTSBURGH, PENNSYLVANIA 15238

Dorrance Publishing Co
585 Alpha Drive
Pittsburgh, PA 15238
Visit our website at *www.dorrancebookstore.com*

ISBN: 978-1-4809-2403-1
eISBN: 978-1-4809-2932-6

Chapter One

Kayla Avery-Battle was awakened at 8:30 A.M. by the alarm she had set the night before in case she wanted to work out at the fitness center. Right before she prepared her second nightcap she bribed herself by saying she could have that last martini if she worked it off in the morning. As she debated whether she was in the mood to honor that promise, she hit the button that opened the electric blinds. There was so much that could be said for modern convenience especially if you could afford to pamper yourself. She could ease herself into the rigors of that day, whatever they might be, without leaving the comfort of her bed. The room was immediately filled with brilliant sunlight. She stretched and enjoyed the luxurious feel of the thousand thread count sheets.

Kayla spent a moment going over her options for the day, and while there were a couple of feasible possibilities, nothing really appealed to her. She knew she should work out because after having two kids, her body wasn't going to keep the voluptuous shape she had when she was twenty, and the figure that men drooled after, without a lot of hard work. On the other hand, she had already worked out four days this week and just one day off wasn't going to have too much of a negative effect.

She reached over and grabbed the computerized remote that used to be Tank's pride and joy. This device controlled not only the TV and the lights but also music in every room. She remembered with a smile how Tank had screamed bloody murder when she had the system installed because it cost over twenty thousand dollars, and after it was installed, he used it more than her.

She scrolled down and selected Kirk Franklin's *Revolution* CD because nobody could integrate inspirational messages with alluring melodies overlaying on a foundation of hypnotic disco rhythms like that little maestro. His music never failed to get her going. Then for a change of pace she selected Lil Wayne's *Tha Carter II* and her latest acquisition, Jay-Z's *American Gangster*. That should help put a little kick in her morning. She programmed the music to be heard in the kitchen, bathroom, the master bedroom, and the bedroom that doubled as her walk-in closet.

As the thumping, throbbing, rumbling bass of *Revolution* started resonating through the bedroom, she again congratulated herself on choosing those Bose speakers because the way they gave the bass-line depth, intensity, and a sense of robustness without dominating the other melodies was almost amazing. It made you feel the music deep down in your soul until the music seemed to be a part of you. As she headed to the bathroom, she cut a little dance step and she started singing along with the music. Turning on the shower, she decided she wanted a hot, steamy shower because the heat would ease some of the stiffness from her muscles after yesterday's workout.

After her shower, she wrapped a towel around her hair because her micro-braids had gotten wet. She preferred the hairstyle she had before this one, but though she liked the look of her weave, it required a lot more maintenance to keep it looking with the degree of perfection that she required. Regardless of the style, having hair that wasn't immaculate and perfectly coiffed wasn't an option she would accept. She had no problem spending the money for the beautician to keep her hooked up, but the two trips a week back to the hood where the beauty shop was located was inconvenient. Maybe when she got tired of the braids and went back to a weave, she would pay extra to have the stylist come to her. It wasn't like she couldn't afford it. Maybe if the stylist was real cool she would even allow her to spend the night in one of the spare bedrooms in the mansion opposed to driving back to Oakland.

As she sashayed into the kitchen, the delicious aroma of the brewing Blue Mountain coffee awakened her senses and she realized that she was hungry. Whoever invented an automatic timer for a coffee machine sure knew what he was doing. This way her coffee could be ready before she realized that she even wanted it. Maybe a big breakfast was called for today and not just her usual bran muffin. Opening the refrigerator, she spied a couple of lobster tails from dinner two days ago. She thought, "That lobster should make a delicious omelet. I'll add some green onions and a little cheese and it should be real tasty."

She poured herself a cup of coffee and opened the blinds and gazed upon one of the most magnificent views in the state of California. This was an awesome way to start your day. It gave you a chance to compose your thoughts, appreciate God's majesty, and be grateful for what her life had become. This view of the Bay was simply breathtaking and the main reason she insisted upon this house in Sausalito despite the 2.3 million dollar price tag. She remembered how Tank had balked at the seemingly exorbitant price and it had taken much coaxing, pouting, pampering, and several nights of mind-blowing sex for her to get her way. But she had held firm and now she had this incredible five-bedroom, four-and-a-half bathroom gem as her reward.

She had met Tank when she was only twenty-three years old and had a promising modeling and singing career which was cut short by the two children she had for Tank. She, now at twenty-nine, could look at herself in the mirror and admit that she may not have been as gorgeous as she was when she first met Tank, but she was still pretty damn good looking and most men still went out of their way for a chance to spend some time with her. She was tall, 6'1", with long, shapely legs that ended at a firm, round ass that wasn't the prototype they desired in modeling but drove Black men crazy. Her narrow waist was still firm and reflected the miles of jogging and countless crunches she did every week. While her breasts weren't as pert as they once were, they were still years away from sagging. She had large, round eyes that reminded you of Diana Ross in *Mahogany*. Her lips were full and shapely and always seemed to be poised for a kiss. The many hours of practicing that art in the mirror until it seemed natural still paid off.

When she first met Tank, he was so enraptured with her that there was nothing he wouldn't have done to get her into bed. She had been wise enough to hold out so long, that he grew accustomed to giving her whatever she wanted. He had plenty of money and she had no problem spending it.

Terrell "Tank" Battle was the third pick of the first round of the National Football League's draft by the San Francisco 49ers. A 6'4", 265-pound defensive end, he was one of the most ferocious players in the league. He was signed to a four-year 16 million dollar contract with a 5 million dollar signing bonus out of Southern University.

He was from a small parish in Louisiana and had never been off the bayou until he left for college. He was a large man from a small town and not prepared for the bright lights of the big city when he arrived in San Francisco. Tank had never met anyone like Kayla, and he was not prepared for her beauty, style, and polish. His mission in life became twofold: to become the best defensive player in the NFL and to do whatever it took to make Kayla his. So it was a simple solution to him; if Kayla wanted a diamond necklace—he got her a diamond necklace.

Finally, after weeks of courting, he and Kayla took their relationship to the next level and a few weeks thereafter she moved in with him. Of course, his townhouse was insufficient for their purposes and he brought her the first house, followed shortly thereafter by the vacation house at Lake Tahoe and later the mansion in Sausalito. Tank was playing some of the best football in the league, and Kayla went a long way to filling out the image in his mind of what a success was. The only drawback was she refused to marry him, which made him question whether she loved him or was devoted to him.

These doubts were appeased when she gave birth to their first child, Terrell Jr. Tank felt on top of the world even though Kayla still wouldn't marry him and do the honorable thing for his son. As Tank travelled around the country with the 49ers and met more people in and out of football, he became more worldly and sophisticated and he became more aware of Kayla's flaws. He wasn't quite as impressed with her. Sometimes she seemed very selfish and self-absorbed and wasn't as high-class as he previously thought. They started to drift apart to the point where, when his daughter was born two years later, he doubted whether she was even his.

Things grew worse between Tank and Kayla, probably because he no longer felt the need to pamper her and give her everything she wanted and Kayla never had to work at pleasing Tank, other than in bed, and she sure wasn't going to start now. If either one of them had been working on the relationship, even if for no other reason than the sake of the kids, the relationship might have survived, but it wasn't to be.

Tank met a beautiful lady of Asian descent, fell in love, and moved out of the house. This was followed by a nasty custody battle that ended with Kayla being awarded not only custody of the kids and the Sausalito home but also 30 percent of Tank's net worth, which equaled somewhere in the 12 to 14 million dollar range when you calculated Tank's salary, investments, and endorsements.

Tank was enraged at what he felt was the unfairness of this settlement because he was positive that he wasn't the only one who had strayed outside the relationship. He was right. Kayla had enjoyed several romantic liaisons while Tank was on the road, but she was smart enough to remain discreet and not allow any of her lovers to get attached.

The only good thing for Tank to come out of the settlement was that he could see the kids whenever he wanted, which was the case this week. He had picked up the kids and taken them to Disney World in Orlando, Florida. He got an extra bonus because Kayla was enraged that he had also taken his current girlfriend and she didn't want her around the kids but she no longer had any control of whatever he did.

So while the kids were back East having a great time at Sea World or Magic Kingdom or someplace like that, Kayla was sitting in her kitchen enjoying her coffee and the view, though a part of her missed her kids. Kayla knew that if the day continued to progress as it started, she could get very bored if not depressed. She felt the need to do something different and exciting.

Maybe a drive down to LA for some shopping and clubbing would be just what the doctor ordered. She wasn't in the mood to go alone so she decided to call her friend Keisha from her hanging and banging days back in Oakland. Though Kayla had moved up and out from those days, Keisha was still in Oakland living that same old life she left behind. Sometimes Keisha's frivolous ways annoyed Kayla, but when Kayla wanted to just cut loose and party, Keisha had the perfect personality.

Keisha answered her phone on the third or fourth ring. "Hello"

"Hey, girl, what you up to?"

"Oh hey, Kayla, I'm not up to too much. I might go get my hair done? Why? What are you up to? You heading up this way?"

"No, but I had a great idea. Tank has the kids for the rest of the week maybe longer, why don't we shoot down the coast and hit Rodeo Drive and just hang for a couple of days?"

"Kay, my ends aren't talking paper like that. You were the one who had the football player, sugar daddy, remember?"

"Girl, you know I got you. The whole trip is on me."

"Kay, I'm not trying to spend your money like that."

"Look, I need a break and I don't want to go alone. Since you're my road dog, my first thought was to call you to go with me. Come on girl, you know I can afford it. Plus, we haven't celebrated my winning my court case yet."

"True that, but what about my kids?"

"See if your mother will watch them for you. Tell her if she does we'll bring her back something real nice from LA. Tell her we'll bring her something from Dolce and Gabbana or a trinket from Tiffany's."

"Okay, let me call her and see what she says. I'll call you right back."

While Kayla waited to hear back from Keisha, she finished cooking her breakfast, ate, and went to her closet to select several outfits to take with her to Los Angeles. She had some new red sling-backs from Ferragamo's that were sexy whether she wore them dressy or causal. She also had five or six new pairs of shoes from Prada that she hadn't gotten a chance to wear yet. She figured she should wear a couple of them on this trip because she knew she would be buying more shoes on this trip as she didn't want too many new, unopened shoes in her closet. Someone might see it and think that she was too carefree with her money. Just as she was picking outfits to go with her shoes, Keisha called her back.

"Okay. Mom said she would keep the kids but we better be back in no more than three days because she has a doctor appointment and she doesn't want to take the kids with her."

"Okay, we're good then?"

"Yeah, I just got one more thing I have to do."

"What's that?"

"I have a date with Justice tonight, so I have to call him and let him know we're going out of town."

"Who's Justice?"

"You remember that real cute brother with the dreads that rolled up on us when we were eating at the *Wharf*?"

Kayla was a little surprised that Keisha was dealing with him. The brother was quite attractive in a rugged, streetwise kind of way while Keisha wasn't exactly ugly but she was plain and ordinary at best. And she was more than a little overweight though she wasn't exactly obese. In fact, when the guy approached their table she thought he was trying to rap to her but he was too *ghetto* for her taste. She would have to be having a serious dry spell before she would consider giving him some. Though there was something sexy about his eyes because they were kind of intense and maybe deadly. She was long out of that *bad boy* phase. She didn't need or want the type of drama they tended to bring.

"Yeah, I remember him. I didn't know you two were kicking it?"

"Yeah. He's got a real smooth style and he can really put it down in bed, Girl."

"I guess he's a keeper then?"

"I ain't committed to anything yet, but we'll see how things go. How are we getting to LA? Are we flying?"

"We could, but I'm in the mood for a nice leisurely drive down U.S. 1."

"Girl, you know I'm not a fan of the Pacific Coast Highway."

The Pacific Coast Highway was a 650-mile marvel of the ingenuity of man combined with the wonders of nature. It runs north and south along the coast of California, and it offers some of the world's most spectacular views of the sun setting against the Pacific Ocean. It isn't dangerous per se, but there are areas where drivers should respect the potential perils of hairpin turns and cliffs bordering the beaches along the coastline.

"Aw come on, Keis, the views are great. Plus, I haven't really broken in the new Benz yet. I need to put it on the road where I can really open the motor up."

"I guess it will be all right if you don't speed too much. I got to be honest, I'm a little scared of those curves and some of those cliffs don't even have guardrails."

"Don't worry, I'll take it easy."

"I guess it should be all right then. It will be cool to help you break in the Mercedes. What possessed you to buy a fire-engine red luxury car?"

"I loved how bright and pretty it is. I had to have it custom made and that wasn't cheap. An added advantage is: people can see me coming long before I get there. Plus, red and gold are the 49ers colors and indirectly I have to thank them for my financial security."

"You mean you have Tank to thank, don't you?"

"Who gave Tank the money and Tank would have given me just enough to survive if it was up to him. You know that fool even tried to get him some when he came and picked up the kids. I guess he thought having to give me all those millions entitled him to some extra loving."

"So did you give him some?"

"I got ready to because I thought it might make him less surly and mean. Plus, I haven't got my swerve on in a minute and a girl can get real stressed, you know."

"So, why didn't you rock his world?"

"Because the kids were up and all over the place. They're getting big now and you can't just tell them that Mommy and Daddy have business to discuss. TJ would have been all up in our business. But don't worry; I'll get my groove on soon enough."

"I hear that, so what time are you picking me up?"

"I don't see the sense in picking you up. Since it's on the way, why don't you drive over here and leave your car in my garage. That way you don't have to worry about it. We can even do lunch at Spinnaker's before we hit the road."

"I don't want to leave too late because I sure don't want to drive on the Highway after it gets too dark."

"Don't worry; I know how you are scared of U.S. 1. If it gets dark because we started late, we can pull into a hotel after we get down the highway a bit. "

"Okay, the kids are almost ready. I'll drop them off and see you in an hour."

That hour turned out to be a little more than three hours and by the time they finished a delicious seafood lunch at Spinnaker's complete with a couple of glasses of Chardonnay, it was starting to approach early evening. Kayla wasn't worried about it though because she was on a mini-vacation and she wasn't going to rush or be pushed for time. She knew they could always get an extra couple of days out of Keisha's mom by simply buying her something a little extra special and slipping her a couple of dollars for her trouble. So, she was gonna kick back, relax and really enjoy the next couple of days.

She put the 'pedal to the medal' and could feel the SL 550 eat up the miles. Keisha seemed a little up-tight but she ignored her because she knew Keisha would relax when she got used to the car's speed and power. Kayla was delighted because the handling of the car at high speeds was extraordinary. Kayla thought "this car is really worth every penny I spent on it." Keisha surprised her by taking her cell phone and discreetly making a call.

"Who are you calling?" Kayla asked.

"Justice. He wanted to know when we left."

"He's clocking you like that? I thought y'all had just started dealing?"

"He's not clocking me. I guess he wants to know when we left so he would know when we should get there safely. I guess he's a little worried about me. I think it's kind of sweet."

"I hope you're not going to keep checking in over the next couple of days."

"Now girl, you know me better than that. I'll hit him back when we get there and after that, I'll only take calls from my Mom or the kids. I ain't going to LA, the land of fine, rich brothers and having somebody back home keeping tabs on what I'm doing. We're both free and single for the next couple of days and I'm sure gonna enjoy it."

Kayla said, "I hear that" as they slapped each other five.

Keisha reached over and turned up the volume on the CD player as the sounds of Kanye West's latest CD coursed through the car. She reached in her bag and pulled out a couple of blunts and lit one up. After inhaling deeply a couple of times, she offered the joint to Kayla "You want some of this?"

"I really shouldn't because I have to concentrate on my driving but we're on vacation and a puff or two won't hurt." Kayla said as she took the joint and took a couple of drags. Then she said, "This is really good stuff. Where did you get it?"

"Justice gave it to me. He said it was his contribution to our little getaway. It's primo stuff, right? A couple of puffs and I'm mellow as hell. Put on that Best of War CD. It's great music for driving and a little old school will be a nice change of pace."

"You put it on. You're the navigator and DJ. I'm the one doing the driving."

Keisha put on the CD and sat back with her head against the headrest, grooving to the music and enjoying the feel of the wind on her face. Kayla said, "Check this out. This CL 550 comes with vibrating seats to help ease your muscles on long trip. Let me know if you like it."

"Wow, Kayla this is the bomb. I love the way this feels. This car is unbelievable. You should get your best friend one."

"You must really want Tank to blow a gasket. Let just chill out for now and enjoy the next couple of days and see what the future holds." Kayla relaxed like she wanted Keisha to do and they let the car burn up the miles.

Keisha must have dozed off because she was shaken awake when the car abruptly jerked around a curve. At first she was disoriented and not sure of where she was. Some time must have passed because it was completely dark outside. As they went around another curve the car was filled by the blinding, white lights of a massive truck behind them with its bright lights on.

Keisha looked at Kayla and saw the look of intense concentration on her face. In the strange, bright light from the truck which backlit Kayla's face, it gave Kayla a ghoulish and gnarled appearance. Still not convinced that she was awake and not asleep and dreaming, Keisha wiped her face as she brushed away the cobwebs and the aftereffects of the marijuana. She glanced at the speedometer and was shocked to see that Kayla was going over eighty and the truck was still keeping pace behind them.

Realizing this was not a dream, a nightmare maybe but certainly not a dream, Keisha had to ask, "Kayla, what the hell is going on?"

"I don't really know. This idiot got on my bumper about three miles back and he's been pushing me ever since."

"Did you cut him off or do something to piss him off?"

"No, I haven't had that many people to pass. The highway has been mostly empty and I sure haven't passed any trucks. I don't know what his problem is."

"Maybe he wants to pass you. Slow down and let's see what he does." Kayla gently decelerated until she was going a little less than forty miles an hour. Unfortunately, the truck also slowed down and kept the same amount of distance between him and the Benz. Keisha sucked her teeth and said, "This shit is getting ridiculous."

"Tell me about it."

"How long has this been going on?"

"Well, he started with the lights maybe five or six miles back but he picked us up about a half hour ago, right around the time we passed Santa Cruz, around Route 17. "

"Did you see the driver?"

"No, I don't remember passing the truck even though there was a black truck pulled over on the side of the road. I really didn't pay it any attention until I noticed it keeping pace behind us."

"Maybe it's some rednecks from down this way who decided to give a couple of sisters in the fancy car a hard time."

"Well, if this is their idea of a joke, it stopped being funny about five miles back. Keisha, see that button right there? It controls the rear-view camera. Hit it and see if we can pick up a license plate or at least what kind of truck that is."

"Your car has a rear-view camera? What is this, James Bond's car or something?"

"No, it was designed to help you with your parking. Look, will you hit the button and stop playing. I'm starting to get a little stressed by all that's going on."

Keisha activated the camera and spent a moment studying the screen. After a few minutes, she said, "I can't see the license plate because of the headlights, but I think the truck is a Toyota Tundra. That's strange. I think one of Justice's partners drives a Tundra."

"Don't tell me one of your stupid ass boyfriends is pulling this stunt?"

"I'm not even sure he drives a Tundra or if this truck is even a Tundra. Kayla, you're bugging. That's jumping to a hell of a lot of conclusions. Why don't you pull over at the next turn off and let us get to the bottom of this?"

"Are you crazy? What if this isn't your boyfriend or one of his stupid ass friends? I'm not pulling over out here in the middle of nowhere, with no way to defend myself. That's how a lot of people get missing. You got his cell phone number, right? Call him and see if that's him or his partner, and if it isn't, call the state troopers. This has stopped being cute a while back."

Keisha dug in her bag and pulled out her cell phone. Kayla could see her getting upset as she dialed several different numbers. "Damn, I can't get a signal. It must be these stupid ass mountains."

"Keep trying, maybe we'll get clear in a few minutes. But look here, Keisha, it gets real winding and narrow up ahead with some serious drops and I'm not gonna keep playing with this asshole while I have to handle that road. Hold on, this car is a V8 with something like 380 horsepower, I'm gonna do some serious speed to see if I can leave this fool behind us."

Kayla pushed down the gas pedal and her car seemed to take off like a rocket. Within seconds she was doing speeds upward over ninety miles per hour. She was relieved to see the truck rapidly fade into the distance. "I'm going to hold this speed for a few more miles, I want to put some distance between that asshole and us. Maybe then we can pull off the road and go get some help or at least someplace safe to spend the night. That was some scary shit, for real," Kayla said as she took a deep breath and let it out.

After about three miles, Kayla tried to relax and concentrate on her driving as she felt that the danger had passed. She was shocked to look in her rear-view mirror and see that the truck was less than two car lengths behind her. She was not aware that it had even gained on them because the truck had turned off its bright lights, which strangely enough made it more threatening and ominous.

"Oh shit!" Kayla muttered, but then fell silent as her speed approached a hundred miles an hour and that speed on this road was reckless under other circumstances and extremely dangerous under these. She felt the right rear wheel catch some gravel on the side of the road as the car fishtailed just a bit, then righted itself just as she approached another curve. Mario Andretti or another Indy racer had nothing on Kayla as she drove with far more skill than she ever knew she processed. Her heart was pounding in her chest with paralyzing fear but she refused to give in to it. Her focus and concentration were completely in charge, as she struggled to maintain her speed and keep her car on the road. Her basic instincts had taken over and she knew her very life could depend upon how she handled the next few minutes.

Keisha was so terrified she wasn't able to utter a word. She was so scared she couldn't remember a single prayer, not even the Lord's Prayer. So she just closed her eyes and said, "Oh God, Oh God, Oh God!" over and over again. She opened her eyes when she heard the screeching sound of metal scraping metal. Her heart went into her throat when she saw the truck was right beside them and forcing them toward the edge of the road. She tried to look into the truck to see if she could see the driver but the truck was so much bigger than them, that her eye level came to the middle of the door on the passenger side. She looked to her right and saw that a few yards past the end of the road was a rocky cliff of several hundred feet leading to the ocean at the bottom.

Time seemed to stand still for Kayla. It seemed she had been fighting this truck forever though it had only been minutes. Kayla could feel the oppressive size of the truck next to her and almost sense its enormous tonnage as it shifted more and more into her lane, making it more and more difficult to maneuver her car. In a brilliant move born out of desperation, Kayla slammed on the brakes, hoping the truck would continue on past them and then she could hit a U-turn and head back the way they came and get a lead before the truck could find a place to turn around. Every ounce of strength she had went into her slamming on the brakes. The car shivered and shook as the machine tried to fight against the momentum that propelled it forward. Any lesser vehicle with a lesser driver would have flipped over and rolled like a tumbleweed across the desert flats but the Mercedes was stopping and righting itself when the left front end hit the right rear bumper of the truck. That little collision threw the Mercedes into a series of spins that slammed the car into the guardrail and flipped it over the guardrail and toward the cliff.

The awful screeching of the Mercedes as it ruptured the metal of the guardrail mixed with Keisha heart wrenching screams as they headed over the cliff. The last conscious thought that Kayla had was how much she loved her kids and was going to miss them so much.

Chapter Two
1993

Brandon Barnett came out of the building as if he had lived there for years and joined a group of teenagers sitting on the bench. He didn't sit in the midst of them but rather on the outer fringe, which would give anyone looking the impression that he was with the rest of the teenagers when in actuality he was a stranger to them. In the course of his new vocation, he had mastered the art of being seen but not noticed. He didn't want to join their group because he didn't want them to realize that none of them knew or recognized him and start asking him questions.

As a scantily clad girl passed by, Brandon (who was known in the street as Pred, short for Predator) engaged her in conversation. The young lady didn't usually speak to guys she didn't know, but Brandon was so attractive that she decided to bypass her normal rules. Brandon stood about 5'11", with a lean but muscular build of about 177 pounds. Even though he was approaching seventeen years of age, he looked to be about two years younger. His smooth, unblemished skin was the color of milk chocolate, almost like a cup of deep, dusky cocoa with a heavy dollop of whipped cream. His teeth were even and very white, which seemed even brighter because of their contrast to his complexion.

Brandon's most striking feature was his eyes. They were a dazzling shade of green with just a hint of light brown around the outer rim of the irises. A person looking at Brandon's eyes could become so absorbed with the color of his eyes, they could easily miss the fact that they were absent of warmth and reflected the coldness of his soul.

Though Brandon was giving a good impression of flirting with the girl, a romantic liaison was not what he was after. The conversation was intended to be just another part of the disguise he used to hide the fact that he was keeping a very close watch on the entrance to the building that was immediately to his right.

In the years after World War II, housing in New York City underwent major shifts. Increasing numbers moved to the suburbs of Long Island and Westchester, while the inner city filled to the point of bursting with immigrants from Europe and the Caribbean, among other places, as well as the continuing migration from the Southern states. In an effort to control and accommodate some of its new population, New York City started building low income housing projects. These projects or complexes could number anywhere between six and twenty buildings, most of which were arranged in groups of four or five around a grassy quad which were lined with benches for people to sit to escape the summer heat. Most of the buildings were at least sixteen stories high and some even went as high as twenty stories. The exteriors were made of bricks and the interior, cinderblocks that were often painted a mundane shade of beige. The building materials were intended to be low maintenance, but they only succeeded in keeping the cold trapped inside in the winter and the heat in during the summer.

Most buildings were built with at least two entrances and some were built with a front and back entrance. The front entrance led into a small lobby area where the mailboxes were usually located. There were two elevators in the lobby and a neighboring staircase on both sides of the elevator. Most buildings had ten apartments on each floor. As was the case with lower level houses, the City did not spend an elaborate amount of money maintaining the upkeep of the buildings and grounds. It was not unusual for one elevator or the other to be broken or disabled for weeks at a time.

These housing complexes, or projects as they came to be known as, came to represent the residential identity of many of America's inner cities. Not rows of two-story townhouses but the large, brick behemoths that could house or confine tens of thousands of people in a small radius of several blocks. Over time they came to be havens of broken dreams, shattered hopes, and crime.

Not girls, not hanging out with other teenagers, and not the desire to expand his social circle brought Brandon to this section of Queens. Crime and the money that criminal activity could bring was what brought Brandon to this project. Brandon was a member of one of the most successful and deadly group of young assassins in New York City. Brandon was a part of a crew of four men, with Brandon as the youngest and Truth the oldest and the leader at twenty-two years of age. The founder of the crew was Truth, who worked under belief that killers who appeared young and relatively innocent could be very effective. They could catch their targets off-guard and unsuspecting and by the time they realized their error it would be too late. Finding young men, cunning, treacherous, and hungry enough to commit murder wasn't hard. Life as hustlers on the street made many jaded and desperate and served to provide Truth with a steady supply of willing participants. At this point they had seven kills to their credit, and the only time they hadn't completed a contract was when their prey disappeared from the streets of New York and the contract was withdrawn after three weeks.

Today their target was a drug dealer by the name of Wee Willie Wakefield, who ruled a large section of Jamaica, Queens, with a ferocious control that belied his diminutive stature of 5'5". When Wee Willie first burst on the scene, the dealers who were running things underestimated him because of his appearance.

By the time they realized his true intentions he had eliminated five dealers and had greatly increased his wealth and power. The drug game is the ultimate game of conquer and devour. This is not a fair-trade industry, and whenever possible dealers will try to eliminate the competition in any way possible and that was what Willie did. Some he had killed, others he absorbed into his organization, and some he even gave the police enough information about them that they were arrested and put behind bars. He was completely ruthless and devious, and there was nothing he wouldn't do to accomplish his goals of controlling the drug traffic in Jamaica, Queens.

For the past three years, Wee Willie had made sure that any significant dealing was done either by his crew or by crews that paid him a hefty portion of their profits as a type of tithe or tax to be able to continue to operate in his territory.

Making money through illegal and illicit means is extremely perilous and hazardous. The normal rules of society or code of ethics don't apply. The streets have their own rules and codes, and those rules are enforced by the strongest who also happen to write the rules. The thirst for wealth reduces many to their most base instincts and the term 'urban jungle' is not an exaggeration.

Typical of any jungle, the young male will inevitably challenge the older male for leadership of the herd. Whenever significant money was to be made young lions would arise to challenge the hierarchy of power. A new crew had made a connection to get high grade cocaine from a new supplier in upper Manhattan. They had neither the intention nor the inclination to give Willie a portion of their anticipated wealth just because he had established himself before they came on the scene. They also realized they didn't have the firepower or resources to engage in a war with Willie, so they decided to pay the money to have Willie killed and then attempt to finish off his lieutenants themselves in the ensuing confusion.

Their suppliers had referred them to Truth and his crew, who agreed to eliminate Willie for $25,000. Though Truth wanted two to three weeks to complete the hit, their employers wanted it done a lot sooner so they could start making the major money that would be available to them as soon as Willie was out of the way. Truth usually required a couple of weeks to get a target's routine down and dissect any weaknesses and chinks in their armor. Truth wasn't happy about it, but he agreed to go ahead and do the job in a lot less time.

Truth had inconspicuously followed Willie for three days and realized that while Willie lived in another section of Queens, he came here to visit his chick on the side and one of his numerous children. Once Willie became a minor kingpin of sorts, he wanted to enjoy some of the perks of his newfound wealth and power. Since he couldn't legitimately prove where he got his money from, many of the things he wanted to buy like homes and boats he couldn't purchase without having the authorities down his throat. So he bought cars and more clothes than he could ever hope to wear. He was also able to enjoy for the first time the company of numerous beautiful women who would ignore his physical limitations in exchange for the lavish gifts and lifestyle he would eagerly reap upon them.

Willie had gotten fairly comfortable in his role as a minor kingpin and he didn't see any major competitors in sight though he was aware that many were envious and would gladly take his place. He partially relaxed his vigilance and scaled back on his protection. Willie usually traveled with two bodyguards who doubled as eliminators of anyone that Willie needed taken care of. Willie usually had one bodyguard go with him up to the apartment while the other bodyguard waited in the car. The bodyguard then returned to the car to wait until Willie was ready to go, at which time Willie called the bodyguard who would come back upstairs to escort him downstairs.

Truth had devised a plan that once Willie was safely in the apartment they would take up their positions. Pred's primary responsibility was to be the lookout. When Willie called the bodyguard and the bodyguard left the car, Pred was to beep Truth, who was waiting on the roof. Pred was then to wait four minutes and then kill the remaining bodyguard left in the car. If the bodyguard left the car and tried to enter the building, Pred wasn't to wait any longer but just kill him at that point.

Truth had disabled one elevator earlier in the day, so that only left one available elevator that Willie could take downstairs. In this operation timing would be important if not crucial. Truth would try to time when he thought Willie would be taking the elevator and he would take the elevator down to the girlfriend's floor so he would be in the elevator when Willie tried to get on. If he mistimed things Truth would have to pretend he forgot something in his apartment and ride up and down until Willie appeared. When the elevator opened, Truth would open fire with his Tec-9 on Willie and his bodyguard.

Truth had posted a new member of their crew in the stairwell and after Willie had arrived at the elevator, he was to come up behind him and open fire after Truth opened fire. This new man Cisco, a recent addition to their crew, was of Latin descent and was close friends with the suppliers uptown who had referred this job to them. Truth was reluctant to add Cisco to the crew because he had a taste for speed and crystal Meth. Truth had finally relented and let him in because Cisco had connections that could lead to more lucrative jobs. This was Cisco's third job with them, and so far he had performed satisfactorily despite his desire for high octane drugs.

Justice, the final member of their crew, was to wait in the stairwell that was at the opposite end of the hall. His stairwell had a clear line of sight of the elevator. When he saw the elevator doors open he was to come out firing, thus catching Willie and the bodyguard in a deadly, three-way crossfire.

Justice was closest to Pred in age and his best friend. They had started hanging in the street together, and he was the one who had brought Brandon to Truth in the first place. He had known Brandon for almost seven years. They had gone to middle school together and while Justice was popular with the girls, Brandon was a little on the aloof and shy side. Justice had always been the largest kid of his cliché. Even in middle school Justice was over six feet tall and weighed over two hundred pounds. He was one of those people who maintained good muscle definition without doing a lot of working out. He could easily have been a bully but he wasn't above intimidating anyone and using his size to his advantage whenever he needed to. Justice was handsome in a rugged, backwoodsman kind of way.

Brandon was always the better student. In fact, Justice couldn't figure out how Brandon got almost straight A's, because they had spent so much time together and he never saw him study. He figured Brandon must have had some kind of scam going because no one could be so smart that he got such good grades without any serious studying.

Justice had given Brandon his nickname after they had watched a couple of the *Predator* movies. Justice thought the cold-blooded emotionless way the Predator hunted down and killed people in the movie reminded him of Brandon and how he went about conducting his business. Justice couldn't figure out why Brandon was in this business in the first place. Unlike him, where he had to struggle for every meal, Brandon came from a middle-class family. Though Brandon's father was no longer around, his mother was a hospital administrator and made ample money to provide for her family.

Soon the bodyguard exited the car and went into the building in response to Willie's summons, thus kicking Truth's plan into motion. Pred beeped Truth then started counting the minutes down. After three minutes passed, he retrieved the Glock 19 pistol from his backpack and made sure the suppressor was correctly attached and approached the car. Pred preferred working with a suppressor and its deadly silence and the large degree of stealth it provided. Some members of the crew liked working with overwhelming firepower and the intimidation that could be provided by guns like the Tec-9 and the AK-47. There is lot to be said for that method because many people lose their composure when bullets are flying around them and there are the loud explosions of gunfire.

As Pred causally walked down the street toward Willie's parked car, he was glad that Willie had spent so much time upstairs that now it was dark. The darkness made his approach to the car less noticeable and in these projects few residents hung around after dark. Although the police had removed most of the drug dealers with numerous sweeps, most residents still didn't feel secure enough in the safety of their neighborhood to hang around after dark.

Pred strolled up to the driver's side of the car trying to appear as innocent and youthful as possible, and he knocked on the window. The bodyguard/chauffeur saw the teenage boy standing outside his window, so he rolled down the window to ask "What do you want, boy?" Pred raised his gun and fired two shots into the bodyguard's face, one piercing the forehead and the other through his left eye. At this close range, the bullets exited the back of the bodyguard's head in a spray of blood, gore, and brain matter. Before the bodyguard realized the bullets had entered his head and ended his hopes and dreams and all that he ever could be, Pred had turned and headed back to his position in front of the building, just as casually as he had approached the car though he made more of an effort to be even less conspicuous.

Meanwhile, upstairs, things hadn't gone nearly as smoothly. Most plans have flaws and if Truth had taken more time to examine his plan, he might have realized some of its flaws. The first major flaw was Cisco. He was the wrong man for the role he had to play in this particular assassination. Proper timing was essential to making this plan work, a few seconds early or a few second late could determine the difference between success and failure. This, unfortunately, was not one of Cisco's strengths. Maybe he was anxious because he was feeling the need to get high or maybe just the stress of having had to wait several hours for Willie to appear, but regardless of the reason, Cisco moved into action too soon.

Seconds before the elevator doors opened on Willie's floor and Truth would have opened fire, Cisco sprang from the stairwell with guns blazing. This might not have been so disastrous but whether he was high on drugs or just plain nervous, but the only thing Cisco hit were the wall and the floor around Wee Willie. The chaos that could have ensued from the thunderous boom of gunfire in such a close, confined space, mixed with bullets flying around and the dust and smoke from bullets hitting concrete didn't faze experienced killers like Willie and his bodyguard.

Seeing Cisco come out of the stairwell with vicious intentions, Willie and his bodyguard drew their guns and opened fire. The bodyguard's first three shots caught Cisco square in the chest. The velocity of their gunshots slammed Cisco back against the wall before he slumped to the floor. At that precise moment, the elevator doors opened and Truth was caught in such an unexpected situation that it froze him immobile. He expected to catch an unsuspecting Willie and be able to use the gun in his hand to kill him. Instead he was thrust into the middle of a firestorm of epic proportions.

In the blink of an eyelash, Truth realized the error in his planning. He should have planned the ambush in the main lobby, where he had a means of escape. Instead, he was trapped inside this metal box that eerily reminded him of a coffin. As Willie felt the elevator doors open, he whirled and seeing the gun in Truth' hand, he opened fire as he faced this new danger. Willie and Truth fired simultaneously, both hitting their targets. Truth's shots hit Willie in the right shoulder and upper chest region, where it narrowly missed several vital organs. Unfortunately, Willie's shot was more accurate, striking Truth dead center in the chest, piercing his heart and ripping it to shreds. Truth was dead before his brain could send a message to his body what great danger he was in.

Truth had made the fatal mistake of underestimating his opposition and it cost him his life. Willie and his men had faced deadly violence on many occasions and panic had long been eliminated from their DNA. Did Truth really think that all the people that Willie had killed had gone meekly to their demise? Willie had been at war for years over the streets, and as a result Willie and his men were as battle tested as the hardiest combat troops.

From his vantage point, Justice could not see the far end of the hall so he missed the encounter with Cisco, but he did see the fire exchange with Truth. A few heartbeats too late, he burst through the door, spraying the corridor with a hail of bullets. His Tec-9 had a thirty-three-shot clip and he was determined to use every bullet to try and save the other members of his crew and complete their assignment.

The bodyguard turned to face Justice, and his aim was thrown off by trying to turn and fire simultaneously. Whether it was luck or skill was irrelevant because his shot caught Justice in the thigh, and as Justice crumbled to the floor he continued to fire. 'It is better to be lucky than good' is a paradox that applied to Justice as his shots caught the bodyguard in the throat and head, more by luck than by skill. Fate had decided to smile on Justice because by falling to the floor it took him out of the line of fire from Willie. From his prone position on the floor, Justice continued to fire but with no degree of accuracy.

The indomitable, survivor spirit in Willie wouldn't let him give in to his wounds. He forced himself to get moving and step over the fallen Cisco all the while continuing to fire over his shoulder at Justice. He staggered and stumbled down the stairs toward the main lobby. Justice tried to struggle to his feet so he could pursue Willie but he must have been wounded worse than he thought because his legs wouldn't support his weight. After several attempts, he was able to stand on his feet. He took one last look at the dead bodies scattered in the hall and elevator and he limped back to the stairwell, leaving a trail of blood behind him.

Willie was seriously but not mortally wounded, and the more he walked the stronger he felt. Soon he was making pretty good time and he quickly made it to the main floor and out of the building. The loss of blood and the pain in his torso made him feel like he was in danger of losing consciousness and he resembled a drunk as he staggered to his car. Pred saw Willie leave the building and start toward the car. Pred started to jog toward Willie and when he got a few yards away he said, "Hey, mister, are you okay? What happened to you? Do you need help?"

"Yeah, kid, I'm hurt. Help me to my car and I'll give you a hundred bucks," Willie replied.

Pred walked toward Willie with his arm extended as if he was going to help him to his car. When he got less than an arm's length away, he raised his right hand and fired several bullets in Willie' torso and head. As Willie slumped to the ground, Pred looked around to see if there were any witnesses or anyone else he had to eliminate. Luckily the streets were empty and no one had seen anything.

Pred had a difficult decision to make. Common sense and survival instincts urged him to leave the premises right away because at any given moment someone could come upon the two dead bodies, but Pred didn't know what had happened to the rest of his crew. He feared the worst or else Willie would not have been able to leave the building. He could assume that everyone was dead, but someone could be wounded and in need of his help. He and Justice were good friends, and he wasn't leaving until he was sure that he was dead.

Pred sprinted into the building and saw the trail of blood left by Willie leading to the staircase. He also noticed that the elevator was still on the floor that Willie's girl lived on. On the dead run, he headed to the stairs and started climbing up. When he arrived at the floor, he viewed the carnage and realized from the pool of blood that all three of them were dead. He noticed right away that Justice was not among the dead bodies, and he saw two trails of blood leading in opposite directions. He followed the trail of blood that led him to the staircase opposite of the one he took up. He immediately surmised that Justice must have made the other trail because he wasn't on the staircase he came up and he was alive at least when he left the scene of the shooting. Pred went into the other staircase and followed the blood down the stairs and after about one flight, he caught up with Justice.

"Here, Justice, lean on me. Where are you hit?"

"In the leg."

Pred reached over and ripped off Justice's pants leg and checked the wound, where blood was still oozing out of the bullet hole. "Just, I'm gonna have to stop the bleeding. Hold on for just a few seconds." Pred took off his belt and wrapped it around Justice's leg and used it as a tourniquet. Hours of watching cowboy and war movies as a child had given him a rough idea of how to handle a gunshot wound. After the bleeding had ebbed, Pred wrapped Justice's arm around his shoulder and helped him down the stairs. "Just, we got to get out of here. The cops will be getting here any minute if they're not here already." They managed to get down to the lobby and looked outside just as two police cars pulled up to Willie's body. As the cops got out their cars and started to assess the situation, Pred and Justice went back into the stairwell. They were at a loss of what to do because they knew it was only a matter of time before the police followed the blood trails and discovered them. They could try walking past the police but with the wounded Justice, that could lead to questions they didn't have answers for. Pred realized their best chance for escape was probably to find a place where they could hold up or hide and wait for the lobby to clear.

Justice always felt that where it pertained to him there were two kinds of luck: bad luck and no luck. Fortunately for him, this time he was wrong and a little good luck smiled on him. As fortune would have it, a woman in her twenties came home from work weary from her labor and tired of waiting for the elevator, she stepped around the blood splatters and headed up the stairs. Whatever her job was must have been extremely strenuous because the woman looked so exhausted she gave the impression it was all she could do to make it home. She barely stood five feet tall and she only weighed a hundred pounds if she had a pocket full of nickels. She was a reasonably attractive woman, but she clearly made little attempt to make herself glamorous for a job that didn't require it. Her hair was pulled back into two long braids, one on each side of her head. She was completely without makeup even lipstick. And her face displayed her fatigue and clearly said she only desired to get home, have dinner, and get to her bed. Though she was disgusted with having to climb the stairs being as tired as she was, she had no other options as her apartment couldn't come to her, so she started the final leg of her journey home.

Pred and Justice went back up the other stairs and looked out on each floor until they saw the lady heading toward her apartment. As the lady was opening the door to her apartment, Pred came up behind her and put his gun in the small of her back and said, "Don't look at me. Keep your head down. Open the damn door." After the lady unlocked the door, Pred pushed the lady inside and walked in behind her. "Is anyone else here?" Pred asked as the lady shook her head no. Pred rapped his gun against the lady's temple, rendering her unconscious.

Leaving the door ajar, he went and helped Justice into the apartment. Then he dashed into the bathroom, wet some towels, and went back out into the hall to wipe up any blood drops that might have given away where they were located. Then he went back into the apartment, locked the door, and tied the lady up, blindfolded her, and put her face down on the floor. Turning to Justice he said, "We'll stay here until things cool off and we can get safely away."

"What if someone else comes here?"

"I hope for their sake they don't, but if they do, we'll deal with that when that happens."

Pred then went through the apartment to familiarize himself with his surroundings. Luckily the apartment was located on the front of the building so he could look down upon the entrance and see the coming and goings of the police. The entrance to the building was a beehive of activity. Nearly a dozen cop cars had arrived and they had cordoned off the areas around the car and Willie's body. Pred could see them wheeling several bodies out of this building and other cops were coming back into the building as they investigated the murder scenes. Meanwhile, other cops had spread off to the other buildings in search of witnesses. As several news trucks and reporters set up shop, Pred realized they might be struck in this apartment for a while.

Pred sat down, composed himself, and tried to come up with a plan. He felt it would be easy for him to leave the building after a couple of hours because the cops probably assumed that the killers were either dead or long gone. Justice, on the other hand, would be a different story. If anyone saw the wounded man trying to leave the building, it was sure to raise some unanswerable questions.

The first thing Pred did was check on Justice's wound since the severity of his injury would dictate how long they would be able to hole up. Pred removed the tourniquet and was pleased to see that the wound was not bleeding profusely, though the bullet, as close as he could tell, was still in the leg. Luckily the bullet seemed to miss any major arteries. There was a discoloring around the leg where the bullet had entered and slight puckering of the entry wound. Pred went into the bathroom and got some clean towels that he used to clean the wound and make a bandage. He also got some aspirin because he heard that with gunshot wounds you had to worry about infection. He didn't have any antibiotics, but the aspirin would have to do for the time being.

Then he went and checked on their prisoner. He thought he saw her stirring but now she was still. He wondered whether she had come to and was feigning her unconsciousness. Pred said, "Lady, I know you're awake. How long we stay here will depend upon how long the cops are outside. If you cooperate we won't hurt you. What is your name?"

"Brenda."

"Who else lives here with you, Brenda?"

"Why are you in my house? What do you want?" Brenda asked in a timid voice.

Pred reached over and punched Brenda in the small of her back, causing Brenda to grunt in pain. Then Pred said, "Now Brenda, I'm gonna tell you one last time. We are in charge here. You will answer my questions without hesitation or I will have to punish you. Do you understand me?"

Brenda had a bit of a dilemma. She didn't know how dangerous the young men in her house were and she didn't want to take a chance on getting hurt. On the other hand, the man speaking sounded like a little kid and he was probably just trying to intimidate her. Maybe because she was angry at getting treated like this in her own home, she decided to try to be more forceful. "This is my house, you young punk. You better cut me loose and get the hell out of here"

"Better? Bitch, did you tell me what I better do? Okay, I'll show you what's up." Pred went into the kitchen and took a dish cloth and soaked it with water and dishwashing detergent. He came back and flipped Brenda onto her back and slapped her across her face. When she opened her mouth to protest, he stuffed the soapy rag into her mouth. Pred turned to Justice and said, "Hey man, give me a cigarette."

"What for, you don't smoke?"

"Light it up for me and you'll see."

Justice lit a cigarette and passed it to Pred, who took a couple of puffs to make the fire grow hotter. He then placed the burning end on the back of Brenda's hand. Brenda's scream of pain was stifled by the dish rag. As she tried to catch her breath she gagged on the soapy water. As Brenda tried not to choke, Pred took the cigarette and burned her on her forearm. Brenda was caught between trying to scream and needing to breathe. Slowly Brenda's screams evaporated into whimpers of despair.

Pred reached down and ripped open Brenda's shirt, exposing her stomach and chest. Brenda froze because she didn't know what Pred's intentions were. She didn't know whether she was about to be raped or if she was gonna be burned again. Truthfully at this point, she didn't know which one was worse.

"Lady, you have such a pretty stomach and a nice set of titties and I would hate to have to mess them up, but don't get me wrong, I will if you keep giving me a hard time. You have to understand, only one of us can be in charge and right now that's me. You give me any more lip and I'll fuck you up real bad and that's a promise. I'm going to take this rag out of your mouth and I don't wanna hear shit but the answers to the questions I ask you. Okay? Nod your head if you understand me." After Brenda nodded her head, Pred removed the gag and continued, "Do you live here alone?"

"No."

"Who lives here with you?"

"My husband and my two kids."

"Where are they? Are they coming home soon?"

"They're down south visiting his family."

"When should they be back?"

"Not until after the weekend."

"Don't try to be slick and lie to me. I would hate to have to hurt your old man or your kids."

"I'm not lying. They'll be back after the weekend unless they think there's something wrong."

"If they are down south, why would they think there's something wrong?" Justice asked. Up to this point he had just been sitting there silent, just observing all that was happening.

"He calls every night and if he doesn't reach me, he might start to worry."

"Old dude probably worries about you messing around on him and then would come home to keep somebody from tapping his shit, huh?" Justice asked.

"He doesn't worry about that because he knows he can trust me, but if he doesn't talk to me, he might worry that something's happened to me because I'm always home to catch his call."

"Well, then, you'll speak to him when he calls and you better not let him think that's anything is wrong, because then he'll be coming home to a dead wife," Pred said.

"Don't hurt me. I haven't done anything to you. Why do you want to hurt me?"

Pred said, "I told you, I don't want to hurt you. If you are cool, then in a couple of days this will all be over and will seem like a bad nightmare. This can be as unpleasant as you make it or it can go smoothly, it's up to you."

"Do you think you can let me get off the floor or remove my blindfold?"

"The blindfold stays, but if you promise to behave we can let you sit on the couch."

"Yo, Pred, what's our next move, man?" Justice asked.

Surprised and annoyed that Justice would be so careless as to give away part of his identity, Pred said, "Come here, let me talk to you." and he gestured for Justice to follow him into one of the other rooms. Once they were alone, Pred said, "Man, what are you thinking about? How could you use my name in front of this broad?"

"What's the big deal?"

"The big deal is up to this point no one has seen us and Brenda still hasn't seen our faces, but now she knows my name. If someone comes to try and get witnesses, Brenda couldn't tell them any more than they already knew. Why do you think I went to all the trouble of blindfolding her?"

"So when we're ready to leave, we'll just kill her."

"That might not be as simple as it seems. We wipe out a couple of drug dealers and thugs and the cops are going to look for us but how much effort are they really going to make? They're probably glad that someone took them out of the picture for them. Now, if we kill someone who's not in the game, especially a wife and mother, and then the pressure brought to bear might be something totally different."

"It seems like it might be a bit of a risk either way," Justice says.

"Yeah, it is but I don't think we need the pressure of a dragnet right now. We got to let things cool down so we can get you some medical treatment."

"Then we just got to find a way to bring her over to our side and make it to her advantage not to drop a dime on us."

"That's a good idea. Let me talk to her, maybe I can make it work."

They went back into the living room and together they lifted Brenda off the floor and placed her in a chair. Pred removed the blindfold and pulled up a chair and sat less than four feet away and looked her directly in her eyes. "Brenda, we have a bit of a problem here. First, I want to apologize for forcing our way into your apartment. It wasn't something we planned on doing or something we really wanted to do but we had no other choice. Now that we are here and you have seen us, we have to figure out what to do with you. Probably the easier thing to do would be to just kill you, but we don't want to have to do that. You seem like you could be a cool person. I don't want to take two kid's mother away from them, but I can't be worried about you turning us in to the cops as soon as we leave."

"Why would I do that? This whole thing is none of my business. If you will just leave right now, I'll forget any of this ever happened. I promise I won't tell anyone anything."

"I wish I could do that, but we can't leave just yet—but we'll leave as soon as we can."

"If you promise to leave as soon as you can, I'll keep your secret but you have to leave before my family gets home. I can't run the risk that you might hurt my family."

"We have nothing to gain by hurting you or your family. If you don't put us in a situation where we have to then we won't."

"I won't. I just want you out of my house so I can get on with my life."

"That sounds good and I'll tell you what I will do, if you cover our backs and never tell anybody anything about this, we'll give you five thousand dollars when we leave. On the other hand, if you change your mind and decide to betray us, I will find you and we will kill you and your husband and maybe even the kids. Don't tell yourself that once the police catch us and put us in jail, you will be safe because that is not the case. I know a lot of people who would do you just as a favor to us and to get on our good side. It seems to me you don't really have much of a choice. You can help us out and end up five thousand dollars richer or you can put us in a position where we would have to do some terrible things to your life."

"Why should I believe anything you say? You burned me just because you felt like it."

"I had to do that to show you I meant business. You took one look at me and decided that I was some young punk you could push around. Ain't that right?"

"What did you guys do in the first place to cause all these problems?"

"You don't want to know. Do we have a deal?"

"Like you said, what choice do I have? So I guess we have a deal."

"I expect you to do whatever you have to do so no one suspects that we're in here."

"I can do that but do I have to cook and clean for you too?"

"You don't have to but we would appreciate anything you do. I'll tell you what: I'll give you an extra hundred dollars for every meal you make while we are staying with you. We're not trying to become the Cosbys or no shit like that, but since we have to be here, let's try to make the situation as easy as possible. I'm sure you don't want to worry about whether we're gonna smoke you at any given moment and I sure don't want to worry about you trying to turn us in at your first opportunity."

"I won't cook for you. It wouldn't feel right me doing something like that. I don't care how much you decide to pay me. I'm not your enemy, but I ain't your friend either."

"That's up to you."

Pred went to the window to get a closer look at what was going on outside. While things weren't as busy as they were before, there was still quite a few police and news crews milling about. These few moments of quiet gave Pred opportunity to slide back into his Brandon persona and a few moments of personal reflection as he needed to assess things.

Though the situation was turning out as well as he could hope after things had went so terribly wrong, that didn't negate the fact that the operation had gone far worse than planned. Even though they completed the hit and would still receive their fee, it had cost them two vital members of their crew. In fact, Truth was their leader, the planner and the one who had brought them both into the assassination business. Before hooking up with Truth, he and Justice had worked as low level drug dealers, which he was eager to quit because it required too much time and earned too little money for the effort it took.

In the less than three months that they had worked with Truth, they had been able to pocket almost twenty thousand each, not including the money from this job. Brandon considered it easy money that usually didn't take more than a couple of hours of work. The only down side before tonight was you couldn't feel bad about ending someone's life. Brandon didn't take pleasure from killing but neither did it bother him. He saw it as a means to accomplish his ends. Some people saw it as evil, but if brought him the money he wanted and needed, then it wasn't really an evil.

In his opinion, the lack of money was the only true evil in America. It was the lack of money that took his mother out of the house to work incredibly long hours and put him in the clutches of his lecherous uncle who did things to him no seven-year-old boy should ever have to endure. He could still feel the ponderous weight of his uncle as he lay on top of him. He could smell his stinking, rancid, hot breath on the back of his neck. He could still fell the burning, white-hot pain of his uncle as he repeatedly thrust into him. He could still feel the immeasurable hatred he felt for his uncle. What he didn't feel any longer was the abject feeling of helplessness the small Brandon felt back then. He would never feel weak or helpless again. And he would never misunderstand what the true evil in this word was.

It was the lack of money that made his step-father *have* to work that second job as a cab driver where he was killed by some robbers. Even though he didn't remember his father, he was sure that if his father was around he would have killed his wife's brother for daring to put his hands (and worse things) on him.

He had seen the situation with Truth as a good opportunity to solve his cash flow problem; at least, he did until today. For the first time, he saw that it was a real possibility that the death he tried to bring to other people could also be visited upon him and that wasn't attractive in the least. He didn't know a single dead person who could buy new alligator shoes or sneakers or leather jackets. Having all the money in the world would do him no good if he wasn't alive to spend it.

He had to find a better way. Maybe Justice and he should pull a couple of more hits to pull in some major money, but the assassination game was not a good long-term plan. Maybe they should do their thing once or twice more and get out before their luck ran out. Or maybe the incident today indicated that their luck had already run out.

First things first, they had to get out of the current jam they were in and then he and Justice could put together a plan. He went to check on Justice and see how he was doing.

"Hey, Just, how are you doing, big fella?"

"It hurts like hell, but I'm all right. Pred, I was thinking. There's nothing that is keeping you from just walking out of here. It's dark outside, and I doubt if anybody saw you. Even if the cops do see you, they would think you were just some kid who lived in the building going out for Chinese food or something. They probably wouldn't even give you a second look."

"What about you?"

"What about me? It ain't your fault that I caught a bullet. It was just bad luck. Maybe I might be able to slip away later, but you should get away now if you can."

"You can forget about that shit. There ain't no way I leaving you here to handle this mess by yourself. Either we both get away or neither one of us does. You're my boy, and I'm not leaving you to rock and roll by yourself. I'm with you through whatever may come."

"I don't think it's smart, but I appreciate the loyalty and I won't ever forget it."

"Don't worry, brother; I'll get us both out of here. It's hard to get a feel for what's going on in the street from up here. Maybe you're right and I should go downstairs and get us some Chinese food and check out what's going on. "

"Pred, that sounds risky."

"No risk, no gain. Don't worry, I'll be real cool and I'm getting hungry anyway. We better get some Chinese food, we don't even know if that Brenda chick can cook."

"Just be careful, man."

"Don't worry about me, I got this. Keep an eye on Brenda; I don't know how much we can trust her. I'll be right back."

Brandon left the apartment and pushed the button for the elevator, not because he wanted to take the elevator but because he wanted to judge how close to normal things had returned. When the elevator hadn't come in a few minutes, he went to the stairs and started down. He was relieved to discover that there were few drops of blood visible on this landing or the one below it. He did see some drops of dried blood where he had met Justice and bound his wound. The lobby was still a buzz of activity with several policemen milling about and a repairman working on the broken elevator because the only working elevator was the scene of the shooting and had to be taken out of service.

As Brandon left the building, a young African American police officer said, "Hey, kid, come here," and signaled for him to come over. Resisting the urge to flee, Brandon composed himself and went over to the officer who asked, "Do you live in this building?"

"No, sir, I'm staying here with a friend of my moms, Miss Brenda."

"Where does she live?"

"3J."

"Why are you staying with her? Is your mother out of town?"

"No, my mother sent me over to help her do some things around the house, but I think my mother had to work late tonight and she didn't want me to stay home by myself." Brandon figured he should appear as young and naïve as possible. "Why do you ask? What's going on?"

"There was a shooting and a couple of people got killed."

"Did you catch the guys who did it?"

"It looks like a drug war and they killed each other, though there's a chance that one got away. Have you seen anything?"

"No, I was inside. I thought I heard some shooting and shouting, but I thought it was someone's TV."

"Do you think your mother's friend saw anything?"

"You can ask her but I doubt it. She just got in from the store."

"Okay, thanks, son. If she saw anything, have her let us know."

"Okay, I'll tell her."

"And young brother?"

"Yeah?"

"Be careful out here. These streets can be real dangerous. Don't be so hard on your mother. She's doing the right thing. She's keeping you from getting caught up in these streets. A smart young brother like you should plan on going to college and making something out of your life."

"You know, you're probably right. I'll plan on doing that."

Chapter Three
(2007)

Ebony Delaney planted a vicious roundhouse kick high on the body bag and followed the kick with two savage punches and another kick. She knew if the workout was going to be as effective as she needed it to be, she should go through a *kata*, which is a series of consecutive martial art moves. Unfortunately, right now she was too angry to properly maintain the composure needed to correctly execute the moves. She was hoping that by engaging in a super strenuous workout, she could burn off some of the anger that seemed to have taken possession of her. So far it wasn't working. She knew she should be ashamed of herself because she knew that in order to have obtained a black belt in Tae Kwon Do, she possessed enough discipline to control her emotions but today discipline and tranquility and composure were all evading her.

She had a damn good reason to be angry. Ebony was a detective and sergeant with the New York Police Department who was on special assignment with the FBI. She was part of a task force investigating a serial killer known as the Street Stalker, who had been abducting, raping, and murdering prostitutes. It was Ebony and her street contacts that had broken the case and led to the apprehension of the killer.

Maybe because Ebony was a twenty-nine-year-old African American female with a reputation for fairness and honesty, that some of the recalcitrant prostitutes had finally agreed to talk to her. They had confided in her that one of their friends who had been abducted had escaped from the killer. Unfortunately, the girl had fled New York and none of the girls knew where she had gone. Ebony had met with the girl's reluctant pimp, Blue, and convinced him to provide her with the address where the girl was living.

At first Blue, playing the tough guy, was unwilling to cooperate but Ebony had put her .38 in his mouth and threatened to blow his brains all over his pretty, blue Jaguar. Blue suddenly came to the realization that it was in his best interest to help get this killer off the streets.

A quick trip to Bridgeport, Connecticut, that resulted in a visit with the reformed prostitute that was very productive. The girl was able to provide Ebony with some pertinent information, including a description of the Stalker and his lair. Within hours an All Points Bulletin for the killer was issued up and down the Eastern Seaboard. Though the killer had tried to flee, it took less than two days for him to resurface, which led to his immediate arrest.

Ebony couldn't be in on the actual capture because the FBI had found him in Baltimore, where they quickly put him into custody. At first Ebony felt elated because they had taken an evil, vicious killer off the streets and everyone on the case knew she was the one who had uncovered the clues to break the case open.

Ebony was not the type of person who did what she did for accolades, praises, or credit, but when the FBI held a press conference and didn't even have the courtesy to invite her, it pissed her off. She had broken several laws, violated numerous police procedures, and put her career in serious jeopardy to take this villain off the street. She sure didn't do it so some Federal agent could use it to boost his career. And what about the girl? She had put her life at risk and challenged a very real personal fear so she could help them.

The fact that somebody was using that sacrifice for personal gain irritated her to no end.

She understood the politics of the situation and that the rival FBI was scrambling to get as much credit as possible, but right is right. The sight of the white FBI agent in charge standing in front of the camera, fielding questions with his chest puffed out like an enraged fighting cock, really irked her. The fact that they were giving the false impression that their agency was responsible for uncovering his identity and address as well as arresting him really bothered her.

It raised a couple of questions that she didn't want to face. Yet it seemed they kept cropping up every time she made some progress with her career. What did she have to do to get the respect and recognition that she had legitimately earned? Did the FBI disrespect her so thoroughly because she was an African American, a female or because she was an NYPD detective? In her mind, it really didn't matter because none of these reasons were even close to being legitimate.

As an African American female, she was no stranger to having to outwork everyone else or having to buck the odds without recognition or accreditation. When she earned an academic scholarship at Dartmouth University and when she earned her Master's degree in criminal justice from John Jay College, no one had given her anything. She had used a brilliant, analytical mind coupled with strenuous, hard work and incredibly long hours to graduate from both schools in the top two percent of her class.

Many people would describe Ebony as beautiful but she would not let her beauty define her. Though she knew she had what many would call crowd-stopping beauty, she was determined to let the world know there was more to her than a beautiful face and a desire invoking body. She was a petite 5'3" on a 119-pound frame that had less than 5 percent body fat. She not only enjoyed being fit, but she knew that being able to defend herself against some of the unsavory characters she dealt with, would come in handy.

She had a bewitching smile that hid behind luscious, kissable lips, even though her upper lip was a little thin for her taste. When she smiled, it revealed deep dimples below her cheeks. Even though she had beautiful hazel-colored eyes with the most disarming twinkle, her smile was her most striking feature. It was warm and comforting and when she chose to share it, it made you feel like you were awarded a special treat.

Her skin was the color of café au lait with extra cream, and there were barely visible freckles lightly scattered across her pretty pug nose. Her hair was a thick, coarse, tawny brown with flecks of hair so light it almost looked blond. The dreadlocks of her youth were replaced by a tight, curly afro of about two to three inches in length. It was hard to tell whether she kept her hair short for convenience or as a fashion statement. Either way it worked and was very attractive on her especially when she wore hoop earrings reminiscent of the style from the 60s.

Her legs were stunning. They were lithe and shapely and her calves were very well developed because of miles of jogging and hours of martial arts. Her breasts were not small but neither were they voluminous, and she had pert, alert nipples that more than compensated for any lack of size. As a teenager, she had a few embarrassing moments when her nipples chose an inappropriate moment to get erect. She grew up a little self-conscious of them, but now as an adult, she wore a padded bra and kept it moving.

Usually she worked out in the basement of the precinct with her fellow officers, but today she wasn't ready to deal with her co-workers. Many knew how close she was to the case, and she feared they might see the hurt and anger on her face. She was by nature a private person when it came to her emotions, and she felt she might need a day or two to put her public face in place. She feared that many of her fellow officers would see her as a weak female if she displayed too many of her feelings. Though it wasn't fair that women weren't treated like male officers, it didn't matter because that was the world she chose to work in.

Even though there wasn't a karate class in session, she chose to work out at the dojo even if she had no one to work out with but herself. She again assaulted the bag with a series of kicks and punches which consistently increased in speed and intensity. The sound of her blows striking the bag resounded throughout the empty room. After about fifteen minutes of steady blows, she was sweating profusely and she paused to catch her breath.

She felt a hand on her shoulder and turned to see her sensei or teacher standing beside her. He didn't smile but his eyes seemed bright like morning stars while at the same time, exuding a sense of peace and calm. He gestured and said, "Come, little one." Ebony followed him to the edge of the mat where he beckoned her to sit beside him. He sat there still and silent and gestured for her to do the same.

After a few moments, Ebony grew antsy and impatient and seemed to be bursting at the seams to talk about what was bothering her. As she started to speak, the sensei put up a hand to have her remain silent. After a few minutes, he finally spoke. "You are troubled, little one. You are out of sync with the universe. You need to relax and breathe. Find your center and focus. Remember who you are, what you are, and all things work as they have been designed."

Ebony decided to try to do as her sensei advised and tried to find her place of calmness and serenity. Even though the situation and how it played itself out was not something she was going to be happy about, her getting further upset was not going to accomplish anything. After about ten minutes, she did start to feel better and more relaxed. She opened her eyes to speak to her sensei but he was nowhere in sight, so she packed her gym bag and headed home to take a quick shower.

After she showered and dressed, she noticed that the light on her answering machine was flashing indicating that she had several messages. She decided she would check her messages later because if any of them were important she would feel guilty for not returning the call right away and she was now eager to get down to the station.

Though she wasn't expected to report back to duty for a couple of days, she figured the sooner she reported to duty the sooner she would get assigned to a new case and the sooner her disappointment over the Street Stalker case would fade. She grabbed her car keys from the key dish by the door and jumped in her three-year-old Volvo and headed for the Manhattan Bridge. Though she lived in Brooklyn, she worked at the Ninth Precinct in lower Manhattan. As she turned onto East 5th Street, she waved to a couple of officers that were leaving as the shift had recently changed. She lucked up and found a parking space almost in front of the building.

As she entered the precinct, she was met with greetings and congratulations from many of her fellow officers. Ebony was a reasonably well-liked woman and even those who weren't crazy about her, respected her abilities and her dedication to her job. She had a well-earned reputation of not only being very bright and quick but also of taking hold of a case and pursuing it like a bull terrier until she solved it. She was one of only two female detectives at this precinct and the other one was on special assignment at Police Plaza.

As she came in, one of the first people she saw was her good friend Stephanie Givens, a younger officer who showed a lot of promise. Stephanie was incredibly beautiful and half the officers in the precinct spent as much time chasing her as they did their cases. Because of her looks, Stephanie was having a hard time getting her fellow officers to take her seriously as a policewoman. Ebony had become a sort of a mentor to her.

Stephanie said, "Hi, Ebony, I heard about the work you did in uncovering the identity of the Stalker. Girl, I'm so proud of you."

"I'm glad someone is. The way the Feds are running around posturing and grabbing credit, you would think I didn't do anything at all."

"Don't let that bother you. The people who really matter know who did what. I know a lot of people around here feel like I do. You really struck a blow for the sisterhood."

"I really don't know how much of a difference I made. There are still a lot of male officers that will never think a woman can be as good a cop as them."

"We can't worry about convincing those that refuse to be convinced even when the truth is staring them right in the face. We just have to be our own support mechanism. We'll just pat each other on the back and keep it moving. Speaking of which, how about I take you out later for drinks to celebrate?"

"That offer sounds good, but I have to ask for a raincheck. I've been so busy, I've been pretty much out of touch with everybody. I need to speak with my parents, and I'm sure Jack is pulling his hair out because I haven't spoken to him in over two weeks."

"I thought you two had gotten divorced?"

"We did, but someone forgot to tell Jack. I still try to at least be friendly."

"My offer still stands. You just let me know me know when it's good for you."

"That sounds like a plan and we'll make it happen in a couple of days. Meanwhile, you be safe out there in those streets."

Ebony went to her desk and started checking her messages. She was correct in that she had three messages from Jack and two from her mother. She picked up the phone to call her mother but hung up when she noticed Lieutenant Melendez signaling her to come into his office.

"Delaney, what are you doing here? We were told you would be assigned to the task force for another couple of days."

"We caught the bad guys and I didn't see any point in hanging around after the paperwork was done."

"I read the report on the investigation and that was some fine work you did there."

"Thank you."

"I guess you're pretty PO'ed at the way things were handled at the press conference."

"I was a little disappointed because I expected better."

"You shouldn't have. You know how this game is played. They brought a lot of resources to bear, and they needed the publicity to justify all the expenditures. You shouldn't take it personally. Those of us in the know are well aware of your contributions. All too often the person who does the grunt work to solve the crime goes unheralded. You've got to take things in stride. At least you got that piece of filth off the streets"

"That is the most important thing, and I feel damn good about that. I must admit that it feels pretty good to be able to protect those women in the street. Just because of the way they are living doesn't mean that anyone should be able to prey on them. You know me, Lieutenant; I don't do this for the glory. I just need people to treat women, especially woman of color, fair or at least like human beings. Someone's got to stand up for them, and if nobody else will, I will."

"I know and that's one reason why you are so good at what you do. Now what do you want to do? Are you going to take a couple of days off, or are you ready to get back to work?"

"I have a couple of personal items I need to attend to, but by day after tomorrow I'll be ready to get back on a case."

"That's good because quite frankly we're kind of swamped right now. Since right now you are the shining princess at Police Plaza and the Mayor's office, you can get some special perks. You can pretty much choose who you want to work with and what you want to work on. I can put you back with Dansby or I can give you a new partner if you rather."

"I like working with Gary; I just hope he's gotten over me leaving him to join the task force."

"He might pout a little bit, but I think that's just to give you a hard time. Dansby's been around a long time, and he understands the politics of this business better than most."

"Then I want to be with Gary. He's a good man, and if the task force had taken him as well, we might have solved the case a lot sooner."

"Hey, don't tell me how good you think he is. I already know. Tell him."

"I intend to, although I thinks he knows how I feel about him."

"Good, I'm glad that's settled. I'll reassign the detective he was working with, and when you come in tomorrow he can bring you up to speed on the cases he's working on. There's talk of a new Special Crimes unit being formulated and when they start it up I'll make sure *both* your names are given heavy consideration."

Chapter Four

Tanya Richardson had discovered something she never thought she would find: a second chance at love. At one of the worst times in her life she had met someone who brought light to her darkness, hope to her desolation, and taught her how to smile again. She had always believed in God, and having Omar come into her life just when she needed him might have been a sign that God was once again smiling on her.

Tanya had only loved one man in her life. When Tanya Moore had arrived at Southern Methodist University as a skinny freshman, she met Larry Richardson. The 6'3" Richardson was a junior and the star of the basketball team. They were two individuals who could not have been more unalike. Tanya was a quiet, unassuming church girl from rural Texas. She was born and raised on the family farm and was an excellent student who majored in Chemistry and Earth Science. Like most dedicated students, she was having no difficulty maintaining her academic scholarship with a B+ average.

Larry was a rough and tumble kid from the streets of Philadelphia. He was a nice enough person, but he had definitely experienced the seedier side of life. He was a high school legend in Philly, and that was probably the only thing that kept him from a life of crime. He could have been a drug dealer or a member of a gang like his brothers and cousins. Even as a young man he was so gifted with the ball that everyone expected him to one day play in the NBA and nothing that happened in high school or college changed that perception. Larry was an able but not devout student, usually only working hard enough in the classroom to stay eligible to play ball.

When Larry first met the quiet, shy Tanya, there was something about her that Larry found very attractive. Maybe it was because she was so different from every girl he had dated. Though Larry aggressively pursued Tanya, it wasn't until the end of her freshman year that she allowed him to take her virginity. They continued to date and go steady until Larry graduated, though Larry did date other girls on the sly. After graduation, Larry's dreams were realized and he made it to the NBA.

At first Tanya was tempted to break up with Larry because she was worried about what the distance would do to their relationship, but she loved him too much to let him go without doing what she could to make it work. To her surprise, their relationship continued to thrive, with Larry proposing marriage during her senior year. Shortly after graduation, they got married, and their marriage yielded three beautiful children.

Tanya had no doubt that Larry loved her, but he had an extensive history of infidelity, and neither scolding, fighting nor counseling had a major effect on Larry's behavior. The straw that broke the camel's back was when Tanya discovered a secret credit card that Larry had and when she investigated the bills she realized that not only had Larry brought his mistress a car, but he also had brought her a townhouse and they took two vacations together the previous off-season.

Though Tanya still loved Larry and could not see herself with any other man, these indignities were not something her pride would let her to continue to accept. She gave Larry an ultimatum: either grow up, act like a husband and stop cheating, or leave once and for all. Finally the one thing happened that Tanya thought would never happen: she and Larry got divorced. Tanya's belief was that when you married, you married for life.

Tanya plunged into the depths of depression. Though she didn't have any money worries because the judge awarded her a financial settlement over ten million dollars, Tanya still was greatly depressed because she felt like it was her lack of sexual experience that forced Larry to seek sexual favors elsewhere. It was only the great love for her children and belief in God that kept her from ending her own life.

One would have thought that being made a millionaire while still in her early thirties would have made Tanya ecstatic, but it brought Tanya no joy. She got married because she loved Larry not because she cared about his money. At first when the judge awarded her that large settlement, she was tempted to give it back. It took a lot of discussion with her mother and a couple of her girlfriends to convince her to keep the money for the sake of the kids. Tanya was still unconvinced because for the life of her she couldn't figure out why three kids would need over ten million dollars.

It wasn't that Larry was hurting for the money, as the judge had left him well over twenty-five million, but she didn't like the mentality that came along with that kind of money and she wasn't sure that she wanted her children raised like that. She was afraid that her children would grow up not just with a sense of privilege but a sense of entitlement as well. She had already decided that the kids would be raised as if they didn't have the money. There would be no nannies or maids or other household helpers even though they lived in a large twelve-room house and keeping it clean was no small task. Larry was never happy about it, but she worked hard keeping their home clean. He felt like she could have had a better use for her time and she did miss working on her career, but she was raised that keeping a clean home was a woman's responsibility and no one else had been able to clean the house to her satisfaction.

So each of the kids had their own chores to perform, and they would earn allowances only if their chores were satisfactorily done. Even the landscaping would be taken over by her son when he became fourteen. Tanya was determined the kids would learn the value of a hard day's work with the proper reward. They were instilled with most of the same values that Tanya was raised with. It took hard work to have a prosperous farm, and to her knowledge, hard work hadn't killed anyone yet.

It was also a fact that excellent grades in school were not an option but an expectation. They were each enrolled in very prestigious private schools, and Tanya expected each to be close to the top of their class. If they weren't, Tanya was okay with that, but they better have her convinced that the lower grades were despite a maximum effort.

Tanya had settled into her life raising her children when she met Omar. She wasn't looking for male companionship, and she never expected to feel love again when Omar thrust himself into her life. He was everything that Larry wasn't, including being attentive, friendly, openly affectionate, and he went way out of his way to make her happy. He even picked her and the kids up and took them to church. He had never attempted to make love to her, saying that though he found her very sexy and attractive, he wanted their first time to be special.

Tanya finally took him up on his offer to take her on an eight-day Caribbean cruise with stops in St. Thomas, St. Maarten, and the Bahamas. At first Tanya was reluctant to leave her children alone for such a long time, but her mother convinced her that she needed a vacation. So Tanya left the kids with Larry and went on the cruise with Omar.

There was something strange about Omar, but Tanya couldn't put her finger on just what it was. It wasn't just that he seemed to be too good to be true, and she could still hear her mother saying "if it's too good to be true then it probably isn't," but it was something else. The way they had met was strange. First she saw him at church a couple of times and then he showed up at the restaurant where they usually went after church and introduced himself to her and the kids, saying that he was new in town and just wanted to meet her because she looked like such a nice lady and good mother.

For the next couple of weeks, he was nothing but a gentleman, and slowly they became friends. He was good with the kids, filling some of the void left by Larry leaving but not trying to take his place. Finally, she had invited him over and they had a lovely evening together as a family, ending the evening playing board games. After that she and Omar started going out alone at least three or four times a week. She didn't want the kids getting any more attached to him in case things didn't work out between the two of them. After a couple of months, they had gotten so close that she was no longer depressed or lonely.

At first, she was scared that Omar might have been after her money, but he never let her pay for anything, not even her own way. But then he had insisted that she pay for the cruise with her charge cards, saying that he didn't have any credit cards and the rate was cheaper when a credit card was used. His explanation that he had recently destroyed all his credit cards when he accumulated a lot of credit debt and hadn't reestablished his credit yet seemed plausible enough. But then who destroyed *all* of their credit cards? Didn't it make sense to keep at least one in case he ever needed it? Despite her misgivings, Tanya was prepared to go ahead and charge the cruise, figuring at least this way she would find out if he was up to no good. Three days later Omar showed up with both their tickets, rendering the whole matter moot.

Then there was the incident with the flight to Miami to catch the cruise ship. Instead of having her charge the tickets, Omar had insisted on getting his own ticket, saying he had some business that might make him take a later flight but he ended up on the same flight. The bad thing about this was their seats weren't next to each other, but Omar had fixed that problem by paying the guy next to her a hundred dollars so he could sit next to her.

At one time, Tanya worried that Omar might be married, but he demonstrated no evidence of any other woman was in his life. After her experience with Larry she knew many of the traits of a man who was cheating. She kept a close eye on Omar, but he demonstrated none of those signals. She had both his cell and his home phone number, and he spent so much time with her it was impossible that any wife would allow him to be away from home that much. Omar didn't have a business address as he said he worked as a consultant out of his house. If he was a dealer, pimp, or other person who made his money in the street, she saw no evidence of that either. Everything appeared to be just as he claimed it to be, but still she had feelings of misgivings. Maybe it was her female intuition or a guardian angel whispering in her ear, but sometimes despite all the evidence to the contrary, she felt that something just wasn't right. Finally, she convinced herself that it was her imagination or her acting out on some strange feelings of guilt, and she proceeded on her trip.

The first day of the cruise was full of so many pleasures that Tanya felt she was living in a dream. The ship's crew and Omar were so attentive to her needs and desires that it seemed as if they were only there for her. It was almost as if every wish was anticipated and fulfilled before she could even express those wishes. After dinner Tanya and Omar went into one of the lounges to listen to a jazz quartet and sample a cognac or two. They then went for a romantic stroll along the promenade desk enjoying the crisp ocean breezes and the soothing moonlight.

As they retired to their cabin, Tanya wondered whether this would be the night they would make love for the first time. Though she was nervous because it had been a while since she had last made love and she had never had sex with anyone but Larry, Tanya still felt a strong desire for Omar's body. Since their room only had one bed, it was a foregone conclusion that they would sleep together, and in Tanya's mind that meant that would probably make love as well. That first night they didn't make love, though. Tanya fell asleep in Omar's arms, and throughout the night she could feel him caress her hair, her shoulder, her back and almost her entire body. But it was not done in a sensuous or erotic way. Tanya woke a couple of times during the night. She laid there looking at the moon through the porthole and listening to Omar's gentle snoring until she dozed off again. Another time she woke up to see Omar looking at her face. After looking in his eyes for a few moments, she gave him a gentle but passionate kiss and she nestled closer to Omar and then dozed off to sleep.

She woke up the next morning fully refreshed and feeling closer to Omar than she thought was possible at this point in a new relationship. Many of her doubts about his motives had evaporated and she dared to think that just maybe he cared as much about her as he said he did. Then she had a thought that erased some of the great feelings she was experiencing. What if Omar didn't make love to her because he didn't find her attractive?

This logic didn't make sense because if he wasn't attracted to her, why would he come on this cruise with her? Even though she told herself that her new doubts about Omar didn't make any sense, she found these thoughts nagging at her like a mosquito in her bedroom on a dark summer night. It was amazing how divorce can destroy a person's self-confidence.

To many Christians, marriage is a sacred covenant. To be successful the institution of marriage requires supreme commitment, obligation, and sacrifice. And if it fails it can wreak havoc at the root of who you are. You can lose faith with institutions, other people and yourself. For someone like Tanya, who lacked confidence in herself in the first place, it was especially traumatic and was destroying the little bit of confidence her marriage to a superstar had started to instill in her. She was so devastated that she often wondered how she could go on. She knew it was only the love for her God and the love for her children that gave her the strength to face each day.

She and Omar had showered and dressed for a leisure day aboard ship. They were sitting out on the promenade desk eating some breakfast and enjoying a beautiful day in the tropics, when Tanya couldn't control her anxiety any longer. The question literally burst from her lips: "Omar, don't you think I'm attractive?"

"Of course I do. I think you're a beautiful, vivacious woman who also happens to be sexy as hell."

"But I'm a mother and no longer a young teenager. How can you still find me attractive?"

"Because I prefer a mature woman who knows her body and what she enjoys. Plus, I don't have the patience for the games that a lot of these young girls play. Some of them are either looking for a sugar daddy or trying to trap you into a relationship by getting pregnant."

"Is that why we haven't made love, because you think I might try to trap you by getting pregnant?"

"No, absolutely not. I explained why we haven't made love yet, and I want to stress the word yet. I didn't want to rush things. I want you to be comfortable and confident in that I truly care about you. I want a long-term relationship with you, not a quick hop in the sack, bust a nut, and go our own separate ways. I want to be a part of the rest of your life and share many happy moments with you. Why do you ask?"

"Because I didn't think you wanted me."

"I can honestly say that having you lay next to me and not making love to you is probably the hardest thing I ever had to do."

"Why is it so important to you that we continue to wait? You had to know that I wanted you as much as you wanted me."

"I thought you did but I wasn't sure and I thought it would be wise to be sure before I made a move."

"Are you sure now?"

"I have a better idea, and if the mood hits both of us again like that, I will take things a little different. Now, what would you like to do today?"

"I want to finish exploring the ship and then we can go down to the casino because I'm feeling lucky. After dinner, I want to go check out the show."

"Your wish is my command. We can do all that and more today."

With her doubts and insecurities eased, the conversation eased into more casual conversation. They had a friendly and enjoyable day including a visit to the casino where Tanya won almost a hundred dollars. She was grateful that Larry had taken her on several cruises or she would have been like Omar who seemed like a country bumpkin as he marveled as the magnificence and splendor of the ship.

Though the ship was less than fifteen years old, it had recently undergone a 10 million dollar renovation, and where it was luxurious before, now it rivaled a floating palace. From the numerous boutiques to the deluxe staterooms to the elegant lounges and dining areas, deep polished wood and smoky etched glass and crystal chandeliers abound throughout the ship. Omar seemed especially impressed by the numerous elevators about the ship. He couldn't believe that a boat would be so big that it would have four elevators until Tanya pointed out that the ship was more than a dozen stories (or decks) high and it would not do to have rich customers climbing several stories multiple times each day.

They relaxed and had a great time bolstered by numerous Mai Tais, which was the ship's drink of the day. Buoyed by the tropical fruit juices and rum concoction, that night when they went to bed, they no longer tried to control their passions and they made love several times during the night. Tanya wasn't impressed by Omar's proficiency in bed, but it had been quite a while since she had come so many times in one night. She wondered whether she underestimated Omar expertise or whether she had such a good time because she hadn't made love in so long. There was no denying she had a lot of passion built up. And though she had slight aching in her loins, she couldn't wait until that night and they made love again so she could find out the truth of the matter.

Over the next couple of days, they made love more times than she could count. The lovemaking wasn't extraordinary but it was satisfying. What it did also was contribute to the overall cruising experience and make it more enjoyable and relaxing then anything she had done in years. After four days at sea, Tanya was disappointed to think that her cruise would soon be coming to an end. She was out on the balcony enjoying the sunrise and a morning cup of coffee when Omar emerged from the cabin.

Omar said, "Hey babe, what are you doing? I woke up and realized you weren't in bed and got to wondering where you were."

"I couldn't sleep and I didn't want to wake you so I figured I would come out here and enjoy the sunrise. Isn't it beautiful?"

"That it is." Omar said as he pulled up a chair and wrapped his arms around Tanya. They sat there for a few minutes just enjoying the beauty of God's work in all its majesty. After a while Omar said, "How come you couldn't sleep? Is something bothering you?"

"No, everything is fine. In fact, I'm enjoying myself so much, I'll be sorry to have to go back home in a few days."

"So why go back home? Why don't you just stay another week?"

"I wish I could."

"Why can't you?"

"Because this is an eight-day cruise and I only made arrangements for the kids till the end of the week."

"Why don't you call Larry and see if he can keep them another week?"

"I think he said he has commitments for next week so I don't know if he could keep them."

"Tell him they're his kids too and to make arrangements for them. Or maybe you can call your mother and ask her to keep them?"

"This is crazy. I just can't stay away like that, I have obligations."

"That you are always handling. I don't think two weeks is too much to ask for. I think you should at least ask your mom. What can it hurt?"

"But what about the ship? Would they allow us to stay another week?"

"If we pay for it they probably wouldn't have a problem with it. The most they would probably do is make us change our cabin. I'll tell you what we'll do. You call your mother and make the arrangements with her, and I'll speak to the cruise officials and take care of that."

"I guess it wouldn't hurt to see what she says. Okay, let's do it. Can I at least pay for my share of the next week? And what about your business? Can you get away for another week just like that?"

"I can take care of things on my end, and I told you this vacation is on me. You can pay for the next one."

"Okay, if you insist. I guess I owe you one. It's a little early to call my mom or Larry, but I'll call them in a couple of hours."

After breakfast Tanya went and made her calls. She was slightly surprised that her mother not only agreed to help out with the kids but she thought it was a good idea. Omar and Tanya went about having a great day enjoying all the pleasures that the tropics had to offer. Tanya assumed that Omar was in such a good mood because he was successful in securing the extra week.

That night they enjoyed a surf and turf dinner, followed by apple martinis and dancing at the disco. They retired to the cabin for some passionate lovemaking while the disco was still in full swing. In the cabin, one deep soul-searching kiss was followed by another. Instead of leading her to the bed, Omar guided her to the balcony. She wondered what was on his mind but she followed his lead. He turned her to face the sea and his groin was seductively pressed against her buttocks. He said, "Look how beautiful the moon is tonight." As he lifted her skirt and removed her panties and entered her from behind. At first Tanya started to resist, as this was the first time she had ever made love in such an open or public place. Then she realized that only the dolphins and fish could see her and the noise from the disco drowned out her cries of passion, so she let herself go. She came with more strength and urgency than she had never experienced before and she rested, spent and exhausted with her head on the railing. She felt Omar grab her legs and she started to stop him because she needed a few moments of rest before they started again. Too late she realized his intentions were not related to passion or pleasure as he lifted her legs and flipped her over the railing. As she plummeted the dozen decks to the surface of the water, her screams mixed with the sounds from the disco.

Omar lit a cigarette as he calmly watched Tanya splash about for several minutes and then her head disappeared beneath the waves. Omar watched to make sure she didn't resurface and he intently listened for cries of man overboard. When none came, he waited fifteen minutes then he returned to the cabin, wiped it down as best he could, and packed his bag. The next morning at the next port of call he left the ship and took a cab to the airport where he caught his flight back to New York.

Chapter Five

Brandon Barnett checked his watch to see if he had enough time to keep both of his meetings. He figured he might be able to make them both, but he would definitely be cutting it pretty close. One of his business practices were to never be late so it would be wise to cancel one of his meetings. He would not have run into this conflict but an earlier business luncheon ran longer than he anticipated. He really didn't mind though because the meeting had been successful. He had made the arrangements for a multi-million-dollar endorsement deal for one of his prospective clients.

Brandon was the CEO of a fledgling agency that currently represented a dozen athletes, a couple of actors, and three recording artists. His agency, International Media Artists, was not one of the heavy hitters in the business yet, but they had only been in business three years. He had a lot of plans that he still wanted to implement, and if they were successful it would make them one of the heavyweights in this business. Locking down that endorsement deal with Coca-Cola from that business lunch should go a long way toward securing his fifth big-name client.

Tank Battle had been among his first clients and obtaining and satisfying every one since then had required a tremendous effort. Brandon knew the importance of having among his clientele certain marquee athletes because that would draw the lesser known athletes as well. Adrian Chase was the second quarterback chosen in the National Football League draft, and he had several other agents pursuing him. He felt that Adrian was leaning toward him, and today's deal could convince him that he could not only negotiate with the best of them but also obtain the type of endorsements that every athlete wanted.

As he was changing clothes Brandon reflected on how far he had come since his days as Pred and the shootout in Baisley Projects. So much had happened since that day when they had to hide out in that lady's apartment. True to their word they had stayed two days and left the lady unharmed and $5,000 richer. Justice had wanted to kill the woman because he felt it would be safer not to leave any witnesses, but Pred had held firm in his belief that it wouldn't benefit the lady to turn them in. The $5,000 in her pocket and the possibility that Pred and Justice would come after her and her family more than outweighed her sense of civic responsibility.

Pred didn't want to take a chance that if they killed the woman and, in the ensuing investigation, the cop who had interviewed him outside the building would remember him.

They had gotten out of the building without anyone paying them any attention, but two days later Justice had to go to the hospital because his wound had become infected. The hospital was required by law to report to the police anyone who is treated for a gunshot wound. Once the hospital turned in the report about Justice, the police obtained a search warrant for his house where they found the guns from the shootout. Though they weren't able to pin the shootout on Justice, they arrested him for possession of a deadly weapon and sentenced him to two to five years in prison.

Brandon had already decided to get out of the assassination game, but he agreed to a few more jobs before he quit. A third of the money earned from these jobs would go to Justice's mother to tide her over until Justice could make it back to the streets. Another third of the money would go to Justice's girlfriend to help support Justice's three-month-old daughter. Though Justice had left them money, he was sure it wouldn't be enough to hold them until he was released. Justice was grateful for Brandon looking out for his family and swore his undying loyalty to Brandon.

Brandon, meanwhile, had put Pred to rest and returned to high school. High school had long since lost any challenge to him, and he was able to obtain excellent grades with very little effort. He instead devoted himself to studying for the SAT'S and when he took them he got near perfect scores. Rather than wait until his senior year, Brandon took and easily passed the G.E.D. He was offered several academic scholarships and the next fall he started matriculating at the University of Pennsylvania, where he entered a five-year program to get a Master's degree in Business Administration.

Throughout his college days Brandon spent a lot of time hanging in Philadelphia. The ambience and culture of the city reminded him of New York City. During his sophomore year Brandon got together with a couple of brothers from Temple and Villanova and started giving parties at different clubs in Philadelphia. Brandon would call friends in New York to bring down some of New York's hottest DJs, MCs, and rap groups to battle the best that Philadelphia had to offer. For crowds aged nineteen to twenty-eight, Brandon's parties became the hottest parties in the city. Brandon made sure his parties were full of the most beautiful women he could find by not only giving them free tickets but also free drinks as well. Brandon even brought down several busloads of gorgeous women and brothers from NYC adorned in their finest hip-hop attire. Brandon's monthly parties became the must-attend events among the party crowd. He made sure that security was tight and no one was allowed in without being frisked and scanned for weapons.

Using the famous Studio 54 nightclub as a model, Brandon did everything he could to make sure his parties were attended by Philadelphian recording stars, college and professional athletes, and other local celebrities. They were treated in a manner that was fitting with their status as celebrities and stars. They were provided not only with free admission but also free food, free liquor, and in a few cases high-grade cocaine and reefer. Brandon knew that people would pay handsomely to party with those people they considered celebrities. The amount of money Brandon made off these parties was more than enough to pay his tuition if he ever needed it to, but he was still on scholarship and was maintaining very high grades. Brandon used the money instead to buy himself a used BMW and to associate with several professional athletes.

As time passed Brandon became close friends with several major athletes. Many of those friends had professional aspirations and expectations. One night three days after the NBA draft, Brandon and his friends went out with Elijah Swinett to celebrate his selection in the draft by the Portland Trailblazers. They were sitting in the VIP section enjoying drinks and greeting well-wishers when Brandon asked Elijah. "Have you signed with an agent yet?"

"Not yet, a couple of guys approached me but I'm not really impressed with any of them."

"You need to take your time and make the right decision because whoever you choose will have a major impact on your immediate future."

"You're right about that and that's why I was thinking, why don't you represent me?"

"Who, me?"

"Yeah, you."

"Man, you're bugging. I'm not a lawyer. What do I know about the law? You see, that's what I'm talking about. You can't afford to put somebody in such an important position just because they're your boy. Any mistake that I or another amateur would make, you would pay for."

"I know you're not a lawyer and believe it or not I'm not putting you on because you're my friend but because I believe you would do a great job."

"How many of those drinks have you had?"

"No, B, I'm serious. I know that you're young and inexperienced in the law, but I've watched you run this party business for over a year now. You've negotiated with these club owners and some of them have even been mob-affiliated and still you have fought for those things you wanted tooth and nail. You have a way with people and you achieve your goals without making enemies. I think that will come in real handy during negotiations. During negotiations, you have to be strong, steadfast, and maybe even confrontational but afterward we will have to be on friendly footing because they are still going to be my bosses and I will still have to deal with them."

"But Elijah, if you show up with a young, inexperienced guy who isn't even a lawyer they might not take you seriously. They would probably try to take advantage of you. I know I would."

"I've considered all that, but on the other hand, I know I can trust you. I know you would be looking out for my best interest and I'm not sure I can say that about those other agents."

"You're serious, aren't you? I see you've given this a lot of thought."

"You damn right I'm serious. After all, this is my future we're talking about here."

"If you're that serious, can I at least have a few days to think about it?"

"You damn right you can. In fact, I would be worried if you didn't think about it for a few days."

After mulling it over for a few days, Brandon ultimately decided not to represent Elijah. They decided that he would act as an advisor, and they remained friends for years after Elijah professional playing days were done. Though Brandon didn't represent Elijah, it opened his eyes to the lucrative world of sports management. Upon graduation, Brandon decided to take a chance and open his own business. He knew if he was going to be successful he had to do things in a way that could compete with the other agents. He opened an office in Manhattan, New York, on the Avenue of the Americas. He supplemented the money he had left from his party giving days in college with a loan from Justice, who agreed to be his silent and invisible partner.

Justice had gotten out of prison after serving two and a half years and had returned to the illegal street life. He not only still worked as an assassin, but he also had one of the most vicious drug posses in New York City. When Brandon approached him about putting some of his money in a legitimate business, he invested the $125,000 without hesitation. He figured if he ever decided to get out of the street life, it would be nice to have some legal money coming in.

Brandon realized the one key element necessary to make the business work was clients. He had several associates from his college days that had jumped at the chance to join his agency and he also had a couple of Elijah's former teammates that Elijah had referred him to but obtaining those high-profile marquee players was more difficult. The standard agent fee was usually between 15 and 20 percent; Brandon charged between 12 and 15 percent. He also put together a very efficient staff.

Leslie was an extraordinarily beautiful woman who also happened to have a MBA from New York University. She was Brandon's second in charge, and she was as much of a mover and shaker as he was. The firm also had Joshua Perkins, who handled all the legal matters and made sure that contracts were understood and reflected what the clients wanted them to. The final executive at the company was Cynthia Dansforth, who was in charge of investment and financial matters. She invested a portion of each client's income, made sure the tax loopholes were appropriate and that all taxes were timely paid. Cynthia had a brilliant financial mind and had worked as an investment counselor for a while but had left Wall Street because of the opposition she felt she encountered because she was a woman.

As Brandon finished changing, he reached a decision: he would let Leslie handle the meeting with Adrian and he would keep his other appointment. He called Leslie on the interoffice phone. "Leslie, I need you to handle the meeting with Adrian. I have another appointment that I cannot reschedule. He's on the verge of signing with us and if you can seal the deal, fine. If not, don't worry about it. It's going to happen. Tell him about the deal with Coca Cola but don't go into specifics. I'll handle that when I see him."

"Should I take Giselle with me?"

Giselle was a beautiful part-time model, part-time call girl who had helped sway a couple of clients for them.

"Yeah, being with two beautiful women will probably help him see the benefits of signing with our agency. I'll trust your judgment whether Giselle should spend the night with him or not."

"Okay, Brandon, I will handle Adrian. Who are you meeting with?"

"It's personal, but I might choose to tell you about it later."

Brandon changed from his finely tailored suit into a rather non-descript outfit, composed of a black leather jacket, black pants and a light blue turtleneck sweater. He put on a pair of aviator shades and drove his car to 79th street where he promptly parked it and walked three blocks to catch a cab up to 149th street in the Bronx. He then went downstairs and caught the number two train to 135th Street. He disembarked from the train and went to a bar on 138th street and Lenox Avenue. They kept it quiet but he and Justice were part owners. He stopped at the bar and got two Jack Daniels on the rocks and went toward the back where he sat at an empty table.

After about fifteen minutes, Justice and Omar entered the bar, and after looking around, they came and joined Brandon at his table. After Justice and Brandon exchanged greetings and handshakes Justice introduced Omar to Brandon.

"How did things go?" Brandon asked.

"They went okay." Omar said.

"Then you thought the plan was okay?"

"I thought it was a little involved and it took way too much time. But other than that, I thought it was okay."

"You didn't think you were paid enough for the amount of time that the plan required?"

"No, I was cool with the pay. I just didn't understand why you wanted me to go through all the trouble of acting like I was her boyfriend and all that crap. If you wanted me to kill her, why didn't I just go up to her and shoot her."

"Is that why you didn't follow orders? Because you didn't understand the plan?"

"What do you mean? I followed the plan."

"Oh, you really think you did? Why is then that you are back in New York and the cruise has been over for two days and no one has reported her missing? An investigation into her whereabouts should have been well underway."

"I convinced her to call everyone and tell them she was going to spend an extra week on the ship. I figured it would give me more of a chance to get away."

"Who in the hell told you to think? You were paid to do as you were told, exactly as you were told. Nobody told you to improvise," Brandon angrily exclaimed.

Justice interjected, "Take it easy Pred."

Ignoring him Brandon continued, "Let me ask you one last question? Did you screw her?"

"What do you mean?"

"Nigger, you know just what I mean. I mean, did you fuck her?"

"I don't see where that's any of your business."

"It's my business because I'm paying you a hundred grand to do a job and not to get your shit off. So I'm paying you for a straight answer."

"I don't see what difference it makes. The bitch is dead whether I fucked her or not."

"Then you admit that you did fuck her?"

"Of course I did. What did you expect? I had to chase that broad for weeks and then I had to sleep in the bed next to her, and you didn't think I would touch her?"

"Justice, you did explain to this idiot that if he wanted to get paid, he had to follow the plan exactly as we laid it out."

"Man, I know you ain't thinking about not giving me my money."

"If you were so worried about your money, you should have thought about that when you were putting your dick in places it shouldn't have been."

"What was she, your old lady or something? You are acting like a jealous bitch."

"Who do you think you're talking to?'"

"I'm talking to you, punk, and I'll tell you one more thing," Omar said as he stood up and placed his hand on his gun. "If you think you can get out of paying me the money you owe me, you're dead wrong."

Brandon stood up as he prepared to bring Pred out of his long hibernation. "If you think I'm some young punk who you can threaten and get away with, you better think again. Justice, you better hip your boy on who he's messing with before he ends up in a world of hurt."

Realizing the situation was only seconds out of spinning so far out of control the damage would be irreversible, Justice intervened, "Both of you, chill out for a second, this situation ain't so deep that we can't fix it. Omar, this is my man and we've been slinging and banging for a lot of years. I need you to chill out and take your ass home. I'll talk with Pred and straighten this shit out. Don't worry, you'll get what coming to you."

Omar said, "Okay, Justice, since you've always been straight up with me, I'm gonna let you handle this shit. But if you don't work it out, you know what I'm going to do," Omar said as he walked out the bar.

Brandon turned to Justice and said, "Yo, Justice, I know you're carrying. Give me your piece and let me go handle that bitch-ass nigger."

"Naw, Pred, take a deep breath and relax. If that nigger has to get done, I'll take care of it but you need to chill out for a few ticks. What's going on, Pred? I know Omar didn't handle things just like the plan, but it seems like you're overreacting a bit. What am I missing?"

"The first thing is that the reason we needed her reporting missing at the conclusion of the cruise was because the client had the kids while she was on the cruise, thus he had a legitimate alibi. He followed the plan and returned the kids to her mother as the cruise was ending because that's where Tanya was supposed to pick up the kids. If it isn't discovered that Tanya is missing for an additional four days due to the ingenious innovation of that fucking idiot, then our client doesn't have an alibi to cover that time until the discovery was made. I realized that something was wrong when her disappearance wasn't reported after two days, so I sent the client and his girlfriend to Hawaii at my expense to provide an additional alibi. That still leaves two days where the client doesn't have a suitable alibi. It probably won't be a problem because the client will be able to account for his whereabouts, but that's not what he paid us for. We promised him when he paid us he will be without suspicion and he probably wouldn't even be questioned more than the routine questioning. Omar has put that in jeopardy because he wouldn't follow orders."

"I can see where Omar made things a little iffy by not following the plan, but what is the harm because he screwed the client's ex-wife. She was getting ready to die anyway. Who did he hurt?"

"In this case he didn't hurt anyone because the timing of what he did and where he did it, but we have to maintain a general policy that no one is to have sex with any of the intended victims. A man may not want his ex-wife but he usually doesn't want anyone else to fucking her and they sure won't pay us a million dollars so someone else can have that pleasure. This is a business and it pays damn well too and we're paying our people a pretty penny to handle their end of what has to be done. This is not an opportunity for them to get high and screw high-powered women. We have to make sure that every last single man who works for us stays disciplined and does exactly as we tell them. That way nobody gets caught and nobody even gets wind of what is going on. I'm not going to jail because some asshole can't follow orders or control his urges. You and I sit down and design this shit so it goes off without a hitch and all of us gets paid if they do what we say."

"I hear what you're saying man and I'll speak with Omar."

"I think it's gone past the speaking phrase. We have to get rid of Omar."

"Are you sure that you don't want to do him because y'all had a beef?"

"If I thought he understood where he messed up and was willing to go along with the program, I would overlook our beef but that doesn't seem to be the case. Right now, he's just a loose end that's not worth the risk. He's got to go, and if you don't want to do it, I'll handle it."

"Naw, I'll take care of it. We agreed that you will stay out of the terminating part of the business because you are the only link to our clients. I'll make sure it's taken care of. Now that's decided, what else do we have to discuss?"

"I have two more cases for us to handle. One is a straight-ahead job. There's a football player in St. Louis who got a stripper pregnant. The girl also works as a hooker, so it should be pretty easy to act like a client popped her and no one will suspect the client because no one really knows about the connection between the two of them."

"If she's living like that, maybe the baby isn't even his."

"I mentioned that to him, but he doesn't want to take the chance and I pointed out that if the DNA confirms the baby is his and the girl is killed then the plan gets much more elaborate, expensive, and risky."

"How much are we charging him?"

"I'm giving him the bargain basement price of only 400 G's because not only should this be a pretty simple job but he also joining our agency and bringing four of his friends with him. The agent that they deal with has lost the five of them major money with bad investments. He has convinced them to come join our agency with him."

"That's cool; things are really starting to come together. If things keep progressing like this, soon we'll be one of the top agencies in the business," Justice said as he gave Brandon some dap.

"Yeah, things are really starting to pick up. I was thinking about adding a person to help handle the investment end of the agency. We've got to make sure the legit part of the business is 100 percent on point."

"Do your thing; you know you have my complete trust in how you're leading the company. What about the other job?"

"That one's much more elaborate. Let me tell you my ideas and you can help firm up the plan."

Chapter Six

Heather Cabernet finished putting the finishing touches on dinner as she grated the Romano cheese to go over the pasta with shrimp and grilled chicken. She knew the boys would be less than thrilled about having pasta for dinner, especially since they thought they had convinced her to prepare hamburgers and French fries. As a wise mother, she understood the art of compromise and had picked up a chocolate layer cake from the bakery, and if they ate dinner with a minimum of complaint, she would reward them with a slice for dessert. As she was fixing their plates, she called to the boys to stop playing in the den and go wash their hands for dinner.

As they came into the kitchen, five-year-old Tyshawn said, "Mommy, Travis splashed me."

Eight-year-old Travis protested, "He splashed me first."

"Travis, you're the oldest. You should know better than to play with your brother when I send you to do something."

"But he splashed me first," Travis said.

"No, I didn't," Tyshawn said.

"Quiet both of you and come to the table. If you don't stop fighting and behave yourself, neither one of you will get any dessert."

Rather than sacrifice their dessert, the boys declared a truce of sorts and adopted their best behavior throughout dinner. After dinner, they sat down and watched a movie together. Then Heather gave the boys their bath and put them to bed before retiring to her room and the novel that she had started the night before.

She must have dozed off because she heard a strange noise downstairs that woke her up. She also must have turned off the lights at some point because the house was dark. She tried to remember if she had turned on the alarm system. She probably had because it was part of her regular routine before she went to bed. Then she clearly could hear someone moving around downstairs. Maybe one of the boys was sneaking downstairs to steal another piece of cake?

Heather got out of bed and walked down the hallway toward the boys' rooms. Though the nightlight in the hallway was on, she didn't need it because she knew her way around the house so well she could have done it with her eyes closed. When she checked in Travis' room she saw that the bed had been slept in but was currently empty. She felt the mystery of who was creeping around downstairs had been answered. Obviously, Travis had gone downstairs to get something to eat. She checked Tyshawn's room and was surprised to find his bed unoccupied as well. For one boy to go downstairs to get food was not unusual, but an organized midnight raid was not something the boys regularly did. Heather headed downstairs with the intention of ending the boy's midnight snack and sending them back to bed. As she got downstairs she was surprised that the boys hadn't turned the lights in the kitchen on. Did the boys really think that they could prowl around the house without waking her up?

As she passed through the dining room she noticed a strange, dark bundle in the middle of the living room floor. As she crept closer she was shocked to realize that the bundle was a bound and gagged Travis, who was either asleep or unconscious. She rushed toward her son but turned as she sensed someone behind her. She was shocked to see a tall, stocky built man standing behind her. He was attired in black and had a ski mask over his face.

Heather exclaimed, "What the hell are you doing in my—"

Heather was interrupted as the stranger raised his silenced gun and shot her twice in the head. The man calmly turned and picked Travis up and headed back out through the garage, pausing only to trigger the alarm as he was leaving. He placed Travis in the back of their unmarked van next to Tyshawn and closed the door as he climbed in the back beside them. As they were pulling out of the driveway they could hear a phone ringing inside the house. The driver of the van asked him, "Did you leave the note?"

"Of course," he said as he climbed in the front seat next to the driver and removed his ski mask as they headed down the deserted residential street.

· · · · ·

FBI agents Alex Waugh and Joseph Schakowsky had to show their credentials to get through the heavy cordon of police and emergency vehicles surrounding the Cabernet house. Agent Schakowsky asked the officer stationed at the door, "Where can I find the officer in charge?"

"That would be Sergeant Desisso. You can find him inside," the officer replied.

The agents had been partnered together on numerous cases over the last five years and had developed a working chemistry. Agent Schakowsky took the lead and asked the questions while Agent Waugh observed and analyzed the information they were given. The agents went inside the house and saw two different teams of officers talking pictures and collecting samples and talking to each other. The agents once again flashed their credentials and asked to be directed to Sergeant Desisso.

"Sergeant Desisso? We're Agents Waugh and Schakowsky from the FBI. We were called in because this is a possible kidnapping."

"It looks like it might be. We found what could be a ransom note upstairs in one of the boys' rooms. The two boys are missing, and we haven't been able to locate the father yet, so it's possible that the father might have the boys. He and the mother were separated with a divorce pending."

"This house seems nice enough but I wouldn't consider it luxurious. Why would someone kidnap the kids?"

"The father is Nicky Burleson."

"The football player?"

"You could call him that or you could call him the star middle linebacker of the Baltimore Ravens, who just signed a multi-year million-dollar deal."

"Isn't the team in Texas preparing for this weekend's game? It should be easy to verify if Burleson is with the team and whether the boys are with him."

"The Texas State Troopers are contacting the team, and they will also inform Mr. Burleson of the situation here if the boys aren't with him. Needless to say, this situation is a little delicate because even if the boys are with him, we have to inform him of his wife's murder while keeping him as a suspect."

"Has he been established as a suspect?"

"Not so much established as a suspect but certainly not eliminated as one either."

"Why?"

"Besides the most obvious reason of him having a serious motive, there are also a lot of troubling things about the crime scene."

"Do you mind us asking you what they are?"

"That depends on whether you are taking over the investigation," Desisso said.

"Not at this point we're not, but if we find out this IS a kidnapping and therefore a federal investigation, we need to be able to hit the ground running. Time is of the essence in cases like this. So if you will cooperate with us, for right now let's say we're just observers assisting you with your case. Does that work for you?"

"It can if you will agree that if this does become a federal investigation, we can do the case together. The Feds can handle the kidnapping and we Locals can handle the murder with the FBI bringing their many resources to bear to help us handle a very high-profile murder."

"We can get approval for that if you agree that if this is a straight murder case, we stay on the case in an advisor capacity."

"Done."

"Okay, now that we've worked out the logistics, what is there about this case that have you concerned about Mr. Burleson's role?"

"The timing of the entire scenario is suspicious to say the least."

"Could you elaborate?"

"The alarm was turned in at 1:26 A.M., a call was made to the home by the security agency at 1:28 with no response, a security detail was dispatched and arrived at 1:37, received no response, and waited until police officers arrived at 1:48. They said that no one entered or left the house until the officers entered the house. If the security company is accurate, and they are very efficient and highly regarded in the business so there is no reason to doubt their accuracy, the perps entered the house at 1:26 rendered the boys unconscious, murdered the mother, and left the house and vicinity within twelve minutes. That's possible but not probable even for highly trained individuals."

"You're right, that's a very close timetable. We'll have to recheck the numbers as the investigation develops. Is there anything else?"

"There are a number of things that have caught our attention, including discrepancies at the entrance point, foreign fibers on the living room carpet, and a couple of other inconsistencies."

"The name on the mail and mailbox says Cabernet, but you say she was married to Nicky Burleson. Was there another man involved? This house is nice but it is not keeping with a million-dollar lifestyle. Did Mr. Burleson live here in West Virginia and commute to work in Baltimore? There're a lot of questions we have to answer before we can get to the bottom of this case," Agent Waugh said. "Let's look at the crime scene and see if we can get any clues as to what was going on. Maybe if we can get a start on solving the murder it will help us get to the bottom of this kidnapping. Can you show us the ransom note?"

· · · · ·

The next morning, Sergeant Desisso, the captain and lieutenant of the local state police, the FBI agents, and several members of the Sheriff's department met for a briefing on the details and developments of the case. As the lead officer, Sergeant Desisso conducted the meeting.

"Since last night we have disclosed numerous facts on this case. Nicky Burleson was with the rest of the Ravens in Texas and has been since they went to Texas two days ago. The boys are not with him and he hasn't seen or heard from them since he left Maryland with the team. Therefore, we will be treating this as a murder and kidnapping and the Feds will be bringing in their people to handle the kidnapping. Mr. Burleson is on a flight back here to be available to help us in the search for the boys. Mr. Burleson and his wife have been separated for four months now, and they were in the process of getting a divorce. Mrs. Burleson was getting a minimal living allowance, which was expected to greatly increase once the divorce was final. Mr. Burleson has a lengthy history of infidelities that Mrs. Burleson had proof of because she had hired a private investigator that has extensive proof, including pictures. I don't know if Mr. Burleson is still a suspect, but he did benefit greatly financially from his wife's demise."

"How did we find out about the detective? Did he come forward?" the captain asked.

"Word of the murder has just hit the media, and it will probably be the big story with the noon news reports. So the detective hadn't heard about the murder yet. No, we got his name and address off Mrs. Burleson's records she kept in her desk. Mrs. Burleson had started using her maiden name of Cabernet, and as close as we can tell there was no male involvement and she had not started dating again. She was renting the house and had enrolled the kids in school here in West Virginia once they moved here from Maryland without her husband.

"What we think happened was: the perpetrators entered the house through the garage and went upstairs where they bound the boys and removed them from the house. The victim heard them and tried to stop them and the perps killed her. Until we have something that would indicate otherwise, it would seem that the motive was to snatch the kids not kill the woman. It appeared she got in their way and paid the price for it."

"What about the ransom note?" one of the troopers asked.

Agent Waugh responded, "We sent it into the lab for analysis. We hope to get some results by later on this afternoon."

"What did the note say?" the trooper asked.

"You each have a copy of the note in your briefing folder. As you can see they are asking for a quarter of a million dollars. They said they will be back in touch with delivery instructions."

"Has there been any further word from them?"

"No, but they may not know who to contact. They probably planned to contact the mother, and now that she's gone they may not have another contact person until the father gets here. We have people manning the phone in the house, but we don't know if they're contacting us through the mail or on the phone. We just have to wait and see."

"Is the father a suspect?"

"Not at this time, but there's no reason to suspect him yet and he has a great alibi. He was halfway across the country and had been for several days."

"Were there any witnesses? Did any of the neighbors see anything?"

"We've had a little good luck there. A woman in the next cul-de-sac said she was up reading and she saw a dark blue or black delivery van come and go. She thought it was strange because it was too late for deliveries and she doesn't think the van belonged to any of her neighbors or at least she's never seen it before. We have a couple of men canvassing the neighborhood to see if anyone has a van that matches that description or maybe someone has someone visiting with that type of van. On the hopeful side, the times do correspond with the estimated times of the kidnapping so maybe we have a substantial clue."

"Should we put out an APB for black or dark blue delivery vans with no identifying markings?"

"It's a long shot but let's go for it within a hundred-mile radius. I'll have someone check our data base and see how many vans meet that description within 150 miles. I'm gonna guess that if the kidnappers are going to return the kids, they will remain somewhere nearby so they can return them quickly."

"But Agent Waugh, they can be anywhere. Both D.C. and Baltimore are less than fifty miles away and can be reached in less than an hour."

"Let's start the search anyway. It gives us something to do besides twiddle our thumbs and wait for the kidnappers to get in touch."

"Let's hit the streets and see what we can do about making some headway on this thing," the captain said.

. . . . .

The dark blue van pulled into the parking lot of the mostly empty strip mall. Two young boys aged eight and five left the van hand and hand and walked into the McDonald's restaurant where they ordered two happy meals and sat down and ate their food. They seemed very quiet and reserved and maybe a touch groggy and dazed. The manager noticed the two boys when they first came in because he thought they were very young to be in the restaurant unaccompanied by an adult. The manager went about his duties without giving them a second thought because he figured their parent must be right behind them. He was surprised to look up more than an hour later and see the boys still sitting there alone. He figured he should get to the bottom of things to make sure they were all right.

He walked up and said to the older of the two. "Are you boys all right?"

"Yes, sir, we're fine."

"Are you here with your mother or your father?"

"No, sir."

"Where are your parents?"

"We don't know."

"Well, how did you get here?"

"Those men brought us here and gave us the money for happy meals and told us to wait inside."

"What men?"

"I don't know their names."

"How many men were there?"

"Two."

"Were these men relatives or friends of your family?"

"No, sir, I haven't seen them before."

Sensing that something was really amiss with these two boys, the manager called the police, who arrived a few minutes later. The police asked the boys their names.

"I'm Travis Burleson, and this is my brother Tyshawn Burleson."

One officer stayed with the boys and the other went to the car and radioed in that the kidnapped boys had been found.

· · · · ·

Omar sat with four members of Justice's crew playing poker. They were waiting for their assignments for that week or the product they were to give to the street dealers to sell. Omar was there because Justice had told him that he needed to speak to him. Omar assumed it was because Justice was going to give him the money owed him for the Caribbean hit. Omar had been waiting almost an hour for Justice, and since Justice was prone to show up when he was good and ready, they were killing time by gambling. Right now, Omar was up three hundred dollars but that was pennies compared to the money he expected to leave there with as Justice still owed him fifty thousand dollars.

After approximately another fifteen minutes, Justice finally showed up with his second in command and two new guys who did hits and handled the violent end of their business. Omar had already done two hits for Justice, but he didn't know either of these guys. Omar was surprised that Justice was travelling with such heavy hitters. Did he have beef in the streets that Omar didn't know about? Justice called the men who had been playing poker with Omar into the back bedroom and dispensed the drugs that they needed to give to their teams. After they left, Justice called Omar into the back room.

"Yo, Justice, what's up, man? Do you have something for me?"

"Yeah, I got you covered, but I don't travel with that amount of cash on me."

"Why not? It's not like somebody is going to try to rip you off and if they did, you had more than enough firepower with you."

"I don't carry product and cash as the same time. You leave with my boys, and they will take you to the cash and pay you off. You lay low for right now, and I'll put you back to work in a couple of weeks."

"If you wasn't gonna have my money, why did you have me meet you here?"

"Nigger, don't go questioning what I do or how I do it or where I do it. Did you forget who the boss is? Now, do you want your money or not?"

"It's fifty G's right?"

"Yeah, I had to argue with my peeps over that though, because he had to lay out another ten G's to cover the change of alibi thanks to your fucking ingenuity. I talked to him, and we agreed for it to come out of my end."

"So he and I are cool."

"I don't know if I would call it cool, but he will hire you again once he's sure you can follow orders. These are the high-profile jobs and they pay long loot, and if you want to deal with that kind of paper again, you've got to convince me that you know how to perform shit the way we lay it out."

"Hey, man, I follow orders. I don't know why you're tripping. The job was handled."

"I'm not going to keep trying to explain this to you. You just don't want to get it, so go get your money and I'll talk with you later."

Omar left the bedroom, and as he was leaving the apartment the two hit men fell into step behind him. There was something about their demeanor that triggered alarms in Omar. Were they there to protect Justice or to eliminate him? Who was Justice's partner and did he have enough juice to have Justice get rid of him just because they had a beef? Was that really their intention or was he just being paranoid?

Omar regretted coming to this meeting without being properly armed. He had to find out their intentions and damn soon, so he could come up with a plan of action. He had no intention of going down without a struggle if they were planning to kill him.

Omar asked, "Where do we have to go to pick up my package?"

"We have to go to a spot over on 127th."

"Why don't I meet y'all there? I got some business that I should have taken care of an hour ago. I didn't think I would be waiting around for Justice so long."

"Naw, that wouldn't be cool. Justice said to take you right there and come right back after we handle your business. He said he has some other stuff for us to do."

"Okay, I'll follow you in my car."

"You need to ride with us. We don't need a parade of cars pulling up at the spot. You ride with us and we'll bring you back to your whip when we're done."

"That doesn't work for me because I told you I'm late for an appointment. Why waste more time having to come here for my car?"

"That's the way it has to be. Do you want your money or not?"

"Well, I need my money, so if that's what I have to do to get it, that's what I'll do. Lead on."

Omar had already made up his mind that there was no way he was going to get into a car with these two guys. They seemed too eager to get him into their car. If they weren't planning on killing him, there was no other logical reason why he had to ride with them. At any rate, it wasn't a chance he was willing to take. If he cut out on them and he was mistaken about their intention, the worst that could happen was they would think he was crazy.

Omar was already visualizing Justice's stash house and where the best place to make his dash for freedom would be. It was a bit of a problem because the stash was on the second floor of this two-family house. The hallway leading to the second floor was a narrow staircase that only one person could comfortably ascend at a time. The door leading outside led to a porch that was raised off the ground by about four feet. As they were walking down the staircase, Omar noticed the bodyguards had positioned themselves so that one was in front of him and one behind him. As Omar cleared the doorway, he realized the bodyguard behind him was still partially in the house. Using the quick reflexes and viciousness that made it possible for him to earn his living as a hit man, Omar stepped back and caught the rear bodyguard in the throat area with a wicked elbow, which left him bent over choking, gagging and trying to catch his breath. The bodyguard in front of Omar sensed the movement behind him and he turned in time to have Omar shatter his nose with a punch that blinded him and sent a spray of blood onto the walls.

Before either man could react, Omar jumped over the fallen man in front of him and he sprang out of the doorway. Then he vaulted over the side railing, turned the corner of the house and sprinted down the alleyway. Omar didn't bother looking behind him, focusing his attention of putting as much distance as he could between him and the other hit men. Omar heard two shots ring out, and it spurred him to greater speed and he started running in a zigzag pattern.

The hit man who was elbowed in the throat stopped the other hit man from shooting and said, "We can't fire around here. We can't bring any attention to the stash house. Don't worry, we'll catch him later."

Omar hurdled the back fence and kept running without breaking stride. The shots confirmed for Omar that they were planning to kill him and he started making plans on how he would leave town and where he was going. Suddenly Atlanta and Houston seemed real attractive to him, and luckily, he still had almost forty thousand left over from the Caribbean hit. It was a shame that he had to leave his car because he really loved that car but he had to figure they would post someone there waiting for him as well as at his apartment. It was a good thing he had his money stashed at his girlfriend's crib.

He just had one more stop before retrieving his money and fleeing town. He knew where one of Justice's lieutenants stopped before distributed his drugs for selling. He would stop there and take his drugs and off the lieutenant, thus killing two birds with one stone. It should bring him another twenty-five grand when he got where he was going and also deliver the message to Justice that he couldn't mess with him without repercussions.

· · · · ·

Sergeant Desisso, Agent Waugh. Agent Schakowsky and Captain Nivens of State Police were holding a press conference with the media and newspapers to bring them up to speed on the development of the Burleson murder and kidnapping. As the lead local official Sergeant Desisso was the lead man fielding the questions.

"I would like to start with this statement, please hold your questions until I am done. At 11:30 A.M., yesterday morning the FBI received a call at their regional office telling them that Travis and Tyshawn Burleson could be located at the local McDonald's on Route 111. A car was dispatched, and the two boys were found safe and unharmed. They were admitted to the hospital for examination and found to be in good health except for traces of a heavy narcotic located in their blood stream. The boys were reunited with their maternal grandparents and their recently arrived father. No further ransom was requested and none was paid. The FBI is continuing its investigation of the kidnappers, and we are also pursuing them for the murder of Heather Cabernet Burleson. We are pursuing numerous promising leads and anticipate apprehending them shortly. Questions?"

"Were the boys able to identify their kidnappers?"

"Though they were able to provide us with some identifying information, the boys are only eight and five years of age and they were unconscious much of the time."

"Is Nicky Burleson a suspect?"

"Not at this time. Mr. Burleson was with the Ravens in Texas at the time of the murder. At this time, Mr. Burleson is with his children making funeral arrangements for his wife. We questioned him and are confident that he had nothing to do with the kidnapping or murder."

"After going through all this trouble, why would the kidnappers return the boys without receiving the ransom?"

"We believe that the murder was not planned as the victim interrupted the kidnapping and the perps panicked and killed the mother. The perps then tried to avoid the intense scrutiny and investigation by releasing the boys. "

"How many suspects are there?"

"There are at least two but it could be as many as three or four."

"Who will be heading the investigation?"

"Local authorities will be the lead agency and though there is no longer a kidnapping, the FBI will continue to lend significant support until an arrest is made. That's all the questions we can handle for now, but we will update you with any additional developments."

. . . . .

Cassandra Pierce was in her alter-ego as Passionate and she couldn't wait for her shift to end. She wrapped her leg around the pole and swung down to the floor where she ended in a split. While still on the floor she gyrated her hips to the thumping, throbbing bass line of Janet Jackson's "Nasty." She moved automatically to the music though her mind was miles away. She had been doing this for so long that she had gotten down the method of dancing while her mind went to other places. Sometimes she went to tropical beaches in a country far away and sometimes she just focused on the problems in her life.

Tonight she was thinking of the life growing inside of her and the effect that it was having on her body. It seemed she was always tired, and she wondered how long she could continue to dance before her pregnancy started to seriously show.

When she first started seeing Reggie around the club, she was immediately attracted to him and the fact that he was a professional athlete and fairly rich was an added bonus. At first, he just saw her in one of the private VIP rooms for a lap dance, which escalated into oral sex, and then she started to see him outside the club at a hotel where she spent several nights making love to him. They had developed a relationship of sorts, though it was mainly sexual and she had secretly hoped that when she told him she was pregnant that he would agree to at least support her financially until after the baby was born.

Instead he had insisted that the baby wasn't his since he had used a condom the majority of the time that they had sex, but as she had sadly found out, it only took one time without a condom for these consequences. Actually, Reggie had gotten quite irate and accused her of not only being a whore but of her choosing him as the father because she knew he had money. Contrary to what Reggie believed, Cassandra was 95 percent sure that Reggie was the father because of the timing and because Reggie was the only man who had unprotected sex with her since her last relationship had ended six months ago. Even though Reggie thought otherwise, Cassandra rarely had intimate relationship with any of the men who frequented the club.

Tonight she was relieved when her shift ended and so she was a little disappointed when the manager told her that a very rich customer who had been spreading money around the club all night had requested her personally to meet him in the VIP section and give him a lap dance. He had even volunteered to pay double her regular rate. Though Cassandra was tired she knew she couldn't afford to let the extra money go, so he agreed to meet him in the room. As she came into the room and after her eyes adjusted to the darkness of the room, she noticed a fairly attractive man of about thirty years of age. He was dressed in an expensive business suit though it seemed ill-fitting, like he would have been more comfortable in a jogging suit or other hip-hop gear.

"Hey, Passionate, come on in. My name is Johnny, and I'm real glad that you agreed to come spend a little time with me. I don't mind telling you that you're so beautiful and the way you moved really turned me on."

"Thank you for the compliment. The manager said you agreed to double our normal rate."

"That's not a problem."

"I'm required to get payment in advance."

"Hey, baby, money is not an issue. You know what? I'm so into you that I don't think that a single lap dance is going to satisfy my needs. I wonder whether it would be possible to get you to agree to spend the night with me?"

"I'm not a working girl."

"I'm sorry, Boo. I wasn't trying to offend you by implying that you are a hooker. It's almost like I was asking you out on a date. Look, I'm in town from Atlanta on some business for a couple of weeks and a brother gets lonely so I was looking for a little companionship. I'm at a pretty nice hotel on the outskirts of town and we could go back to my room and we could order some room service and have a nice meal. If you are feeling me as much as I'm feeling you, you can do what comes naturally. How much do you get paid around here on a normal week?"

"I make about $1,200 plus tips."

"I'll give you $2,500 just for tonight and the money is yours to keep whether we have sex or not."

"And the money is in advance?"

"Sure, I'll give a G to you now and the rest as soon as we get to the hotel."

"This sounds like very nice offer and I'll be glad to accept."

"Are you driving or would you like to ride with me to the hotel?"

"No, I'm driving and I'll follow you."

"Okay, here's your thousand and I'll meet you in the parking lot. I'm driving the black Lexus."

Cassandra got in her car and counted her thousand dollars, which she promptly tucked away in her bra. She saw Johnny get in his car and pulled in behind him. She noticed that Johnny was wearing an expensive Sean John leather coat over his suit and driving a new model Lexus.

"I guess money isn't an issue with him," she thought as she noticed the license plate was from New York. "I thought he said he was from Atlanta. I must have misunderstood him. If he is willing to give up $2,500 just for one night, maybe he would give a couple hundred more as a tip if I really put it on him."

Cassandra thought as she decided to reach into her bag of tricks and really try to please Johnny.

As they pulled up the mid-level hotel, they entered through a side door which Cassandra noticed had been left ajar. She found this to be a little strange since hotels of this quality usually kept the doors locked for the safety of their customers. This was the second sign that things seemed a little out of order, and if there was a third, she was out of there. There were a lot of freaks out there who appeared to be perfectly normal.

When they arrived at the room, she asked Johnny to leave the door open while she checked out the rest of the suite in case there were extra guys hiding there. She wasn't trying to be the victim of a gang rape or worse. Assured that no one else was in the suite, she closed the door and removed her coat. After removing his coat, Johnny took the phone and ordered room service. Without asking her what she wanted, he ordered a steak, cheeseburger, salmon and a chicken dish she had never heard of as well as a bottle of champagne and a couple of bottles of beer. At first Cassandra started to get offended that Johnny didn't check with her about what she wanted before he ordered, but then she remembered that she was not on vacation and was there on business. She also overheard the name that Johnny gave room service and it wasn't Johnny, but she didn't think that strange because she figured Johnny wasn't his name anyway and for the business they were conducting it wasn't necessary.

Almost as if reading her mind Johnny said, "I didn't know what you wanted so I ordered the best of what they had on the menu."

"Thanks, that was pretty considerate of you. Do you want to eat before we start?"

"It should take them at least a half hour before the food arrives."

"So how would you like to do this? Do you want to be in charge, or should I do what I feel will make you happy?'

"How about a little of both?"

Taking the lead Cassandra kneeled in front of Johnny, removed his member, and proceeded to give him oral sex with all the skill she could muster. After Johnny had climaxed Cassandra asked, "Do you mind if I take a shower before the food arrives? It's been a long day and I'm kind of sweaty."

"Sure, go ahead and help yourself."

Cassandra took an extra long and soapy shower while she let the hot water ease the achiness in her muscles. She was glad for the opportunity that had presented itself as the $2,500 dollars would help with her impending financial crisis a bit.

As she came out of the shower she saw that the food had arrived and that Johnny had helped himself to something from several of the plates. She saw where he had smoked about half a joint and had done several lines of coke and already two of the bottles of beer were empty.

"Help yourself," Johnny said. "If you think of anything else you want, let me know."

"Thank you," Cassandra said as she finished the joint and two lines of coke. After she finished eating, she and Johnny started having energetic and rousing sex, which was satisfying but not extraordinary. About a half hour later, Cassandra was lying on her stomach as Johnny took her from behind. Johnny took out his belt and wrapped it around her throat. Cassandra had heard about this, people who cut off the oxygen supply until the person was ready to pass out. They said it led to a very intense orgasm in many people but Cassandra didn't know Johnny well enough to let him do this to her. She said, "Whoa, stop baby. I ain't into that."

"Come on, Passionate. I guarantee you will like it. Help me out with this, baby, I really need it. I'll tell you what, there's an extra two hundred in it for you if you let me do my thing."

"Okay, but be careful."

Johnny started stroking her again with strong, steady strokes as he gradually increased the pressure on the belt. The pressure got more and more intense until Cassandra saw spots start to flash in front of her eyes. She started flail around and instead of loosening the pressure, Johnny increased it and used his other arm placed again her neck and shoulders to hold her in place. Johnny kept increasing the pressure for five minutes after Cassandra had lost consciousness. Johnny got off Cassandra's prone and lifeless body and went and took a shower, after which he got dressed and proceeded to wipe down the surfaces of the room. He looked in Cassandra's bag and found a can of mace, a switchblade, and his money, which he immediately pocketed. He then left the room, and after he drove away from the hotel, he took his cell phone and called Justice.

"Hey, J, it's done."

"Good, dump the car and the credit cards and get a flight back to New York. I got more work for you to do. Good job."

. . . . .

Suzanne Morgan was a little distraught because her latest asthma attack wasn't responding to the medication as well as it usually did. She took another hit from her pump but did not feel that automatic relief that she usually did. Her new friend Allan had filled the prescription at the pharmacy earlier this week so she was confident that the medicine had not expired and should have been more effective. If she didn't feel better soon she was going to go to the hospital, something she hadn't had to do in a few years.

Since she had married major league baseball star Clarence Emory, she had gotten accustomed to the best medical treatment available which was a good thing because she had a lengthy history of respiratory problems. The list of things she was allergic to was very extensive, with everything from strawberries which led to a severe rash to sesame and peanuts, which if she ingested would cause her bronchi to constraint to such a severe degree that it would probably prove fatal. Even as a child, she was jealous of those other children that could eat whatever they wanted and didn't even have to read the label to check the contents. She couldn't even eat at a restaurant unless her mother checked with the cooking staff as to what was in the food before ordering.

She had lived a childhood that was not the envy of anyone she knew and she grew up feeling like she had never gotten a chance to live a normal life. By the time she got to high school she was more than ready to live the life that she thought all of her friends got to live. She wasn't an especially attractive girl, but she was told that she had a pretty good shape. She knew that Clarence was interested in her body when he started dating her. Clarence was a start on the basketball and baseball team, and she liked the prestige it gave her to be known as his girl. She knew she couldn't keep a boy as fine and popular as Clarence unless she let him have his way with her. Not willing to go back to her mundane life, she started having sex with Clarence on a regular basis even though she knew he was seeing other girls. Not wise enough to use protection, it wasn't long before she got pregnant. Though Clarence begged her, threatened her, and coerced her in every way he could, she refused to get an abortion. Of course, once she wouldn't give him his way, Clarence broke up with her.

Shortly after God blessed her with a beautiful baby boy, Clarence came around to visit his son. It wasn't long thereafter that she and

Clarence resumed their intimate relationship and since she must not have learned the error of her way, right before Clarence graduated from high school she got pregnant again. Her mother forgave the first pregnancy, figuring that anyone could make a mistake, but shortly after the second baby was born she insisted that Suzanne get her own place.

Suzanne got a job as a waitress to support herself and her children while Clarence was in college. Shortly after graduation Clarence entered major league baseball and by his third year was an all-star. He signed a very lucrative contract that gave him the chance to be one of the highest paid men in sports.

Suzanne had waited a long time for Clarence to do the right thing by their kids but other than promises Clarence had been slow on delivery. Finally, out of desperation, she had taken Clarence to court hoping to get enough to provide a decent life for her two boys. She had expected things to get better but even she was amazed at the generosity of the judge. He had awarded her a settlement of several million dollars and a monthly stipend of several thousand.

No longer having to live a life of poverty, she had bought a home in the suburbs and had quit her job as a waitress, choosing to stay home and build a better life for her sons. It was in the adult learning class where she went to get her G.E.D. that she met Allan, who had recently joined the class. Allan was an electrician who had dropped out of school to take care of his mother and sisters after his father died and though he had a thriving business, he always felt inadequate without his diploma. They had immediately bonded and Allan was more attentive than she could ever imagine any man being. He seemed to delight in doing the little things that made her life easier, like going to the drugstore and getting her medicine. She couldn't believe that the pharmacist had made such a mistake as giving her such ineffective medicine but that was hardly Allan's fault. Tonight Allan was preparing her a special meal while her kids were visiting with their father.

Allan was very much unlike the type of men she usually associated with. Their relationship was not an intimate one nor did it have the potential to one day become one. In fact, she suspected that Allan was gay and not even interested in her in that way but that didn't lessen how much she enjoyed his company and the way he helped her out. In a way it was refreshing to spend time with a man who was charming and attentive and not interested in getting in her pants.

Tonight Allan was fixing her a special meal and she hoped she started feeling better before he arrived. Her asthma was starting to ease up some though she still had difficulty breathing. It was probably a good thing that Allan was cooking because she didn't know if she could endure the exertion of cooking.

Allan arrived a few minutes early and busied himself with cutting vegetables and he had several pots going all at once as he prepared some Asian dish. He put some oils in a wok and browned garlic and ginger and added spices and then chicken and shrimp and covered it with a special sauce that he had prepared in a separate pot. The aroma coming from the kitchen was so tantalizing that it made Suzanne forget that she wasn't feeling well. She further awakened her appetite with several cups of warm sake. She usually didn't drink when she was taking medication but Allan had insisted and she figured a couple of cups wouldn't hurt much.

As Allan was preparing the plates he asked, "How did you like the sake?"

"It was a little stronger than I thought it would be."

"How many cups did you have?"

"The cups were real small so I had about four or five."

"That's quite a lot. Didn't I tell you to be careful because they had a little kick that could sneak up on you? You shouldn't have had that much on an empty stomach. Let's get some food into you before you pass out."

"What are we having?"

"One of my own secret recipes but I will share it with you if you like it."

They engaged in idle conversation as they sat down and started eating. Suzanne's immediate reaction was that the food was absolutely delicious. The variety of flavors seemed to literally explode in her mouth and she greedily swallowed mouthful after mouthful.

"What is this?" Suzanne asked.

"You tell me," Allan suggested.

"I could taste the chicken and the shrimp but there were a couple of ingredients that I had never tasted before. What were they?"

"It's a secret," Allan said with a wink. "Have a little more, and if you still can't identify it, I'll tell you after we finish."

Suzanne had three more mouthfuls before she realized that something was very wrong. She could feel the bronchial arteries in her lungs constrict and draw up at an incredible rate. Instantly she had hard time breathing and her breathing was becoming more ragged at an alarming rate. In a panic, she rushed and got her pump but as she was squeezing it she remembered how ineffective it was earlier but that didn't stop her from using it now. Unfortunately, nothing had changed and it still wasn't giving her any relief. Suzanne knew she better get help and right away or she was going to be in big trouble. Now she felt like her throat as well as her lungs had completely closed and squeezing oxygen into these vital organs was becoming nearly impossible. She felt like a swimmer who was dying and she was getting light-headed and her lungs were sending urgent messages to her brain to get it some air and now. She stumbled to her phone but was unable to stand upright.

Allan took the phone from her and said, "Are you all right? Who are you calling?"

"I…need…help…call…9…1…1."

"Aw, now that wouldn't do. I'll call them but they'll get here way too late. I think now would be a good time to tell you what my secret ingredients are: sesame seeds. And they give such a special flavor that I added a little paste made from peanuts and sesame seeds." Allan smiled as Suzanne crashed to the floor. "I think we should thank Clarence for giving us such an extensive copy of your medical records. Aw poor baby, you're suffering. Let me help things along just a little bit." Allan said as he covered her face with a pillow off the couch. The last thing Suzanne heard before the blackness engulfed her was Allan saying "Clarence said to tell you 'let's see you enjoy that money the judge gave you now, bitch.'"

Chapter Seven

Brandon had his limousine pick up the rapper from his hotel in mid-town and bring him to his favorite Soul food restaurant in Harlem. The rapper was from Philly and was one of the hottest rappers to ever come from that city. His last two CDs had sold more than 3 million units each. As the rapper and three members of his crew arrived in the restaurant, Brandon stood up to meet them. "I would prefer it if we could talk alone. Some of the things I want to say to you are meant for your ears alone. Please have your people sit and order whatever they like. The bill is on me."

EZ Money directed the rest of his crew to sit at a nearby table while he pulled up to the seat that Brandon offered. "I only agreed to meet with you because my people back in Philly said you are a serious brother who is about business. I remember the parties you used to give in Philly when I was a little kid, so I decided to hear what you have to say. What's up, partner?"

"Did you look over my proposal?"

"Yeah, I peeped it and I had my lawyers go over it. It's a good deal but nothing special. Why should I leave the agency that has been good to me to come and join you? You only handle two other rappers and all the rest of your clients are athletes. Do you even know how to handle someone who does what I do?"

"Speak with any of our other clients and they will tell you that we handle business as efficiently as anyone in the business. We will do your bookings and management for only 18 percent, which is way better than the combined 28 percent you are currently paying."

"Yeah, but their agency is tried and tested and I know what I'm getting with them."

"We have the best investment record in the business. I have at least seven endorsements lined up for you. Everything from sneakers to liquor will have your stamp of approval for a hefty price. We also have a great tax lawyer so there is a great chance if you do what she says you won't end up broke or with the government owning all your money. We're young Black men, not old White farts, who know what the rap game can be and how lucrative it can become. We can help make you one of the driving forces in business as well as the rap game."

"You talk a good game. How do I know you can deliver the things you say?"

"You are not talking to some underling or VP. This is my company, and if I say I can do something, I damn sure can do it. If I say I will do something, it damn sure gets done."

"You're still just talking. How can you prove it? Why should I trust you?"

"I'll tell you what. I'm gonna put my money where my mouth is. I'm willing to tear up the old offer and offer you a new contract that's two years instead of three and I'll only ask for two one-year options instead of three. I'll even make them mutual options, which mean we both have to agree to keep the contract going or it will cease to exist."

"Damn, Mr. Bennett, that sure sounds good but I just don't know."

"*What* don't you know EZ? Talk to me."

"You are asking me to break my existing contract. That agency has been good to me and they took a chance on me when no one else would. You're asking me to break my word to them and believe it or not, my word means a lot to me."

"Damn, a rapper with integrity. I can respect where you're coming from but dig this. You made them a shitload of money and anyone could see you were going to blow up so they really didn't take much of a chance with you." At this point, Brandon paused as he thought strongly on what he was about to say. "There is one other perk that come with our agency that we and only we offer."

"What's that, women? Blow? Shit, everybody throws that stuff my way."

"No, nothing as trivial as that. You are one of the top rappers in the game. You probably got more of that than you can handle."

"So what are you talking about? Come on, Nigger, I ain't got all day."

"First of all, don't ever refer to me using that word again please."

"My bad. No disrespect intended."

"I'm not trying to get funky with you but what we're about to talk about is serious business between men and there's no room for no bullshit, grandstanding, or games."

"Okay, you got my attention."

"First, I need your solemn vow as a man that what we are going to discuss here you will never repeat to anyone. Ever. Our lives may depend upon it."

"You got it."

"No, you have to swear."

"Okay, I swear."

"EZ, I need you to really think about this before I go any further. Don't enter into this lightly."

"Man, you make it sound like a deal with a devil or something."

"Some would call it that and others might refer to me as a revenging angel. You sure you want to swear?"

"Now I feel like I got to, if for no other reason to find out what the hell you're talking about. I swear."

"How much are you worth?"

"About 75 to 80 million. Why?"

"I understand that you have a little problem with your ex-girl-friend. If I understand the situation correctly, she used to be one of the dancers from some of your videos and you and she had two children together."

"One is mine and I'm not sure who the other father is."

"But it might be yours?"

"Yeah, I'm waiting for the DNA results now. Why do you want to know?"

"Just bear with me for a minute. So there's a chance that both children might be yours and I understand that she's suing you for child support."

"That's right."

"How do you feel about that?"

"What do you mean?"

"I mean do you love her? Do you think she's entitled to the money she stands to get?"

"Hell no. I mean we were cool and everything, but the money she's talking about is way out of line. She was never my lady or nothing. Just some freak trying to get on by screwing her way into the business. She was fine and she could do her thing in bed, but there was no way I could ever be serious about her because she had been with a lot of other rappers. I had already been right by her. I bought her a townhouse and I gave her cash every month. So the money she asking the judge for is plain crazy."

"With the way things are going in the courts these days, if both kids are yours she might get anywhere between 10 and 18 million. Do you think that's fair?"

"Hell no. That's a stupid question."

"How much would you pay to make that problem go away?"

"What do you mean?"

"I mean is it worth a million dollars to you to make the problem disappear once and for all."

"Yeah, but how can you do that?"

"That's none of your concern. But if you pay me one million dollars and sign the revised contract, I can guarantee you within two months, she will never bother you again and you will have custody of both kids."

"How will you be able to pull that off? She'll never agree to that."

"It won't matter. She won't be able to fight with you anymore."

"What do you need me to do?"

"Sign the contracts. Do exactly what I tell you to do, and most importantly, never and I mean never, discuss what we discussed here today. Not with your mother or God or anyone. Can you do that? After all, loose lips sink ships."

"Unless my lawyers tell me there's no way out of my current contract, you got a deal. What do you want me to do?"

"You can start by making nice with the young lady. Give her whatever she wants to drop the case and get out of the judge's and the public's eye. If possible, seem to be the happiest couple in America. Does she get high?"

"Just a little weed. Nothing heavier."

"Okay. I'm gonna send by some primo weed. It's going to be off the chain and laced with a little PCP. It's important that neither you or any of your crew smoke it under any circumstances. Am I clear about this so far?"

"Yeah, what else?"

"The rest of the instructions will follow later, but you should plan on taking the kids and just the kids on a vacation so y'all can get closer. We'll tell you when. You'll get the rest of the instructions from a man I will send to you later. You are to follow his instructions exactly. This is the last time we will ever discuss this matter. After this we will only discuss your music career."

"Is this how you hooked up all your clients?"

"That's none of your fucking business. If we're going work together you need to grow up and let us handle our business. Believe me, this ain't no game and we're not playing."

· · · · ·

A little over five weeks later Jasmine Norris was preparing to take a hot, bubble bath as she reflected on how strange life was. She never thought that life would have led her down some of the paths she chose but things were turning out okay. She knew she was a very beautiful woman and had the type of body that most men went crazy after. When she was a young girl she dreamed of being a fashion model or an actress but she was too short to be a model and being a successful actress took too damn long. When she was twenty-two, she appeared in her first adult video. She had thoughts about being a porno star but the business was full of young desperate women and once you were popular there it shut off a lot of other options in the entertainment field.

In a last-ditch attempt to get into the fashion industry she had moved to New York City from Detroit where she quickly moved into the high roller and party crowd. At one of these parties she had met a popular director of rap videos. After spending the night with him in his hotel room, he offered her a job as one of the dancers in a video. It only took Jasmine one video to realize that music videos would probably not be the quickest route to stardom, as there were numerous beautiful women in every video seeking to be a star. When the star of the video showed a distinctive interest in her, she realized that she would be an old worn out woman if she continued to try to sleep with every Tom, Dick, and Harry who she thought could advance her career, but if she could hook just one of these mega stars she could be set for life. The night she bedded the star of the video and though she laid some unbelievable sex on him, he was only interested in her when he wanted sex.

When Jasmine met EZ to do his video, she took a different route. She played hard to get and was resistant to his overture for sex. She had guessed right in that this star was so accustomed to getting his way that his ego had a hard time with being turned down. Instead of becoming bored and moving on to easier prey, he pursued her more aggressively. When she finally relented and made love to EZ, she made sure he used her condoms that she had discreetly poked several holes in the tip with a sewing needle. When she got pregnant, she was reasonably sure that the baby was EZ's even though she had made love to other men. After the DNA results confirmed that the baby belonged to EZ, EZ bought her a modest house in the suburbs of Detroit and gave her a monthly allowance.

While this was generous, it was far less than she knew she would get if she went before a judge but she was wasn't worried about that because she and EZ continued to have a relationship of sorts. EZ lived with her when he was so inclined, but he also had three other homes that he lived in, just staying with her when he was in the mood. She also knew that he dated and slept with other women, which made her feel it was within her rights to sleep with other men.

This went on for over a year before she got pregnant and had another son. When EZ asked her who the father was, she told him he was, but of course he didn't believe her and honestly she really wasn't sure. Responding to rumors that EZ had heard about her sleeping around, he had insisted on a DNA test and had terminated what little relationship they had. She had retaliated by taking him to court, which thrust their relationship into a state of limbo.

She was shocked but pleased when EZ approached her about resuming a serious relationship with her and their sons, and they had even spent the past month at EZ's mansion in the outskirts of Philadelphia. Though she wasn't head over heels in love with EZ, the prospect of a relationship with him was attractive because of the lifestyle he offered her. The month they had spent at the mansion was indeed pleasant, and she had the sense of a feeling of family for the first time in years. It was so good that she had stopped sleeping with Big Steve, a rapper in a different camp. When EZ suggested that he keep the kids for a few days and take them down to Sea World or Busch Gardens, she had readily agreed. She had returned to her house and had already made plans to meet with Big Steve tomorrow night. Tonight she was enjoying a quiet night at home. She was savoring a chilled glass of wine and some of that incredible weed that EZ had given her.

Having gotten the water just the way she liked it, Jasmine put out her joint and went into the bedroom and changed into her plush terrycloth robe. As she reentered the bathroom, she got the strange feeling that someone was behind her. She discounted it because she knew she was in the house by herself, but when she turned she was shocked to see a man clad all in black standing behind her.

As she opened her mouth to scream, he reached out with a blunt hammer-like instrument and struck her in the temple, rendering her unconscious. The man went into the bedroom and returned with an electric hairdryer, which he plugged in and put in her hand. He then unceremoniously picked up Jasmine and dumped her and the hairdryer in the tub. The hairdryer electrocuted Jasmine before it shorted out all the electricity in the house. The man turned on the flashlight which he removed from his pocket. He took a little hair shampoo and spilled some on the floor and smeared a little on the bottom of her foot. The man then turned and left the house locking the door behind him.

· · · · ·

Brandon returned to his office in time for his 1:30 meeting with Larry Richardson. He reviewed a couple of endorsement contracts that were awaiting his signature while he waited for Larry's arrival. When Larry arrived, he was shown immediately into Brandon's office.

"Come on in, Larry, and have a seat. Can I have my assistant get you anything? Are you hungry or maybe something to drink?"

"No, I'm okay. I just ate."

"So how have you been?"

"I don't know. I guess I'm getting by."

"What's wrong?"

"It just that it's been such a major adjustment. My life and everything that I thought it was has changed so much that for the first time I'm not sure whether I'm going or coming. My life used to be so simple. I played ball and let somebody else worry about everything else. And that someone else was usually Tanya. All I had to contribute was a paycheck and everything was straight."

"I thought you had it all worked out. Why didn't you just hire a nanny and a housekeeper or cook? It's not like you couldn't afford it. Or I thought you might leave the kids with your in-laws."

"I did for a while but they're still getting over the loss of their daughter. Plus, I thought it would look better with the kids here with me instead of all the way down in Texas, though if I don't find a nanny I will send them down to spend a week or two. I started interviewing nannies but I haven't found one who satisfies me yet. Plus, the kids are just getting over the loss of their mother. I'm not sure that this is the right time to bring a stranger in their life."

"How can we help? Do you want us to find a nanny for you? I don't know any good agencies but I'm sure if I ask around I can get a few referrals."

"No, I think I can work it out. A few ladies from the church have been coming by and helping out."

"What church? I didn't know you were involved in a church?"

"I wasn't but after what happening I was having trouble dealing so I started going to church. I got saved about two weeks ago. You see, I couldn't deal with what we did. Every time I looked in my kids' faces and saw the hurt there and how bravely they were trying to deal with their mother being gone, I remembered that I was responsible for it. And I couldn't deal with it. That's one reason I came to see you today. I want you to let me out of my contract."

"Why?"

"Every time I see you or do business with you, I'll always be reminded of what we did. I've got to pray the Lord will forgive me and try to put this behind me."

"So you blame me for what happened?"

"If you had never came to me with your proposal, I never would have chosen that course of action. I would have paid the money. I would have bitched and moaned about it, but I would have paid. I have to wonder now whether that would have been better. As for me blaming you, I hold us both equally responsible. When you came to me, I agreed to the proposal. I was so focused on being free and holding on to as much money as I could that I lost sight of everything else. I just think this is a relationship that I must put behind me."

"I don't know if I can do that?"

"Why? If it's a matter of money, you tell me what you think is fair and I'll pay it."

"It's not just the money; even though I was looking forward to working with you in a strictly business capacity, that's not my main concern. I worry whether you're leaving the agency, some people might interpret as a sign of you blaming us for the tragedy"

"Why would anyone blame you? Everyone considers it an accident or suspicious because the guy with her disappeared too. I have heard numerous theories, everything from a joint suicide to a murder suicide to an unfortunate accident where the man disappeared because he didn't want to be blamed. Nowhere has any my name come up in any way, and if they don't blame me how can they suspect you?"

"That just goes to show you how effective the plan worked. I think you need to stay the course."

"I can't. I've really tried to deal with the situation, but I can't."

"Well, if you feel that strongly about it, then I guess we'll give you your release. There won't be any need for any financial restitution. I'll have my assistant prepare a statement saying that we resolve our contract due to mutual consent. I just want to caution you again never to tell anyone about our arrangement. That includes your priest or anyone else."

"Why would I do that? I can't tell anyone without putting my own neck in the noose."

"In that case, we're done and I wish you well with whatever you do in your future," Brandon said as he got up and guided Larry out the door. As soon as Larry was gone, Brandon returned to his desk and reached into a secret drawer and removed a cell phone. He dialed Justice and said, "I need to see you right away. One hour. You know where."

An hour later as Brandon walked into the bar uptown he saw Justice sitting at their usual table in the back. After giving each other dap Brandon said, "We might have a bit of a problem. You remember the cruise job that Omar did? Well, the client is having some second thoughts."

"Second thoughts? Everything is done. How can he have second thoughts?"

"It's more like an attack of the guilts. I don't understand these soft-ass chumps. It's like I told you, a lot of these guys don't really want to kill their old ladies for real. They're just pissed off because the judge is hitting them so hard in their pocket. By the time they cool off and realize what they've done and the true ramifications of the situation, it's too late because the deed is done. If you don't have the heart for the game, then you shouldn't play."

"Is he upset over what Omar did?"

"Naw, he's feeling guilty about taking his kids' mother away. I think he may even be discovering that he still loves her."

"If he felt like that he should have never agreed to the deal. If I remember correctly, you told me he was eager for the deal. Now he's feeling sorry about it. That's some stupid shit."

"That's how I look at it too."

"So Pred, what do you think we should do? Should I have somebody 'touch' him?"

"I don't think so. It might bring unwanted attention our way. I think we want to put someone discreetly with him. See who he talks to and what he says. If he keeps his part of the bargain and keeps his mouth shut, then we'll let him rock for a while to see if he recovers. But if he starts running his mouth, we'll take him out."

Chapter Eight

Ebony and Gary sat in their car outside the suspect's girlfriend's house. They had been waiting several hours, and Ebony could not drink another cup of that awful coffee from the deli on the corner. So far she didn't have to use the restroom but if she had any more coffee she wouldn't need any caffeine to keep her alert. She would be so busy keeping her bladder from exploding, she would surely stay focused. She and Gary had engaged in banal conversation but that had dried up and for the last hour each had been wrapped up in their own private thoughts.

At first Ebony was absorbed with thoughts about her relationship with Jack and what she was going to do about it. She was sure that she didn't love Jack and she had reason to wonder if she ever loved him. Which raised the question that if she didn't love him, why did she marry him? She had an idea about the answer but didn't like what that said about her. Could it be possible that she married Jack just to spite her parents? Did she despise her parents' lifestyle so much that she would hurt an innocent person just so she could prove a point?

Ebony's parents could be summarized as being definitely very Pro-Black. At one time that had been members of SNCC, the Black Panthers, and Black nationalists. They had moved from one movement to another, always in search of equality for people of color or people oppressed by the powers that ran this country. They had moved past being liberal into the realm of being activists when both were in their early twenties.

Ebony spent much of her formative years being dragged from one meeting to another. Ebony's parents had many pictures of Ebony, as a toddler, attending many protests with them. Somewhere along the line when Ebony became a teenager, Ebony discovered that more often than not, she disagreed with her parents and their political philosophies. Maybe it was rebellion on her part, but as she got older many political discussions with her parents turned into arguments, some quite vehement. The differences started with the analysis of the problem and ended with the subsequent solution to the problem.

Ebony's two brothers, upon completion of their college education, had chosen a different path from Ebony's. The eldest had become a civil rights and defense attorney, and the youngest ran a homeless shelter and food pantry on the Lower East Side of Manhattan. Upon completion of her Master's, Ebony chose to join the Police Department instead of entering law school, her father saw it as a slap in his face. To Ebony's father, his precious but strong-willed daughter went from being his pride and joy to being akin to a traitor. He was convinced with every fiber of his being that the American criminal justice system was the greatest oppressors of the African American community and there was a distinctive difference in the way people of color were arrested, tried, and imprisoned. For his daughter to join those oppressors was something he couldn't fathom or understand.

Ebony also felt there were inequalities and injustices in the criminal justice system as it applied to African Americans but she felt that the solution was to not only protest against the system but to also join the system. Ebony felt if you had enough African American officers on the street it would cut down on brutality against other African Americans. The large number of high-profile questionable shootings of African Americans by the police served to provide her father with tremendous ammunition against this philosophy.

Their relationship was already strained when Ebony decided to marry Jack Delaney, a White assistant district attorney. Ebony was never clear whether her father objected to him because he was White or because he was a DA. What was clear was her father was far from giving her his blessing. Her mother had tried to stay neutral and even tried to act as mediator between her warring husband and daughter.

Ebony and Jack were classmates while she was getting her Master's and while they had dated a few times, she didn't consider their relationship to be serious. She greatly enjoyed the time she spent with Jack though. He was a great listener and had the uncanny ability that when she was speaking making her feel like what she was saying was the most important thing in the world. He was one of the rare friends that would disagree with her and tell her the truth even if it wasn't what she wanted to hear. When she was discussing her problems, he told her what she needed to hear even if it wasn't what she wanted to hear.

Despite their racial differences, they had so many things in common. They could talk for hours it seemed. She could be serious with him and more important she could be silly with him. She could laugh with him and joke with him, and she really begun to see him as a good friend. Political discussions and/or arguments were an adventure into the diverse realities of being Black and White in America. Surprisingly, sometimes Jack was more radical and liberal than Ebony. Sometimes his opinion was so diverse that Ebony wondered if he chose an opposing opinion just so he could argue with her. The fact that Jack was so handsome was irrelevant as far as Ebony was concerned because she wasn't attracted to him in that way.

While Jack was studying for the Bar exam, his mother had succumbed to a long bout with cancer. Considering herself a good friend of Jack's, she was there to help him deal with his grief, and at some point, and she wasn't clear how it happened, they became intimate. When Jack proposed marriage, to say she was shocked would be an understatement. Not wanting to hurt the wounded Jack any further, she accepted his ring. Deep inside, she figured they would have a long engagement and after some time had passed the relationship would peter out and she could call the engagement off.

After an especially vicious argument with her parents, she was bitter, angry, and resentful, and when Jack came over to console her, she agreed to get married that week. The next day they went and got their license and two days later a civil judge married them. Ebony didn't marry Jack to spite her parents, as least not consciously. She really thought she loved Jack, and in a small way she probably did. It didn't take her long to realize the marriage was a mistake, and the amount of love necessary to make a marriage successful she just didn't have. Though Ebony felt the marriage was a mistake, she nonetheless remained faithful and made a concentrated effort to be a good wife. Though the efforts were sincere they were futile and the distance between them grew greater. The fact that Jack wanted children and Ebony refused to bring children into such a tenuous situation might have been the straw that broke the camel's back. Ebony was willing to admit the mistake in marrying a man that she wasn't hopelessly in love with but she was not willing to bring children into such a tenuous situation.

After a year and a half Ebony realized that the marriage was hopeless and there was no chance of it working, they separated and shortly thereafter got divorced. Unfortunately, the damage had been done and her relationship with her parents remained distant and almost estranged.

As Ebony sat in the car reflecting upon her relationship with Jack and her parents, her partner Gary was absorbed with his own thoughts. Murder investigations could often be long, drawn-out affairs, but this case wasn't one. An arrest hadn't been made yet but they had a suspect in mind who most probably was the culprit. The victim was a college student from upstate New York whose well-off parents had rented him an apartment in the Lower East Side. To make extra money the victim had rented a room to an unsavory character and there was evidence of drug usage by at least one if not both of them. There was a dispute among the two men that turned violent and resulted in the death of the victim.

The reason why the crime was discovered after only two days was the victim had the habit of speaking to his family every day and sometimes twice a day. After the victim didn't speak to his family for twenty-four hours, they came to his apartment and discovered his body, which was hidden under his bed. Most of the evidence pointed toward the roommate, who couldn't be located. The victim's car couldn't be located either, and the roommate had been seen driving the roommate's car around the city. Ebony didn't think that was conclusive evidence that the roommate killed the victim until the family pointed out that the victim's car was a vintage Mustang that he never let anyone drive under any circumstances. Friends of the roommate had given them his girlfriend's address and now they waiting for him to show up.

"I hope we're not wasting our time waiting for him to show up here," Gary said.

"I think he'll show up. He can't go back to the apartment. We have an APB out for the car. How many other places could he have to go?" Ebony responded.

"He could have skipped town," Gary said.

"He might have if he had any idea that we were looking for him, but he doesn't even know that we found the body yet. If he did, I would hate to think that he would be so stupid as to keep driving the victim's car."

"We know he's not too smart or he wouldn't have killed the guy in the first place. Hey, Eb, there's something I wanted to talk to you about."

"What's that, Gary?"

"How do you think I would fit in with the Feds?"

"What do you mean?"

"I mean, do you think I could get along if I was a Fed?"

"Why are you asking me?"

"Because you know me pretty well and you just spent quite a bit of time working with the Feds."

"Why do you want to work with the Feds?"

"I just get so frustrated working with our department. They make it so hard for us to do our job, it makes you wonder whether they really want to solve any murders. They deny us the support we need to nail down a lot of crimes. I just get so sick of some of the interoffice politics that I have been thinking about leaving to join the Feds."

"The Bureau is no picnic itself. There is a lot of red tape and bureaucracy in that agency as well. I think that you will—hold up, isn't that the suspect that we're after? Let's go." They sprang from the car and approached the suspect. As they drew closer Gary said, "James Riordan? NYPD. Can we speak to you for a minute?" Riordan took one look at the two officers and took off running as fast as he could in the opposite direction, with the two officers in hot pursuit. They chased the suspect for five blocks before the cops started to close the distance. The suspect and Gary were both starting to tire but Ebony appeared to be getting stronger. As the suspect was giving in to fatigue, Ebony launched herself at the suspect's legs and the two ended up tangled in a heap on the ground. Gary came up with his revolver drawn and quickly had the suspect handcuffed and searched as they headed back to their unmarked car and the precinct.

· · · · ·

Larry Richardson met his cousin Rashid Jenkins at his office in lower Manhattan and the two drove up to Harlem where they had dinner and drinks at one of Larry's favorite restaurants. The restaurant was a combination bar, restaurant, and nightclub where you could catch one of New York City's hottest jazz combos on Friday night and a jamming R&B or Reggae group on Saturday night.

As you entered the first thing you noticed was a long, mahogany bar that could comfortably seat fourteen to sixteen people on the left side of the club. Along the right wall were six plush, leather booths that could each seat six to eight people. There were also about a dozen tables that could seat four or five people. The back room could either be used for special events or the tables could be cleared for dancing. The club was lit in a way to create an intimate but relaxed atmosphere.

The chairs were of a dark, sultry wood with thick, burgundy leather seat cushions that hinted of intimacy and elegance. The tables were covered by fine linen tablecloths colored a light salmon which perfectly matched the Spanish ceramic tiles that covered the floor. The ambiance of the restaurant was sophisticated, trendy, elegant, and comfortable at the same time. Coupled with scrumptious food, it was the perfect place for eating, meeting, or just kicking back and enjoying a long intimate or casual conversation.

Since his meeting with Brandon five weeks before, Larry was still having a hard time getting his life back on track. He had gotten a new agent and had resumed playing but his guilty conscience was making his personal life a wreck. Though his play was inconsistent and far below his regular standards, his team was sympathetic of what he was going through and wasn't putting any pressure on him. Larry wasn't used to such poor performance either. In the past, basketball was the one area of his life that he didn't have to worry about and his skills on the court helped him to forget his problems off the court. He now found that to be the case less and less.

Since Tanya's death he felt like every aspect of his life was falling apart. He thought that he would enjoy having his kids around him all the time but dealing with them and their needs on a consistent, day-to-day, twenty-four-hour basis was more difficult than he ever imagined. Watching his young children trying to deal with their grief over the loss of their mother brought forth a feeling of guilt in him that was so profound he was having a hard time facing himself. He had tried to turn to his newfound discovery of God to help him deal with his internal turmoil but he couldn't overcome the overwhelming feeling that after committing probably the greatest sin imaginable how could he ask God to forgive him?

He wanted to discuss the situation with his pastor but he was scared of the legal repercussions. He wasn't sure that his pastor wouldn't have felt compelled to tell the police if he confided in him his role in Tanya's death. If he talked to someone and Brandon or his people found out, he was worried about what they might do. They already had proved that they could be very deadly, and if the preacher went to the police, they probably would find out and he had little question about what they would do to him if they did find out.

Larry was not a coward and he didn't normally fear too many things and he wasn't scared for himself. Rather he was worried about his children and how they would react if they lost two parents in such a short time frame. He had provided for the kids and they would be very well taken care of financially. Their grandparents would provide a good home but the emotional toll might be devastating. He was in an emotional quagmire and he didn't feel like he could move left or right. He was wound so tight and so stressed that Rashid had decided to take him out for drinks to see if he could help him.

"So, Cuz, what's happening with you?" Rashid asked.

"Nothing happening, I'm really just trying to deal with life," Larry replied.

"C'mon, man, I've never known you to act like this. I know it's something. What's going on?"

"I rather not talk about it."

"Why not? Maybe I can help or talking about it will make you feel better."

"I doubt that very seriously."

"You've got to do something; you can't keep going on like this."

"Like what? I'm telling you there's nothing going on."

"Larry, we've been close ever since we were little kids. I know you like I know the back of my hand. Don't tell me nothing's going on, I know you too well for that."

"Then you should know enough to leave it alone and let's enjoy our meal. How do you think the Yankees are going to do next year?"

"You want to talk about the Yankees?"

"Yeah, you know I'm a Yankee fan. Can't we try to relax and just kick back for one night? Maybe that's what I need."

"If you say so then that's what we will do. Maybe you're right and that is what you need. There are quite a few lovely honeys in here tonight. Maybe you need to just let go and get your swerve on? What are we drinking?"

"I don't care. You pick," Larry said.

"Do you want to try something different like tequila shooters or stick with cognac?"

"It's your choice, man."

"Let's have tequila before dinner and some Remy afterwards."

Rashid signaled the waiter and they ordered dinner and drinks. Rashid was surprised that Larry was drinking double shots of tequila straight. Rashid noticed that though Larry had drunk three double shots he really hadn't eaten much of his dinner. Rashid felt he better say something. "Yo man, you better slow down or it's going to be a short night."

Though Larry did slow down he didn't stop drinking all together. He just picked at his food and he really didn't do much talking. During dinner, he finished another two doubles and the effect of all that tequila was starting to show. His mood was deep and sullen, and Rashid was at a loss to try to figure out how to bring him out of his enveloping depression. Rashid noticed a couple of women he knew near the front of the restaurant in the bar area. Rashid excused himself and went to talk to them. After ten minutes Rashid returned with the two girls.

"Larry, I want to introduce you to Monique and Paula. They're big fans and when they found out I was your cousin, they couldn't wait to meet you."

"Do you mind if we join you?" Paula asked.

"Suit yourself," Larry said.

"Larry, I'm your biggest fan. Are you going to lead the Knicks to the championship this year?" Paula asked.

"I don't know. We'll have to see."

The girls stayed at the table while they tried to engage Larry in conversation. The more they talked, the less Larry had to say, leaving Rashid to keep the conversation going. If the girls' intention was to entice Larry into a romantic evening, they soon realized that wasn't going to happen and after about twenty minutes the girls gave up and left the men to return to the front of the restaurant.

After the girls left, Rashid turned to Larry and said, "Man, what is wrong with you? Don't you know those girls were trying to get with us?"

"I ain't thinking about them chicks. They weren't really interested in me. They're interested in my paycheck. Fuck them gold-digger bitches."

"I don't know if they were only about the money, and what does it matter anyway? We could have got some sex and then sent them on their way."

"I don't want to be bothered with them chicks, man. They ain't about nothing."

"Man, I can't figure you out. Ever since Tanya ran off with that guy, you've been impossible to deal with. You need to get over her. I mean, why are you tripping? Y'all weren't even together when she left."

"You think Tanya ran off? Is that what you think?"

"Isn't that what happened? If she didn't run off, where the hell is she?"

"Man, you don't know what you're talking about."

"Why are you getting funky with me? It's not like it's a reflection on you. You had broken up with her long before she left."

"Rashid, I love you man but you don't know what you're talking about."

"Then what don't I know?"

"Rashid, leave it alone."

"Naw, nigger, your ego is so big that you can't deal with someone not trying to be with you, moving on with her life and trying to be happy. Is that's why you're walking around here looking like a lost puppy?"

"Like I told you Rashid, you don't know what the fuck you're talking about."

"If I don't know what I'm talking about you tell me what you think is the deal?"

"Leave it alone, man."

"Naw, man, tell me. You know so damn much. Tell me."

"Okay, man, you think about it. Tanya was the most honest and principled woman I knew. She was a great wife and a better mother. I was just too busy running the streets to appreciate her. You know what type of person Tanya was. Do you really think she would desert her kids? Do you think she would leave her babies without so much as a goodbye, just to be with a man? Any man?"

"Well, when you put it that way it doesn't really sound like Tanya. But if Tanya didn't run off then where is she?"

"Probably at the bottom of the ocean."

"Aw, man, don't think like that. Tanya has to be somewhere safe and happy." Rashid noticed that Larry had gotten very quiet as he sat there with his head bowed. When he lifted his head up Larry had tears in his eyes. Rashid said, "Hey man, I'm sorry. I shouldn't have said what I did."

"That's not what's bothering me."

"Then what is bothering you? Come on, man, talk to me."

"When I said that Tanya was at the bottom of the ocean, I wasn't guessing. I know that's where she is."

"How can you know that, man? Don't start blaming yourself for things you couldn't control."

"I wish to God I wasn't to blame, but I am."

"Don't do that, Larry. Don't start beating yourself up for something that's not your fault. I know you're thinking that if you hadn't broken up with Tanya she wouldn't have gone on that cruise in the first place."

"That ain't it. I wish it was but it's not."

"Then what is it?"

"I had Tanya killed."

"What are you talking about?"

"You wanted to know the truth, so I'm telling you the truth. I had Tanya killed."

"*Had* her killed? Larry, what are you saying? You need to start at the beginning."

"After Tanya and I split up, I signed with a new agent who for a million dollars made sure that Tanya disappeared. The guy who was with Tanya I think was one of his people and he did the job. Exactly what he did I don't know, but I do know I paid a million dollars and Tanya hasn't been seen or heard from since."

"Do you mean the agent you just signed with?"

"No, Brandon Bennett, the agent I recently fired."

"Why would you agree to something like that?"

"Tanya and I had just separated and she stood to get about half of everything I owned. I wasn't thinking clearly, and I was just seeing her becoming a millionaire based upon my hard work and I got so damn angry I lost sight of what really matters. So when Brandon approached me with an easy way to get out for only a million dollars, it seemed like a good idea."

"Are you sure that your agent was behind Tanya's disappearance?"

"What other reason could there be for Tanya not to contact the kids or her parents? Plus, Brandon took the million dollars and he wouldn't do that if he hadn't handled the dirty business."

"Did Brandon do this to anyone else?"

"I think so, even though I can't prove anything. The whole thing went down too smooth for this to be the first time they did it."

"So what are you going to do about?"

"Do about what? He did what I paid him to do. If I didn't pay him to kill her, they wouldn't have done it. It's my fault."

"But you said that they've done it before. Those weren't your fault. This guy is running around bumping people off and getting away with it. You got to do something."

"What can I do about it?"

"Go to the police."

"Rashid, have you lost your mind? How can I turn them in without admitting my own guilt and role in the whole situation? Any prosecutor would lock me up and throw away the key."

"But these guys are committing a horrible crime in killing innocent women for money. Somebody's got to do something."

"It won't be me. I owe it to Tanya to raise up the kids as well as I can. My thirst for justice or revenge will have to wait. My feelings of guilt will have to wait while I try to atone by being the best father I can."

"Okay, man, I got your back. Just let me know what I can do to help."

"You can pray for God to forgive me. Let's just spend the evening chilling. I'm not up to dealing with female companionship just yet."

"If that's what you want, Big Man, that's the way it will be."

Larry and Rashid were so absorbed in their conversation that they didn't notice the couple sitting in the booth adjacent to their table, finish their meal, pay the check, and leave the restaurant. The couple appeared to be a quiet married couple enjoying their dinner without paying them any mind at all. The man appeared to be a young businessman who was taking his wife out for dinner before retiring for the evening. The man was dressed in causal business attire and was wearing what appeared to be a Bluetooth cell phone in his left ear. In reality the device was a highly-sophisticated listening device that enabled the user to hear any conversation in the room.

As soon as they got in the car, the man pulled out a cell phone and placed a call and told his boss he was coming into the office. An hour later he met Justice in the back of his variety store where he conducted non-drug related business. He said, "You were right, Boss; he was running his mouth like he had shit on his mind he couldn't wait to tell."

"Who was he with?"

"Some cat named Rashid. I think they were family."

"So what did he tell him?"

"Every damn thing he knew. He talks about some agent named Brandon something and how he paid him to kill his wife."

"Did he say whether he planned to tell Five-O?"

"The other cat wanted him to but he said if he did he would go to jail too."

"Did he say anything else?"

"Nothing significant, a lot of bitching and moaning about God and guilt and shit like that."

"Thanks, Tonio, here's your money. If I need your assistance further, I'll let you know."

After Tonio left, Justice called Brandon and said, "Get to a secure line and call me back."

When Brandon called Justice back from the cell phone that he had purchased and only used to talk to Justice when they needed to discuss things that couldn't be overheard by anyone else, he said, "What's up, partner?"

"That party you were worried about is telling everything he knows."

"To whom?"

"Right now just his cousin but no telling who else he will tell. He's getting weak just like you thought he would. What do you want to do about it?"

"He's got to be eliminated. I warned him to keep his mouth shut. Plus, this will serve as a warning to our other clients to adhere to the arrangements and keep their mouths shut."

"How do you want it done? Do you want to do it and make it appear a robbery that went bad?"

"Naw, that would draw too much attention and too much heat from the police. After all, he is a celebrity especially here in New York. Remember that other plan we were kicking around?"

"Yeah."

"Let's go with that one. It will take a little more time, but it should not bring about much of an investigation."

"Are you sure that's the way you want to go?"

"Yeah, I'll call Mendes to get the product you will need to pull it off. Use the spot up on Southern Blvd."

. . . . .

As the team finished practice and headed for the locker room, one of Larry's closest friends on the team, James, pulled him to the side and asked, "How are you doing, man? You've been so down lately I am worried about you."

"It's been an adjustment, but I'm hanging in there."

"A bunch of us are heading out for some drinks, why don't you join us?"

"I wish I could but I got a new nanny for the kids and I don't want to leave her with them too long."

"Why not? She's a live-in nanny, right? That's what you are paying her for. She's capable of taking care of the kids for a couple of hours while you go out. I wouldn't make a habit of it, but once in a while can't hurt. You still are entitled to a life. Why don't you come hang out for an hour or so?"

"Well, let me call her and make sure she doesn't have any plans."

After Larry called the nanny and cleared things, he told his teammates he would meet them at the bar.

James said, "You want to ride with me?"

"That's okay. I'm not going to drink that much and then I can head straight home from the bar without having to come back here to pick up my car."

"So tell me about this new nanny. What is she, a cute little senorita? There's nothing wrong with having a fine piece of ass under your roof."

"Actually, she's from Eastern Europe, and I don't think anyone would consider her a fine piece of ass unless you're into the grandmotherly type. She's real good with the kids though."

"What's up with you, man? Have you even been on a date since that thing happened with Tanya?"

"Not really."

"I would offer to hook you up, but I know you always had plenty of women begging for your attention."

"That's all right. I'm good for now. I decided to cool out for a bit while I get my head together. It wouldn't be fair to start a relationship now because my head is a mess. I think it might be too soon."

"Have the police or the investigators found out anything more about Tanya?"

"No, we still don't have a clue what happened to her."

"That's a shame because I'm sure not knowing must be a bitch. I admire how well you're taking care of your kids."

"As hard as it is for me, it's got to be twice as hard for them. Especially the youngest, they were very close," Larry said.

"Don't worry, Big Larry, things will get better once some time has passed. Kids are amazingly resilient, and they will recover faster than you ever imagined. And given enough time, somebody will discover what happened to Tanya and reaching some closure will only help them and you."

"I hope you're right."

"I am. Come on, let's go, the fellas are waiting."

The two friends continued talking as they left the arena and headed to their respective cars. As they were leaving the parking lot, Larry was busy adjusting the stations on his radio and didn't notice the dark blue Nissan that fell in behind him about two or three blocks back. Larry considered himself pretty lucky to find a parking space around the corner from the sports bars they were going to on the Upper East Side.

Larry went into the bar and was surprised at how crowded the place was. It was after 5 o'clock, and the bar was filling up with the usual Manhattan after work crowd. Quite a few people recognized Larry and his teammates, and a few women started hanging around casting flirtatious glances their way. One tall exotic beauty who appeared to be from Brazil or some other Latin country walked into the bar and got immediate attention because everything about her presence was dazzling. She seemed to be waiting for someone because she went to a small private table in the back and ordered a drink as she was sitting there alone. Larry noticed her from the minute she walked in and he was impressed by her beauty and cool demeanor.

Larry got James' attention and asked him, "Who is that girl?"

"I don't know. I've never seen her before and we come here quite a lot. She's definitely not a regular but she's bad. Why don't you go rap to her?"

"No, she seems to be waiting for someone."

"If I had a woman that fine, I sure as hell wouldn't keep her waiting for me."

Over the next half hour Larry had three drinks while he kept an eye on the beautiful Latin lady. He probably would have approached her already but he noticed at least five guys had tried to talk to her and all of them had been turned away. Noticing the lady was still alone, Larry had a final drink to boost his courage and headed over to her table.

"Excuse me, ma'am, but I noticed you sitting here alone. Are you waiting for someone?"

"I was supposed to meet a girlfriend but it looks like she isn't going to make it."

"Do you mind if I join you?"

"Well, I was planning on leaving since she's not going to show."

"At least let me buy you a drink."

"Well, maybe just one,"

"What are you drinking?"

"This was a peach martini, so I guess I should stick with that."

"That's fine. Since the waitresses seem to be busy I'll be right back," Larry said as he went to the bar and got the girl's drink and returned to the table. As he sat down he said, "A peach martini as the lady requested. I took the liberty of making it a double. I hope you don't mind."

"No, that's fine."

"Not as fine as you. May I ask you your name?"

"Consuela."

"No last name?"

"Rivera. My name is Consuela Mendez-Rivera. You ask me my name but haven't told me yours."

"I'm sorry, I thought you might have recognized me. My name is Larry Richardson."

"You thought I might have recognized you? Are you famous?"

"I'm not exactly famous, but I'm a professional athlete and a couple of people in here recognize us."

"Oh, you are an athlete. What sport do you play? Baseball?"

"No, I'm a basketball player."

"Oh, Gary, are you any good?"

"My name is Larry not Gary and some people think I'm very good and some say I play basketball pretty good too."

"Okay, *Larry*, what else are you very good at?"

"I could tell you but I much rather show you."

"Can you show me here?"

"I could but it would be much better in private."

"Sounds interesting almost enticing, but how can I know that you can deliver the things that you are implying?"

"I come with a money back guarantee unless you are completely satisfied. Take a chance on me; after all, what do you stand to lose?"

"Why should I take a chance on you?"

"Because I think you are the most attractive woman I've seen in a very long time, and I would really like the chance to get to know you better."

"That's what you want, but what's in it for me?"

"Pretty much anything you want."

"Sounds promising, but I'm not sure I'm convinced. Let me finish my drink while I think about it."

Larry sat down as Consuela finished her drink and they engaged in casual conversation. During a lull in the conversation Larry took a long look at Consuela as he tried to figure out what there was about her that made him so eager to make love to her. Her face, while attractive, was not classically beautiful and her face had a bit more make-up on it than he usually found attractive. Her legs were shapely but her breasts weren't very large. Her glossy black hair was thick, long, and luxurious, and she wore it so that it partially obscured the right side of her face which made her appear exotic and mysterious. Perhaps the most attractive thing about her was she seemed to have an air of sex about her. There was something about her that hinted she was very passionate and to make love to her would be an experience one wouldn't soon forget. She seemed to exude sex and a love for sex. Larry allowed his imagination to run wild and he could easily envision an incredible night of love-making in her arms. So while he talked with her about meaningless things and putting his most charming side forward, his secret mind was absorbed with very erotic fantasies.

After Consuela finished her second drink she prepared to leave. As she slowly and tantalizingly wet her lips, she looked Larry deep in his eyes and said, "Well, Larry it's been a pleasure meeting you and talking with you."

"It doesn't have to end. I would really like to spend more time with you."

"Just talking?"

"Of course I would like more than that, but if that's all you're down for, I guess I can settle for that."

"You're not trying to get me into bed?"

"I would like to, but it doesn't work if you're not with that plan. But I'm not rushing you. If you spend some time with me and get to know me better, I think soon you will be as eager as I am to make love."

"You sound very confident."

"I am but I have good reason to be."

"Which is?"

"For the answer to that you have to get to know me better. Didn't your ride fail to show up?"

"No, she didn't make it."

"So how are you going to get home?"

"I'll catch a cab."

"Why don't you allow me to drive you home? No strings attached, and if you want me to, I'll go home as soon as you are safely in your home."

"Can I trust you?"

"I'm as trustworthy as a Boy's Scout."

"In that case I would appreciate a ride."

"My car is parked right around the corner. Would you like to wait here while I bring my car around or would you rather walk with me to the car?"

"I can use the fresh air to clear my head. I'll walk with you." Consuela wrapped her arm around Larry's arm as they walked to the car. Larry helped her into his car and made sure the seatbelt was securely fastened. He noticed that her skirt had hiked up her thighs, giving him the most tantalizing view of her stunning legs. Larry was so wrapped up in the amazing view that he noticed nothing else. He saw Consuela digging in her handbag but thought little of it when she pulled out a cigarette and lighter and asked, "Do you mind if I smoke?"

"Normally I don't allow anyone to smoke in my car, but you're such an exceptional person that I will make an exception to my rules."

Consuela proceeded to light her cigarette and smoke it in a way that could best be described as seductively. Now Larry's attention was divided between the way Consuela was smoking the cigarette, her gorgeous legs, and keeping an eye on the road. He never noticed that Consuela had removed another object from her bag and had hid it underneath her leg. As they pulled up to where Consuela said she lived, she leaned over as if to give him a kiss good night as she said, "Thank you for the ride."

"I thought you were going to invite me up?"

"Come closer," Consuela said as she pursed her lips. As Larry leaned over and closed his eyes as he prepared for his kiss, Consuela took the object in her right hand that she had hid under her leg and jabbed the hypodermic needle into Larry's thigh. Before he could yelp out in pain the strong sedative had rendered him unconscious. Within seconds Consuela had opened the car door and left the car. She headed to the navy blue Nissan that had been following them. Two men got out of the Nissan and shoved Larry out of the driver's seat and into the back of the car. They then drove Larry's car off in one direction and Consuela drove the Nissan in the opposite direction.

. . . . .

Two days later, Larry's teammate James called Rashid and asked, "Have you seen Larry? "

"I haven't seen him in a few days. We got together last week but I haven't heard from him since. Why? What's up?"

"He missed practice yesterday and today and no one has heard from him."

"What do you mean he missed practice? Larry doesn't ever miss practice without calling the coaches."

"I know, that's why I'm a little worried."

"When was the last time you heard from him?"

"He went out with some of the guys from the team two days ago. He left with this chick so we didn't think anything of it until he didn't show up again yesterday."

"What girl did he leave with?"

"I don't know her name. None of us had seen her before."

"Didn't any of you think that was strange?"

"Why? Tons of women go to that spot because they know they can meet us there. Some of them are even married women who are just looking for a fling."

"Let me call his house and see whether he's home and when was the last time his kids heard from him was. I hit you right back."

. . . . .

Malik and Ronell sat in the living room playing a game of high stakes blackjack worth $50 a hand. Malik, the older of the two at twenty-three years of age, was roughly $600 ahead. Ronell probably could have played better, but he was unaccustomed to such sedentary activities. He was used to being in the street hustling and making moves. They were hoping that playing cards for large sums of money would help defeat some of their boredom, but it was an exercise in futility.

Malik and Ronell finished the hand and Malik said, "Let me go check on that sucker."

When he came back Ronell asked, "Is he awake?"

"Naw, he's still out but he's stirring."

Ronell asked, "Is it time for his next shot?"

"Not for another hour."

"How many more days did Justice say we had to babysit this dude?"

"Justice said we could give him the hotshot after six or seven days."

Ronell said, "This is some boring-ass shit sitting here all day just watching this cat nod. Why don't we just give him the hotshot now and get on with our lives?"

"Because Justice was very specific about this, he said we are to shoot him up every four hours for no less than six days and then he can OD. Look I've been trying to move up in Justice's crew and I'm not trying to fuck this up because we're trying to take a shortcut. When was the last time you got paid 10 G's just for shooting up a guy fix or six times a day? Would you rather be out on the streets slinging rocks?"

"No but—"

"Well, then, nigga, just chill and let me make this easy money."

"Can we at least get some bitches up here to hit me off? A brother gets horny and I don't know if I can go a week without some pussy

"If we bring some hoochies up in here and they see that cat, they will recognize him because after all he is a local sports hero. Then we would have to kill those girls. It ain't worth the risk to me. I would suggest you get your hormones under control, and if you can't do that, go in the bathroom and handle your business."

"Hell no, I ain't jacked my shit off since I got out of the joint and I ain't starting now. I can wait."

"Well, then, stop whining about it."

"Seriously, doesn't it bother you bumping this cat off who never did nothing to you?"

"Not at all. Justice said the fool is a snitch and was gonna rat him out on some business they handled together. If the nigga is a snitch, I would do him for free but to get paid 10 G's to kill him is free money to me. Plus, I met the sucka at a club in Midtown and he was playing the big NBA star and shit and the cat walked past me without even speaking. He's just a creep who thought he was all that. Helping him get his is going to be pleasure."

"This shit is harder than I thought it would be. Having to feed the nigga and take down his pants so he can shit is some real domesticated bullshit."

"Justice said he couldn't be roughed up, and if we took off his straitjacket he probably would have tried to kick our ass. The straitjacket kept him in line until the junk could take over. Now my man is cool as long as we give him his shot when he needs it."

"Do you think he's addicted to the heroin already?"

"I don't know, it's only been three days, but that is some pretty high grade shit and a lot of it has been running through his veins."

"Are you sure that hotshot will do the trick?"

"It should because it is damn near pure and I don't think it's been cut at all. If it doesn't work, we'll mix his next shot with a little rat poison and the cops will think he just got his hands on a bad batch."

· · · · ·

"Good evening, this is Tom Gorman with a special report for Channel Six News. The NYPD just announced that a body found in a deserted tenement in the South Bronx has been identified as missing NBA superstar Larry Richardson. We now go to Edwin Ruiz who is on location in the Bronx. Edwin—" "Thank you, Tom. Police this morning identified a body discovered this morning in this building to be the body of missing basketball superstar Larry Richardson. The six-time All-Star was reported missing seven days ago by his family and team after he missed several practices and games. Preliminary autopsy reports seem to indicate that Mr. Richardson died as a result of a drug overdose. At this time foul play is not suspected. The NBA is scheduled to issue a statement later this afternoon reputing the NYPD's findings. Back to you, Tom."

Chapter Nine

Ebony was not in the mood to be in the precinct because she hated having to do the excessive paperwork associated with her job. While she acknowledged that it was necessary she still disliked having to do it. She would much rather be out on the streets solving crimes. She considered the drudgery of paperwork to be a useless punishment so a bunch of bureaucrats with nothing better to do could justify their salaries. She had been putting off completing the paperwork for four or five days, and since she was expected in court later that afternoon to testify at a murder trial that she had investigated, she decided to eliminate as many unpleasant tasks as she could in one day. She really didn't mind testifying in court but she considered it a waste of time, since the prep had very clearly committed the crime and even had tried to kill her and her partner when they came to arrest him.

The American justice system was an incredible thing, and the presumption of innocence was essential to making the whole process work, but as a homicide detective Ebony had a chance to see the entire process from a different perspective. As an investigator by the time she got to court, she was usually very convinced that the suspect was guilty or she wouldn't have arrested him. She was aware that sometimes people were arrested on skimpy or questionable evidence but that wasn't how she operated. She dug and dug and searched and interrogated and questioned witnesses and was relentless until she was able to obtain enough proof to remove any doubt that the person was guilty even in court.

She was also aware that sometimes when officers were convinced of the guilt of a suspect but couldn't obtain sufficient evidence to prove that guilt that some officers would invent or create the necessary evidence to prove their case. Ebony was determined that she would never become that type of police officer. To her that kind was the exact opposite officers seeking after justice and empowered officers to set themselves up as judge and jury. She was no stranger to that deep rooted feeling of absolute certainty that investigators could get when they concluded that someone had committed a crime. Like Denzel Washington said in his Oscar winning performance in *Training Day*: It's not what you know but what you can prove. With the monumental decision of fabricating evidence or letting culprits go, many officers sold their souls in the search for justice and did what they had to do to get the conviction. In Ebony's opinion, what those officers gave up in terms of their principles and integrity just wasn't worth it.

Ebony found it hard to envision a scenario where she would feel compelled to behave in such a manner. It wasn't that Ebony couldn't understand why another cop would feel like he had to do whatever was necessary to obtain what they thought was justice, but Ebony had watched her parents fight such atrocities. In that matter she agreed with her parents. If officers of the law subverted the laws and rules they were paid to enforce, it opened the door to all sorts of abuse. If you didn't follow the law consistently, it left it up to individuals what laws you would follow. So she had a different perspective on the true damage it did to justice.

Ebony was wearing a navy blue, pleated skirt suit with a cream-colored silk blouse that she wore open at the collar. She had dressed with great care wanting to appear both feminine and professional at the same time. She was very careful to make sure she gave the jury the proper impression. It was important to impress upon them that she was an authority and highly proficient in the testimony that she was giving. As she removed her jacket to hang it on the back of her chair, she spied another detective Nick Fernandez, who happened to be the biggest practical joker in the precinct, preparing to make one of his snide remarks. Beating him to the punch Ebony said, "Don't even try it, Fernandez."

"What are you talking about, Delaney?"

"I saw you getting ready to say something, and I'm warning you not to start."

"I think you getting paranoid in your old age, Delaney."

"It's not that I'm paranoid but it's bad enough that I have all this stupid paperwork to do and I have to get my head right for court. We all know how you can be."

"Aw, darling, you hurt my feelings."

"Fernandez," Ebony said with a smile as she warned him.

"Aw mommieeee, you hurt me so but I can't resist you. You are so beautiful and sexy and your eyes are so lovely and I love your legs. I can't help myself. I must have you. I must," Fernandez said in a highly exaggerated Latin accent, sounding almost like a South American version of the Frito bandito.

Laughingly Ebony picked up a pen and threw it at Fernandez, who was retreating from the squad room, but as he was leaving he said with best Humphrey Bogart impersonation, "My dear, I have to go now, but I will meet you later at the Kasbah and we will wine and dine and I will fulfill your every dream when I make love to you."

Still laughing Ebony said, "Nicky, you're a fool. I'll get you when I see you later. Are you catching up with us later for drinks?"

"You know it. Be cool, Delaney, and I'll see you later. Have fun in court."

"Yeah, right. You be careful out on those streets."

"Don't you worry about me. You know I handle my business. Oh yeah, I left a message on your desk. He said it was urgent that he speak with you."

"Who was it? Jack?"

"Read your message. Later, chick."

"How am I supposed to find one little piece of paper with all this junk on my desk?" Ebony thought. "It was probably Jack because I didn't return his call from Monday." Rather than search through the clutter of paper on her desk, Ebony placed a call to Jack's office. His secretary said he was busy in court but she would make sure he got the message that she called. Since her attempt at a pleasant diversion had failed, Ebony decided to buckle down and complete the report she was working on. As she was completing the report and returning the dossier to her files, she noticed the memo from Fernandez saying that Rashid Jenkins had called.

Ebony was more than a little surprised because she hadn't spoken to Rashid in almost a year. While they were in college, she and Rashid had gone out for more than six months. At one time she thought their relationship was turning serious until she caught Rashid leaving another girl on campus's room in the wee hours of the morning. After the ensuing argument followed by months of her not speaking to him, Rashid had shown up at her room the next semester with a bouquet of flowers and a sincere apology. Though they were never intimate again, they did become fast friends through the remainder of their college years. There weren't so many Blacks at Dartmouth that Ebony could afford to not speak to one of the finest and most popular brothers there. More importantly, now that Rashid wasn't trying to get in her pants, she really enjoyed hanging with him. He was not only good looking but also ambitious and smart as hell, and their conversations were often stimulating and provocative. Rashid could argue his point with the best of them. Many evenings were spent in the student union's lounge with pitchers of beer or carafes of wine or coffee as they were part of a group who argued everything from the validity of hip-hop opposed to R&B, to the impact of the Black Power Movement on the Civil Rights Movement. Sometimes even a game of bid whist or spades was thrown in for good measure. While they both continued to date numerous people on campus, they never tried to get together again as a couple. In time, she came to see Rashid as one of her best friends and maybe even like a brother.

After graduation, Rashid went to Howard to get his Master's while she stayed in New York City and they kind of drifted apart.

After graduation Rashid returned to New York but they both were so busy with their individual lives that though they tried to get together, it didn't happen very frequently. When his cousin Larry was traded to the Knicks, Ebony assumed that Rashid spent a lot of time with him. Ebony felt a little guilty after Larry died because she intended to call Rashid and offer her condolences but that was just one of the many things that she couldn't seem to find the time for. Ebony made a mental note to call Rashid as soon as she got a chance but as she was putting the note aside; she noticed that it was marked urgent.

As much as Rashid meant to her and if he needed her, she could at least take the time to call him right away. Intending to leave a message she called Rashid at home and was surprised when he answered the phone.

"Hello."

"Rashid?"

"Yeah."

"This is Ebony."

"Oh hi, Eb, how are you doing?"

"I'm doing fine, but the question is, how are you doing?"

"It's been rough, baby girl, but I'm trying to keep things together. I've been trying to be there for the kids. You know they recently lost their mother, and this is hitting them pretty hard."

"Are they staying with you?"

"No, we sent them down to Texas to live with Tanya's parents on their farm. So not only do they have to deal with losing both their parents. They have to get used to a whole new life in a different state with a different school and losing all their friends on top of everything else."

"You sound a little bitter."

"I guess I am a little bit. I'm not sure it's the best thing for them, but I really didn't have much say in the matter because that was what the will stipulated and they were given custody. So I guess that's what Tanya felt would be for the best."

"Well, hang in there, maybe they can come and see you during the summer."

"That's my intention. As they get older I'll bring them up to New York to go shopping and see the sights like the Bronx Zoo and the Statue of Liberty."

"That would probably be good for you and them. You know if you need my help you only have to reach out."

"I know, that's why I called you."

"Because you need help with the kids?"

"I need your help, but not with the kids."

"What do you need my help with?"

"I can't talk about it right now."

"What's going on, Rashid? Why can't you talk about it now?"

"I rather not talk about it over the phone."

"Is it that important or that personal?"

"Both."

"So when do you want to talk about it?"

"As soon as possible."

"Would you like to get together this weekend?"

"I was hoping we could get together sooner than that."

"If it's that serious, I have to go to court this afternoon and I could see you afterwards."

"That would be great, Ebony. I really appreciate it."

"That's okay. Would you like to meet me here at the precinct?"

"I would rather not. How about I take you out to dinner?"

"You're not trying to ask me out on a date, are you?"

"Come on, Ebony, stop playing."

"I was just making sure."

"It's just I'm trying to be discreet and I want your complete attention and you know how many distractions you have at the precinct."

"Okay, where do you want me to meet you?"

"Why don't I pick you up at the precinct and we'll decide where we want to eat then?"

"Okay, that will work. About 5:30?"

"Great, I'll see you then."

That evening Rashid and Ebony was sitting in a quiet, intimate Italian restaurant in the Union Square section of Manhattan. They had ordered mussels in a white wine sauce and fried calamari as appetizers followed by a main course of chicken parmigiana and veal with peppers and mushrooms as well as a robust red wine to help their food digest.

Though Ebony was more than a little curious, she was willing to wait for Rashid to discuss what was on his mind, so they discussed casual issues over dinner. Finally, as they were enjoying some espresso after dinner Ebony said, "As much as I enjoyed seeing you again and sitting and kicking it with you like old times, I know that's not why you asked to see me."

"I didn't want to discuss anything so heavy during dinner. I wanted you to be able to enjoy your meal."

"Well, I'm finished eating now. What is all this about?"

"My cousin Larry."

"Oh yeah, Rashid, I'm sorry that I didn't call you to tell you how sorry I was to hear about Larry. I knew y'all were real tight."

"That okay, Eb, I was caught up in my own thing at the time anyway."

"I know it must have been hard."

"You don't know the half of it. Ebony, I don't think that Larry killed himself."

"Pardon?"

"I'm sure that Larry didn't commit suicide."

"I didn't think that was even an issue. My understanding of that situation was that Larry died of an accidental drug overdose. I've never heard anyone imply that the overdose was intentional."

"I know my cousin, and he never would have used heroin under any circumstances."

"I heard that Larry was depressed because of the disappearance of his wife."

"Larry and Tanya had been separated for months after Larry left her to be with another woman. Why would Tanya's disappearance upset him to the point where he would start using drugs and jeopardize his health and his career? Plus, Larry was very concerned about being there to take care of the kids."

"So you think that someone killed Larry?"

"I'm sure of it."

"Why would someone kill Larry?"

"Because of Tanya."

"You think that Tanya's family killed Larry?"

"No, not Tanya's family, they're not those kind of people."

"Then who do you think is responsible for Larry's death?"

"His agent and business partner."

Ebony took a long hard look at Rashid as she tried to read his emotional stability. Rashid had large, round eyes that were considered romantic or bedroom eyes by some but others thought were a bit feminine. Ebony considered them very sexy and how a certain look from those eyes used to put her in the mood to make love for half of the night. She also remembered the time she planned to look into those eyes for the rest of her life. Ebony looked in those eyes but now she didn't recognize the look she saw coming from those eyes.

Could that look be the beginning of madness? What it possible that the loss of Larry had affected Rashid so profoundly that he lost his grasp on sanity? Rashid had a very sharp, analytical mind, and he had done a great job of juggling the straight nine-to-five life and still being hip to hang with the street cats. At one time she thought Rashid had the potential for greatness, and now she wasn't sure if that still was the case but the leap to insanity was an unlikely one. Before she determined that Rashid was slipping, Ebony figured she should have the whole story.

"Rashid, why don't you start at the beginning and tell me everything?"

Rashid took several moments while he appeared to be deep in thought before he said anything. "As everyone knew, after Tanya's disappearance Larry seemed to taking it very hard. Like everyone else I thought that Larry was feeling dejected because it looked like his ex-wife had run off with another man, so I took Larry out for dinner and drinks. Larry confided in me that rather than feeling rejection he was suffering from guilt brought on by watching his children suffer over the loss of their mother. The reason Larry felt guilty was because he knew that their mother hadn't run off with some guy she had been dating and that she had been murdered while she was on that cruise."

"Did he feel like she was murdered or did he know she was murdered?"

"He knew."

"How could he know?"

"Because he had paid a million dollars to have her killed."

"Paid who? Did he go out and get somebody to kill his ex-wife?"

"Not directly. He was approached by his new agent, who made all the arrangements in exchange for Larry signing with his agency and paying a million dollars."

"Why would Larry agree to such a heinous act?"

"He was pissed of that Tanya had taken him to court for a divorce and child support and it looked like the judge was gonna give her a hell of a lot of money, probably more than twenty million."

"So Larry was willing to kill the mother of his children to save some money?"

"Yeah, that's about the gist of it."

"That's pretty messed up, Rashid."

"Hey, don't get mad at me, I agree with you. I didn't know anything about it until long after the fact."

"After doing such a horrible thing, why would Larry tell you about it?"

"As well as dealing with his guilt, I think he had a newfound discovery in his belief in Jesus Christ."

"If he was feeling so guilty, why do you think it's not possible he killed himself?"

"Several reasons, the first being that he was determined to provide a better life for his kids to make up for costing them their mother. Two, I think his belief in God was sincere and suicide is almost as great a sin as homicide. Three, I think he wanted to bring his agent to justice."

"If that was the case, why didn't Larry come to me and help me bring down this agent?"

"How could he implicate the agent without confessing his role in the whole thing? And like I said, he was obsessed with being there for his kids. If he told you, he would have had to go to prison, and what would have happened to the kids while he was serving life in prison?"

"We might have been able to work out a deal."

"That wasn't a chance he could afford to take."

"You still haven't told me why you feel like someone killed Larry."

"Because they must have found out somehow that Larry was thinking about going to the cops. According to Larry this wasn't the first time they did something like this, and at a million dollars a pop, this operation had to be very lucrative for them."

"Who is this 'they' you keep referring to?"

"I don't know exactly, but the agent had to have a lot of people working with him to pull off an operation of this scope and magnitude."

"Rashid, what do you want me to do?"

"You're a cop. I want you to go after this guy. This guy should be brought to justice."

"So you want justice for your cousin?"

"You damn right I do."

"Excuse me for saying it, Rashid, but Larry was far from innocent in this matter. In fact, some would say if he was murdered he got what he deserved."

"That's a pretty messed up thing to say, but I can understand why some people will feel like that. But what about the other people they killed? Who's gonna stand up for them? Even if you feel that Larry got what he deserved, what about all those innocent women? What did they do to deserve being killed? They were innocent wives and mothers and they were killed just so somebody could save some money? Is that fair? Are you gonna let that shit go down like that, Ebony? I could go after the agent myself and do what I gotta do, and believe me I thought about it, but what about those people who are in this with him?"

Ebony sat there deep in thought because Rashid had given her a lot to think about. Was it possible that such an extensive conspiracy was going on without being detected? How could she find out the truth about the situation? Did she even want to? This wasn't her job and should it be her concern? Then Ebony got mad at herself for even thinking such a thought. If someone was killing innocent women just so they or their client could save money, then she damn sure was going to do something about it.

"We don't even know if things went down the way your cousin said."

"But you can find out. You're a damn good cop, and if anybody can get to the bottom of this whole thing, I'm sure you can."

"You still think flattery will help you get your way with me," Ebony said with a smile.

"I'm serious, Ebony, this means a lot to me."

"I know, Rashid, I'm just trying to help you lighten up. I'll tell you what, I take a long hard look into the situation, and if I find that things went down the way your cousin said, I won't stop until I nail his ass to the wall."

"Thanks, Ebony."

"I haven't done anything yet but I promise you I will get to the bottom of things."

Chapter Ten

Brandon was in the guise that he liked to call his "chameleon role" in that he adapted to his environment and presented whatever image people expected to see. Tonight he was accepting an award from the Urban League as one of the top businessmen of the year. He was accompanied by one of his numerous girlfriends, Stacy. Stacy was an attractive and classy businesswoman who sold real estate and ignited zero passion in Brandon, but she was the proper type of woman he felt he should be seen with at this type of event.

Stacy turned to Brandon and asked, "Are you spending the night at my place or are we going to yours?"

Brandon looked at Stacy and realized that right now she was boring him nearly to the point of tears. The last thing he wanted to do was spend the night having empty, passionless sex with her. Stacy was proof of the philosophy that just because someone has a dynamite body, it doesn't make them a great lover. When Brandon made love to Stacy, he felt like he was just going through the motions because she neither excited him nor seemed overly excited herself. He needed a woman who either loved to make love or was adventurous and willing to try new things or both. When they made love, Brandon felt like they were both checking their watches to see when they should be done so they could both quit. On the other hand, Stacy did serve a purpose. He moved in a high-class circle, and many people considered him a sharp and up and coming businessman. Taking a lesson from the Mafia, Brandon had given several very high-end and luxurious receptions for a couple of the top young Black congressmen.

They were very successful fundraisers that increased the congressmen's coffers by thousands. Brandon didn't expect to get the congressmen in his pocket, but he hoped that it would help them look upon him favorably. It was part of creating a positive public image. He wanted to appear to be part of the top, young business elite. He would never marry Stacy but she did fit the picture of the successful companion.

She fit the image of the type of woman who should be with him. She knew which fork to use at dinner, had impeccable taste in her clothes, and could conduct an intelligent conversation with anyone on almost any subject. Through his illegal and legal endeavors Brandon was now a millionaire several times over. When he needed to reinforce the opinion that he was a serious businessman who had a brilliant future, he brought Stacy with him to a public event. He considered her part of the window dressing much like he would consider a tailor-made suit. He was just annoyed that Stacy couldn't be removed as easily as his suit when he no longer needed her.

Brandon had several women who filled a number of different roles in his life. There was Anita, who was the best lover he had ever had, and whenever he wanted to get his groove on she was ready and willing and more than capable. There was Towanda, who was a lot of fun and he would hang out with when he just wanted to have a good time. His second in command at the agency was even a woman, so he had no problem with women performing a significant role in his life. He just didn't have anyone that he was in love with.

As he matured into manhood Brandon was still an extremely attractive man with his stunning eyes and beautiful smile and he had a detached air about him that many women found irresistible. He was nearly six feet tall at 5'11" and he weighed around 217 pounds. He was fairly muscular, as he went to the gym to work out two or three days every week. He had a cool, controlled demeanor about him that helped him appear to be in charge. He exuded strength and confidence and had an air that those in the know interpreted as dangerous.

It wasn't that Brandon didn't enjoy sex, because he very clearly did, but it was that he had found something that filled him with even greater passion. Murder. There was something about engineering and committing murder that ignited feelings in him that nothing could compare with. Brandon was an avid chess player, and he loved the game so much that he played every chance he got. He even played against the computer and other players on the internet, sometimes playing as many as four games simultaneously. Brandon enjoyed the strategy of devising a plan to conquer and defeat your opponent. He especially enjoyed formulating plans that were invisible until it was too late for his opponent to do anything to counter them.

Brandon saw his well thought out formulas for death to be akin to a devious game of chess. Brandon wasn't fascinated by death itself but rather by planning and committing murder without being detected. He didn't have strong feelings about death because he saw it as inevitable. Everybody dies. The only question is when. The plan. That was the big thing for him.

Brandon was a few weeks short of his fourteenth birthday the second time he killed someone. It was during rush hour and he was on his way to school when a harried businessman shoved him out of the way in an unsuccessful attempt to catch his train. An irate Brandon started to curse the man out as he was standing there waiting for the next train, but though he chose to hold his tongue, it didn't do anything to lessen his anger.

Brandon stood a few feet behind the man trying to decide whether to tell the man what he thought of him or just punch him in his face when he noticed the man standing right at the edge of the platform as the train was pulling into the station. Without thinking about the consequences of his actions, Brandon walked past the man and bumped him into the path of the oncoming train. Amid the horrified screams and panicked confusion, Brandon worked his way through the crowd rushing to see the accident as he headed above ground.

Once Brandon was outside he realized the incredible stupidity of what he had done on an impulse. Though he had used this method before, that didn't mean it would work again or be less risky. The fact that he ended another human's life didn't bother him near as much as the realization that he could easily have been caught and sent to prison for more years than he would have cared to think about. He made the decision right then that he would never again kill anyone spontaneously or for any other reason other than financial rewards. If he felt that someone deserved to die he would take the time to make sure that death happened with a minimum of ramifications that could affect him.

· · · · ·

Ebony sat at home that night enjoying a glass of merlot trying to decide whether she thought that anything that Rashid told her had even a small degree of possibility and if so what she should do about it. Her initial thoughts were that Rashid was responding to his feelings of guilt and a sense of loss of the death of Larry, but there was something about the whole thing that just didn't sit right with her. One of her greatest strengths was the way she analyzed a problem. She would write out the facts of the case as she knew it to be on one side and the questions and things she didn't know on the other side. She preferred to break down problems that way. Not only did it take emotions out of the equations, but it also gave her a course of action as she tried to answer those unanswered questions.

If someone had seen Ebony, they would have remarked that she looked much like she must have been when she was a high school or college student. She was wearing a tee-shirt and cut-off jeans and she sat on the couch with her legs curled up under her and a studious and pensive look on her face. Something that became clear to her right away was that she didn't have enough information to properly reach a decision as to whether there was something strange going on with Brandon Barnett.

Ebony pulled out her computer and started pulling up information on International Media Artists. Ebony was immediately impressed by the graphic design and artwork of their website. Ebony wasn't able to obtain a complete list of all their clients; rather the website just revealed a few of the high-profile clients. At first things seemed completely normal and above board, then Ebony realized that many of the clients came from different aspects of the urban culture. There were a couple of rappers and musicians as well as several high-profile athletes.

She found that a little strange because most agencies stayed within a specific specialization. An agency usually focused on clients with the same areas of expertise. Most agencies either dealt with athletes or people in the entertainment field. Ebony assumed it was because their needs weren't necessarily interchangeable though they did have certain things in common. A football player didn't have any need for concert bookings and a rapper didn't have a need to deal with a salary cap but they did have contract negotiations and endorsement deals in common.

Ebony spent a little over an hour researching International Media and Brandon Barnett and while she had seen a few things that had given her a reason to pause and ponder, she hadn't found anything that she would consider a red flag or a sign that something suspicious was definitely going on. Before she decided to close the issue as Rashid's overzealous imagination, she decided to obtain a complete client list and see if anything jumped out at her.

The next morning on her way to the precinct, Ebony stopped at the International Media's office in lower Manhattan. Ebony entered the luxurious and sophisticated lobby of the high-rise and took the elevator up to the 17th floor which housed IMA. As Ebony entered the reception area of International Media, she made special notice of the classy elegance of the office.

The walls had wall-to-wall wood paneling of an exquisite wood with a deep reddish-brown hue that with the block brass letters spelling out the name of the agency gave you a feeling of not only casual comfort but also business-like sophistication. The floors were composed of Spanish mosaic tiles that were cream-colored with reddish veins that gave it an appearance similar to marble. Luxurious goldenrod leather sectional couches complemented the walls and floors perfectly and invited the visitors to the firm to wait in ease and comfort until they saw their representative. "Things must be going pretty well around here," she thought as she approached the receptionist.

The receptionist was an attractive African American female of about twenty-eight years of age with a voluptuous figure that was very enticing despite her conservative dress. She addressed Ebony in a friendly manner: "Good morning, welcome to International Media Artists. How may I help you?"

"My nephew is a young, up-and-coming rapper who has just signed his first record contract and is seeking representation. I told him I would help him look at different agencies and help him make a decision. Several people recommended your agency so I figured I would come by and get some information on your agency. Do you have a pamphlet or some literature on your client list?"

"If you wait a minute, I'll see if I can get someone to talk to you."

Ebony took a seat and waited about five minutes until one of the junior executives came to see her. The executive was another attractive woman of about twenty-eight years of age, who was tall, statuesque and of questionable ancestry. She looked to be a mixture of Asian and African descent. She had almond-shaped eyes and her skin was the color of creamy cocoa. She had glossy, jet black, straight hair that fell halfway down her back. When she spoke, she had an accent that Ebony couldn't quite place, though she thought it was oriental. She said, "Good morning, may I help you?"

"I was interested in obtaining information about your agency."

"Would you like to come with me to a conference room?"

"Sure, that would be nice."

Ebony followed the lady down a corridor past about a half dozen offices into a room that was large enough to accommodate maybe twenty people. The room was also very luxuriously decorated and was dominated by a large wood conference table made of a wood that seemed similar to the wood paneling and complemented it perfectly.

The woman turned to Ebony and said, "Won't you please have a seat?" As Ebony was sitting down she asked, "Can I offer you something to drink? Maybe some coffee or some juice?"

"I appreciate the offer but no thank you," Ebony replied.

Taking a seat across from Ebony the lady said, "My name is Naomi Cailoxto. How may we be of service to you?"

"As I explained to your receptionist, my nephew is an up-and-coming rap artist who has recently signed a record deal and we are seeking representation."

"That is usually taken care of by the record company."

"That's what he said but I feel like that might be a conflict of interest."

"May I ask you what company he signed with?"

"It's a small, new company, but I think it's a subsidiary of Def Jam Records."

"Well, ma'am, I would like to thank you for your interest but IMA chooses those artists we decide to represent. Our agency has to feel that we can best represent the interest of artist and that the relationship would be mutually beneficial."

"I completely understand where you're coming from and you don't know my nephew from a hole in the wall, but trust me one day he is going to be one of the biggest artists in the business. He had numerous companies after him before he decided on this one."

"May I ask you your nephew's name?"

"His name is Philip Baptiste Remy but he will be going under Remy P."

"You're right, I haven't heard of him."

"Don't worry, you will soon enough. They are predicting great things for him. I'll tell you what, if you could give me a brochure or a list of your clients we could research your company just in case you do decide to represent him."

"I'm sorry, ma'am, we do not have nor give out brochures and I can't tell you the names of our clients because we like to respect their confidentiality and their privacy. I'll tell you what I can do though, if you can tell me when and where your cousin will be performing I will send someone to check him out and see if he's someone we would be interested in representing."

"He's my nephew not my cousin and I'm sorry but I don't have his itinerary with me, but if you give me your e-mail address I will have it e-mailed to you."

"Here's my business card, my e-mail address is on the bottom."

"Thank you. I must tell you I'm very impressed with the decor of your office. This desk is absolutely gorgeous. Do you know what type of wood it is?"

"Yes, I do, it's Brazilian cherry."

"It's beautiful. Is the wood paneling Brazilian cherry as well?"

"No, it isn't. I believe its American Redwood, but I can't say for sure."

"It's very beautiful as well. I must say the appearance of this office gives the impression this is a very prosperous and successful company."

"We take pride in the fact that we're one of the more successful companies in our field. Our clients are very well taken care of."

"Well, thank you for seeing me. I appreciate you taking time out of your day. I know you must be busy so I won't take any more of your time."

"It was my pleasure. I'm sorry, ma'am; I didn't catch your name."

"I didn't throw it, but my name is Janice Baptiste. Thanks again and you have a great day."

Though Ebony hadn't been able to obtain a list of their clients, which was her primary reason for going to IMA, Ebony wasn't sorry that she had gone to the agency. As soon as she got back to the office, Ebony had taken a moment to write down her impressions of IMA, the strongest of which was the richness that it flaunted. As she thought about it, she realized that made a lot of sense because if you were trying to lure in big-time athletes and recording artists, it was probably necessary to exude money and wealth. If you wanted them to give you a percentage of their earnings, then you should show them that you had money, which meant somewhere along the line you had made someone a lot of money. Which also raised the questions: where did IMA get their money and approximately how much had they spent to decorate the office? Sometimes it looked like you spent a lot of money and it really didn't cost that much.

Ebony used the computer on her desk and pulled up information on American Redwood and Brazilian Cherry wood. She pulled up price lists and saw that even at wholesale prices, the wood was every bit as expensive as she had suspected. Estimating how much wood it took to do the paneling, she figured the cost would run in the tens of thousands, and that was just for the walls and didn't include the furniture.

The tried and tested method by which Ebony approached a case was by writing extensive notes on the case. She made a list of the things she knew, the things she didn't know, the things she suspected, her impressions and the things she needed to find out. As Ebony started organizing her notes, she realized one of the most important things that she needed to proceed forward one way or the other was a list of the clients. That would help her begin to answer a lot of questions about the agency, like where did they get their money. Did they have a lot of very wealthy clients giving them seventeen percent? Were there a lot of clients who had endured personal losses and tragedies? Now that some of the major questions had revealed themselves, she sat and pondered how to solve the most immediate problem: the client list. She wondered "Who else would have a list of their clients and how could she get it?"

She knew there was an answer to her question, but it seemed to be perched just beyond her reach. And then the answer occurred to her.

If IMA was a legitimate business and they made the type of money that would justify having such a luxurious office, they would have had to file their taxes. Their resources would have to have been itemized and filed with the IRS. It would have listed their clients individually and how much money they paid the firm. But how could she get a copy of his tax returns? It was not typical of the IRS to disclose the information of private citizens and corporations, and she couldn't formally request the information because there was no investigation going on.

Since she couldn't go to the IRS directly, after a quick mental checklist she realized the only federal agency that could help her was the FBI. For the first time, she had reason to regret having turned in her credentials when her assignment with the FBI ended. If she still had her credentials she would have access to the computer labs and classified files, now she had to figure out another way to get the information.

Ebony was an extremely attractive single woman who usually garnered the interest of different men she worked with. It happened so often that it rarely fazed and didn't affect her as she went about her business. Her short stint with the FBI was no exception. While she worked with them, she received several offers for dinner or romantic trysts of different degrees of intimacy, all of which she ignored or politely declined. There was one agent, Teddy Delaphine, who was especially persistent, asking her out to dinner several times or giving her the option of going to a bed and breakfast in Montauk where he claimed they could each have their own room and didn't have to be intimate. He contended it would be a chance for them to get to know each other better. Ebony found his offers very easy to turn down because she got the impression he was something of a ladies' man who was probably interested in bedding her as a tribute to his male ego.

When she left, he made it a point to tell her that if she ever needed anything to get in touch with him. She didn't know if she wanted this information bad enough to play these games with him. She decided she could contact Teddy, and if the conversation started to take a turn she couldn't control, she could terminate the conversation. After fishing out Delaphine's number out of her rolodex she called his office number, after he didn't answer she left a message on his voice mail asking him to call her back. Figuring she had spent enough time dealing with the Barnett issue that wasn't even a case yet, she started doing her regular paperwork on one of her pending cases. She got in almost two hours of consistent hard work analyzing her notes and perspectives on one of the cases before Delaphine called her back.

"Detective Delaney, how have you been?"

"I've been fine, Agent Delaphine. How have you been?"

"I've been fine as well. I don't mind telling you this place hasn't been the same since you left the task force."

"I did what I came there to do so it was time I returned to my regular mundane job."

"You don't belong with the NYPD. You should put in an application to join us on a permanent basis. I know quite a few of the right people over here and I could put in a good word for you."

"And what would that cost me?"

"Nothing, I would be glad to do it. In fact, you would make such a fine agent that you would make me look good for recommending you."

"I don't think the Bureau is the place for me. Some of your policies and procedures would be more than I could bear."

"Ebony, I know you got screwed by how things were done around here but I don't think you should judge the whole Bureau on that one little incident."

"I don't think it was such a small incident when someone else takes credit for your work."

"I can understand why you see things that way, but I still think if you joined us you would make a heck of an agent."

"I appreciate the compliment, but I think I'll stay put for now."

"Since I haven't heard from you since you left and it's obvious you're not seeking a job and I wouldn't dare dream that you're after a date, why are you calling me?"

"I'm working on a case, and it appears I could use some help."

"Really? Well, if it's advice you're after, I'm at your command."

"Though I might need some advice later, right now I need some information."

"On what?"

"I'm looking into a sports and entertainment agent and I need some information on their agency."

"Why are you looking into a sports agent? What are you on to?"

"I would rather not say just yet since I'm really just chasing down a rumor, but if it turns out to have some substance I will bring you into the loop as soon as I find out if any federal laws have been broken."

"What do you suspect them of?"

"I would rather not say at this time but it could be big. You will have to trust me."

"I think I could do that. Who are we talking about?"

"International Media Artists and their founder Brandon Barnett. Have you ever heard of them?"

"Not off hand, they don't ring a bell. Are they a big company?"

"I didn't think so but there seems to be a lot of money floating around there."

"So you suspect drug involvement?"

"Nah nah nah nah, there you go asking questions again. You're a little too slick and crafty for your own good. I have to be on my toes around you."

"What's wrong, don't you trust me?"

"Only when I've got both eyes right on you."

"Aw, Ebony, that was just a little slip."

"Ted, I don't think you ever even heard of a slip not to mention having made one. I think you are well aware of everything you do."

"Is that why you wouldn't go out with me, because you didn't trust me?"

"Maybe a little but the main reason was because I don't date where I work. It can lead to too many complications."

"Well, you don't work for the Bureau anymore, would you have dinner with me?"

"You really have a one track mind."

"When you encounter a special and beautiful prize, it's worth the effort to try to obtain it."

"So you see me as a possession now?"

"I didn't mean it like that."

"Then how did you mean it?"

"Aw, Ebony, don't be so sensitive. You know that I just meant that you are very beautiful and I would not hesitate to go to the extra effort to get to know you better."

"I'll think about what you said. Now, what about the information I need?"

"Is my cooperation necessary to get you to go out with me?"

"Careful, you almost sound like I'll be selling my body to get you to help me with a case."

"You know it wouldn't be anything like that. You know I don't see you like that; it's just that I hope you would begin to see some of my better traits. I'm not such a bad guy as you think."

"How do you know what I think?"

"I think you must not trust me because you won't go out with me."

"Maybe I just don't find you very attractive."

"Wow that never occurred to me. Is that the case?"

"It could be, but I must say it would be more attractive to know that you would be there for me with no strings attached."

"That's pretty naive of you, Ebony. You know that nothing in this world is free."

"They say that love is free."

"Is that what you're looking for? Love?"

"Isn't everyone?"

"Right now I can't deal with everyone else. I am just focusing on you and me. I'll ask you again, are you looking for love?" Ted asked.

"I don't know. I thought that love grows out of friendship?"

"Let me get this straight, you want me to do this favor for you out of friendship? People are going to wonder why I want this file, and if there is ever any fallout over this situation, there are going to be questions asked that I don't have answers for. "

"First of all, why should there be any fallout? If everything with International is on the up and up, I return the file to you and we'll put the matter to bed with a clear conscience. If not, it will be part of a criminal investigation and you were just helping out the local authorities with resources we didn't have access to. Secondly, I think you're underestimating the value of friendship. Friendship often endures when love or passion fades away," Ebony countered.

"Even though I'm not sure I agree, I can see some validity in some of your points. Out of fairness to me since you asking me to step out on friendship and trust, I think you should trust me enough that at least to tell me what you suspect them to be guilty of."

"You have a point there. At this point I don't have any evidence, just an accusation, but I can tell you it's a murder investigation."

"You think someone at this agency has committed murder?"

"At least one, possibly several."

"You're joking."

"That's what I'm trying to find out, if this agency has been up to some serious misdeeds."

"Are you sure about this? You know how this business is. If something was fishy up there we would have at least heard rumors. I haven't heard a peep."

"That's why I'm looking into it, because there has been nothing whispered about them, but I can tell you, I got my information from a source that I completely trust."

"You really think there's something there?"

"I owe it to my source to at least find out."

"Okay, I'm in. What did you want from me again?"

"Anything you may have on them, but I especially need a list of their clients and their tax returns for the last five years."

"That would mean involving the IRS and that could get dicey."

"I know, that's why I'm asking."

After a few moments' pause Teddy said, "Okay, give me three days and I'll courier over whatever I can get."

"Thanks, Teddy, just send it to the precinct and I'll keep you posted on any developments."

"I'd appreciate that. Take care, my *friend*."

· · · · ·

Three days later Ebony received the envelope from Teddy, which she promptly put away until she got home and could review the material thoroughly. The envelope was about three inches thick and included a list of the clients, tax return, and brief biographies of Brandon Barnett, Cynthia Dansforth, and Joshua Perkins. Ebony decided to start with the client list to see if any names popped out. As she looked it over, a couple of names of seemed familiar but she wasn't sure if they stood out because of their exploits in their professional careers or because of something more notorious. The name Nicholas Burleson seemed very familiar, but she couldn't remember why, so she took her laptop and googled his name. The early information detailed his accomplishments on the football field but then a paragraph told how his estranged wife was murdered in a botched kidnapping attempt. Right away this struck her as more than a little coincidence.

Ebony finished reading about Nicky Burleson and opened the files on Nicky's ex-wife. She went to the newspapers from that date and read several news accounts of the incident. She remembered the slaying of Heather Cabernet and how upset she became when she first heard of this mother who was killed trying to keep her children from being kidnapped. Maybe because of the difference in names she hadn't previously made the connection between this incident and Nicky Burleson, but now she had reason to seriously question Burleson's involvement.

Despite the fact that Burleson was allegedly cleared as a suspect, she knew that this might only be the official response and might not reveal the opinion of the investigators. Was it possible that Burleson would have someone kidnap his kids? This didn't seem like a reasonable conclusion, but this did make at least two clients of IMA whose former spouses had died or disappeared under extremely suspicious circumstances. Could Burleson have hired somebody to fake a kidnapping to murder his wife? If he did, why would he do something like that? What kind of man would jeopardize his children by exposing them to such an unsavory element as kidnappers?

This didn't make sense and it raised more questions than provided any answers but nonetheless there were two clients at the firm which raised some serious questions within her. She was getting a strong feeling that all wasn't as it appeared to be at IMA. Could there be an innocent reason why these two clients were both at IMA? Maybe they were more sympathetic and compassionate than other agents or maybe this was merely a coincidence? Ebony really didn't believe in coincidences and thought it more feasible that there was more here than met the eye. Due to the lateness of the hour and the fact that she had to work the next morning, Ebony closed down her files for the night with far more questions than she started with. Ebony knew if she was going to get to the bottom of things she was going to have to slow down and take a thorough look at her files.

It took Ebony three days to go through the history of IMA's client and compile a list of what she felt might be suspicious deaths. There was Larry Richardson and Rashid's ascertain that Brandon Barnett kidnapped Larry and killed him with a drug overdose. There was Larry's ex-wife Tanya, who disappeared during or after a Caribbean cruise and allegedly the reason why Larry was killed after he threatened to disclose how he and Barnett had arranged for Tanya to be killed. There was Heather Cabernet, ex-wife of Nicky Burleson, who was killed in a botched kidnapping attempt. There was also Jasmine Norris, the ex-live-in girlfriend of one of IMA's few non-sports related clients, a rapper, who died when she accidentally fell into a bathtub with an electric hairdryer in her hand. There was Kayla Battle, the ex-wife of Terrell Battle, who drove her car off a cliff on the Pacific Coast Highway. Finally, there was Victoria Coulter, the wife of baseball star Rodney Coulter, who died in a horseback-riding accident.

As Ebony looked over the list, a couple of facts glaringly stood out that convinced her Rashid could very well have been telling the truth: an unusually high number of ex-wives had died, and they had all died in bizarre accidents. After all, how many people died every year in accidents while riding horses or died falling into a bathtub while holding an electric appliance? Ebony was not scared to bet that each were very rare occurrences, and the fact that they were clustered here together alerted every alarm in her that something very wrong was going on here.

Now that Ebony had determined that there was a very strong possibility that IMA was engaged in some very sinister and illegal activities, she had to decide what to do about it. What should be her next move and how should she proceed? At this point she didn't have any tangible evidence that Brandon Barnett or anyone at IMA had done anything wrong or illegal. She knew in her heart that Rashid wasn't crazy or jumping to some preposterous conclusions, but did she have enough evidence to get approval to launch an investigation?

Ebony decided that if someone was killing innocent women or having them killed, she was going to do whatever was necessary to bring them to justice with or without official approval or assistance. There was no way she was going to stand idly by while these wives or mothers were murdered for the sake of convenience or any other reason. One thing she wasn't able to draw any conclusion about yet was motive. She was looking at at least four women who had all died under extremely mysterious circumstances and she didn't know why. Was the only thing they had in common was they were involved with clients of IMA or was there another common bond? Why were these women being wiped out? Was it because their former husbands and lovers didn't want them moving on and having happy and successful relationships? That might be plausible in one case and maybe even two but in four or possibly more cases it was highly doubtful.

This irritated Ebony because she felt that the answer lay right in front of her but she just couldn't see it yet. It was annoying like an itch in a place that you can't scratch and it was really bugging her. She knew that she had to get at the truth of the matter if she was going to be able to launch an investigation. She was going to have to convince her superiors and the first question they were going to ask was: why. If she was going to be able to build a case against whomever the guilty parties turned out to be, the first thing she was going to have to establish was a motive.

The analyst in Ebony knew she had to approach things with her emotions in control but with resolve and determination. Ebony started to break things down into categories and to make lists. The lists help serve two purposes at this point: 1) to help clarify her thinking, and 2) to help her establish a course of action. One other thing became clear to her in that the investigation was larger and going to be more involved than she previously thought. If she was going to investigate into the situation, it was going to take a lot more time than she earlier anticipated, and if she was going to look into it the way she should, she wouldn't have the time to do so and carry her usual caseload at work. Therefore, it would help a lot if she could convince her superiors of the crimes being committed and get them to assign the investigation to her. The first thing she figured she should do would be to speak to her lieutenant. The thing she wasn't sure of was whether she had enough evidence to make her boss as sure as she was that this was a situation that they should make a priority.

Roberto Melendez was a third generation of Puerto Ricans who had migrated to the United States. He was a firm believer in the American way of life and felt that America had fulfilled its promise to those people who had come to its shores seeking a better way of life. He thought that anyone could achieve to any degree of success they wanted in America if they were just willing to work hard enough. His philosophy was unlike many African Americans and other minorities who felt that the American dream was denied to them and they were outsiders in a country they had made and were struggling to have America repay the debt it had incurred with their people. Roberto didn't bleed red, white, and blue when cut, and he could see many of American's faults and flaws, but he felt that the good far outweighed the bad. He was proud to call himself an American and had even served in the U.S. Marines and had achieved the rank of sergeant.

He brought this philosophy with him to the justice system upon his discharge from the military and through hard work and perseverance had reached the rank of lieutenant. He probably could have gone higher and in less time, but he was unwilling to play the political games that were so much a part of any bureaucracy. As soon as Ebony arrived at the precinct she went to see Lt. Melendez so she could talk with him before her shift started. "Lieutenant, may I speak to you for a minute?"

"Sure, Delaney, what's up?"

"Something important has come up and I need to speak with you about it."

"I can spare a few minutes. Come on in and have a seat." After Ebony had sat down opposite his desk he asked, "What's on your mind?"

"I was recently made aware of a murder conspiracy that might involve as many as five people."

"Excuse me? Did I hear you correctly? Did you say that there have been five murders?"

"Yes, that's correct; I believe there have been at least five, maybe more."

"You believe? You don't know? Ebony, you're not making a lot of sense. Why don't you start at the beginning and tell me the whole story?"

Ebony took her time and told as much of her story as she could, minimizing much of what she suspected and relying on things the evidence indicated. When she finished, she sat there silently while she waited for a response from the lieutenant. Surprisingly, the Lieutenant didn't have anything to say for a couple of minutes while he appeared deep in thought. Then he got up and went to the coffee machine he kept in his office, made himself a cup of coffee, and took several sips before he responded. "Delaney, that's a hell of a story. My question is: what do we do with it. What do you think we should do about it?"

"I think you should assign it to Gary and me to investigate."

"Investigate what? We don't even know if a crime was committed. All we have is hearsay evidence from your former boyfriend, and that wasn't even evidence. It was something he allegedly was told by his cousin, who as far as we know either could have had a nervous breakdown or was using drugs at the time."

"LT. Melendez, every instinct I have is telling me that something is going on at IMA that is highly illegal. You were the one who taught me that coincidences rarely happen and are usually an indication that something very fishy is going on. Come on, Lieu, five women dead on all these unusual circumstances and all these exes are clients at the same firm. That doesn't strike you as very strange?"

"Of course it does, but strange does not mean that a crime has been committed."

"But Lieu, what if someone is murdering these innocent women and every one of them were mothers? Can we let someone commit such atrocious acts and get away with it?"

"Do you think that the fact that they were all mothers is related to why they were murdered or is this just another coincidence?"

"My gut tells me 'Yes.'"

"How?"

"I don't know."

"That's my point exactly, there's just too much that we don't know."

"That's why I want you to assign us to the case so we can get the answers to these questions."

"I understand your frustration, Ebony, I really do, but how can I justify assigning two of our best detectives to a case where we don't have a body, proof of a crime being committed, or indications that even if a crime was committed it was even in our jurisdiction?"

"Then just assign me. Gary wouldn't mind working our cases alone for a couple of days while I determine if there is enough there to launch a full investigation."

"I would like to, Ebony, but I can't. Everyone here is overburdened as it is. There's just not enough to go on for me to justify that course of action if the Captain or anyone downtown starts asking."

Melendez took a long, hard look at Ebony. He recognized that look on her face and shook his head. The look on her face made you disregard how attractive she was and look beyond it to what lay underneath. He knew that it was a look of stubborn determination, resolve, and tenacity. He realized that Ebony had made up her mind to investigate the case with or without his approval. It was that look and the emotions that lay behind it that made her such a good detective. He could order her to ignore her feelings and focus on her work, but he knew that whether she verbally agreed or not, Ebony would follow the course of action she had already decided on. Now he had to decide whether to fight with her on the issue or find a way to assist her and appear to keep the official position that he could sell to his superiors.

"I wish I could help you, Ebony, I really do but I have to do what best for all the detectives."

"I understand, Lieutenant."

"I'll tell you what I will do. If you square it with Dansby to cover for you for a couple of days, I'll approve vacation days for up to ten days while you do the investigating that we both know you're going to do. If during or after that time you come up with enough *facts* and not suspicions to launch an investigation, I'll assign you both to it and give you back the vacation days. Fair enough?"

"Yeah, that's better than I hoped for."

"Okay then, go clear it with Dansby and start proving that both our instincts are as sharp as they ever were."

· · · · ·

Ebony discussed the situation with Gary who reluctantly agreed because he felt he should be accompanying Ebony on the investigation but he went along because he didn't think Ebony would be facing any serious danger at least in the preliminary stages. As soon as they finished talking Ebony finished any paperwork she had pending on cases she was working on. After promising Gary she would keep him abreast on any developments in the case, Ebony left the precinct and headed for Rashid's job. She had phoned him and he promised he would meet her for lunch at a restaurant around the corner from his job. Ebony went into the restaurant and got a table and before she could order her food Rashid had joined her. Rashid said, "Ebony, it is usually fantastic seeing you but I don't know how I feel about seeing you today. Have you decided what you are going to do about Larry and Brandon Barnett?"

"I can't believe you have problems with seeing me today."

"Not problems, just a little uncertainty; depending upon what you say will determine the path my life will take."

"How so?'

"Barnett cannot be allowed to get away with what he's done. If you're not going to do anything about him then I will have—"

"Stop right there, don't forget I'm a law officer. Don't say something to incriminate yourself or that would make me have to come after you. If something should happen to Barnett, don't say anything that would make you a suspect."

"That's amazing. Knowing what this guy has done to Larry and God knows how many people and you threaten to come after me."

"No one is above the law; if you break the law, you should pay like anyone else."

"What about Barnett paying for what he's done?"

"The key word here is: what do we *know*. You are working with what we think or suspect and not what we can prove. So far there's a lot we suspect but little we can prove. But if you tell me you're going to do something then I would have to investigate you like anybody else. That's how our justice system works."

"Not for Black people."

"I don't believe that and I don't think you do either at least not deep inside. Plus, what does race have to do with this case? Both involved parties are African Americans."

"Then you've decided to investigate Barnett?"

"Why did you think I wanted to meet with you?"

"You could have finally realized you missed me and it is pointless to try to further resist my charm."

"And I also could have decided I'm sick of men and become a nun, but neither one is the case. What I have decided is that I'm going to find out the truth about this matter and if Brandon Barnett is guilty of murdering or having innocent women murdered, I won't rest until his balls are in a jar on my desk."

"Wow, you are even scaring me and I haven't done anything to hurt anybody."

"If Barnett has done even half of what we think he did, then he's the one who better be scared."

"I hear you. So how do we begin?"

"Whoa, there is no 'we.' I'm the police officer and I will be doing the investigating and you will stay out of the way and away from Brandon Barnett until I'm finished my investigation."

"I thought you needed my help and that's why you wanted to see me today. "

"I wanted to see you because I have some more questions for you, not because I want you involved in the investigation. I know how much you want to help and how much you want Barnett brought to justice but this is no game and nothing to play with. Several lives are on the line here and if we are right there are numerous people who deserve justice for them and their families. We're not cowboys or superheroes swooping in to bring the bad guys to justice. It's going to take some grueling hours and a lot of hard work, but I will get to the truth of the matter and that I promise you."

"Okay, you've made your position very clear. I'm here to do anything I can to help. You said you have some questions for me?"

"Yeah, a few," Ebony said as she pulled out her notebook and started taking notes. "Did Larry tell you how Barnett killed Tanya? Did he do it himself or have someone else do it?"

"He didn't get into the specifics. He just said that Barnett asked him if he wanted Tanya eliminated and he said yes and paid the money."

"Did he say how much money he paid?"

"I really don't remember if he said exactly but for some reason I seem to remember it being a million dollars."

"That's a lot of money. Did Larry say why he was willing to pay so much money to get rid of Tanya?"

"Yeah, he said he was pissed of that Tanya got so much money in the divorce settlement. He said he later regretted it but by then it was too late."

Ebony paused as she wrote divorce settlement and underlined it several times.

"Did Larry tell you anything about the other murders?"

"Nothing specific, just that this wasn't the first time that Barnett had did this."

"Were Barnett's partners involved in the criminal operation or was he in this by himself?"

"I don't know."

"Is IMA a legitimate agency or just a front for their other dealings?"

"Again, I really don't know, but I got the impression that they are a legit agency and this was just a side deal."

Ebony continued to question Rashid for several minutes until she was sure she had most of the information he had on the incident. What became clear to her was Rashid had very few facts or details that would help guide her in her investigation. However, he remained convinced that Barnett had a hand in Larry's apparent suicide so Ebony decided to probe in that direction further and maybe she could get to the bottom of why he had that opinion with such strong conviction.

"Rashid, there is nothing linking Barnett to Larry's death other than the fact that he was his agent. We don't even know for a fact that Tanya is even dead, but you seem convinced that Barnett is at the bottom of both deaths. Why? What do you know that you're not telling me?"

"Nothing, Ebony, I'm telling you everything I know."

"Are you sure you're not withholding anything to protect Larry's image?"

"You're kidding, right? What I already told you if it comes out, and it will come out if Barnett is arrested, will picture Larry as a greedy, selfish athlete who killed his wife and the mother of his children just to protect some of his fortune. And you think that I would withhold information to protect his image? What could be worse than the way he's pictured now? No, Ebony, I'm telling you everything I know."

"But what do you have that links Barnett to this? Couldn't Larry have done this himself and blamed Barnett so that you wouldn't think badly of him? Couldn't Larry have been lying to you? You said that Larry was feeling very guilty. Couldn't he have blamed Barnett because he couldn't face what he had done and when that didn't appease his guilt because he knew the truth, start using drugs?"

"It could have been like that but it wasn't."

"How do you know? What makes you so certain that's not the case?"

"Because I know Larry. You think that he was just my cousin but we were more like brothers. We stayed at each other's house for weeks at a time. When we were little before I developed into the strong, confident Rashid that you knew, Larry took care of me and protected me and took me under his wing. Even in junior high school Larry was the man in our neighborhood because everyone knew that one day he would be a basketball star. Larry could go into even the worst neighborhoods and no one messed with him. The thugs and the gangsters not only didn't mess with him, they wouldn't let anyone else mess with him because everyone knew he was special on the court. And even though I played ball, I wasn't very good at it and still no one messed with me because I was Larry's cousin and he looked out for me.

"You don't know how important that could be in our hood. As a girl, I'm sure you had guys trying to push up on you but you don't have any idea how rough it can be for young men in our hood. There are always guys trying to take your shit, take your girl, or even try to take your manhood and punk you, but because of Larry I didn't have to go through any of that crap. Larry shared everything with me. Even when girls were trying to get with the basketball star, he brought me along and I got what little game or rap I have from hanging with him."

"I understand how much he meant to you and maybe he did so much for you that now you want to repay him for all he did by blaming someone else for the way he fell?"

"Ebony, you don't get it. It's not what he did for me that I'm trying to describe for you; it's how close we were. We helped each other define who we would be as men. We spent many a night talking and just rapping about the future, making plans and helping shape images of what a real man would be like. I know Larry like I knew myself. Larry messed up royally by doing what he did with Barnett, but I'm certain that Larry did not try to escape what he did by using drugs. I'm as sure of that as I am that the sun will come up tomorrow. The last thing Larry said to me was the only way he could atone for what he did to Tanya was by being the best father in the world to their kids. Make sure they honored and never forget their mother and make sure they didn't need for anything. Now, does that sound like someone who would bail on them by using drugs?"

"I think it's ironic that he wouldn't want the kids to do without anything after he had deprived them of the most important thing every kid needs—a mother."

"That was after the fact, and Tanya was gone and there was nothing he could do to bring her back. I'm not trying to say that what Larry did wasn't a horrible thing. It was one of the most heinous acts I've ever heard of and I'm deeply ashamed that Larry was part of it, but he didn't do it alone. Barnett was in this crap with him, and then when he got scared that Larry would come clean, he killed Larry. Even if you wanted to prosecute Larry and I wouldn't blame you, but you can't because he's gone and facing a bigger judgment than anything Man could impose on him. But Barnett is still here and enjoying the fruits of having done this vile act. Plus, Larry was only involved in Tanya's murder; Barnett had several people killed, if what Larry said was the truth. You're the cop and you want me to stay out of it; well, you find out the truth about that shit."

The more Rashid talked, the more emotional he became and the louder his voice became until he was literally yelling. In an attempt to calm him down, Ebony placed a soothing hand on his chest. "Calm down, Rashid, I hear everything you're saying and feel what you're feeling. I'm on your side."

Rashid took his glass and took a deep draught of his beer as he tried to compose himself.

"Look, Ebony, I'm sorry I got upset but when I think this guy killed Larry, Tanya, and God knows who else and meanwhile he's parading around giving Congressmen receptions and stuff, it pisses me off."

"Don't stress yourself, he might have got away with some stuff before but now we're on to him. Trust me, it won't be long before he gets what coming to him."

"One way or the other," Rashid said in a threatening tone of voice.

"Rashid, you have to trust that everyone gets what's coming to them eventually."

"I know Karma and all that good stuff. So has the department formulated a task force to look into Barnett?"

"Not yet."

"Really? Well, how many people have been assigned to the case?"

"For now, I'm the only one."

"Why is that? Didn't you tell anyone what I told you about Barnett?"

"I told my lieutenant."

"So what happened? Didn't he believe you or doesn't he think this guy is dangerous?"

"It's not that, it's just that right now we don't have enough information to launch an official investigation. After I obtain some concrete evidence we'll put the entire weight of the NYPD after this bastard."

"You're doing the entire investigation by yourself?"

"Yeah, but I'm enough. Trust me. In fact, most of the time I prefer to operate that way. That way no one gets in my way."

"Is the NYPD putting their resources behind you at least?"

"They can't until it's an official investigation, but I have an incredible amount of resources on my own, including federal resources if I need them."

"Are you sure that you won't let me help you? I can at least do some leg work and I'm damn sure not scared of Barnett or whoever is working with him."

"If there is anything you can do, I'll let you know."

Rashid took out his checkbook and wrote Ebony a check for $5,000 and passed it to her.

"Rashid, what is this? You know I can't accept any money for doing my job."

"It's not payment for you. Use it to help in the investigation. You might need it for expenses or to loosen some tongues. If you need any more, you let me know."

"I still can't accept this."

"Honey, look, if you won't let me help you with the investigation, I have to do something. Larry's will left me a whole lot of money. Let me use a bit of it to help bring his murderers to justice."

"Well, if you put it like that, I guess I can make an exception."

"Thank you."

"Oh, and Rashid?"

"Yeah?"

"Don't call me honey."

. . . . .

After leaving Rashid, Ebony returned to the precinct because she had some calls to make and she didn't want to make them from her cell phone because some of the parties she didn't want to have her cell phone number. She didn't want to go home because she had a couple of errands to run and it would be easier if she didn't go home and have to come back out.

As soon as she was at her desk, she called Agent Ted Delaphine at the FBI.

"Agent Delaphine, this is Ebony Delaney."

"Hey, Ebony, how are you doing? Did you receive the packet I sent you?"

"Yes, I did, I wanted to call and say thank you."

"No problem, how is the investigation going?"

"It's progressing but it's slow going right now."

"What do you need, Ebony?"

"How do you know that I need anything?"

"As charming as I may be, I'm not telling myself that you are calling me solely because you can't resist my charm or just to say thank you."

"Maybe I was keeping my word and keeping you up to date on the investigation?"

"Okay, so bring me up to date."

"I'm getting a distinct feeling that a certain prominent sports agent has been engineering and conducting murders across the country."

"How many murders?"

"Maybe as many as five or six."

"You're not sure of how many you suspect him of?"

"He's very good at covering his tracks and making things appear like an accident.'

"Then how do you know it was murder?"

"I don't know, but that's what I'm trying to find out."

"Okay, Ebony, you've succeeded in piquing my interest. What do you need?"

"I do need a couple of things that you could be helpful with. I want to know if you could get me copies of a couple of official files. A couple of them may not be Federal cases but you guys might have an informal file on them. I'll fax you the list. Also, could you arrange a meeting for me with the agents who handled the Cabernet/Burleson kidnapping?"

"Whoa, that one might not be so easy."

"Why is that?"

"Because that case is still a sore spot around here. There are not that many high-profile cases that aren't solved. Is that case part of your investigation?"

"There are certain things that link it to my guy."

"Ebony, give me twenty-four hours to get what I can on those files. I meet you for dinner tomorrow night at Theresa's, it's an Italian restaurant on Mulberry Street. Is seven o'clock good for you?"

"I'll make it work."

"Good, I'll see you then."

After making a couple of calls, Ebony headed up to the Bronx to talk to the two detectives that handled the Larry Richardson case. After she arrived at the 42nd Precinct, Ebony was introduced to Thomas Brennan and Anthony Jackson.

Together they went into an interview room to discuss the Richardson case.

Detective Brennan asked, "We were told they you wanted to speak to us about the Larry Richardson case?"

Ebony replied, "That's true. I appreciate you taking the time to speak with me."

"It's not a big deal. Consider it professional courtesy. What do you want to know?"

"Did your investigation reveal anything that was a little suspicious?"

"What do you mean?" Detective Jackson asked.

"The official conclusion was that his death was an accidental heroin overdose. Was there anything that made you question whether this was the case?"

"All the evidence indicated that Richardson died as a result of a heroin overdose."

"Was there anything to make you question whether it was self-inflicted?"

"Not really. It seemed like a pretty open and shut case," Jackson said.

"Are you sure there wasn't anything that made you suspicious?"

"I'm not sure what you're looking for."

"I'm a detective like you are, and sometimes there are a few minor details that just don't seem to fit. I've had a few cases where every fact seemed to point in one direction but there were a few little things that just didn't seem to add up. Sometimes it was nothing more than just a feeling in my gut, but even after the case was closed I couldn't get away from the feeling that I was missing something. Was there anything like that?"

"Sure there was, and that's usually the case, but there just wasn't enough to make us change our conclusions."

"Could you share with me some of the things that didn't quite fit?"

"There was evidence of lividity that would seem to indicate that where the body was discovered was not where he died," Detective Brennan said.

"I often wondered why someone who had several houses like Richardson had would choose to die down here in such a shithole. The way we figured it, he was probably getting high with some friends and after he overdosed had to dispose of his body because it might raise questions they didn't have answers for. So they brought the body down here to dispose of it. He was probably getting high with some of them high-profile, celebrity types," Detective Jackson said.

"Did you look at any other theories?" Ebony asked.

"Not really because there are few other possibilities unless you subscribed to the theory that someone murdered him and therefore dumped his body down here. But that theory would raise the question: if somebody wanted to kill him, why would they do it by giving him a heroin overdose?"

"And you don't buy that possibility?"

"No, I don't. Who would do something like that and why?"

"There was one more thing that I thought was a little strange," Detective Brennan said.

"Which was?" Ebony asked.

"When the toxicology report came back, it indicated extremely high levels of opium derivatives. To reach levels that high, a person would have had to use heroin almost non-stop for several weeks. This guy was a professional athlete, not a heroin addict. To have reached levels that high, he would have had to be trying to kill himself. Also, the report indicated no traces of cocaine or marijuana. Usually when the rich and famous use heroin, it is because they are partying and using a mixture of drugs and alcohol, but that wasn't the case here."

"Didn't you think that was enough to warrant further investigation?"

"Investigate what? That the guy liked to get high off heroin and not other drugs? Look, Detective, this was a high-profile death up here in our precinct. That doesn't happen up here too often. Administration was eager to get this case closed as this was media attention that no one wanted. To keep the investigation open we would have needed a lot more than a strange toxicology report or the feeling that all the pieces didn't quite fit."

Ebony said, "I'm sorry, Detectives, I didn't mean to imply that I thoughts you guys took a shortcut or didn't do your job. I was just trying to understand your impressions and thoughts on the investigation."

"Let me ask you a question, Detective Delaney? Why are you looking into this closed case?" Jackson asked.

"I promised one of Richardson's relatives that I would look into the case to ensure that everything really was as it appeared."

"Did he have reason to think there was more to the case than a simple drug overdose?"

"Well, you know how families are in the case of tragedies. They just don't want to believe that their people could die through some foolish mistake. But a promise is a promise so I'm looking into it. I want to thank you gentlemen for your time and I know you're busy, so I'll be going."

After Ebony got back home she took a few moments to think about the case. She wondered why she didn't tell the detectives about her real reason for investigating the Richardson death. Was she looking to protect Brandon Barnett's reputation in case he was innocent? Did she think that there was a chance that Barnett was innocent of the things she suspected him of and the entire case was just a web of unusual coincidences? She knew that was possible if not probable.

Maybe she was approaching the case from the wrong angle. She was looking for the facts to convince her of Barnett's innocence or guilt because as a top investigator she was convinced that no one could commit multiple murders without leaving traces somewhere. Barnett would have to be a genius of epic proportions to have committed several murders without leaving a trail or a loose end somewhere. Her challenge was to find that loose end and pull it until Barnett whole case of deception was exposed.

Ebony remembered that the place to get to the bottom of the entire manner was at the beginning and not at the middle, like she was doing now. The beginning of the Richardson case was at Tanya's death not Larry's. What if Tanya wasn't even dead? It was certainly not unheard of for someone who was declared dead to reappear years later after joining a commune or some other Bohemian lifestyle. Was Tanya even dead or had she just decided that she couldn't deal with the many pressures of this life and had run away from everybody and everything? Maybe the place to begin should be at Tanya's disappearance.

Ebony took out Tanya's file to see what cruise line she was on when she disappeared and checked to make sure they had a New York office. That would be her first stop tomorrow. Then she called Rashid. "Rashid, who has custody of Tanya and Larry's kids?"

"Tanya's parents. Why?"

"How's your relationship with them?"

"It's okay. Why?"

"I want you to call them and see if I can see them the day after tomorrow?"

"Okay, I can do that, but why do you want to talk with them?"

"Damn it, Rashid, will you stop questioning everything that I say or do? You wanted to help with the investigation, this is how you can help, but I don't have the time or energy to bring you up to pace on every move I make or why I'm doing what I'm doing."

"Okay. Okay. Chill out. I'll call her people and get right back with you."

Fifteen minutes later Rashid called back and said, "They said okay. They said for you to call them with the time your flight will arrive and they will meet you at the airport."

"Great! I got their number in the file and I'll call them when I know my flight information. Thanks, Rashid."

"Have a good trip, Eb. I'll see you when you get back."

Next Ebony placed a call to the cruise line where Tanya disappeared. After being transferred from department to department she was finally transferred to a vice president. It took quite a bit of coaxing and a little arm twisting to have him agree to a meeting the next day at one o'clock.

Having coordinated her plans for the next day, Ebony decided to take a few minutes of personal time to unwind and relax because she knew she would have to be sharp to handle her business over the next few days. After enjoying a hot bubble bath and a cold glass of wine, Ebony read the newspapers to catch up on the current developments in the world. While reading the society section she saw where Brandon Barnett was giving a special invitation-only Black Tie reception for a State Assemblyman. This might be a good occasion to observe Barnett without him being aware of it and therefore get a better feel for what type of person he was, but the problem was how to get into the special invitation event. Since this was a political event and her father used to be political activist, she placed a call to her dad to see if he could be of assistance.

"Hi, Dad."

"Ebony? How are you, honey?"

"I'm fine, Dad, how have you been feeling?"

"I was fighting a cold earlier this week but it was nothing serious. How are you?"

"I'm feeling fine. How is Mom?"

"She's fine. Do you want to speak to her?"

"I called to speak to you about something. I'll speak to her when we're finished."

"Okay, what's up?"

"Were you invited to Assemblyman Green's reception?"

"Yeah, if you want to call it that. Even with an invitation, a ticket costs $1,000."

"Are you planning on going?"

"I wasn't planning on going. Why do you ask? Are you interested in going?"

"I was thinking about it."

"Why? That doesn't seem like something you would be interested in."

"I'm not usually but this might be an exception. Plus, I'm not sure if I'm interested in the event as much as someone at the event."

"Oh yeah, who?"

"Brandon Barnett."

"Really? He's a pretty dynamic young man and not too bad looking either."

"Then you've met him?"

"Yeah, a couple of times."

"What did you think of him?"

"He's a pretty sharp young man with a lot on the ball. He doesn't seem like your type though."

"Don't start, Dad. Do you want to go?"

"I don't have a thousand dollars to feather a politician's nest right now."

"I think I can cover it."

"Ebony, you have two thousand dollars for a political event?"

"I told you I got it. I came into a little extra cash."

"And you can't think of anything better to do with it then to give it to Assemblyman Bradford Green? You must really want to meet Brandon Barnett in the worse kind of way to give up that kind of money."

"Do you want to go or not?"

"I guess I'll go with you. I can't let you go into that den of snakes by yourself."

"Okay, I'll drop the money off before I go out of town."

"You're leaving town? Where are you going?"

"I have to leave town on a case."

"Okay, I'll see you when you come by then. Hold the phone and I'll get your mother for you."

· · · · ·

The next day Ebony started her day by booking her flight to Texas and making the arrangements to rent a car. Though Tanya's parents had volunteered to pick her up at the airport, she felt it may have been inconvenient and a bit too familiar. Though Tanya's parents weren't suspects in any way, her investigative protocol would not allow her to be at anyone's beck and call while researching or conducting an investigation. Ebony had found that a lot more information was gathered when the proper psychological parameters were maintained. Ebony wanted to make sure that Tanya's parents viewed her as a legitimate investigator who was trying to uncover the truth and trying to get them justice and not a friend of the family who was doing them a favor.

After getting her clothes together for her meeting/date with Ted Delaphine later on that evening, Ebony headed to her meeting with the cruise line. Though she showed up more than an hour early, she was escorted into the vice president's office right away.

"Detective Delaney, my name is Alberto Orengo and I am here to help you in this grave matter in any way I can. Yesterday you indicated that you were assigned to look into the Tanya Richardson disappearance?"

"That is correct."

"I have taken the liberty of having our Director of Security fly in to attend this meeting. He should be here shortly. Can I offer you some coffee or light refreshment while we await his arrival?"

"No thank you, I'm fine."

"Detective Delaney, I must say I'm curious why the NYPD have developed interest in this case after all this time?"

"New evidence has recently been uncovered that indicated that Ms. Richardson's disappearance may have been the result of foul play."

"It was always questionable at best, but I still don't understand why the NYPD is interested? It does not appear to be within your jurisdiction."

"It is part of a larger investigation that involves numerous victims and suspects."

"Are we talking about a serial killer here?"

"I'm not at liberty to disclose that information at this time."

At that moment the door opened and a tall, swarthy man of about 6'3" entered the room. He was brown-skinned with a Latino or East Indian complexion.

"My name is Patesh Hapuaragy, and I am the Director of Security for this cruise line. Excuse my tardiness, but I was perusing the dossier that just arrived from our corporate headquarters in Miami, as that was the ship's port of origin so all pertinent information on that cruise is in that office and had to be brought here by overnight courier."

"May I see the file?"

"Sure. Take your time and read the file, and I am available to answer any questions you may have."

"Can I take the file with me?"

"I'm afraid not, but I am authorized to provide you with a copy of anything that I feel is pertinent to your investigation."

Ebony took the file which was about twelve pages thick and it took her about fifteen minutes. Afterwards she asked several questions. "The first time that Mrs. Richardson was noticed to be missing was when she failed to check out of the ship before disembarking?"

"That's correct. She and her companion had failed to show at their assigned seat at dinner, but that was not unusual as many passengers choose to eat in their room or at one of the many restaurants and cafes on board."

"Did her companion check out of the room?"

"No, he didn't. At first we didn't think it highly unusual because although it is uncommon, sometimes passengers get off the ship at one of the ports of call and spend so much time on the island that they miscalculate the time and the ship leaves without them. They will either catch a flight and meet us at the next port of call or make their way home. We first became aware of the problem when no one contacted us to pick up her luggage and belongings that were left behind, including some very expensive jewelry."

"I noticed in the file several photos of Ms. Richardson and her companion."

"The cruise line has professional photographers on staff who takes pictures of many of the special events on the ship like passenger's arrival, the captain's dinner and other events. The passenger then has the option of purchasing as many of the pictures as they want. Ms. Richardson ordered and paid for the deluxe package but she never picked it up."

"Will it be possible for me to get a copy of those photos?"

"Sure, that shouldn't be a problem. Actually, you can take these copies. I'll have duplicates made from the negatives which we still have on file."

"Is the ship equipped with security cameras?"

"Yes. Many of the common areas and some of the passageways have cameras."

"What about the cabins or balconies?"

"None of the cabins have cameras. Our clients pay a lot of money to have the vacation of a lifetime. We pride ourselves on providing a very safe environment while also allowing privacy within their living quarters."

"Are one of the filmed common areas the egresses on and off the ship?"

"Yes, they are."

"Has someone viewed the tapes to see if Ms. Richardson or her companion left the ship?"

"I personally reviewed all the tapes and was able to see a gentleman who looked very much like her companion disembarks the ship in St. Maarten. I was not able to find any evidence of him reentering the ship."

"Have we been able to establish the identity of Ms. Richardson's companion?"

"We've run into a bit of luck there. After the 9/11 disaster, a passport is required on all international travel. Our records indicate that her companion was named Omar Kareem Douglas."

"Might it be possible for me to view the tapes myself? I might spot something that was missed earlier."

"I brought the tapes with me so if you want to view them it's not a problem. I'll have them set up a screening room for you."

"I would appreciate that."

Several hours later Ebony left the cruise line's offices and started home. At first she was going to stop by the precinct and run the picture of Omar Douglas through the data bank to see if anything came out, but she was a little tired after spending hours looking at film and she still had to prepare for her meeting with Ted Delaphine that night. Though she was tired she was not discouraged because for the first time she had tangible evidence that a crime probably was committed and not just circumstances that could be a coincidence. She had concrete proof that Tanya never left the ship and wasn't off somewhere living a new secret life. She also had a picture and identity of her last known companion. Tomorrow she would contact the airlines leaving St. Marten on the date that Douglas exited the ship to see if he took a flight from there, which might help her begin to track his whereabouts starting with his destination.

Arriving home, Ebony decided to take a bubble bath while she organized her thoughts on the case and prepared for her meeting with Ted that evening. She dressed in an olive green Ann Taylor business suit with a white silk blouse and green leather sling-back pumps. She wanted to look like she was about business while still looking sexy and elegant. As she still hadn't decided the complete parameters of her relationship with Ted, she wanted to dress in a way that left all options open but did not invite an intimate relationship. It wasn't that she didn't find Ted attractive; it was that she didn't want to be just another conquest for Delaphine in the rumored long list of ladies who couldn't resist his charm.

She also didn't need the additional complication of a questionable relationship with all she had going on in her life. Her parents still hadn't forgiven her for marrying outside her race as well as outside the acceptable social system, and if she was to come to them with another relationship with a White man who was also a federal agent, it might damage their relationship to the point where it couldn't be repaired. It wasn't that she needed her parents' approval to have a relationship, she just wasn't sure that Delaphine was worth the trouble.

In recent years, she and her parents didn't see eye to eye on many issues but that didn't mean she didn't love and respect them or that she didn't want their love or respect in return. It was hard maintaining a relationship with so many cultural differences when everybody was on the same page, but throw in their parent's disapproval and it got infinitely worse. There were a few times when her marriage fell on difficult times that she wanted to go to her parents for advice or maybe just a listening ear and maybe a shoulder to cry on before being told to go back to husband and try to work things out, but she couldn't. While her parent tried not to interfere, they made it very obvious they felt that Jack Delaney made a poor choice as a husband.

Before he even met Jack, her father was convinced that because Jack was White he could not have legitimate feelings for Ebony. He feared that Jack was acting on some forbidden taboos and that his fascination was not with Ebony but with the mystique of an interracial relationship. In his opinion, for centuries the only place for Black women in White society was in a White man's bed and he just couldn't believe that things had changed dramatically.

Ebony knew better. She knew that Jack didn't love her because of her color neither did he despise her because of her color. To him it just wasn't very much of an issue one way or the other. She tried to convince her father of as much but gave up when she realized that a person's mind has got to be open if you were going to have a chance to change it. She could describe her father's mind as brilliant, creative, or innovative but not open. He had very distinct opinions about most things, and it damn near took an act of God to get him to change those opinions.

For quite some time her relationship with her parents was strained with bad feelings on both sides. Her parents resented that she had deviated so far from the things they believed and the plans that they had imagined for her and she had just as much resentment that they didn't trust her to live her life the way she saw fit. They felt that children should work to finish the hopes and dreams of not just the parents but also their people. Ebony, on the other hand, felt that family should love and support you in whatever path you chose to take. She felt that her life was hers and she should be able to live it however she wanted. Not history, not her people, and not her parents should have more than some influence and the degree of influence should be determined by her. She and her parents had been at an impasse for years with neither side budging from the island of their opinion.

Finally things were starting to get a little better. Ebony didn't know if things were healing with time or if her divorce from Jack was a determining factor, but now that things were getting better she realized how much she missed the support and warmth of her parents, which was just one more reason not to deal with Ted on anything but a professional basis.

Having reached new resolution on her relationship with Ted, Ebony arrived at the restaurant and was directed to Ted's table. After Ebony was seated, Ted asked, "Would you like something to drink?"

"Maybe I'll have a Grey Goose Martini."

After Ted had ordered the drink he asked, "Are you hungry? Would like to eat before we discuss business?"

"No, I can wait. Why don't we discuss business first then we can relax and enjoy our meal."

"That's fine with me."

"Did you bring the files I asked you for?"

"Sure I did, but don't you think it's time you told me what the hell is going on?"

"I was asked by a friend to investigate the death of Larry Richardson."

"The NBA star?"

"The one and only."

"Wasn't his death considered an accidental drug overdose?"

"That was the official story but Richardson told his cousin that he and his agent, a Brandon Barnett of International Media Artists, engineered the death of his estranged wife, Tanya Richardson who disappeared on a Caribbean cruise. Richardson was preparing to confess to the authorities and therefore Barnett had him killed."

"What happened to Mrs. Richardson?"

"I met with the cruise line earlier today, and there was no evidence of her exiting the ship. It is safe to assume that Mrs. Richardson either fell or was thrown overboard. We have film evidence of her companion exiting the ship in St. Maarten. We need to check the flight records for all flights leaving St. Maarten within forty-eight hours of the ship leaving to see if he left the island by plane and if so where he went."

"Do you have a name or a face?"

"We have both. In order to take a cruise in international waters, you have to have a passport."

"How does the Cabernet kidnapping fit in?"

"Her husband, Nicky Burleson, was also a client of IMA."

"Some coincidence."

"If you think that's a coincidence, at least five of IMA's clients have lost a recent spouse under mysterious circumstances."

"Whew, and you think that Barnett or someone at IMA is behind the deaths?"

"They all appear to be accidents and none of the accidents have a direct link to the spouses so I really don't know what I think yet, other than its one hell of a coincidence. I don't know about you, but I don't believe in coincidences, and even if I was to admit that one is possible, I still wouldn't believe five."

"Maybe they joined IMA because of some type of support or therapy group?"

"Maybe so, but don't you think we need to do some type of investigation to make sure that's all it is?"

"We? Do you realize that you said we?"

"I don't mean necessarily you and I. I meant 'we' as in some type of official authorities."

"Oh. I had started to get my hopes up."

"Ted, I have no objection to your working this investigation with me. This investigation is starting to be far more extensive than I thought it was going to be and I could use your help and the federal resources could prove to be very helpful. But I have to stress that I'm not ready for a relationship just yet so any dealing we have will have to be strictly business."

"Let me ask you a personal question. Do you find me attractive?"

"Ted, I think that we both will agree that you are a handsome man and I can say that I find you physically attractive, but I don't know you as a person well enough to determine whether I find you attractive as a potential partner."

"That's what I have been saying. I think that if you get to know me as a person you will find that I'm not half as bad as people make me out to be."

"I don't think you have been listening to me, Ted. So I will tell you again. Right now there is so much going on in my life that I don't have the desire, interest, or inclination to start a relationship. I know I've told you this before, but you seem incapable or unwilling to believe me."

"It's not that I don't believe you, it's just that I don't think you appreciate how difficult it's going to be working with you while I'm so strongly attracted to you."

"Aw, Ted, grow up. I'm not the first woman to tell you 'no' so stop pouting and stomping your feet trying to get your way. I'm looking at a fiend here who may have murdered as many as five women, for reasons of money or convenience or for whatever damn reason. Someone has got to stand up for these women since the men they married and entrusted seem to be involved in getting them murdered. Who speaks for them? Doesn't anybody even care?"

Ebony started getting her things together and stood up as she prepared to go. "Ted, I know you're a damn fine agent and I thought you would want to get this son of a bitch as bad as I do. But if all you can think about is getting in my pants then I was wrong about you. I know that you have a strong sense of justice. Don't you think these women and their families deserve some of that justice?"

"Ebony, why don't you calm down and sit down back down? I understand what you are saying, and I do feel like you do. I wasn't saying that I wasn't going to work with you on this case. I just thought I was doing the honorable thing by letting you know how I feel about you.

"After I looked at the files I got for you, I got a sense of where you are going with this case. I believe in it strongly enough to have gone to my boss and requested that we open a case on it. I want to tell you, I'm in on the investigation whether they approve it or not. You're not the only person who can get enraged at someone murdering innocent women. Now, where are we at with this case?"

"I think we have to establish that we do in fact have a case. The first thing we are missing is a motive. Why is Barnett having these women killed? Then we can look into the how and who else might be involved with him."

"Didn't you tell me that Richardson said he paid to have his wife murdered?"

"Yeah, that's what I was told, and I believe that the figure was a million dollars."

"I think that I will contact some people I know at the IRS and in the banking communities to see if we can access his financial records. If he did five or more murders at a million dollars plus for each, he has to have that money somewhere. Even if he has a partner that he has to share the money with, that's a lot of money to try to hide at home under a mattress."

"Is there a way we can access his accounts in foreign banks?"

"We could, but we would have to go through a lot of red tape and we would have to know the countries and which banks he was doing business with. I think I'll also make some calls to Immigration and have them send us a record of his comings and goings in and out of the country. If he left the country, he had to have used his passport. What are your plans for tomorrow? We need to coordinate our plans and I think we need to set up one central office where we work the case. That way our left hand will know what our right hand is doing."

"Does that mean you are formally in the case?"

"I'm in whether it is official or not."

"I've set up a work area in my home, but I'm not sure we'll be comfortable working there."

"I'm sure I can get us some space in my office. I'm hoping that tomorrow my superiors will decide that we have enough to open the case and they will assign a couple of more agents to us."

"That would be fine but I'll be moving forward if it's only the two of us. I'll be leaving tomorrow to go to Texas to talk to Tanya Richardson's parents. I want to eliminate any suspicions that she might be alive somewhere. It would be good if you could arrange the meeting with the agents who handled the Cabernet kidnapping for the day after tomorrow so I could see them on my way back to New York."

"I'll make a call tomorrow to see if I can make that happen. Come on, let's enjoy our dinner while you bring me up to date with where you are with the investigation. You said you have a picture of Tanya Richardson's travel companion?"

"Yeah, his name is Omar Douglas."

"Why don't you give it to me and I'll see if I can match it with anything in our files as well as seeing if he's on any flight manifests coming out of St. Maarten. I should have that information for you when you get back from your trip."

Chapter Eleven

As Ebony pulled up to the Moore farmhouse, she was surprised at how modern the facilities were. Like most New Yorkers she had imagined that farm looked like was something out of the old TV show *Green Acres*. That was so far from reality that it was almost laughable. This farmhouse was a beautiful green and white, five-bedroom ranch-style house that was spacious if not luxurious. There was a long driveway up to the house that was lined on both sides by large trees which succeeded in giving the house an appearance of being comfortable and welcoming as well as providing shade. The front of the house had a large porch across the front with two swings as well as a couple of rocking chairs.

A few hundred feet behind the house and to the right was a long building that was a combination of metal and wood painted white. There was another building, similar but smaller behind that building but equally as modern and efficient looking. Both buildings were enclosed by a white wood fence that ran for quite a way until it disappeared in the distance over a hill. Ebony realized that if the fence signaled the boundaries of the farm, then this was a very large and prosperous farm. Since she had first entered what she assumed was the

Moore's farm, she had seen numerous black and white cows. In the distance, she could see several horses grazing in a picturesque meadow.

As Ebony parked her rental car in the parking area to the right of the porch and exited her car, she was met by a middle-aged woman who came out of the house to meet her. The woman looked to be in her late fifties, and was stoutly built with her salt-and-pepper hair pulled back into a bun. The woman had a complexion resembling honey-roasted almonds with cherubic cheeks that revealed dimples when she smiled. She had on a floral dress and an apron that had several splotches and areas covered with flour. As she wiped her hands on her apron she said, "Detective Delaney? Hi, I'm Juanita Moore, and thanks for coming to see us. It wasn't necessary for you to rent a car. We could have had someone pick you up at the airport."

"It's wasn't a problem. I didn't want to inconvenience anyone."

"Well, now that you're here, won't you come inside out of the heat?"

As Ebony followed Juanita into the house, Juanita said, "Do you mind if we talk in the kitchen? I'm putting the finishing touches on the desert for dinner. My granddaughter and I are making a Brown Betty as an extra treat to LJ for doing so well in school."

"LJ?"

"Larry Junior. He's the oldest and probably having the hardest time adjusting to everything that has happened. He was especially close to his mother. I think after the breakup he took over trying to take care of and protect his mother. He took it as his personal failure when she disappeared. We tried to convince him it wasn't his fault, but he doesn't really believe us. At first he wouldn't do his schoolwork or much of anything, but lately his grades have been excellent. I asked him about it and he says he wants to do real well so when his mother comes home she will be proud of him."

"He thinks his mother is coming home?"

"I don't know if he really believes it or if he is trying to convince himself because he can't deal with the possibility of never seeing his mother again."

"Mrs. Moore, do you think that your daughter might be coming home one day?"

Instead of answering Mrs. Moore glanced at the most darling little girl that Ebony had ever seen. She was about three years of age with soft, silken skin the color of warm caramel. She had round, black eyes that, despite the innocence of her age, hinted at just a touch of mischief. She had the cutest little pug nose and round lips that Ebony would bet she could get anything she wanted with just a pout. She was also blessed with the largest, curliest afro that Ebony had ever seen.

Mrs. Moore asked, "Can I offer you something to drink?"

"Thank you, that would be very nice."

"Would you like a nice cold soda or some iced tea?"

"Some iced tea, if it's not a problem."

"Of course it's not a problem. Detective Delaney, would you like to stay for dinner?"

"Please call me Ebony."

"If you'll call me Juanita."

"Thank you for the invitation, Juanita, but I wouldn't want to intrude."

"It wouldn't be an intrusion at all, and in fact it might be nice to have a little adult company. Are you flying back to New York tonight?"

"No, my flight is in the morning. I didn't want to take a chance on missing your husband because I was rushing to catch a flight."

"Then it's settled and you'll be having dinner with us. Would you like to spend the night? We have plenty of room."

"Thank you for the offer, but I've already gotten a hotel room though I will gladly accept your invitation for dinner." Turning to the little girl, Ebony asked, "And what's your name, angel?"

"Jaleesa," the little girl replied.

"And how old are you dear?"

"Three."

"This is my youngest granddaughter. She's the spitting image of Tanya when she was that age. Tanya had three kids: LJ, Jaleesa, and Zoe, who is eight years old. LJ and Zoe should be home from school shortly. The school bus usually drops them off around three. Jaleesa finished her lessons early so I'm letting her help me with dinner."

"Does Jaleesa attend pre-school?"

"No, Jaleesa will be raised just like I raised my children. I will teach them myself. By the time she's ready for kindergarten, she will know how to count to 100, her ABC's, and be able to read on a second grade level. Miss Delaney, Rashid told us you were investigating Tanya's disappearance and Larry's death and I know you have a lot of questions for us, but I rather not discuss it in front of the children. As you can imagine, the whole thing is very upsetting to them, and my main goal is to get them adjusted and living a normal life as soon as possible. I don't know how we can help, but if you can wait until after dinner, we'll gladly answer any questions you have."

"That would be fine because I wanted to speak to your husband as well. I kind of barged in on you anyway without a lot of advance notice. Plus, this will give me a chance to get to know the kids."

"It's okay if you talk to them but please don't ask them a lot of questions about their parents," Juanita said.

"I understand, and I wouldn't want to upset them any further. They've already been through quite a lot. I'll just be a friend of the family who's come to visit."

While Ebony was talking, Juanita noticed that Jaleesa had succeeded in getting more flour or herself than anywhere else and started using her apron to clean her up so Ebony offered, "Would like for me to take her and clean her up?"

"Sure, if it's not too much trouble, there's a bathroom right down the hall on the left."

While Juanita was listening to Ebony and Jaleesa laughing and talking as Jaleesa was washed, LJ and Zoe arrived home from school.

"Do we have company?" LJ asked.

"Yeah, a friend of your Uncle Rashid was in town so she stopped by to see you."

Ebony and Jaleesa reentered the kitchen from the bathroom and upon spying LJ, Jaleesa dropped Ebony's hand and ran over and gave LJ a hug.

LJ said, "Hey, Lee-Lee, were you a good girl today?"

"Uh-huh, I worked on my numbers and I helped Nana make you a surprise."

"LJ, Zoe, this is Miss Delaney from New York," Juanita said.
"Please call me Ebony."

"It's nice to meet you, Miss Ebony," LJ said. "Nana, I'm hungry, can we have a sandwich?"

"You may have a piece of fruit. We are going to have an early dinner, and I don't want you to spoil your appetite. Zoe, are you hungry? Would you like a piece of fruit?"

"No, ma'am, I'm hungry but I think I can wait until suppertime."

"Okay, then I think y'all should get started on your homework."

LJ took his apple and they headed upstairs to their bedrooms to do their homework. Jaleesa jumped down from her stool and started following her brother and sister upstairs.

"Lee-Lee, you leave your brother and sister alone and let them do their homework. Don't you be bothering them."

"I not gonna bother them. I gonna work on my ABC's," Jaleesa said.

"Don't worry, Nana, she won't bother us. I don't have a lot of homework so I can help her with her penmanship."

"Okay then, if anyone needs any help just let me know," Juanita said as she turned to Ebony and informed her "LJ is very protective of his sisters, especially the little one. Zoe is still pretty much a pain in the neck to him, though there is no doubt how much he loves her."

Juanita and Ebony engaged in small talk about life on the farm until about ten minutes later they heard a ruckus from upstairs that sounded like the kids were trying to dismantle the house around their heads. Juanita went to the bottom of the stairs and called "Get down here, all three of you. Right now!"

The kids came downstairs with a forlorn look on their faces and tears were flowing down Jaleesa's cheeks.

"What the heck is going on upstairs? Didn't I tell you to do your homework?"

"We were doing our homework," LJ said.

"No, you weren't, not unless your homework involved destroying my house. Now what was going on?"

"I'm sorry, Grandma, it was my fault," LJ said.

"That still doesn't tell me what was going on. Why are you crying, Lee-Lee?"

"Because Zoe hit me."

Juanita gave Zoe a look that indicated she was in big trouble so Zoe said, "I didn't hit her, Grandma. I was trying to get my new Barbie doll back and I might have pushed her. By accident! She had the new designer Barbie that Mommy brought me. And you should see the mess she made of my room. I just cleaned it up last night and now everything is all over the place."

"What do you have to say for yourself, young lady?" Juanita asked Jaleesa.

"I didn't want to play with it. Angela wanted to play with Barbie," Jaleesa said in her defense.

"Don't you know that the rules are you can't go in your sister's room or play with her things without her permission?"

"But I didn't want to play with her. Angela did."

"Well, if your doll wanted to play with Zoe's doll you should have gotten permission for her."

"But I wasn't going to hurt her. I was gonna put Barbie right back."

"So how did you mess up your sister's room?"

"I couldn't find Barbie and I had to look for her."

"Okay, young lady, you may not watch TV after dinner tonight and you cannot have any dessert until you have helped your sister clean up her room."

"But, Nana, that's not fair. I didn't do nothing wrong."

"Would you like to not be able to watch *Yo Gabba Gabba* or *Sesame Street* for a week?"

"Oh no, Nana, please."

"Then apologize to your sister."

"I'm sorry, Zoe."

"Zoe, you may not go to dance class for one week."

"But why?"

"Because you know as well as I do that we don't hit each other in this house and you should remember that your sister is only three years old."

"She causes as much trouble as if she was ten. She's always getting away with stuff."

"If I were you, I would watch my mouth before you get a lot more than one week punishment. Now go finish your homework and if you're finished with that, start cleaning that room."

As they were leaving, LJ put his arm around his sister's shoulders and said, "Come on, sis, I'll give you a hand."

"You want to help me? Keep *her* away from me. If she gets me in trouble one more time, I'm gonna clobber her," Zoe muttered. LJ gave her a playful shove as the two headed back upstairs with Jaleesa close behind.

Juanita turned to Ebony and with a smile she said, "They're quite a handful but to be honest, they bring a life to this house that hasn't been here since my youngest left for college." Ebony responded with a smile and a hug and she could feel the warmth of a beginning friendship. "Come on in the kitchen and help me finish getting dinner ready."

"Are their other grandparents involved in their life?"

"Yeah, they still see them a lot. We decided that it better if they stay with us during the school year and spend a month or two with them during the summer. We're making the arrangements for them to come and spend Thanksgiving week with us. They are good people even if they are a little citified. Right now they're on a trip to China or someplace. Larry left them quite a bit of money, and they're trying to enjoy some of the things they missed in life."

"Didn't Tanya lea—"

"Nita, whose car is out front? Is everything okay?"

"Jasper, we're in the kitchen. Stop all that yelling. Everything is okay." Juanita turned to Ebony and said, "That man arrives like a summer storm sometimes—a lot of noise and flashes of lighting till he calms down."

Two men entered the kitchen. Both were attired in heavy plaid shirts and work jeans with dusty work boots. While neither was dirty, it was clear that both had spent the day working at hard physical labor. The oldest was a dark-skinned man of about 6'1" weighing about 211 pounds. He was clean shaved with a strong, dominant chin underneath sharp and quick eyes that seemed to see everything and miss nothing. The younger man seemed to be in his late twenties, and his face resembled his father's, though he had Juanita's lips and nose. He was also tall but seemed leaner and more muscular. His head was clean shaven, and he had a closely trimmed beard and a diamond earring glistened in one earlobe. Ebony thought that he was quite handsome in a rugged, down-home kind of way. He reminded her of the rapper/actor Common. Ebony shook her head slightly to get refocused. She had come to Texas on business, not in search of romance.

Juanita said, "This is my husband, Jasper, and our son, Malachi. This is Detective Delaney from New York."

Jasper took a seat but for some reason he seemed to collapse in the chair as he said, "Has there been any word about my daughter?"

"No, I'm sorry I don't have anything new to tell you yet."

"Jasper, you remember I told you that Larry's cousin had a police friend who was going to look into what happened to Tanya and Larry. She wants to talk to us after dinner. Why don't you go wash up? Dinner is almost ready."

"What's for dinner?"

"Nothing if I burn my food waiting for you."

The calm of the kitchen was disturbed as a three-year-old starburst of energy exploded into the kitchen with screams of Grandpa as Jaleesa ran across the room and leaped into her grandfather's arms. After covering his face with kisses, she took his face in her little hands and in the most serious voice imaginable said, "I missed you soooooo much."

Juanita said, "Let your grandfather alone so he can get ready for dinner."

"But, Nana, I missed him."

"Come on, Pudding, you can help me clean up for dinner," Jasper said as he tucked Jaleesa under his arm and rubbed her face into his armpit. "Maybe you can tell me if I'm sweating and need to change my shirt."

"Yeech, Grandpa!" Jaleesa protested as she laughingly tried to get away.

"What? No love for me?" Malachi said.

"Hi, Uncle Mal. Save me from Grandpa."

"Nope, you jumped up there. Now you figure out how to get away."

"Aaawww save me. Save me!" Jaleesa said as the three laughing and talking headed upstairs.

Juanita turned to giggling Ebony and said with a shrug "He dotes on her so much."

"It's seems impossible not to," Ebony noted.

"Like most three-year-olds, she makes sure she gets the love she needs. I just wish I could say the same about her sister and brother." Juanita went to the foot of the stairs and called "LJ. LJ, come and help Miss Ebony set the table. Since we have company, let's eat in the dining room and use the good dishes."

"Should I use the good china?" LJ asked.

"No, baby, we'll save that for formal occasions." Juanita turned to Ebony and whispered, "He likes using the china because he went with his mother to buy it as an anniversary gift. I guess he likes using anything that reminds him of his mother. I think it makes him feel closer to her."

"That's understandable."

"I guess it is, when you think about it."

Juanita and Ebony busied themselves completing the dinner and getting it on the table. It was obvious that Juanita was enjoying the adult, female companionship as Ebony found she couldn't resist feeling close to this very special woman. Dinner was an altogether enjoyable experience. Not only was the food delicious, but the conversation was friendly, warm, and loving. Malachi spent much of the meal entertaining the kids with a variety of riddles and jokes. Even when LJ knew the answers, he didn't respond, preferring to give his younger sisters a chance to figure out the brain teasers. Ebony observed that as much attention as the grandfather heaped on Jaleesa was how much extra attention Malachi gave Zoe.

After dinner LJ led the girls upstairs to entertain themselves with games or television until they had to get their baths and go to bed. After the kids were upstairs Malachi said, "Ebony, if you do not need to talk to me, I'll think I'll be headed home."

"I'm pretty sure that whatever I need I can get from your parents."

"Well, in that case, it was a pleasure to meet you. If you do find that I can provide any useful information, please do not hesitate to contact me."

"It was nice to meet you too."

After Malachi had left, Ebony turned to his parents and said, "I thought that Malachi lived here with you."

"No, Malachi has his own place in town. He was engaged to marry a nurse in Houston, but after Tanya disappeared and the kids came here to live with us, Malachi moved back home to help out with the kids. Malachi is our youngest, and he and Tanya were very close. He is taking all of this pretty hard so he is spending a lot of his free time with the kids and helping them adjust to the loss of their parents," Juanita said.

"Does Malachi work here on the farm?"

"He helps out sometimes, but mostly he is working on getting his doctorate from A&M. He is working on developing a better grade of chicken without using hormones or additives. He's trying to find an organic and completely healthy chicken that cost less than the standard chickens in the industry at this time," Jasper said.

"Where did he get his degree?"

"He got a BS in chemistry from Princeton and his Master's from A&M. If you were staying longer, you should have him show the lab he set up in the chicken barn," Juanita said.

"Nita, you know Mal would have a fit if he knew you were referring to his facilities as a chicken barn." To Ebony he said, "He takes a lot of pride in what he does? He thinks what he's working on can be key to the American farm industry. I think he might be right."

"How does it work?"

"I don't know all the details, but it has something to do with improved crops and feed and cross-breeding with the more successful types of chicken. I'm sure if you ask him, he will give you a full tour of all the facilities."

"It sounds very elaborate and expensive."

"I guess it is, but Tanya significantly upgraded all the facilities when she got that ridiculous settlement from the divorce," Jasper said.

"You don't approve of the settlement Tanya got from the divorce?" Ebony asked.

"No, I didn't. That amount of money was absolutely insane. I mean, why would anyone need that many millions? The kids sure don't need that much money. All it can do is mess them up. Tanya didn't approve of it either. In fact, she was in the process of giving Larry most of it back."

"Why do you feel that the money will mess up the kids?"

"Because it will change their value system. It will make them lose sight of what is important. For example, they will not experience the sense of joy and achievement of doing a hard job well. Look at those celebrity kids out in Hollywood and New York. You hear about their developing drug and alcohol problems and going to wild parties and stuff. They have lost their way. It's quite sad really," Juanita said.

"So you haven't given the kids the money?"

"The vast majority of the money is in trust for the kids when they graduate from college. We make sure the kids have whatever they need. I must point out that this farm has been turning a modest profit for many years. This farm has already put four kids through college, though all of them received at least a partial scholarship."

"You haven't taken any of the money for yourself? I mean, Larry's parents are taking trips and trying to enjoy their lives. No one would have any problem with your spending some of the money."

"We donated $50,000 dollars to the church to build a new roof and make some other improvements. We know that Tanya would have done that if she was here."

"That's all the money that you've spent?"

"We really don't need anything, plus that's Tanya's money," Juanita said.

Ebony paused as the gravity of what Juanita said sunk in. Finally, she asked, "Have you heard from Tanya?"

"The last time we heard from Tanya was when she called us from her cruise."

"Do you think that Tanya will be coming back?"

"If our daughter could come back, I'm positive she would have been back long ago. Not only was our daughter very close to our family, but she also was a fabulous mother and she loved her children very, very much. There's no way she would let these kids suffer the way they have if she had any other choice. The kids miss her so much and we do the best we can but we give them so much less than what they need emotionally. LJ feels guilty because even at his young age he tried to take care of and protect his mother. Zoe is angry because I think deep down she feels she is the reason her mother left. Lee-Lee is probably in the best shape, though she often cries for her mother at night. We've discussed it and realize that at some point we are going to have to get the kids some therapy," Juanita said.

"Detective, I tell you I would give every cent I owe including the damn settlement money just to see my daughter walk through that door," Jasper said.

"Ebony, do you think you can get to the bottom of what happened to our daughter?" Juanita asked.

"I promise you I will do everything I can to get you and the kids as many answers as I possibly can. If someone has done something to hurt your daughter, I won't rest until I bring them to justice. You don't know me from a hole in the wall, but I am very good at what I do and if someone did something to those darling little kids' mother, believe me, they are going to pay."

"We really appreciate anything you can do," Jasper said.

"You folks have been great and I really appreciate your hospitality, but I'm going to go now. I will keep you posted when I find out anything significant. Please tell the children 'goodnight' for me and that I will see them when they come visit Rashid in New York. Maybe I can take them to the zoo or something."

Ebony left the farm and using the car's GPS system navigated her way back to the hotel. As she entered the hotel's lobby, she was surprised to see Malachi sitting in the lobby reading a book. Ebony said as she approached Malachi, "I'm surprised to see you here. Is everything all right?"

"I wanted to talk to you without my parents being present. Do you think I could buy you a drink?"

Ebony was curious as she said, "Sure," and followed Malachi into the bar in the hotel.

"What would you like to drink?"

"I'll have a rum and coke."

Malachi ordered Ebony's drink and a Jack Daniels for himself and they took their drinks to a table in the corner. Ebony was curious what Malachi wanted to tell to her about that made him meet her here at her hotel. She remembered the attraction she had felt for Malachi earlier and she wondered if he felt the same way and if that was the reason why he was here. Rather than be anxious, she decided to wait patiently because she was sure he would discuss what was on his mind when given the opportunity. They engaged in idle conversation for a few minutes until finally Ebony said, "Malachi, it's been a long day and I'm getting a little tired. Is there something you wanted to talk to me about?"

"I wanted to speak with you without my parents being present. They've been through quite a lot and if I can spare them any of this, I would prefer that. I think that Larry had something to do with Tanya's disappearance."

"Why do you say that?"

"Tanya and I were very close. One reason I went to school at Princeton was because she hated living up North and I went there so I could be close to her. I think it made her feel better to have someone in the family relatively close by. Even after graduation and I came back home, we would talk on the phone just about every day. We talked about everything. She was my girl and my best friend, not just my sister. I remember when I hooked up with Adrian she couldn't stand her and told me all the time to get rid of her. She said that Adrian was selfish and didn't really care for me. Boy, was she right." Malachi paused deep in thought as he struggled with his feelings.

Ebony sat patiently and waited until Malachi was ready to talk. As an experienced interrogator, she had learned that when people had something to say if you gave them time, they would get around to saying what they had to say. "Anyway, after the judge gave Tanya that enormous settlement, Larry was pissed. He told her a couple of times that he would get her and she would never get the chance to spend *his* money. The funny thing is that Tanya didn't even want the money. She was going to give it back to him, but after he threatened her, Tanya didn't give it back to him just out of spite. I mean, she was going to give it back to him; she was just going to make him wait a bit. Larry forgot how stubborn and strong-willed Moore women can be. And then things happened with that other guy, Omar Smith. I don't know how he fits in this whole thing, but he's in there somewhere."

"Did you say Omar Smith?"

"Yeah. That's the name he told her."

"Did you ever meet Omar?"

"Yeah, I met him once or twice."

"What did you think of him?"

"I didn't like him, and I damn sure didn't trust him. There was something about him that just didn't seem right or legit. He seemed like a big fake to me. I thought he might have been after Tanya's money, but she insisted that he never asked for any or would let her pay for anything."

"Are you sure his last name was Smith?"

"I'm fairly certain that's the name he gave me. Why? Is that important?"

"I don't know. We'll see. What happened to Tanya's money?"

"Why do you ask?"

"Because if this becomes a murder investigation, whoever benefitted financially could be significant."

"Tanya left a will, and in it she left most of the money to the kids and then a couple of million to my parents and $500,000 to each of her brothers and sisters. No one has gotten any money yet because none of us want to have Tanya declared as legally dead. Even though all the evidence indicates otherwise, we all still hope that Tanya will one day come back. It's possible, isn't it?"

"Anything is possible, but I like you and your family and I don't want to offer you false hope. The investigation is just beginning, but I'm approaching it as a murder investigation not as a missing person case. I know that's not what you want to hear, but I have to be honest with you."

"I appreciate your honesty, but I need to believe that maybe Tanya is alive somewhere and just can't get back to us yet. I mean, you hear about women who are stolen into slavery in the Middle East and Africa. I would hate to think that something like that happened to her, but I think it's better than her being dead. Wait a minute. You asked about Tanya's money. You don't think that one of us had anything to do with her disappearance because we were after her money?"

"I have to look into that possibility."

"Let me remind you that we got millions of dollars from Larry's estate and my parents haven't touched very much of that money yet."

"Don't forget that Larry's money came after Tanya's disappearance. Theoretically, Tanya's disappearance could have been arranged before Larry died. Let me be honest with you. I don't think that you or anyone in your family had anything to do with Tanya's disappearance. I didn't think that before I came to Texas, and after meeting everyone, I'm just that much more convinced. *But* I wouldn't be a good investigator if I wasn't open to the possibility, regardless of how remote it may be."

"I'm not worried about it, Ebony, because I know the truth and I believe that the truth will win out. I know you're tired because it's been a long day so I'll be going. I want to thank you for seeing me. If there is anything we can do to be of assistance in your investigation, please let us know."

"This is my cell phone number; if you think of anything to add that might help please give me a call."

"Ebony, I'll be in New York in a few weeks, would it be okay if I see you?"

"Socially or about the investigation?"

"Maybe both?"

"Call me when you getting ready to come to town and we'll discuss it."

"I'll do that."

Chapter Twelve

The next day upon her return to New York, Ebony called Ted as soon as she arrived at her apartment to bring each other up on what developments that had in the case. She explained in great details her impressions of the Moore family and how she was convinced that Tanya had been killed. She told him about the strong family unit that she had just spent the day with and that in her mind there was no question that Tanya would never have voluntarily deserted her kids and family.

What she didn't share with Ted was her emotional attachment to the Moore family. She had developed an intense affinity for the entire family, including those brothers and sisters she hadn't even met. She genuinely like the mother and father and was determined to get them answers and through those answers a sense of closure and maybe a bit of peace. Her heart bled for those three little kids who would have to face the world without the love, support, and guidance of their mother and father. She was more determined than ever that whomever brought about such a cruel injustice would not go unpunished.

"Ted, did you come up with anything on Omar Douglas?" Ebony asked.

"Actually, we came up with quite a lot. We got an address up in the Bronx but the apartment has long been vacant. He has a record for a couple of minor offenses. He has an arrest in '99 for possession of crack with intent to sell and an arrest in '02 for assault. I made an appointment with a couple of undercover cops up in that precinct to see if they have any additional info. I figured you might need a day to recover from your trip so I scheduled it for tomorrow at two. I'll pick you up at one."

"Did you make any progress with the agents on the Cabernet kidnapping?" Ebony asked.

"Oh yeah, bingo again. We have a meeting with them set up for the day after tomorrow in D.C. I booked two tickets on the shuttle for seven in the morning so no hanging out tomorrow. You need to be sharp and on your game because they will probably have as many questions for you as you will have for them."

"Ted, I'm really impressed. You've gotten quite a lot done in a short time."

"I told you I was not just a pretty face and that I'm a pretty decent agent. I may not be the heaviest hitter, but I do carry a little clout and influence in certain circles."

"Well, in that case I'm damn glad you're on my side."

"Why don't I pick up some Thai food and come over later and we can go over the case and get our questions ready for the agents and detectives?"

"I can't. I have a date."

"A date?"

"With my father, knucklehead. I figured it was time I met Mr. Barnett and got a chance to check him out up close. My father is taking me to a reception Barnett is giving for Bradford Green."

"Oh!"

"Don't tell me you were getting jealous?"

"Not jealous, but I was wondering how you got me working my ass off and meanwhile you are enjoying your social life."

"Trust me, right now this case has my total attention and focus. I'll tell you what, why don't you give me a rain check on the Thai food until tomorrow after we meet we the detectives. We can compare our notes and get ready for D.C."

"That sounds like that might work."

"Good, then that's the plan. Let me go and get myself together for tonight. "

A few hours later at six that evening, Ebony's father picked her up at her house. Attired in his tuxedo, he was elegant and distinguished and further proof that a tuxedo lends dignity to any occasion. He was an old experienced player in the New York political arena, and he knew how to wear the fixtures of the game and could play the game with the best of them.

Ebony had spent a lot of time and effort selecting her dress for the evening. She went through more than half a dozen dresses before deciding on an elegant but sexy grown by the designer Cassandra Stone that was a subdued but energetic red, one-shoulder dress made of a taffeta material that seemed to cling to her body and flow at the same time. It was form-fitting through the torso and hips with legs that flowed in folds and swirls. There was a slit to the mid-thigh that revealed Ebony's gorgeous legs. The dress was attached at the shoulder by several sequin hoops that allowed Ebony to move without fearing that the dress would reveal more than she wanted but still implied a degree of elegance. She complemented the dress with four-inch high heels with a crisscross ankle strap and a rhinestone toe strap. She finished the outfit with a silver sequin clutch bag that was just large enough to hold a few personal items.

The reception was held in the banquet room of one of New York's five star hotels. As they prepared to enter the Grand Ballroom, Ebony and her father paused and took in the spectacle of the event. There were close to two hundred people milling about attired in tuxedos and evening gowns. Ebony relaxed and grew confident as she realized she was as attractive as any woman in the room. She took her father's arm and together they entered the room. They greeted about ten people with her father introducing her to his political associates until they got to one of the three bars positioned at different, convenient places around the room. They got a couple of cocktails and continued making the circuit around the room. Most of the men, though they stopped short of flirting, looked at Ebony with appraising and admiring glances. Ebony remained polite and friendly but slightly aloof and remote. She didn't forget her main reason for coming to this event, which was to meet and assess Brandon Barnett. She wondered whether she made a mistake in getting so dressed up because she was drawing a lot of attention. It might have been smarter to have blended into the crowd a little more and she could have observed Barnett undetected.

At this point it really didn't matter, as it was too late since she had already made a first impression. Rather than worry about something over which she had no control, Ebony took a seat and enjoyed the band that was playing a mixture of everything from Duke Ellington to Stevie Wonder and Usher. As she was tapping her foot to the rhythmic bass line of "I Wish," she had to remind herself that she was there for business and not just to enjoy herself.

Her father had introduced her to more than a dozen of his associates when he introduced her to Assemblyman Green. "Bradford, this is my daughter, Ebony Delaney"

"James, I didn't know you had such a beautiful daughter."

"Well, you know what predators you politicians can be. I thought it best to keep my baby away from the political arena."

"Now, James, I know you can't be talking about me. You know my life has been devoted to my constituents. " Ebony noticed that Assemblyman Green had the strange penchant of addressing her father by his last name as if it was his first name. She wondered how well he knew her father and if he was mistaken about his name or if this was an intentional slight or just a habit the Assemblyman used to make him seem familiar or friendly. She would check and see if he kept the same pattern with everyone else. She questioned how smart it was for an aspiring politician to not have the method down of how to remember people's names. She also noticed that her father didn't correct him. Was that because he knew that was the Assemblyman's way or was it because he held him in such low esteem that he didn't care what he called him?

Ebony realized that it was the detective in her nature that made her notice and analyze the little things. She chided herself to stay on task and remember why she was here tonight. Brandon Barnett.

"That's open to a debate that we can have at a later time. I see your beautiful wife has joined us."

"Hello, dear, I was wondering what was keeping you? This is James's daughter, Ebony. Ebony, this is my wife, Doreen. Excuse me for a second, I see someone I need to speak to. Why don't you come with me, James, I would love to introduce you to him," Bradford said.

"It's a pleasure to meet you, Mrs. Greene."

"Please call me Doreen. Ebony, it's nice to meet you too. I was admiring your dress from across the room. You look stunning in it."

"Thank you. Your dress is beautiful too. Is that an Oscar de la Renta?"

"Yes, it is. How did you know?"

"Because I was thinking about buying one along the same lines but I didn't think I could pull it off."

"Young lady, as fantastic as you look in that dress, I don't think you need to worry about that."

"You're way too kind but I appreciate it. Have you seen the sponsor of tonight's event?"

"Oh, do you mean Brandon Barnett?"

"Is that who has given this event? One man? This event must have been very expensive."

"Believe me it was, and Brandon has been very generous."

"Are he and Assemblyman Green good friends?"

"I don't believe so. I think they are of recent acquaintance. I think he really believes in Brad's mission and agenda."

"Which is?"

"To make the government more accountable to the people of our community."

"Locally or nationally?"

"Wouldn't you agree that both need to be? For now, Brad is focused on city and state government, but who knows, maybe one day he will be able to fight on a national level. Events like tonight will one day make this possible. Are you a supporter?"

"Not yet, but I'm weighing my options."

"So you came tonight because you're interested in Brandon Barnett?"

"Maybe a little, but mostly I came as my father's escort. He doesn't like to come to these events alone."

"Well, if I see Brandon, I'll make sure to introduce you to him."

"Please don't go out of your way. It's not that big a deal."

"Well, I see Brad beckoning me. I have to go but it was a pleasure talking to you. I hope you decide to come and join us. There is a lot of work to be done, and we can use all the help we can get."

"I will strongly consider it, and it was nice meeting you too."

Ebony refreshed her drink and sat down and listened to the band wind its way through jazz classics and smooth love songs. A few minutes before dinner was served, Ebony noticed a striking couple enter the room and start to greet many of the guests. Since Assemblyman Green was already present, she assumed this was Brandon Barnett. The woman on his arm was so beautiful that Ebony wondered if she was a model, but she wasn't the focus of her attention. She looked at Barnett and could easily see why he was considered by many to be very handsome.

She took her drink and leisurely strolled into Barnett's vicinity. She did not walk up to him, but she was causally close enough that she could overhear his conversations. After overhearing two or three conversations, she became convinced that Barnett was not only good-looking but he was very articulate and smooth and could control conversations like a master politician. At one point Barnett noticed her standing close to him and she looked directly into his eyes. She was immediately taken by their unusual color but then she realized they were cold and totally devoid of any feelings or emotions. She was reminded of stories of people who had looked a crocodile in the eyes just before it attacked them. Realizing that she may have brought a bit more attention to herself than she had intended, Ebony walked away. Her intention was to stay under the radar while she conducted her investigation without the suspect realizing that he was being investigated, but now it might have been too late. As Ebony walked away, she cast a look over her shoulder to see if Barnett was watching her and was not surprised to see that he was. Luckily the announcement was made that dinner was served and that everyone should find their seat, so she didn't have to wonder if Barnett would have followed her.

After a delicious dinner featuring broiled lobster tails, prime rib, and salmon steaks with butter saffron sauce, the band kicked up the music and the dancing started with a vigorous "Electric Slide" followed by the "Cha Cha Slide." As the dancing broke into couples, several men ventured over and asked Ebony to dance, a couple of which Ebony accepted. After an extremely energetic dance to an extra funky version of the O'Jays' "For the Love of Money," Ebony was sitting and enjoying a cool drink while catching her breath and looked up to see Barnett standing over her. He was looking at her appraisingly as he was clearly sizing her up. Ebony couldn't tell if it was for a fight or a romantic tryst. After several prolonged seconds during which nothing was said, Ebony asked, "Can I help you?"

"I was wondering why you were looking at me," Barnett said.

"Pardon me?"

"I thought that you were staring at me."

"I'm sorry, but you must have been mistaken."

"Well, maybe it was wishful thinking on my part. My name is Brandon Barnett, and I attend a few of these events and I don't think I've ever seen you before. As a matter of fact, I'm sure that I never seen you before because if I had, I'm sure I would have remembered."

"I don't usually attend too many of these events."

"Are you a supporter of Assemblyman Green?"

"One of the reasons I'm here is because I'm looking into some things."

"I'm sorry, but I didn't catch your name."

"I didn't throw it. My name is Ebony Delaney."

"It's a pleasure to meet you. Is that Miss or Missus Delaney?"

"Does it matter?"

"It doesn't to me if it doesn't to you. Are you here alone?"

"Do I look like the type of lady who would come to such an elegant affair unescorted?"

"Not at all. I guess I was just hoping again."

"Speaking of being escorted, the very attractive young lady who came with you is trying to get your attention."

"Don't worry about her, she's not that important."

"I wonder how she would feel about what you are saying about her."

"She's well aware of where things stand between us. I want you to know where things stand between her and me."

"I don't think that's necessary, and actually I think we both need to get back to our dates," Ebony said as she walked over to where her father had engaged several people in a spirited discussion of a new federal housing bill. About a half hour later Ebony and her dad said their goodnights and headed home.

· · · · ·

Early the next afternoon Ted picked up Ebony to head up to the Bronx for their meeting with the undercover detectives. Ebony was surprised that Ted was driving a Buick LeSabre. She thought that a man who wanted to maintain an image as a man about town would be driving something like a Porsche or a Beamer.

"How did things go last night?"

"They went all right."

"Did you meet Brandon Barnett?"

"Briefly, we spoke for a few minutes, but I didn't want to speak to him too long. I feel I may have drawn too much attention to myself. He seemed to be something of a ladies' man so he might not even remember me, plus there were a lot of people there."

"I seriously doubt there was anyone there who looked better than you. So what was your impression of Barnett?"

"He was very smooth and slick, but he seemed cold and calculating to me and completely capable of doing the things we suspect he did. We don't have anything conclusive yet, but I'm convinced we're heading in the right direction."

"Don't worry, we'll get everything we need. We're just getting started," Ted said.

A few minutes later they arrived at an apartment on Davidson Avenue just off Fordham Road in the Bronx. The area was a very heavily trafficked area because it was just around the corner from numerous clothing and variety stores. They took the elevator up to the third floor and knocked on the door and entered when the door was opened.

"Hey, Ted, it's good to see you. Come on in. Don't worry, this is a safe house. Nobody in the streets knows that this place exists. Can I offer you some coffee?"

"Naw, Jocko, we're good. Ebony, this is one of the DEA's best agents, Edward Santiago, known in the streets as 'Jocko.' Jocko, this is one of NYPD's finest detectives, Ebony Delaney. We're working on a special project together."

"It's nice to meet you, Ebony. If Ted vouches for you, you must be one heck of a detective. Ted told me you were looking for some information on one of the dealers up here. I'm not really familiar with him so I called in one of the Narcs who handle this area. If anyone knows who is who up here, he sure would. He's on his way and he should get here any time now."

Shortly Frankie Cohen, the detective they were waiting for, arrived. After showing him the picture and giving him all the identifying information they had, he said, "I'm a little familiar with him. His name is Omar. I didn't know his last name, but he started out as a small-time street-level dealer. He is part of a pretty powerful and well-organized posse up here run by a guy named Justice Permentier. Omar recently moved up from the street level to the enforcer part of the organization. I hear that he's pretty cold-blooded and that he doesn't hesitate to touch anyone that Justice wants him to. He was moving up pretty good but then he kind of disappeared from the scene."

"Do you know what happened to him?" Ted asked.

"Not really, I know he wasn't busted and I don't think he was bumped off or I would have heard something about it."

"Have you ever heard of a Brandon Barnett?" Ebony asked.

"No, I haven't. In what context do you mean?"

"I was wondering if he was associated with Omar or this guy Justice."

"No, I haven't heard of him, but if you think it's important I could ask around."

"It could have some significance. Could you put some feelers out in the streets and see if you come up with anything? Also, any word you can get on the whereabouts of Omar would be greatly appreciated," Ebony said.

"How extensive is the dossier you have on this guy Justice?" Ted asked.

"We don't have a lot on him. He's become the object of pretty intense investigation. His organization was able to stay pretty much under the radar, and we're playing catch-up because we just realized how big and powerful he's has become. We thought he was a mid-level player but recently we realized his organization is one of the largest in the Bronx. We're talking about formulating a task force to bring them down before they get any bigger."

"If we decide he is part of our investigation, we may want to attend some of the task force's meetings," Ted said.

"That shouldn't be a problem. I'd have to run it through channels, but I don't see where it should be a problem."

"Can we get a copy of the dossier on Justice?" Ebony asked.

"As I said there's not a lot there, but you can probably get a copy of what we have built so far but you definitely would have to go through channels to get that. There is some information there that would have to remain confidential for the safety of the undercovers on the case. We take great care to make sure that certain information doesn't slip into the wrong hands."

"Are you trying to imply that you don't trust us?"

"Personally, I trust you or else I wouldn't be here but office policy is to venture on the side of caution."

· · · · ·

"Ted, what in God's name is all of this?"

"Food, knucklehead."

"But there's only the two of us, why did you get so much?"

"I wasn't sure what you liked so I brought a combination of things."

"Ted, I hope you're not trying to wine and dine me again."

"Relax, Beautiful, its food not a Cartier watch or a tennis bracelet. The food is for me as well as you because when I eat Thai food I like a large variety. I think the combination of flavors enhances the experience. Plus, when we're through working here I have to go back to the office and finish some work since I'm going to be out of town tomorrow. Until this investigation takes off and this becomes my only case, I still have to manage my caseload."

"Okay, my bad. So what did you bring?"

"Thai food is my favorite so indulge me if I elaborate. We have Yum Hoi Mang Pu which is a mussel salad, Pad Thai, Kow Neon, Goong Gah Tiem or garlic shrimps, Chicken Satay, and this restaurant has a specialty which is pan fried fish with a lemon herb sauce."

"That sounds like a lot of food," Ebony said.

"Well, let's dig in while everything is still hot," Ted said as he prepared the plates.

They commenced eating, and for the first few minutes no one said anything as they both enjoyed the food then Ebony said, "This is really quite good. I didn't realize how hungry I was."

"I told you Thai food is one of my favorites. Maybe at some point I'll cook Thai food for you."

"You cook?"

"Quite well, actually. Do you cook?"

"I know my way around the kitchen."

"I bet you cook better than that."

"Maybe one day you'll find out when the investigation allows us a spare moment."

"Ebony, I take my work seriously too, but you still have to eat. Ms. Delaney, you seem so serious all the time. What do you do for enjoyment?"

"You're right I do take my work seriously, especially in a case like this one where I feel someone is being victimized but there are quite a few things I do that I enjoy."

"Such as?"

"I love live performances like the theater or R&B concerts or jazz at the City Center, and I try to catch the Ballet whenever they are in season. I love watching artists who work so hard at their craft as they perform in front of people. I just think it's something special and something you catch an artist in that special moment that they are creating something extraordinary."

"Do you have any favorites?"

"Not really, though I caught the O'Jays a couple of times and their lead singer, Eddie Levert, was just bringing it. Oh yeah, about a month ago, I saw this double mallet vibe player named Stefon Harris, and he was amazing with the joy and passion this little guy was bringing to his art. It is things like that that make music something special."

"Maybe one day you'll take me when you go check some of it out."

"I sure will as soon as we finish this case."

"This case sure seems to have become very important to you."

"You're right it has because not only is he killing innocent people but he seems to be thumbing his nose at us."

"At us? At you and me?"

"No, I mean 'us' as in law enforcement."

"Then let's get this bastard. Do you know what questions you want to ask the agents tomorrow?"

"I have some, but I figured I would mostly play it by ear. Tomorrow is pretty much a fact-finding mission. Here are my notes on my Texas trip and the Richardson case. Let me know if you have anything to add or if you have any questions."

Ted busied himself reading the notes and making notes of his own. Ebony, meanwhile, cleaned up after dinner and started doing the dishes, and then she asked, "Ted, would you like another beer?"

"One last one would be good. Three is pretty much my limit when I 'm working."

Ted and Ebony sat down over their beers and compared notes on the case. After almost an hour the phone rang and Ebony answered it. "Good evening."

"Ebony?"

"Yes, who's calling?"

"This is Malachi Moore."

"Malachi, it's nice to hear from you. Is everything all right?"

"Everything is fine. I just wanted to make sure you got home okay. Did you have a nice flight?"

"It was fine, thanks for asking."

"Did I catch you at a bad time?"

"Actually, my partner and I were going over the case."

"I'm sorry to disturb you. I'll call you tomorrow."

"Tomorrow we're headed out of town on the investigation."

"Okay, I didn't mean to bother you," Malachi said.

"It's no bother really. I'm glad to hear from you. Can I call you back in an hour or so?"

"Please do, I would like that."

"Okay, should I call you at this same number?"

"Yes, that would be fine. It's the number to the lab, and I will be working late."

"I'll talk to you then."

Looking up from his work, Ted said, "You didn't have to end your conversation. I'm getting ready to leave. I need to get back to my office. I'll see you at LaGuardia in the morning at nine."

After Ted left and Ebony secured her apartment, Ebony called Malachi back.

"Malachi?"

"Ebony, I'm surprised you called me back."

"Why? I said I would."

"Well, I'm glad that you did."

"How are your parents and the kids?"

"They're fine, and you've made quite a few fans here."

"Really?"

"My mother has been asking about you. Zoe wants to come see you when she visits her uncle Rashid in New York, and Jaleesa has been drawing you pictures that she wants me to mail to you. Are you used to having such a profound effect on people wherever you go?"

"They're very sweet people, and they made an incredible impression on me as well."

"I've been thinking about you a lot myself," Malachi said.

"Well, I came back and got back to work on the investigation. I made a little progress, but like I told you it's going to be slow."

"I'm not worried about the investigation because I know it's in good hands—yours—and I don't expect you to update me on every move you make. I gave the investigation some thought but mostly I've been thinking about you. Look, I'm not good at beating around the bush and so I'm going to come right out and say what I have to say. I think you're a beautiful and fascinating woman, and I would love to get to know you better."

"How are you going to manage that with you in Texas and me in New York?"

"If you are interested, then I can find a way to make it work. First, I need to know if what I am feeling is even slightly mutual."

"I must confess that I am attracted to you and I felt some type of chemistry between us but I didn't deal with it because of the distance factor between us."

"What if I told you I have been offered a fellowship at Princeton and a chance to teach there for two years?"

"What about your work?"

"I have the money to set up a duplicate lab in Jersey."

"I don't want you moving your life around because of me."

"I was on the fence about accepting the job even before I met you, and you are just one more great reason why I am strongly considering accepting the position."

"Malachi, I think you're a great guy but we've only met for a very short time. I don't think I should be a factor in why you make any decision you make."

"Actually, I couldn't disagree more. Great jobs come around frequently and I can do my research anywhere, but a woman like you may only come around once in a lifetime. I have no intention of letting something so precious slip through my fingers until I have fully examined how far a relationship can go."

"Wow, you can be very flattering. You better be careful or I will get a big head."

"I sincerely doubt that. I didn't tell you anything you didn't already know. I will be in New Jersey next week for a meeting with the head of my department and some trustees. Can we meet one night for dinner?"

"I would love to but I have to go to D.C. to meet with some federal agents and then it's off to California to meet with the State Police there. I'm not sure when I will be back to New York."

"Is all that part of the investigation into Tanya's disappearance or another case?"

"Both."

"It's that big a case?"

"Yeah, but Malachi, I need to tell you this will be the last time I will discuss this case until I conclude it. Can you live with that?"

"Yeah, but under one set of circumstances."

"Which are?"

"You agree to call me Mal and not Malachi."

"I think I can agree to that."

"Good, then I'll wait in New Jersey until you come back to New York. Will you let me know when you expect to be home?"

"I can do that, and I will also call you from my travels because I think I might enjoy talking to you."

"Great, that will give me something to look forward to."

"Good, then let me go because tomorrow will be a long day and I have to get up early."

. . . . .

Ted and Ebony arrived at the Baltimore district office and after Ted flashed his credentials were shown into a conference room where they were joined by Agents Waugh and Schakowsky. After introductions were made all around, as the agent who had initiated the conference Ted took over the conversation before turning it over to Ebony.

"I really want to thank you agents from taking the time out of your busy schedule to talk with us. It would appear that a case you are working might overlap with an investigation that we are conducting."

"And what case is that?" Agent Waugh asked.

"We'll really not at liberty to discuss because our investigation is in the very early stages. We are just beginning the investigation and we are still identifying where the crimes are committed and who the suspects are."

"Yet you feel it's okay to ask us to discuss our case with you?"

"Only because we're not sure if a crime was committed and whether it ties in with your case, but if we find that a crime was committed, we will agree to send you a copy of our entire file. Is that fair?"

"It could be. What do you want to know?" Agent Waugh asked.

"We've already seen the official file on the Cabernet kidnapping. What we are interested in is your personal impressions of the case and the things that were not in the file."

"I have to tell you, Agent Delaphine, that I have a lot of problems with this meeting," Agent Schakowsky interjected.

"Maybe if you tell us where you have problems with this meeting, we can address those problems and make everyone a little more comfortable."

"You have to understand, we only agree to see you in the first place because we were instructed to do so by our supervisors. You show up with an officer who is not even in the Bureau. Then you want to pick our brains and get our *personal* reflections on one of our worst unsolved cases and you won't even tell us why you want us to jump through all these hoops. This whole thing smells like bullshit to me."

"First things first, this is not some civilian who is a causal bystander. This is Ebony Delaney, who has a lengthy history of working with the Bureau in solving some of our most difficult cases. She was the one who solved the Street Stalker case in New York. She has one of the most distinguished records in the NYPD and has turned down a position in the Bureau on more than one occasion. The reason why we chose not to tell you about our case is because we didn't want to indicate to you that we think our suspect is involved in your case and send you off on what could very well be a wild goose chase."

"Agent Delaphine, my partner—" Schakowsky started to say.

Ted interrupted, "Please call me Ted. After all, this is not an official investigation. Right now you're just extending a courtesy to us, and I appreciate it."

"Well, Ted, as I was saying, my partner and I have been with the Bureau more than a dozen years apiece, and I feel that we are more than capable of determining whether your case should be part of our investigation or if we would be wasting our time pursuing a case that has nothing to do with us."

Ted looked Ebony, who nodded her assent then said, "Fair enough. We don't have any evidence yet, but we are looking into a sports agent who appeared to have arranged several deaths of the ex-wives of some of his clients. Nick Burleson was one of his clients. We're not sure yet how much he's responsible for, if anything, or whether it is just conjecture or coincidence. We've read the report on the kidnapping, but I'm well aware that there are always things that you can't prove and impressions that don't make it into the official record. Those are some of the things we wanted to ask you about."

"I know what you mean, and this case bothers us a little more than most. We have a lot of forensic evidence but not one viable suspect. We have hair samples, fabric, footprints, and a witness who could probably identify one of the suspects if we had someone who she could choose from," Waugh said.

"A couple of things in this case just didn't make sense. Why let the boys go? They didn't attempt to contact the father or family for ransom, just left the boys in a McDonald's and kept it moving," Schakowsky piped in.

"Maybe they were scared of getting caught," Ted suggested.

"Then why do the kidnapping at all if they were that afraid. They went through all the trouble of getting the boys and then just let them go without even trying to get the money. True, the kidnapping was amateurish and they left too many clues to indicate this was done by real professionals, but to pull this off they must have had some plans for a ransom and a drop point for the money. Why let it go before they even attempted to get the money?"

"Maybe they panicked after killing Heather," Ebony said.

"Maybe, but why should that change their plans? They had already killed her, and letting the kids go would not lessen the search for them since they had already committed murder and they had to know that letting the boys go wouldn't affect the search for them. They had killed the wife of a millionaire and a sports legend, and only an idiot wouldn't have anticipated the media frenzy to find them. These guys were sloppy, but they weren't idiots. They disarmed the security system and got in and out undetected," Waugh said.

"I thought you said you had a potential witness who might be able to identify them?"

"That was from when they dropped the boys off, not the kidnapping itself," Waugh replied.

"That's another thing that bothers me. Why kill her at all?" Schakowsky said.

"Wasn't she killed trying to prevent them from taking the boys?" Ebony asked.

"All the evidence didn't fit together. There was evidence of a struggle, but we found a bloody partial footprint leading to one of the boys' bedrooms. Did she come down and see an intruder in the house and start fighting or was one of the boys still in the room or after killing the mother did they go back up to the boy's room? If they let the boys go because they panicked, why after killing a woman would they go back upstairs if they were the type to get scared enough to call the whole thing off after successfully getting away with the boys? Anyway, why kill her? Why not try to subdue her and kidnap her as well or knock her out and get the money from her because she was a millionaire several times over. It just doesn't make sense. That's not even talking about the issue of why make the kidnapping in the house. They had to know in the house there was a strong chance that the mother might break in on them. Most kidnappings are done in the street or coming or going to school or catching the boys playing outside. Why even plan on making the kidnapping in the house, and if you did decide to do that, why not have a plan to subdue the mother? "Schakowsky said.

"If we're dealing with cold-blooded killers, why not kill the boys as well? Three murders wouldn't get a much greater sentence than one, and it would be two less witnesses who could identify them," Waugh said.

"So, you're thinking that this might have been a murder case and not a kidnapping?" Schakowsky asked.

"It's possible," Ted said.

"So why do the kidnapping at all?"

"Maybe to cover up that this was a paid assassination," Ebony said. "You said that she was a millionaire as well. Do you know where she got her money?"

"Burleson went out of his way to keep it secret, but she got a shit-load of money as part of a divorce settlement." Ebony looked at Ted, and Waugh saw the look so he asked, "Does that mean anything?"

"It could because it could definitely establish a motive," Ted replied. "We would have to check and see if there is a pattern, but we do know that at least one other victim received a pretty hefty divorce and child custody settlement."

"Let me get this straight. You think that this guy might have murdered Heather Cabernet and set it up to look like a botched kidnapping?" Schakowsky asked.

"We're looking into that possibility. What do you think?" Ebony asked.

"It would answer some of these nagging questions that remain. That might just make sense," Schakowsky said.

"Look here, Ted, if you think that is the case and there is evidence that points that way, I want in," Waugh said.

"Whoa, we don't have a task force yet, and I can't get you reassigned because we don't even have a formal case yet," Ted said.

"I really don't care about that. This guy played us and the Bureau for a fool, and he thinks he's gonna get away with it? It ain't gonna happen. If I got to work this case on my own spare time, I'll do it," Waugh said.

"Me too." Schakowsky agreed.

"Quiet as it's kept, that's what we're doing," Ted informed them.

"So if you are using your vacation time and coming out of your pocket to fly down here, you must really think that this is what's been going on."

"We're not positive, but we feel it is a very strong possibility."

"We want in. You tell us what we can do and where you are at in the investigation," Waugh said.

"Why don't we do it like this? Why don't we finish our preliminary investigation and then report back to our superiors and see if we can make the investigation a formal one. If it does then I can pull some strings to get you on the task force," Ted said.

"And if it isn't?"

"Then we can bring you up to date with our investigation and you can decide if you still want to be in and how much of a part you want to play."

· · · · ·

Ebony and Ted waited until they were on the flight back to New York before they discussed what had transpired in the meeting. Ebony said, "You really exaggerated my role with the FBI and in the NYPD."

"Exaggerated? I don't think I did as much as you may think. Ebony, you are very highly regarded by the higher-ups at the Bureau, and when I asked you if you were interested in joining the Bureau it was partially at their urging."

"Really?"

"Really. They usually don't have a lot of regard for most city police agencies and they feel that your vast abilities are being largely wasted there."

"Well, that's flattering, but right now I am going to stay focused on this case and not worry about future ambitions. The one thing that was bothering me about this case is: I understand what Barnett's motives were—money, of course—but why would the clients want to kill their ex-wives? Jealousy? Some weird type of possession thing like 'once you belong to me you can never be with anyone else'? Maybe in one or two cases it might be possible, but not in this many cases. I just couldn't see that, but this makes sense."

"So you think that the clients were killing their exes to get out of paying hefty divorce settlement amounts?"

"Doesn't that make sense to you?"

"But what about Tanya Richardson? Didn't you tell me she intended to give her husband the money back?"

"Yeah, but I don't think she told him she was gonna give it back. Remember, he was acting like such an asshole that she was gonna let him suffer for a little while."

"Are you sure she didn't tell him?"

"I'm not sure, but I can check right now." Ebony took her cell phone and called Malachi. "Malachi, this is Ebony."

"Good afternoon, Ebony, are you back in New York already?"

"No, Mal, I'm still on the plane coming back to New York, but I had a question for you. Did Tanya tell Larry that she was going to give him the money settlement back?"

"She tried once or twice, but every time she opened the subject he got so angry and started behaving like such a fool that she hadn't got around to it. She even had me help her figure out how much of the settlement she and the kids would realistically need and the remainder, which was the vast majority, she was going to just give it back to him."

"But did Larry know her intentions?"

"No, he didn't. She was going to have her bank just transfer it into his account and then accept his apologies, but she disappeared before she could complete the transactions. Why do you ask? Is it important?"

"Mal, I'm still in transit and I'll talk to you before I head out again."

Ted gave Ebony a strange look and he said, "You're on a first name basis with the brother of one of the victims?"

"They're people too. There is nothing wrong with me being sympathetic and compassionate."

"You also have him on speed-dial in your cell."

"And your point is?"

"Nothing, I'm just observing. So did Tanya tell Larry?"

"No, she intended to but didn't get the chance."

"So the possible motive would still appear to be intact. What's our next move?"

"I'm headed out in the morning to Arizona and California to talk to the authorities in those states. Why don't you check the financial records of our suspected victims and see how many were the beneficiaries of divorce settlements?"

"I can do that. If you need any help opening doors out there just give me a call."

"Thanks, Ted. We should be back to LaGuardia by four; would you like to do dinner tonight? My treat."

"I got some things in the office that demand my attention."

"Okay, afterwards?"

"I can't, I have a date."

"Oh, okay. Maybe we'll do it after I get back from the Coast?"

"That would be good." Ted sat there in an uncomfortable silence for several minutes until he felt he had to say something. "Ebony, you know how I feel about you. If I knew you wanted to get together, I would be with it in a flash."

"No, Ted, I'm glad you're going out to have a good time. I like things where they are with us right now, and I'm very thankful to have you working with me on this case. Already your insight, experience, and connections have been invaluable. As to your having a date, you're a man and I'm sure you have needs," Ebony said with a sly smile.

Though Ted was thinking, "I'm sure you have needs too," he kept that comment to himself and immersed himself in reading some reports for the remainder of the flight. After landing and exchanging hugs, they took separate cabs to their different destinations.

· · · · ·

Ebony's cell phone rang a few minutes after she entered her apartment and she was catching up on reading several days of mail.

"Ebony?"

"Oh hi, Malachi. I'm sorry I couldn't finish our conversation but my associate was listening to every word I was saying."

"That's okay; I figured you couldn't talk then. Was the trip productive?"

"Yes, it was, the pieces are starting to come together. Is everything all right? I told you I would call you when I got back home."

"I guess I appear to be impatient, but I wanted to know if you would like to join me for dinner."

"That would be a neat trick. What do you suggest, we eat at the same time while we talk on the phone?"

"No, we could go out to a restaurant or I could come over and cook dinner for you."

"You're in New York?"

"Yeah, I came in this morning."

"But I talked to you on the phone?"

"That was my cell phone and people usually carry them with them."

"Very funny. For some reason I thought that was the phone to your lab."

"It is, but it is also my cell phone."

Ebony laughed. "Thanks for the lesson on modern technology. I thought you weren't coming to New York until next week?"

"I wasn't, but I wanted to see the latest August Wilson production before it closed."

"So you came in a week early just to see a play?"

"There also might have been a certain young lady I couldn't wait until next week to see."

"But Mal, I have to leave tomorrow for Arizona and California."

"You are coming back though? Right?"

"Yeah, I'll only be gone for a couple of days."

"Don't worry, I'll find plenty to do to occupy myself until you get back. Meanwhile, you haven't answered me about dinner tonight."

"Of course I would love to join you for dinner. Can you cook? "Ebony asked.

"I'm no stranger to the kitchen. My mother made sure all of her kids could cook."

"Since I have to leave early tomorrow, it would give us more time together if we cooked here in the house, but I've been on the go so much my house is a little short of provisions."

"I would love to cook for you. I make a pretty impressive Texas chili. If that sounds good to you, I'll pick up everything we need and I'll see you in an hour?"

"That sounds great. Are you driving?"

"No, I'll jump in a cab."

"Okay, here my address." Even while Ebony was giving Malachi her address, she had started straightening up her apartment. Her place was usually in pristine condition, but as she said, she had been on the go the past week or so. After she finished tidying up, she got in the shower. She wanted to take a bubble bath to relax herself, but she really didn't have the time so instead she used a scented shower gel which smelled like gardenias and jasmine. As Ebony took extra care rubbing the YSL lotion on her body and the spots where her body was most sensitive, she thought about why she felt a little nervous. There was no doubt that she was very attracted to Malachi, but did she subconsciously plan on sleeping with him? She told Ted that he was human and had needs, but was she speaking for herself as well? It was more than six months since she last had sex, and though she kept herself busy with work, there were times where she felt very strong urges.

Deciding to dress causal and comfortable but sexy, Ebony dressed in a pair of snug low-rider jeans that gave subtle glances of the turquoise throng she wore underneath it with a turquoise halter top and coral blue sandals. She didn't wear a bra so she checked the mirror to make sure her nipples weren't too prominent. Even if she decided not to have sex with Mal, she didn't see anything wrong with raising the level of desire in him. If nothing else she would see how he functions under pressure and whether he was as much a gentleman as he appeared to be. She barely had enough time to finish her preparations before Malachi rang her bell. As she opened the door, Malachi entered with his arms so full of bags and packages that you could barely see his face.

"Are all these bags just for us or are you expecting a small army to join us?" Ebony asked.

"If we are going to eat at home then we have to do it right," Malachi said as he put the bags down and reached in the bag and handed Ebony a bunch of flowers. "Here, these are for you."

"Thank you," Ebony said as she kissed Malachi on the cheek. Malachi responded by turning to face Ebony and gently caressing her cheek with the palm of his hand. This gesture was so gentle but provocative that the intimacy almost made Ebony shiver. Malachi took a long look at Ebony and breathlessly said, "Wow, you look absolutely beautiful." Ebony took a step back because for a moment she was greatly tempted to step into Malachi arms and give him a deeply, passionate kiss. To distract her from the thoughts she was thinking, she asked, "What do you have here?"

"All the fixings for a fine Texas dinner. If you will guide me to the kitchen and your blender, I can get started on making the Margaritas so we can have something to drink while dinner is getting ready. Do you like guacamole?"

"Yeah, why do you ask?"

"Because you can't have legitimate Tex-Mex food without fresh made guacamole. We'll start with guacamole and nachos with my own specially made salsa sauce."

"You sound like you're going to be in the kitchen all night."

"Actually everything should be prepared very quickly. Why? Are you worried that I might spend too long preparing the food?"

"I was hoping that we could spend some time talking and getting to know each other better."

Malachi stepped closer to Ebony and swept her up in his arms and gave her a deep, soul-searching kiss that she felt from the top of her head to the bottom of her feet. When after nearly a minute, he released her it was Ebony's turn to say "Wow."

"I know that was a bit presumptuous of me, but I have been thinking of that moment since I first met you and I wouldn't have been able to relax and cook at my best anticipating that kiss. So now the pressure of our first kiss is out of the way. I hope it won't be our last."

"You keep kissing like that and you truly won't have to worry about that."

"Why don't you have a seat at the breakfast nook and let me get busy preparing the food."

Ebony took her seat and enjoyed the view of Malachi's strong back and broad shoulders as he busied himself preparing the food. Ebony thought Mal was very well developed to be an academic. His body reminded her of someone who did physical labor for a living not poring over beakers and test tubes. Ebony decided that there was something very sexy and intimate about a man working his way around her kitchen. In less than five minutes, Malachi gave her a delicious Margarita complete with a salted rim of her glass. Maybe it was the erotic thoughts she was thinking earlier, but the drink was cool and soothing going down and then she could feel a warm glow permeate through her body.

"How is your drink?"

"It was delicious."

"I didn't realize you were finished. Would you like another?"

"Maybe one more. I'm pretty close to my limit, but it's been a hard week and it was just what the doctor ordered. No pun intended."

"Real funny, but be careful with them because they pack a little punch and they can sneak up on you."

"Yeah, I wouldn't want you to take advantage of me."

"Do you think I would do something like that?"

"If I did, you wouldn't be here."

"Not that I wouldn't be tempted, but I'm not that type of man. Here's your drink and a little guacamole to wash it down with."

"I feel guilty just sitting here while you are slaving away in the kitchen. Is there something I can help you with?"

"No, I would rather that you just sit back and relax. Let me prepare this meal for you."

"You better be careful or you'll spoil me."

"I wouldn't mind spoiling you. Maybe I think you need to be spoiled a little bit. I haven't known you for long, but I think you are a pretty special lady and should be treated as such."

"You better ease up on all the compliments or I'll get a big head."

"Naw, you wouldn't, you're too pretty to become that ugly."

Maybe it was the liquor but Ebony, who was usually immune to compliments, was finding the compliments from Malachi to be sincere and heartfelt. Ebony was surprised at how much she was attracted to Mal. She was sure it wasn't because of the things he was saying because she had been hearing men flirt and flatter her and try to run every game imaginable on her ever since she was a teenager. What she had to decide was whether it was because of Mal or just something as simple as her being horny because she hadn't made love in quite a while or both.

"Ebony, did you always want to be a police officer?"

"Not at all. When I left for college, I was leaning toward becoming a lawyer but I realized that there are a lot of bad people out there doing a lot of mean, evil things. The only way they could be tried and the victims receive justice was if someone caught them and arrested them."

"So the need to help people obtain justice was why you became a cop?"

"That is the primary reason but not the only reason. I also enjoy the intellectual challenge of being a cop and breaking down the mystery of who did it and how a crime was committed. It involves a degree of psychology in that I need to understand the workings on a criminal mind. It involves a bit of chemistry and biology in that we have to use the sciences in the forensics development of most cases. In many ways being a cop can be very rewarding. What made you become a scientist?"

"I became interested in the technology of farming because I saw how important being a farmer is to America. The population of this world is growing by leaps and bounds and someone is going to have to feed all those people. It's damn shame that, in this day and age, there are children somewhere in the world going to bed hungry. I want to help feed them.

"There are some corporations out there that are giving animals these growth hormones and chemicals to make them grow bigger and reach full maturity quicker. I'm not convinced that some of those chemicals don't have negative side effects that we aren't even aware of yet. Some of the government regulations on testing before approving it for public consumption are a little lax for my taste. So that is one of the things that I'm doing research on before in a couple of years we have a whole generation of kids born with a third eye or something."

"You don't really think it will be that bad? Do you?"

"Not really, I was only joking about the third eye, but I am serious about developing a larger, healthier chicken."

"How are you doing that?"

"Without going into too many details, I'm looking into the DNA of different species including capons and turkeys and even ostriches. Some of my findings have been pretty interesting."

"Are we talking about developing a new species altogether or adapting changes to existing species?"

"Right now, the field is pretty open so I'm looking into both and some other things as well, but I didn't come here tonight to talk about my work."

"Why not? I thought you wanted to get to know me better."

"I do."

"Well, I want to get to know and understand you better too, and our work is a large part of who we are. Plus, I'm finding this whole subject pretty fascinating."

"Not many people would find what I do that interesting."

"I'm not like most people."

"I was aware that you're not like most people, but now I'm discovering just how truly unique you are. Fascinating is a word that you used for my work but I think that word would apply to you even more. Ebony, stop looking at me like that."

"Like what?"

"With that look in your eye."

"Why?"

"Because it makes me want to do certain things."

"Oh really, things like what?"

"Things like this."

Ebony didn't know how it happened, but at some point Mal had moved across the kitchen and now was standing only a few feet from her. As he was speaking, he bent and took her chin in his hand. He then moved his hands to her cheeks and pulled her closer to him. They were standing mere inches from each other, and Ebony's mind was a whirlwind of thoughts, emotions, and observations. She saw that his eyes were a brown so deep that they looked to be almost black, but they were warm, gentle and very intelligent. They seemed to be peering into her soul as if looking for answers to questions that haven't even been asked yet.

She saw his nostrils flare as he was breathing deeply and holding his breath as if trying to gain control of his breathing or his pounding heart. His full and sensuous lips were slightly parted as if he was poised to say something important, maybe urgent. She felt him pull her in even closer, and before she could tell him how strong and soft and comforting his hands were, her lips were covered by his as he kissed her, long, hard and deep. Though his mouth was slightly parted his tongue did not venture out seeking her. It almost seemed to be waiting for her tongue to cross this great divide and come to him. She hesitated, not because she was scared but because she knew once she crossed it where it would lead and she wasn't sure she would want to come back. She felt his need (or was it her need) overwhelm her and engulf her and her body seemed to float closer and closer until it melded with his.

Her hands touched, stroked, and caressed his back that she had admired for what seemed like eons though it was only moments ago. She felt the muscles of his arms, so strong and tense but yet so gentle. She had no doubt that he could crush her if he chose to, but she had no idea that he could be so gentle or that she would feel so safe and secure and so much a part of something she wanted to be a part of for too long. She could feel herself slip away as she lost herself in him and she just relaxed and enjoyed the sensation.

She could feel her hunger start to build as Mal's hands caressed her back and slowly worked their way below her waist. As much as she wanted this and could feel that Mal wanted it too, she could see where this was leading and she wasn't sure that this was smart at this time. She reluctantly took a step back and looking Mal directly in the eye said, "You better be careful or you'll burn your food."

"Right at the moment that's not my concern."

"What is your concern?"

"My main concern is wrestling with these feeling and desires that I haven't felt for many months. I've been attracted to you since I saw you at my parent's house, but I didn't expect these feelings to be so hard to control."

"How long has it been since you were with a woman?"

"That's a very personal question."

"And what we were about to do wasn't personal?"

"I guess you're right about that. It's been several months since my last girlfriend and I broke up. Why do you ask?"

"Because I need to know if what you were experiencing was your desire for me or just your physical urges taking over."

"Ebony, I can honestly say that what I'm feeling is my overwhelming desire for you. I kind of got the feeling it was mutual."

"It is, but I can't afford to just go on my feelings."

"Then what should we go on?"

"I need a large degree of understanding about what this is, where we think this is going, and what is going to happen tomorrow. I mean, is this a one night stand or the beginning of a relationship that we're not sure that both of us want."

"I can't speak for you, but I know that this relationship has so much potential that I want to pursue it with every fiber of my being. I don't want you to think that I'm some horny country boy who came to New York because I thought I could score. That's far from the truth. True, I haven't been with a woman is months, but that is by choice not by necessity. I have had more than my share of opportunities, but the act of physical intimacy is too special to do it with just anyone. When I first met you, I knew that there was something about you that draws me in and I couldn't rest until I see if there's a chance for us to have a real relationship. That means if you feel the way that I do even to a small degree, we can take this as slow or as fast as you feel you need to."

"You are not alone in your feelings. I'm feeling things for you that I haven't felt about a man in quite some time, but I'm not the type of person to causally jump in and out of bed with anyone, regardless how I feel about them."

"I didn't expect anything different. I just got carried away with my feelings."

"Does that happen to you often?"

"No, almost never in fact. I consider feelings and emotions a very good thing but only if you are controlling them and not them controlling you."

"So what happened to you?"

"A combination of things, none of which I'm eager to discuss, but dinner smells like it is almost finished. Can we set the table and eat or do I need to finish being embarrassed first?"

Chuckling, Ebony said, "I didn't mean to embarrass you."

Laughing Malachi responded "Really? I didn't notice us talking about *your* loss of control of your emotions but I like you so I'm gonna give you a pass this time. Do you want wine or another Margarita with your dinner?"

"If I have another Margarita without something substantial in my stomach, I'll be the one throwing you down and pouncing on you." With a wink, Ebony turned and walked toward the table, leaving Mal standing there with his mouth hung open. Recovering, Mal responded, "Then by all means let's have a couple of double-strength Margaritas."

"No, I think we'll have water with our meal and then the Margaritas after dinner and we have better control of our composure."

"Shucks, I guess that means I have no choice but to just enjoy my food and maybe after something close to a cold shower I can get back to just enjoying your beautiful company."

"You make that sound like a bad thing."

"Actually, I think it will still be the most enjoyable evening I've had in quite some time."

"But not as enjoyable as it could be?"

"Ebony, I'm not going to even think about that or what it might be like to make love with you. Rather I will focus on the pleasures at hand and leave the pleasures that could be to their proper time and place. Let me fix your plate and I hope this food is one of those pleasures."

"I'm sure it is going to be good. It smells delicious."

"I'm not so sure. Usually my chili is out of sight but tonight I was a little distracted."

"Very clever, blaming the food on me in case it doesn't turn out as well as you bragged that it would be. I see you're intelligent, devious, and handsome," Ebony said with a wink and a smile.

"It's nice to know that you think I'm handsome."

"Of course I think you're handsome or else you might not be here in my home and you sure wouldn't have been grabbing my butt."

"I didn't grab your butt."

"You would have if I hadn't stopped you."

"We'll never know, now will we. Meanwhile, I'm sticking to my story that I would have stopped before then," Malachi responded laughing as well. "Ebony, would you like some extra cheddar and Monterey Jack in your chili?"

"Fix mine the way you like yours."

"Your wish is my command."

"Thank you, I'll keep that in mind," Ebony said before she settled in and started to really eat and enjoy her food. She was surprised to discover that either she was famished or the food was pretty good. Ebony was almost finished before Mal asked, "How do you like the chili?"

"It's surprisingly good. I mean, I'm not a big Tex-Mex fan, but this is almost as good as any gourmet meal."

"Thank you, I appreciate the compliment. Would you like some more?"

"Even though I usually don't eat anything heavy this late, a little more would be nice."

As Mal was fixing the food he said, "Ebony, tell me about you."

"What would you like to know?"

"Why don't you tell me about your family?"

"I'm the youngest of three children of Maxine and Lester James."

"If your parents' name is James, why is your name Delaney?"

"That's my married name."

"Are you still married?"

"No, Jack and I are divorced."

"You married someone named Jack Delaney?"

"Yeah, what's wrong with that?"

"I don't know, but that name sounds like a superhero's alter-ego in the comic books."

"Not quite, he was an assistant DA."

"If you don't mind my asking, what's happened to the marriage?"

"That is a little heavy for a first date."

"My fault, I didn't mean to pry and I wasn't trying to condemn or reach any type of judgment. I was just trying to understand. It's not like I've done so well in my relationships that I can look down on anyone else."

"It doesn't really bother me but we've having such a good time that I don't want to spoil it by talking about something that didn't go so well. I would much rather talk about something else."

"Family is very important to me and you seemed to really take to my parents and the kids. Is family important to you?"

"I clearly see the value of family, but I'm not as close to my family as I would like to be."

"Why not?"

"My father and I don't see eye to eye on a lot of issues politically, and I'm not willing to change who I am to get along with him. I have two older brothers and we're cool and everything, but I think that still see me as their little sister who they need to protect and look out for. I know they respect what I do, but I don't think they truly appreciate how good I am at my job."

"Sometimes the people closest to us are the last ones to see us for who we really are."

"I know your parents are really proud of the work that you do."

"I'm not so sure of that. I know they are proud of my degrees, but I don't think they fully understand my vision of where I think things can go."

"You couldn't be more wrong. It was very clear to me how your parents feel about you and your work, and immensely proud would be an understatement."

"I think we are usually the last one to know how those people close to us really feel about us and our work. I wonder if that's the case with you and your family."

"I wish that was the case, but I don't think it is."

"Tell me more about your parents and your brothers."

Maybe because Mal was such a good listener and seemed legitimately interested in what she was saying, Ebony found herself talking at length about her family and her relationship with them. Though Ebony had an early flight to catch the next morning, the conversation was so relaxing and stimulating that she found herself talking for hours after she had planned on being in bed. As she was kissing Malachi goodnight, she realized what a great time she had and resolved to see Malachi again as soon as she returned from the coast.

· · · · ·

"What time did you say you expected Sheriff Guillermo to return to the station?" Ebony said with just a touch of irritation because she had been waiting for more than an hour to see the sheriff. Her day had started at 6:30 A.M. when she had taken a cab to LaGuardia Airport to catch an 8:00 A.M. flight to Phoenix where after an hour layover she had caught a commuter flight to Flagstaff, Arizona. She then rented a car and drove for hours to a small town somewhere between Selgman and Walapai, Arizona, just to speak to this sheriff.

Ebony had called ahead for this appointment, and the lack of professional courtesy was not only unexpected but also disappointing. She was there looking into what appeared to be a horseback riding accident when the wife of another IMA client, baseball player Jason Woodbury, was killed when she was thrown from her horse. The case didn't fit the profile of the other deaths in the IMA file in that Woodbury and his wife, Camille, were not divorced or even separated and seemed to be happily married, but so far little on this case was as it appeared on first glance, so Ebony felt compelled to check it out.

Ebony waited another fifteen minutes before the Sheriff finally arrived at the station. The Sheriff was a tall, handsome, Hispanic man of about 6'1", 220 pounds with a very fit and lean physique and a Fu Manchu mustache that made him look forbidding and mysterious. If Ebony wasn't already annoyed, the way Sheriff Guillermo sauntered into the station oblivious to the fact that he had kept her waiting almost two hours, sipping a cup of coffee and behaving as if he was a feudal lord inspecting his manor. He stopped and looked Ebony up and down slowly and almost lustily as if he was evaluating a prized thoroughbred for purchase. Ebony half expected him to walk over and either grab her ass or examine her teeth. After a few more seconds, he turned and headed toward his office. Before entering his office he stopped and engaged an attractive assistant in an intimate conversation that did not appear to be work related.

A few minutes later Ebony was shown into the Sheriff's office.

"Miss Delaney, how can I help you?"

Ebony saw how this was going to go. He was evaluating her as if she was a potential sexual partner. She had to stop this and put things in the proper perspective. "Actually, it's Detective Delaney," Ebony said as she stood up, looked his firmly in the eyes and shook his hand.

Guillermo sucked his teeth as he said, "That's right, you are a New York Detective. How can I be of service?"

"I wanted to speak with you about the death of Camille Woodbury."

"You have questions about it?"

"I just wanted to cross check a couple of facts."

"Are you an insurance investigator? I thought you were a New York City police detective." Seeing that Ebony was not swayed by his masculine charms and would not be enticed into his bed, he took a tack very close to intimidation or at least an attempt to establish who was in charge here. He picked up a silver dagger that was on his desk and probably served as a letter opener and started fiddling with each around his fingers while he intently tried to stare Ebony down. Ebony returned his stare with a smile.

He reminded her of so many bullies she had seen, trying to act tough or macho and he would probably piss his pants at the first sign of real danger. Ebony took a second to adjust her attitude. She wasn't here to get in a pissing contest with some rural sheriff, drunk on his own power. This was part of a larger investigation and she had bigger fish to fry, but she wasn't about to let him push her around.

"I am a NYPD detective first grade."

"Then why are you interested in the Woodbury case?'

"I think that it might be part of a larger investigation that we are conducting."

"What kind of investigation could an accident be part of?"

"Are you sure that it was an accident?'

"Did you read the file?"

"Yes, I did."

"Then I don't understand your question. If you read the file, then you should know that it was an accident."

"I was wondering if there was more there than met the eye."

"Let me get this straight. You think that there is a chance that this was more than an accident? That it might have been murder?"

"I am mainly here to eliminate that possibility."

"Look, Ms. Delaney, this may not be New York City, but my department is good at what they do and believe me but we do a very competent and thorough investigation."

"I did mean to insult or imply—"

"I am insulted though. But since you have questions, let me answer them for you. I personally conducted the investigation, and there was no question that it was misfortune and damn bad luck, but it absolutely wasn't murder or planned. Camille Gibson, or Woodbury as she became known after she married Jason, was born and raised in this town. We were grateful that she and Jason made their off-season home here. They helped put our little town on the map. I have known Camille ever since she was a little girl, and when they were little kids, my younger brother was her boyfriend. She met Jason in college and married him and I have not known two people who were more in love, and despite that I still did a very thorough investigation. Do you know the particulars of the accident?"

"She died in a horseback riding accident".

"Not just a riding accident but an incredible misfortune. She was out riding on her favorite horse with the kids one evening after dinner, the horse reared. Camille was thrown from her horse, which usually would just result in some bumps and bruises. Unfortunately, they were riding along the rim of a canyon, where Camille and the oldest daughter were engaging in their passion of photography and Camille stumbled partially down the canyon, breaking her neck in the process."

"Was Camille an experienced rider?"

"Pretty much, but most people in this part of the country are."

"Isn't it unusual for her to be thrown from her horse?"

"As I said, the horse reared, probably from a rattlesnake."

"Did anyone see the snake?"

"One of the girls thought she did, but she wasn't sure because so much was happening with her mother falling and all. Rattlesnake makes sense, though, because they frequently come out around that time of day."

"Is there any other reason why the horse could have reared?"

"Such as?"

"Maybe an electric device of some kind placed under the saddle? A few years ago, they discovered that certain jockeys were giving their horses an electric shock for a burst of speed. Could someone have used something like that?"

"First of all, I checked the horse and his gear for any irregularities and found none. Secondly, for a device of that type to work someone would have to be in a close proximity to be effective especially because there are so many canyons out there and not only didn't the kids see anyone but there was no evidence that anyone else was within miles. Plus, why would anyone use such a device?"

"Maybe they would if they wanted to kill Camille."

"That would be a highly ineffective way of killing anyone. First of all, there is no way of knowing if the horse would rear or just bolt and run off. Then there is no guarantee that an experienced rider like Camille would be thrown, and even if she was thrown, there would be no way of knowing if she fall down a canyon or even a cliff and then if she fell how would you know if she would break her neck and not just a leg or an arm. Not only is there no one that I could find who would want to kill Camille, but this would be a cockeyed plan to do so. I am confident that this was an accident and nothing more."

"But—"

"There is no but. I've told you we've looked at this from every angle possible and it is what it appears to be. Plus, whom do you think would want to kill Camille?"

"Jason?"

"*Jason*!? Why in the hell do you think Jason would want to kill Camille?"

"For money maybe."

"Are you sure you're a detective and not just some lunatic who escaped from the loony bin. Jason was a millionaire many times over. It's not well known, but Jason gave countless millions every year to his church and numerous other charities. Jason is a devout Christian and was completely devoted to Camille. I've never seen any man more devastated by the loss of his wife. He even took a year off from baseball to grieve and be there for his kids. I don't know about you, but I don't think that's how someone who would murder his wife for money would behave. If you think that maybe he killed her because of another woman, forget it. Not only isn't there any sign of any infidelity, but even after she's been dead all this time, there still isn't a girlfriend. Have you ever met Jason?"

"I can't say that I have."

"If you did, you would know right away how ridiculous any thought that he had anything to do with Camille's death is."

"Maybe I should meet with him while I'm here."

"I would not suggest it, and in fact, I forbid it."

"Forbid? Who do you think you are to forbid me from doing anything?"

"I'm the man who will lock your fucking ass up with so many violations of city ordinances that it will be months before you get out of my jail. I will *not* have you harass one of our leading citizens and a man who has become a damn good friend, simply on some crazy whimsy. In fact, I suggest you go back to New York or wherever you want to go and leave this man and his family to continue to rebuild their life. They deserve at least that much."

"In New York we don't rest until we get the truth."

"I'm beginning to wonder if you would know the truth if it got up and bit you on the ass. The truth is there looking you in the face. All you have to do is read the report. Did you even bother reading the report?"

"Then if this is the truth, it should bear up to some investigating."

"I'm not concerned about something else coming out. I'm concerned about you stirring up some bad memories and a very rough time for some good people simply based upon some crazy notion. Plus, I resent the shit out of you telling me that my department and I aren't capable of running a thorough investigation."

"Maybe because you've shown so much professional courtesy."

"I've let you see our files on the case, haven't I? That's all the courtesy you're going to get and maybe a little more than you deserve. I think it's time for you to leave my office and I suggest my town but I can't make you leave. But I will tell you I will assign a deputy to watch you, and if you go anywhere near the Woodburys, you will be brought back to this station on not such pleasant circumstances. Good day, Miss Delaney."

Though Ebony was angry at the way the Sheriff spoke to her, she couldn't see any reason to stay and argue with him further. She was tempted to ask to again examine the file, but she didn't see what else she could get from looking at it again that she didn't get the first time, especially in her present state of mind. Right now she was obsessed with an overwhelming desire to get his ass on the dojo mat where she was positive she would kick his butt six ways to Sunday. She had to get her anger at Sheriff Guillermo under control so she could look at the facts of the case from a non-emotional perspective.

After she calmed down she realized that what the sheriff said had a large degree of validity and that planning this murder would have too many intangibles to make it feasible. Maybe this death was an accident and any correlation to IMA was just a coincidence. Ebony decided that the only smart thing she could do was move on to California and her meeting with the state troopers. She could conclude that there was nothing really to indicate this death was part of her investigation. If she changed her mind and decided that this was part of the conspiracy, she could always have Ted send some agents to pick up any information they needed.

Ebony pulled out and was getting ready to head back to Phoenix to catch her flight but then she noticed a police cruiser pulled in behind her. Ebony remembered the Sheriff's threat to have her followed and decided that she would not give him the satisfaction of thinking he chased her out of town. Even though it didn't accomplish anything but make her feel better, Ebony drove to the diner in the center of town and had a fairly lengthy lunch before she headed out of town and back to Phoenix still with time to spare before her flight.

· · · · ·

The next morning Ebony woke up in her hotel room amazingly refreshed and alert. Usually when she went to bed angry or frustrated, she didn't sleep well, but that wasn't the case in this instance. True, she was aggravated to the point of violence but she slept soundly nonetheless. Maybe it had something to do with her flying almost across the country and then driving for numerous hours and thus she was exhausted but just too pissed off to be aware of it. Or maybe it was the fact that she had good reason to look upon today with a lot more promise.

She had swallowed her pride and called Ted and had him place a call to the California Highway Patrol using some gentle federal persuasion and urging them to agree to meet with her as his representative today. Ebony really didn't want to utilize Ted or his connections, but she realized she was running out of time before she had to report back to her superiors and she couldn't afford another wasted day. Plus, she didn't feel like having done all this traveling without accomplishing anything of significance. So she submerged her ego and went about trying to get the most positive things accomplished today she could.

She had a big, hearty breakfast complete with fresh melons and fruit before jumping in another rented car and driving down to the California Highway Patrol office in Salinas. As close as she could figure, that was the closest major office to the site of the Kayla Battle crash. When she arrived, she was shown into a modern and efficient conference room where she was greeted by two agents from the Highway Patrol's Accident Investigation Unit. They had recently arrived from Sacramento and one of the corporate headquarters and were patiently having coffee and Danish while they waited for her to arrive. "This is more like it," Ebony thought as they greeted her with smiles and warm handshakes.

"I'm division specialist Sergeant Kevin Wiggins, and this is Tom Newkirk who was the lead investigator on the accident you were inquiring about."

"Good morning, I am New York Police Department Detective first grade Ebony Delaney, and I am serving as a liaison between our department and the FBI on a special task force. It is a pleasure to meet you gentlemen, and I want to thank you in advance for your cooperation. I know you both are plenty busy, and to take time out of your busy schedule to come down and meet with me is very much appreciated."

"Will we be joined by other agents today?"

"Not at this point. This is pretty much a fact-finding mission today and the other members of the task force are scattered across the country handling other aspects of the investigation, though if we determine that subsequent investigations here are needed, I'm sure that several of them will join us. I can tell you that I'm fairly confident that the information your office has obtained will be so extensive that we might not have to bother you further."

"We have brought the entire file on the accident, including whatever forensic evidence we were able to obtain. If you would prefer, we can leave you alone with the file, though we will remain available to answer any questions or provide clarification should you need any."

"Thank you, I would like to do that, but then I'm sure that I would need to talk to Officer Newkirk and obtain any observations that are not part of the official file."

"I'm not sure that there are any, but I will gladly answer any questions you may have," Officer Newkirk said.

Ebony spent the better part of an hour closely perusing the file and making notes of the facts she felt were pertinent. Things at first seemed to be fairly simple and pretty much as a simple traffic accident, but the more she read the file the more inconsistencies arose. She thought she saw a clear pattern which indicated that these young women may have been forced off the road, but then she saw the autopsy reports and she had more questions about what really happened. Ebony had been so engrossed in the file that she didn't realize that the other officers had left the room and she was alone. She went to get the other officers and saw them standing outside the conference room talking with other patrolmen. Not wanting to appear unfriendly or standoffish, Ebony joined the throng and spent a few minutes engaging in small talk until Sergeant Wiggins said they needed to get back to work and headed back to the conference room. Once inside the room, Ebony said, "I see that this incident was classified as an accident and not a homicide. Who made that determination?"

"We collectively made the determination, and as lead investigator I had to sign off on it, which I did with reluctance," Officer Newkirk said.

"Why?"

"Because there were factors that didn't fit together. I felt like something happened that wasn't a typical accident but what it was and proving that it was intentional was impossible."

"Let's talk about the factors that led to the conclusion of an accident first. I assume that the autopsies played a major part?"

"That's correct; there were traces of alcohol and marijuana in both their systems."

"But the levels were so low that I have questions about how much it would have impaired their ability to drive," Ebony pointed out.

"On most highways, yeah, but not on that stretch of the PCH at night. Being even the slightest bit impaired is not a good idea. They must have been high to drive the speeds they were driving on that stretch. According to the skid marks, they had to be driving at speeds of over eighty miles an hour."

"Wasn't there another set of skid marks a couple of hundred yards down the road?"

"That is correct."

"So they were driving at a high speed, temporarily lost so much control of the car that they had to brake hard enough to leave skid marks, but they then resumed those high speeds? Why?"

"That's one of the things we don't know."

"Are we supposed to assume that they were so high that there were unaware of the speed they were traveling or the consequences of traveling at those speeds?"

"It is a bit of a stretch."

"Correct me if I'm wrong, but doesn't marijuana often make the user paranoid?"

"That is frequently known to happen."

"So logically wouldn't they have gone slower not faster, especially after almost losing control of the car a few seconds before?"

"That's what I would have done, but then I would have been thinking clearly. Plus, there were the other drugs in their system."

"Was there speed or meth in their systems?"

"There were very faint traces of PCP in the blood of the passenger."

"But none in Mrs. Battle's blood?"

"None that could be detected."

"So even if the passenger was speeding, how could she convince Kayla to drive faster at speeds close to dangerous?"

"No way that I can imagine."

"In the pictures there was another set of skid marks adjacent to the skid marks identified as the Battle marks."

"Yes, according to the measurements, it was to a large SUV or a truck. What the pictures don't show is that there was another set of skid marks a couple of hundred feet further down the road. The width of the skid marks clearly show they didn't come from the Battle vehicle. Also, the rubber samples show that they are from different manufacturers. What we don't have any way of knowing is if the skid marks were made at the same time as the Battle accident."

Referring to her notes Ebony asked, "I saw the pictures of the car and it seemed pretty well torn up. Was the car itself recovered?"

"We lucked up and it landed above the tide line so we were able to get to the wreck and take pictures, but it was logistically impossible to haul it back up the cliff just to bring it back to the lab. So we don't know if damage was caused in a collision with another vehicle or if it was caused in the crash," Newkirk said.

"I don't envy you at all in this case. I must compliment you because under the circumstances, it seems that you did an outstanding investigation. Like in most investigations, there are a lot of questions but what is different here is I don't know how you could have obtained factual answers."

"It wasn't easy closing this case without answers that I felt in my heart were the true answers beyond any doubt. But I sincerely believe that we came as close to the truth as we could."

After her bad experience with Sheriff Guillermo, Ebony didn't want to get on the wrong foot by insulting another investigator so she wanted to phrase her questions as sensitively as possible. Ebony was silent while deep in thought and then she directed her question to Sergeant Wiggins. "Please forgive the implication in my question because I don't mean to insult you, but I really need to ask this question. In the NYPD to the rank and file statistics carry a lot of weight. One of the things we are judged on is the amount of open or unsolved cases. Is it possible that this case was listed as an accident because the higher-ups didn't want an unsolved case on the books? Especially a high-profile case like this one was."

"How can I answer that?" Wiggins said.

"Pardon me?"

"I mean, if I say that it was closed for political reasons, then I implicating the higher-ups as incompetent or worse. If I say it was closed because we all agreed that was the truth or proper decision, I'm not sure that's accurate."

"That question is not for any official report or file. It is for my own personal knowledge. Like I said, I'm very interested in your opinion and impressions. To me there's a world of difference between thinking that two girls were out partying and drove off a cliff or someone somehow helped them go over that cliff."

"What I can say is that bureaucracies are the same, be they in New York or California. The same issues and stats that are of such importance there have the same degree of importance here. The state of California is a big ass state. Finding one little truck that may or may not have forced those girls off the road would have been a task that would have been damn near impossible."

"Would it serve any purpose for us to drive over and look at the site of the crash firsthand?"

"Other than to see how difficult that turn was and therefore assess how skilled a driver she might have been, it serves no purpose. I can tell you that in spots the PCH can be a bitch to drive and it should be taken seriously. This turn was one of those spots. It would be entirely possible to go off the road at that spot under normal circumstances. If someone was trying to force you off, it would have been impossible not to."

· · · · ·

On the plane ride back across the country toward her next stop, Ebony spent some time thinking about the developments of the past few days. There were quite a few things that she was convinced had happened and nothing that she could prove. She felt like she was haunted by Denzel Washington in the movie *Training Day* and the line "It's not what you know, but what you can prove." She was sure that Barnett was behind as least four murders and couldn't prove that he was involved in even one. On the other hand, she didn't have to prove that he was behind multiple murders just that he was responsible for one. Life in prison was the same if it was for one murder or for a dozen.

Ebony knew it was time to move her investigation from whether murder had been committed into proving that murder was done, by whom and how. Barnett was the only common thread in these deaths, but that still was a far step from proving he was responsible for them. Ebony had four days left before she had to meet with the officials to see if she could convince them to turn this into a formal investigation. She hadn't decided what she would do if they determined there wasn't enough to launch a formal investigation yet. She did know that she was positive that Barnett was dirty as the day was long and no matter what the authorities said she wasn't going to let him get away with it.

As the plane was touching down at Detroit-Metro airport, Ebony stretched because after all this traveling in such a short period of time, the fatigue was starting to set in. Though she had planned on one more stop before going home to New York, she was having thoughts about changing her itinerary. Ebony's goal was not to tour the whole country or to build up her frequent flyer miles, though they were increasing at a pretty impressive rate, but she did feel she should follow down each of these cases because there was no telling what those cases would reveal. What was becoming clear to Ebony was that Barnett had committed what appeared to be some pretty airtight crimes and he probably didn't think that anyone was on to him.

Ebony knew there was no such thing as the as a perfect crime and there were always some loose threads. Ebony's job was to find those loose threads and tug on them until the whole conspiracy unraveled. History taught her there was no way of knowing which thread would be the one to bring the whole house of cards tumbling down so she had to give each suspected murder thorough research until she found that thread. She was going to look at every accident related to a client of IMA until she found the weakest ones and then she would intensify the investigation on those.

She wondered how Ted was making out with his search for Omar and the investigation into Justice's operation. She didn't know why but she had a sneaky suspicion that could be the weak link in the root of the whole case. She made a mental note to try to find a connection between Brandon Barnett and Justice and not just Omar and Justice or Omar and Barnett. As she got in her rental car and headed toward Farmington Hills, an affluent suburb of Detroit, she called Ted's voice mail and left a message asking him to see if he could find any link between Justice and Barnett.

Chapter Thirteen

Ebony was deep in a peaceful and restful dream full of dreams of summer flowers and spring romance when it was disturbed by an angry and incessant buzzing. She searched through the meadows for the bees or hornets that were causing such a major disturbance in her peaceful slumber. As she begrudgingly came awake, she realized that the buzzing that invaded her sleep was the intercom to the entrance to her building.

She was so tired she didn't even bother trying to find out who was trying to get, just pushing the button so they could have admittance. Deciding against going back to bed and risking that whoever wanted to get in wanted to see her and would just wake her up again, she went into the bathroom and splashed some water on her face. She got out the bathroom just in time to answer Ted's knock at the door and let him in.

"Hey, Ted."

"Wow, Delaney, you look like you've been through the wringer."

"Aw, shut up and put on some coffee while I jump in the shower."

"Oh, I excite you so much you have to take a cold shower?"

"Not hardly. I just need to clear my head from all of these cobwebs."

Ebony had no intention of taking such a long shower, but the hot, steamy water was working wonders on her stiff and aching muscles. Though she didn't ignore the fact that Ted was waiting, the temptation to pamper herself just a little bit was overwhelming. As she was applying lotion to her body, a delicious aroma from somewhere in the vicinity made her aware that she was almost as hungry as she was tired. Hoping that Ted had surprised her by having food delivered, she emerged from the bathroom casually dressed in jeans and a t-shirt. Though Ted didn't have food delivered, the smells were coming from her kitchen.

"I thought you might be hungry so I took the liberty of throwing together a couple of omelets from some of the stuff I found in your refrigerator. I was surprised at how well stocked it was with you having been out of town for so long. I found a couple of steaks so I grilled them and there was a lot of cheese, so I'm having T-bones and a cheese omelet if you care to join me."

"Only you, Ted, could sound gracious offering me my own food."

"It may be your food but it's my recipe and expertise."

"I'll determine the degree of your expertise," Ebony said as she sat down and joined Ted in enjoying the meal. Any attempts at idle conversation soon died as both settled in and enjoyed the food. After finishing her food, Ebony cleared the plates from the table and busied cleaning up after the meal as she said to Ted, "I don't know whether it was because I was starving or whether you can really cook, but the food was very good."

"Thank you, but I must confess that I don't cook a lot of things but those things that I can cook, I cook very well. How was your trip?"

"Productive and eye opening. Oh yeah, thanks for the assist with the California Highway Patrol."

"Did it work?"

"Yes, they were very cooperative."

"What did you find out?"

"The accident in Arizona for all intents and purposes appears to be just that an accident. However, in the Kayla Battle case there is a very strong possibility that they were forced off the road. There was nothing that we can prove, but both the investigators and I agree that it was probably an accident caused by somebody forcing them over the cliff."

"Why does the official record have it listed as an accident?"

"That classification was a result of interoffice politics. The higher-ups didn't want a high-profile case on the books that they had little chance of solving."

"If they have little chance of solving the case, what can we do with it?"

"We'll just add it to the overall case and file of evidence against Barnett."

"Was there any link to Barnett?"

"Other than the husband, Tank Battle, was a client of Barnett and the judge awarded her a lot of money in the divorce settlement? No, but it might come in handy as we build a case against Barnett. There's no way of knowing how much information it might contribute and if nothing else, it helps us create a profile."

"That's a little disappointing. I was hoping we could get something a little more substantial on Barnett."

"I was too, but my last stop was more promising. In the case of Jasmine Norris, they still have classified it as a homicide. Whoever did that murder got a lot sloppier than was the case in the other murders. Once again they tried to make it appear to be an accident but this time they left a lot of loose ends. First, there were signs of forced entry. Then, in order to have slipped on the shampoo on the right foot but have a contusion on the left temple, the lady would have had to slip, do a 180-degree pirouette in the air, hit her head, and then do another pirouette in the opposite direction in order to land flat on her back and then pull the hairdryer in the tub with her. Plus, what a lot of White people may not realize is: a Black woman would not wash, press, and curl her hair and then take a hot bath because the steam would negate a lot of the hard work she put in. A woman might wash and curl her hair, but she would leave the curlers in until after her bath was done."

"How is Miss Norris related to Mr. Barnett?"

"The father of her children is the rapper EZ Money, another client of IMA."

"Did she also receive a large amount of money in a divorce or child custody settlement?"

"Their relationship seemed to be on again, off again, and at the time of her death they appeared to be on again."

"Was EZ established as a suspect?"

"No, he was out of town with the kids on vacation."

"Did they have any suspects?"

"No, that's why they were so interested in our investigation."

"Ebony, we're building a pretty impressive list of victims, suspects and locations. I think it time we established a chart to help us keep things straight."

"Too late, I already have one. Come on into my den and you can help me update it."

They spent the next half hour working on and discussing a gigantic chart that took up most of a wall. At the top of the chart was Brandon Barnett and under his picture was a giant map of the United States with names and pictures at the different locations where the suspected murders were committed with the name of the victim underneath.

After they were finished, Ted stood back and studied the chart and then said, "Let me get this straight. We suspect Barnett of orchestrating or committing murders in New York, the Caribbean, and Maryland, California, and Michigan, plus a couple others that we don't know anything about yet. My question is how did he pull it off? Did he have someone contract the killers in each of these places, or did he get the killers here and send them to commit the murders? I can't see him having somebody arrange killers in each of these places. That leaves too many loose ends. This means he got the killers here and sent them to where the murders were committed. Let's check his financial records and see if he did significant business with a travel agent and if so find out if he brought airlines tickets to some of these places. I'll have one of my assistants check into that."

"That's a good point, Ted. I missed that one."

"That's okay, Delaney, you would have noticed it. It was only a matter of time and you probably would have thought of it already, if you weren't so tired."

"Thanks for the confidence, Ted. This case is starting to frustrate me. We know that Barnett is behind these murders and that he had to make a mistake somewhere. It's just catching that mistake. Sometimes I feel like we're trying to catch a will-of-the-wisp."

"Be patient, Ebony, and keep doing what we're doing. It will pay off in the end."

"Have you come up with anything on Justice Permentier?"

"Quite a lot actually, but nothing related to our investigation."

"Can you do me a favor and shift your search away from a connection between Omar and Justice and shift it toward any connection at all between Permentier and Barnett? You said that someone had to be contracting all those killers. What if Permentier is that someone?" Ebony asked.

"That's a great idea, partner; I think you might be on to something. It's worth at least a look see. What's next for you?"

"To meet with my superiors and see if I can get them to make this investigation official."

"Good luck with that. Do you think we have enough?"

"No, but I'm out of time and I have to try to convince them to see things my way. We need more resources and that would make this investigation go much quicker."

"I spoke with my section chief and he is willing to trust my instincts and he is giving me some leeway but he fell short of making this an official federal investigation."

"That's good, and I'll let you know how I make out tomorrow."

· · · · ·

"Delaney, you've got to be kidding me. I know you're not serious. You want us to launch an investigation based on this. You do not have one piece of concrete evidence. Even if I give that a crime *might* have been committed, there's nothing linking any of it to Brandon Barnett," Lieutenant Melendez said.

"That's why we need an investigation," Ebony said.

"But why Barnett? Why not Mayor Bloomberg or the seven dwarfs or even me?" Melendez asked.

"I don't think it was a joke and I damn sure don't think it's funny," Ebony countered.

"I don't think it's funny either. I just want to point out how ridiculous you're being. You want us to launch a major investigation that would cost us thousands of dollars and countless man hours, against one of New York's more successful businessmen and who also happens to be a mover and shaker in the political arena, based on evidence so sparse that we couldn't convict him of jaywalking. *And most of the crimes weren't even committed here in New York.* What are you thinking?"

Ebony had scheduled an appointment with her lieutenant and CO, Captain Riley, to try to convince them of the need for a full-fledged investigation. Ebony knew the evidence was thin and sketchy at this point but she was surprised at the degree of opposition she was receiving from them.

"I was thinking that this man has killed at least five people that we know about and he is still walking the streets."

"But, Detective, what makes you so convinced it was Barnett who committed these crimes?" Captain Riley asked.

"One, I was told by one of his victims—"

"He told you directly?" Riley asked.

"No, he told his cousin who told me," Ebony said.

"Who you were romantically involved with?" Melendez asked.

"What does that have to do with anything? That was years ago."

"It matters because maybe he was upset about his cousin's death and felt that someone had to pay. Knowing that you had an emotional attachment with him, he decided that you could help him with his vendetta," Melendez said.

"You act like I'm some love-struck teenager. You know I'm a competent and efficient professional. If I pursue a suspect it's because the evidence indicates he's guilty."

"What evidence? You have no evidence."

Captain Riley interrupted the debate. "Okay, that's enough out of both of you. It doesn't matter what the cousin told you because all of it is hearsay. What else do you have? "

"Two, he's the only common link between all the victims." Ebony said.

"That we know about. There might be another link and we just don't know about it yet or it could be a coincidence," the Captain said.

"Now, Captain, I know you don't believe in coincidences," Ebony argued.

"No, I don't believe in them but I would have to be an idiot to think that's it's not possible."

"Captain, you know me and my record speaks for itself. I got a feeling deep down in my gut that this guy did this."

"I'm sorry, Detective, but as much as I respect you and what you've done, I can't justify a major investigation based on a feeling. You know better than that."

"I know, we can't let him get away with this."

"Detective, why are you so passionate about this? It makes me wonder what's going on with you."

"Meaning what exactly, sir?"

"Meaning that I wonder if you got so accustomed to the limelight that you need a high-profile case like this. Maybe your ego needs for Barnett to have done this crime so you can be the big, bad sheriff that brings him to justice."

"I'm insulted that you would even think something like that. I don't give a shit about publicity or ego and all that nonsense. The only thing I care about is innocent women are being murdered and no one is doing a damn thing about it."

"Okay, I'm sorry, Detective Delaney, but I had to say that to test your reaction. I'm sorry, Detective, but even if I believed you, and right now I'm less than fifty-fifty, I can't justify opening an investigation."

"So you just want me to let this go?"

"You have to."

"I can't."

"So what do you want to do?"

"Assign just me and my partner to the case and give us three weeks to bring you some conclusive evidence."

"I can't afford you and your partner away from our regular caseload. Can't do it."

"Then just me. Give me one month and I'll solve the case and bring in an arrest."

"Three weeks, Delaney, and you better come in with an airtight case."

Not wasting any time Ebony left the precinct and went straight to Ted's office to bring him up to date on the results of her meeting with her bosses. After waiting fifteen minutes Ebony was shown into Ted's office.

"Good afternoon, Ebony, how did it go?"

"Not as well as I hoped it would. They refused to make it an official investigation, but they did give me three more weeks to try to make a case. So I got some time to work with, but we need to intensify our investigation."

"My office hasn't opened an official file because we can't prove that a federal crime was committed. But they are giving me a lot more leeway. They're going to allow full use of their facilities and use of whatever resources I need within reason. I have been using a couple of analysts to do some of the groundwork and research."

"Have you been able to establish a link between Barnett and Permentier?"

"It's a coincidence that you should ask me, but the analyst who was tracing their histories hasn't got back to me yet. I'll e-mail him to get his report back to me as soon as possible. You're putting a lot of emphasis on Permentier. Do you know something that I don't know?"

"It's just a feeling. We know that Omar killed Tanya Richardson probably at the behest of either Barnett or Permentier or both, so there's got to be a link between the two. I'm guessing that Barnett has gone to great lengths to cover his tracks but I'm willing to bet that Permentier hasn't made nearly as much effort. Maybe by turning up the focus on Permentier we may be able to uncover the entire conspiracy."

"Then I'll make sure Amir does a real thorough search, and if nothing comes up right away, I'll have him run a more extensive search."

"I'll have a couple of errands to run and I'll speak with you in the morning. If Amir comes back with anything conclusive before then, just let me know."

"I'll speak to you as soon as I hear anything one way or the other."

Ebony left Ted's office and called Malachi from her car. "Good afternoon, Malachi."

"Good afternoon. Whom may I ask am I speaking with?"

"Ebony Delaney."

"Ebony, it's great to hear from you. Where are you? Are you back in the city?"

"Yeah, I got home day before yesterday."

"You got home two days ago and you didn't call me until now?" Malachi said, sounding disappointed.

"I was exhausted when I got in, and I had to bring my partner and supervisors up to speed on the investigation. You okay? You sound a little annoyed."

"It's just that I have been thinking about you so much, I was kind of hoping that it was reciprocated."

"When I tell you about how many states I visited and how many meetings I have had since I saw you, you'll understand. It doesn't mean that I didn't think about you, it's just that this investigation isn't as simple as I would have thought it would be. I warned you that I can get obsessed with my work."

"I guess that's a good thing because that means that you're gonna get the guy who killed Tanya."

"I'm gonna get him and the guy who put him up to it.

"Sounds like you have a lot to tell me."

"No, I don't. I have a firm rule that I don't discuss a case until it's done. Is that okay?"

"Hey, rules are rules. How are you doing?"

"Other than still being a little tired, I'm good. How are you?"

"Other than missing you, I'm great."

"That's sweet. Are you still in New York?"

"No, I'm down here at Princeton, but I can get back to the city if you want to get together."

"I would love to see you, but I can't ask you to drive back up to the city. I'll tell you what. Why don't we meet in Newark? That's pretty close to halfway. I know this really great Spanish restaurant there. How does that sound?"

"That sounds fantastic, just give me the address and the time you want to meet and I'm there."

· · · · ·

Ebony got home around ten thirty, which was early for her but seemed a lot later because she was so tired. She saw where she had several voice messages but fatigue was Lord of the Day at that point and she just went to bed without checking her messages. She was awakened early the next morning by the shrill ringing of the phone.

"Wake up, you sleepyhead."

"What's going on Ted?"

"I got some good news for you."

"Really what's that?"

"You have to be fully awake for this so wash your face, get your coffee, and call me back."

"Trust me, I'm awake and alert. What's the good news?"

"Guess who attended the same junior high school and high school?"

"Barnett and Permentier?"

"Correctomundo, and furthermore they were good friends at least until Permentier went to youth detention and later prison and Barnett finished high school and went to college."

"I knew it. I knew there was something between those two."

"Wait, there's more. Guess what Permentier went to jail for?"

"Assault? Or better yet murder?"

"Not quite. He went to the hospital for treatment of a gunshot wound and a subsequent search of his house turned up a gun used in a shootout and death of a couple of drug dealers."

"That's some pretty heavy shit for a kid in high school. Was Barnett suspected of being part of the shootout as well?"

"There's no evidence that he was involved but that doesn't mean he wasn't. What might be notable is that Barnett was considered a brilliant student but was underachieving and failing everything until Permentier went to prison. Then he seemed to get his act together and got his G.E.D. and went to college."

"Interesting. Did he learn from his friend's mistakes or did he clean up his act because his road partner was no longer on the street?"

"Those are some pretty intriguing questions, but it doesn't change the fact that there was a significant link between Barnett and Permentier."

"What about after Permentier's release from prison? Did he and Barnett resume their friendship?"

"We really don't know if they hung together, but Barnett was a party promoter while he was in college and we know that Permentier went down to Philadelphia for a couple of his parties. Though we can't prove any wrongdoing or anything illegal on the part of Barnett, we can establish the relationship between the two. How do you want to handle it?"

"I think it might be a good time to spend a couple of days following Permentier to see if I can establish a pattern or connection between him and Barnett or our victims."

"Whoa, Ebony, this guy is a drug dealer and considered by the DEA to be dangerous. Barnett might go out of his way to cover his tracks, but this guy is a hoodlum and he might come straight at you if he feels threatened. Do you think following him is a good idea?"

"Do you think I'm scared of this punk? Remember that I'm not some defenseless woman they can throw off a cruise ship. I don't want them to come at me, but if they do, I think I can handle myself."

"I still think you need to be extra careful. What do you need me to do?"

"What can you do about getting those financial records? A whole lot of money changed hands and if we can get proof of the transactions, which can establish the motive."

• • • • •

Three days later Ebony was again talking with Ted as they were comparing notes on the cases "This just isn't working. I'm been following this sleazeball for three days and I'm no closer to having any concrete evidence that will bring us any closer to proving what these guys are doing. How are you making out with the financial records?"

"We're working on it hard and our friends at the Treasury Department are helping as much as they can but I'm sure he has the money in a foreign account and without knowing what bank he was dealing with, we're looking for a needle in a haystack."

"I might have a couple of leads that might help the DEA if they ever want to investigate this guy, but I haven't come up with squat that helps us. These guys are either laying low because their radar has kicked in or they don't have a hit planned, but either way nothing is going on. At this rate, we can go for three months rather than three weeks and not have anything substantial on them. We're gonna have to find a way to turn up the heat. I think it's time I turned up the pressure on Barnett. I think I will meet with Barnett and see how he reacts if he knows we're on to him."

"What if he just goes even further underground, which is what I would do if I knew you didn't have anything on me."

"Then I have to make him think I have more on him than I have."

"If you identify yourself and let him know you're after him, how are you going to follow him or Permentier?"

"That's true."

"Ebony, this course of action reeks of being desperate. I think we just need to be patient and wait for them to make a mistake."

"We don't have that kind of time. This can go on like this for months. I see the flaws in confronting him, but I don't see where we have a lot of options. Do you have any guys that can take over following Permentier?"

"No, I have resources but not that kind of manpower."

"That's why the NYPD is pissing me off. If they had made this official, we would have the bodies to do what we need to do."

"I understand your frustration, but that doesn't help our situation."

"I do have some resources that I haven't called on and I think that now is the time to call on them."

. . . . .

"Rashid, this is Ebony Delaney."

"Ebony, how is it going girl?"

"It's going but things are far more extensive than I had anticipated."

"Are you close to an arrest?"

"Not nearly as close as I would like to be. I need your help."

"Just tell me what you need."

"I need to hire a private detective firm to follow a suspect 24/7 for about three weeks."

"Why are you hiring private detectives? Don't the police have enough officers to cover that? Don't tell me the NYPD still isn't helping with this case?"

"Rashid, you said that whatever I needed to catch this cat to just let you know. Did you mean it or do you just want to ask me a lot of questions?"

"You're right just tell me how much you need and I'll take care of it tomorrow."

. . . . .

"Gary, I want to thank you for coming with me."

"I don't think I had much of a choice, Delaney, once you told me what you are working on. I thought we were partners. I didn't appreciate you leaving me in the dark again."

"It was all I could do to get Melendez to give me the time to work this case. There was no way he was going to let you go too."

"I would have worked it anyway. The hell with them. I do what has to be done, and I support my partner come hell or high water."

"I know that, Dansby, and I count on you a lot more than you know. I just didn't want to bring any heat down on you while I was doing the preliminaries. I figured I would bring you in like this when things started to get hot and heavy."

"Are they hot and heavy yet?"

"No, but I hope this will serve to turn things up a bit."

"Let's do this then," Gary said. Gary and Ebony took the elevator up to IMA's offices and entered the reception area. The same voluptuous receptionist that had greeted Ebony on her previous visit asked, "Good morning. May I help you?"

Ebony and Gary flashed their shields and credentials as Gary said, "We would like to speak to Brandon Barnett." Ebony and Gary had agreed that Gary would be the lead detective and conduct most of the questioning because as the person who was conducting the investigation, the less attention Ebony drew to herself the better. She didn't want to alert Barnett any more than necessary as to who his true adversary would be.

"Do you have an appointment?"

"No, we do not but we need to speak to him regarding a matter related to a criminal investigation. I don't think an appointment is necessary."

"Mr. Barnett has a very full calendar. I'm not sure that he's available."

"I think he will want to be available because if I have to come back, I will come back with a warrant and things won't be nearly as pleasant." Gary knew he had absolutely no chance of obtaining a warrant to interview Barnett, but he also knew the receptionist had no way of knowing that.

"I'll see if Mr. Barnett is available."

"I would appreciate that," Gary said as the receptionist went into Barnett's office.

The receptionist returned and said, "Mr. Barnett said he will be with you as soon as he completes this international call. Please have a seat. Can I offer you some coffee or refreshment?"

"No, thank you." Ebony and Gary sat and waited until about fifteen minutes had passed then Gary said to the receptionist, "You can tell your boss that he has exactly sixty seconds and then we're leaving and returning with the proper paperwork that will require him to come down to the precinct to speak with us."

The receptionist again retreated into Barnett's office, but this time she returned and said, "Mr. Barnett will see you now."

Ebony and Gary walked into Barnett's office with authority. They realized that Barnett had kept them waiting in an attempt to control the meeting and show them who was in charge. They were equally determined to show that this was their meeting and they were the ones in control. Brandon Barnett was sitting behind a large, elegant desk made on an exotic wood, maybe teak or Brazilian Redwood. Barnett was dressed in a stylish, expensive gray Armani suit with a tailored pale blue shirt and a colorful tie that brought out the color of his eyes and complexion. Standing in a way that made him appear almost regal, he said, "I'm Brandon Barnett. How can I help you?"

"I'm Detective Dansby, and this is Detective Delaney. In the future, we would appreciate it if you didn't keep us waiting to speak with you."

Brandon's antenna was raised by the "in the future" comment, which indicated they intended to speak with him again. While not giving up the guise of being in control, he immediately became more alert. "I'm sorry, but I wasn't trying to be rude. I was on an intercontinental call as I was trying to finalize an endorsement deal for one of our clients with a corporation in Japan. The time difference made it impossible to end the conversation any sooner. How can I be of service to you?"

"One of the reasons we are here is about an investigation into the murder of Tanya Richardson."

"Murder? I was under the impression that Ms. Richardson had run off with her lover."

"*Mrs.* Richardson's companion was seen disembarking from the ship and he has since disappeared and is part of an extensive search. Evidence indicates that Mrs. Richardson may have come under foul play while aboard the ship. The ship is registered in the Bahamas, so their police department who is in charge of the investigation has determined that it was a homicide"

"I'm really not sure what this has to do with my agency."

"I'm sure you're aware that Tanya Richardson was the wife of Larry Richardson, one of your clients."

"I'm aware that Tanya Richardson was the ex-wife of one of our former clients Larry Richardson. I'm sure that you're aware that Larry died as a result of a drug overdose during a binge that was probably brought on by his wife deserting him. So are you assisting the Bahamian Police with their investigation and is this a routine background check?"

"Not quite. We're working in conjunction with the Bahamian Police as their investigation seems to be part of a larger investigation that we are conducting."

"I'm still not clear on what all this has to do with me," Barnett asked.

"Mr. Barnett, are you aware that the wives of six of your clients have died under mysterious circumstances?" Ebony asked.

"Really? I didn't know that."

"Five of those deaths occurred after the clients had signed a contract with your agency. Three of those deaths are considered suspicious by the investigating agencies and are still open cases. Do you have an explanation why such an unusual amount of deaths are associated with your agency?"

"Excuse me, Detective Delaney, wasn't it? Do we know each other?"

"No, we do not."

"I'm sorry, but you look hauntingly familiar. Are you sure we haven't met before? I'm usually very good with faces."

"I'm sure we are not acquaintances. Will you answer my question?"

"Which was?"

"Do you have an explanation for the huge number of deaths associated with your agency?"

"I would think that it is a coincidence or bad luck."

"Do you know that fifteen kids are left without a mother because of your bad luck?"

"I didn't know that. I'm not that involved in the personal lives of my clients. I'm especially not involved in the private lives of their ex-wives."

"How do you know they were ex-wives?"

"Pardon me?"

"I *said* how do you know they were ex-wives? How do you know that all of these women who had these strange *accidents* were the ex-wives of your clients? Especially since you're not involved in the *personal* lives of your clients?" Ebony said.

"I really don't know how I knew that. Maybe I read it somewhere."

"Where? Where could you read something like that?" Ebony blared as she started to lose control of her temper.

"Detective *Delaney*, do you have a problem with me?"

"Yes, as a matter of fact, I do. You are sitting there lying to us which means you either think you're smarter than us or you think we're just stupid."

"Are you sure that's the problem you have with me? *Delaney*? Isn't that an Irish name? Is your mama or daddy Irish and your half-white ass has a hard time dealing with a successful Black man? Or is it that you're a butch and you are threatened by my manhood? It's no new thing for you so-called *officers of the law* to have a problem with successful Black businessmen and fabricate such preposterous charges."

"You're trying to play the race card with me? You got to come way better than that if you think you're going to get away with this."

"Get away with what? What are you accusing me of, Ms. Oreo?"

"Do you really think you're going to get off the hook by insulting me?"

"What hook? Am I on a hook? In fact, either arrest me and charge me with something or get your Uncle Tom asses out my office. I don't have to speak with either of you."

Standing up and leaving, Ebony said, "We'll leave for now. But you will see me again. I know just what you did and I promise you, you are going to pay for it."

· · · · ·

In the apartment across the street from Justice's apartment where the DEA had set up surveillance and wire taps on Justice, one agent signaled to another, "I think this is that call that Agent Delaphine alerted us to be on the lookout for. Listen."

"Hey, Justice, this is B, we got problems man. I think I know a way to handle it but I think I need to bring you up to date on what's going on."

"What do you want to do about what? Do you want to tell me about it now?"

"No, I think we need to talk face to face. Can you meet me at spot one in ninety minutes?"

"Is it important like that?"

"Yeah, I think so."

"Then I'm there."

"Cool."

As soon as he hung up the phone, Brandon started changing clothes and preparing himself for the long ride to the Bronx and the roundabout trip to the meeting place in Harlem. Especially after his meeting with Ebony, Brandon was not about to desert his practice of being cautious. Justice, on the other hand, had never seen a need to be cautious about his comings and goings. He did not know that the DEA had become aware of how large and prosperous his drug operation had become and had launched a major investigation into his operation.

When Justice and his bodyguard left his headquarters and headed toward Harlem, he had no idea that his every movement was being followed by two undercover agents. Justice and his bodyguard parked in front of the bar and entered the bar where the two separated and the bodyguard took a seat at a table near the front and Justice headed toward his customary table in the back. The two DEA agents parked down the street from the bar, and after waiting a few minutes, one agent followed Justice into the bar. He took a seat at the bar and ordered a beer. He seemed oblivious to Justice or anyone else in the bar. He was wearing what appeared to be an MP3 player but in reality was a powerful microphone and transmitter and was capable of picking up any conversation within the bar and sending the signal back to the tape recorder in the car. He appeared to be just one of the guys from the neighborhood stopping in for a couple of cold ones before heading home from work and he appeared relaxed and nonchalant because he knew they were capturing anything that would be said on tape that they could go over later.

Within the hour, Brandon entered the bar and headed straight to Justice's table and took a seat. "Yo, Pred, what's going on man?"

"I was visited by a couple of cops today."

"Why?"

"Somehow they have put together the pieces of the puzzle. They are hip to our little side hustle."

"How much do they know?"

"I've been thinking about this since they left and I think they suspect that we're somehow behind the accidents but they just haven't figured out the how or why. I'm not sure whether they know all the particulars of our operations, but clearly they can't prove anything or else they would have arrested me instead of just questioning me. I think this is proof that it was a wise thing that we took such strong efforts to make sure none of this could be traced back to us. There's only one thing that worries me."

"What's that?"

"That punk Omar. He's the only weak link that's left out there that we have no control over. Have any of your people heard from him or got any word about his whereabouts?"

"No, and that kind of surprises me. He must've left town or else he would have turned up by now."

"Does he have someone or a relative that might know his whereabouts?'

"I don't know, but I don't think his family would tell us anything."

"If you find a member of his family, we'll make them tell us where he is."

"I'll see if any of the crew know about him or his family and get back to you. What are we gonna do about the cops?"

"Like I said, they probably can't prove anything, but I ain't too cool with them prowling around because sooner or later they might turn something up. There's this female pig that really seems to have something against me. I'm gonna have to back her up off me."

"You want to send some people after her?"

"No, that shit would be crazy. The NYPD would really come after us if we touched her. You know how crazy they get when someone kills an officer. That might bring more problems than she's worth. I don't think she enough of a threat to bring about such drastic measures."

"I'll follow your lead, but I think we should eliminate her before she becomes a problem."

"Let's hold up on something that drastic for now. I have another plan that might accomplish the same thing without putting us at risk. Let me handle it for now."

"You got it, but if you decide to go another way just let me know because I got a couple of cats who would jump at the chance to make their mark against a pig."

"I don't know, but I'm thinking we're gonna have to be real cool with that shit from here on in. If they're on to what we did, then we sure can't take a chance or doing another hit."

"That's a shame because that was some sweet paper we got from that."

"True, the money sure was great, but we knew it couldn't go on forever. Luckily the agency is making so much money we might not even miss it. Plus, I know you should still have at least a million or two in the bank because you couldn't have blown all that money."

"You know I still have most of it, plus I still have my street operation."

"Maybe you should think about getting out of the life all together. You should have enough cash to last you the rest of your life."

"And do what?"

"And enjoy your hard-earned riches, that's what. We have more than enough money to last us the rest of our lives especially if we don't go crazy spending it on stupid shit."

"This street shit is all I know. I ain't built to do anything else. You're the one who went to college and got a serious shot at the legit life. I ain't ready to live the retired playboy lifestyle. That crap would bore me to death. You know me, baby. I got to be out here in these streets making moves and making things happen."

"You're my man for life. You could come and work at the agency. You could work with EZ and the other rappers. Hell, nobody knows the streets better than you."

"That's something to consider, but I don't think I'm ready for the straight life yet."

"Well, think about it. It's there for you if you want it. Meanwhile, let me put that other plan in motion and I'll let you know how it works out."

. . . . .

Ebony walked into Captain Riley's office and, although he was on the phone, took the seat that he gestured her into. She was surprised to see that Lt. Melendez was here as well. As the captain was hanging the phone up, Ebony said, "I got your message. It said that it is urgent that I see you right away so I came right in."

"You're killing me, Delaney. I broke every rule in the book to give you a chance to conduct that investigation that was so important to you and you do this to me.'

"Captain?!"

"Don't look at me like you don't know what I'm talking about. I tell you it was only because your record was so damn good that I gave you such incredible leeway and now you got my ass in a sling."

"Captain, I don't know what you're talking about."

"I'm talking about the Commissioner calling me downtown and chewing on my ass for an hour like it was a piece of week old beef jerky."

"But why?"

"Because that's what he usually does when he's called on the carpet by the mayor."

"Captain, I don't want to appear dense or anything, but could you start at the beginning because I'm not following what happened."

"You went, confronted and insulted Brandon Barnett, who complained to State Assemblyman Green, who complained to the Mayor about rogue police running out of control and launching personal vendettas."

"How was it a personal vendetta because I'm against his murdering innocent women?"

"According to Barnett, it was a personal vendetta because you have a thing for him and you propositioned him at the reception that he had for Mr. Green but he rebuked your advances and you just won't take no for an answer. So now like a woman scorned you are after him. Did you go to the reception he had for Assemblyman Green?"

"Yeah, because I wanted to size him up and get a feel for our adversary and whether he did the things I suspected he did."

"Did you sleep with him?"

"Absolutely not. Is that what he said?"

"He sure implied it. My question is: why did you even go to see him? Is that how you usually run an investigation? Do you usually alert the suspect that we think he committed a crime?"

"No, but I was afraid that they were going to go to ground. I did it to ratchet up the pressure a little bit. Obviously it must have worked."

"It doesn't appear so obvious to me. Why do you say it worked?"

"He must be panicking. Why else would he go to such drastic measures to get me off his trail?"

"And it worked. How do you think it appeared to the Commissioner? Here's one of our top detectives, who happens to be out on personal leave, accusing one of the city's top businessman of all types of crimes, none of which can she prove. In fact, they were talking about suspending you."

"Shoot, if they are going to fall for such a simple gambit, let them suspend me."

"Now, Ebony, don't overreact," Melendez said.

"Overreact my ass. I have been one of this city's top detectives and received numerous commendations and citations and they're taking that piece of filth's word over mine?"

"They're not taking anybody's anything. They only heard one side of the story."

"Which they assumed to be true."

"Look let me talk to them and tell them what going on and see what they say about that."

"You do what you have to do. Meanwhile, *I'm gonna handle my business and bring this asshole down.*"

After leaving the precinct Ebony headed back home to have a little lunch and regain her composure. On one hand, she was starting to feel like she was making a little headway in the investigation because she had turned the pressure up on Barnett and he had reacted in a way that reeked of desperation. She was confident that if she continued it was only a matter of time before she got a big break in the case. The NYPD higher echelon may have forgotten it, but that's how successful investigations occurred. You kept pounding away and picking away until you got a break that would solve the whole thing. It was rarely a stroke of genius or some suspect who developed a conscience and confessed to the crime, but it was perseverance and hard work that accomplished the deed.

She was sure that the higher-ups had either forgotten or never knew how this was done. She was getting damn tired of the political games and the other nonsense that they engaged in that had nothing to do with solving crimes. If they thought she was going to ease up on Barnett because he was friends with some politician or had that politician in his pocket, they had another think coming. She knew Barnett had done this, and there was nothing short of illegal activities that she wouldn't do to bring him to justice. The move that he tried not only pissed her off, it also made her more determined.

Maybe because she was in such a foul mood, she decided to give herself a treat and stopped at the fish market and got herself some lump crabmeat and was making some delicious crab cakes when the phone rang. She answered the phone like she was expecting more bad news from downtown with a somber if not grim "Hello."

"Hey, Ebony, this is Malachi. How are you doing?"

"Oh hi, Mal, I've had better days. How are you?"

"Is everything all right? Is it anything I can help you with?"

"Thanks for caring, but it's just the regular departmental bullshit and it's getting on my nerves. Not only aren't they giving me the kind of help we deserve, but now they're getting in the way."

"Come on, baby, you know how the system is. It's not designed to be efficient and get the job done. The hardest job sometimes is to not let it frustrate you and still be productive. This may not be of much comfort, but I have complete confidence in you and I know that Tanya and those other women will get some measure of justice because of you. Meanwhile, I have something that might make you feel a little better."

"Don't tell me you're going to again volunteer to give me a bath and a massage?"

"Even though giving you a massage sounds damn good to me, that's not what I have in mind."

"Seeing me naked and being able to run your hands all over me is not what you have in mind?"

"Believe me, that would be more like a dream come true, but I have something else on my mind today. Are you available for me to stop over in about three hours?"

"I can be."

"Good, I'll see you then."

Ebony didn't want to stop and analyze the situation, but more and more of late she always felt a lot better after her conversations with Malachi and usually after one of their dates, she was eagerly looking forward to the next one. It was true they hadn't made love yet, but secretly she was starting to anticipate what it would be like. She was still enjoying the afterglow of their last conversation and anticipating his visit as she tried to decide whether she had the time to shower and change clothes when the intercom rang as someone was trying to gain entrance into her building. Figuring that maybe Ted had stopped by to discuss the case, she just buzzed him in without asking who it was. Opening the door and expecting to see Ted, she was surprised to see her father coming up the stairs.

"Dad, what are you doing here?"

"Don't you know better than to buzz people in without asking who it is first?"

"Be serious, Dad, who would try to break in here? If a criminal wanted to rob somebody, I think they would find an easier target than the house of a cop."

"Still, you can't be too careful."

After her father entered her home and she closed the door behind him, she turned and gave him a hug. She was surprised because he only half-heartedly returned her hug. "What brings you here in the middle of the day?"

"I needed to talk to you."

"Have a seat. Would you like a cup of coffee or tea?"

"No, thank you, I just had lunch."

"Well, at least make yourself comfortable. What's on your mind?"

"You know I love you, just like I love all my kids. Each of my kids is special in their own right and I try to stay out of the way and let them find themselves and who they are going to be. You were always my brightest and smartest child and I always thought you would go the furthest. Let's be honest, there's nothing that you couldn't accomplish if you put your mind to it. I guess that's why I thought you were so rebellious. Sometimes it seemed you went out of your way to do and be the opposite of everything I stood for or what I thought you would be. I never said anything. I just tried to let you do your own thing. I figured it would be something you would outgrow. But the older you get, the worse you get."

"Dad, what are you talking about—"

"Ebony, let me get this out. I've had this in me to say for a long time but I can't keep biting my tongue not any more. When you went to college, your mother and I figured you would be a lawyer, and we knew if you did, you would be a brilliant one with the potential to one day be a judge. Just when I felt that I could deal with you becoming a lawyer and not a doctor or an engineer like you always talked about. Remember when you said you wanted to become a scientist and design limbs for people who had lost theirs?"

"Dad, that was when I was ten years old."

"I know, but you can see how I thought you were on a different path, and I must admit I was kind of excited about it. What does our community need more than people in the medical field? Then not only didn't you become a doctor or even a lawyer, but you became a cop. Not only didn't you become someone who could be of service to our people, you became one of *those* people the system uses to oppress our people."

"You know I don't agree that's the role of the police."

"I don't see how you can disagree. If they put in a cruel or unjust law and the people refuse to obey it or take to the streets to protest it, the police are the ground forces that will enforce it by arresting or imprisoning the people."

"Dad, this is an old argument and we stand to gain nothing by fighting about it again."

"That's true, so anyway as if your being a cop wasn't bad enough, you had to go and marry a White man. And a DA on top of that. What happened that you started hating Black men so much? Was it something that happened to you or did you hate me that much?"

"I don't hate Black men, and I sure don't hate you. We disagree a lot, and we argue because both of us strongly believe in our opinions."

"Then why did you marry him? I don't know if you thought you loved him or just married him because he was White but you had to know that marriage had no chance of working. I didn't disown you and I tried my best to accept that marriage, but I won't lie and say I was disappointed when y'all got divorced. I thought you had finally come around and accepted who and what you are in the grand order of things when you showed interest in Brandon Barnett. But now you're harassing him because he is not interested in you?"

"Excuse me? Where did you get such a preposterous idea?"

"Brandon called Assemblyman Green who asked me what your problem was. He remembered that you're my daughter and that I brought you to his reception and his wife saw you talking to Brandon. When did you get like the rest of those cops and start abusing your power as a policewoman? Just because a man isn't interested in your advances, you think it's okay to ruin his reputation? Why do you hate Black men so much that you will go after a Black man just because he doesn't want you, or was it because he's so successful? When did you get so arrogant, or is it desperate?"

"*Stop*! Hold it right there. Where did you get such a ridiculous idea? First of all, I did *not* proposition Brandon Barnett nor did I ever have or express a romantic interest in him. You're treating him like he is some kind of hero. Yeah, I find him repulsive but not because he's Black but because he's a low-life piece of shit. You take such pleasure in looking down on cops and seeing them as your enemies and true there are some cops who are just as you say but not all cops. There are some people out there who rob, rape, and murder Black and poor people, and some of the people who do it are Black. Who do those victims turn to?

"If a cop kills a Black kid there are protests in the street, as there should be. But Black kids are killing other Black kids and who is protesting that? When a Black person comes home from work and someone has broken into their house, who do they call but the police? They want and deserve the same justice that a White person wants and deserves and I try to give it to them. When—"

"Ebony, I—"

"No, don't interrupt me, Dad. I've listen to you pop this bullspit for too long and I've taken far too much of it. I've never really explained myself because I didn't have to and I shouldn't have had to because as my father you should have trusted me, but now you come in here accusing me of things based on the word of that low-life piece of filth. Do you want to know why I became a cop? Do you remember my good friend Julie Morales that I hung with in high school? She went with her cousins and some friends to a club in midtown to celebrate the cousin's birthday. Someone must have slipped something in her drink because when her cousin wasn't looking, she went outside with a guy she was dancing with to smoke a joint and they made her go to one of the guy's house. They found her three days later, beaten and raped. She was barely hanging on to life, but she was able to tell the cops that she was taken by seven to nine guys who made her take drugs and took turns having sex with her during that time. She said she had been raped over twenty times. The guys were Black *and* White. Because one of the boys was the son of a rich businessman, no one was ever arrested for that crime. The police said that because she had a reputation for sleeping around at the high school and she couldn't say who gave her the drugs, no crime had been committed.

"They told that eighteen-year-old girl that because she wasn't a virgin and had three different boyfriends her senior year in high school, she must have wanted it or asked for it. That she wanted to be drugged and raped repeatedly over three days by a bunch of pigs that she had never seen before. She never recovered. She had a nervous breakdown and tried to kill herself and has been in and out of mental institutions ever since then. The guys, meanwhile, were able to go about their lives and attend college and work on careers with just a stern admonishment from a judge. No one was ever arrested or convicted of a crime. Where was the justice for Julie? Where were the protests for her? Did the cops investigate and try to build up a case to give that girl some justice, or did they just say that's what that Puerto Rican deserves?"

"I didn't know, Ebony. You never told me."

"Telling you or anyone else wouldn't have done Julie any good, but what might do some good for the next Julie or other victim is a cop who tries to bring those people who hurt people of any color or age or sex to justice. That's what I vowed to do and that's what I do, and whether you like it or not, I'm damn good at it. That gives my life new meaning and that is why I'm after Barnett. Trust me, I get plenty of offers from Black, White, and Brown men. My only interest in Brandon Barnett is in bringing him to justice."

"So you think he committed a crime?"

"Barnett is *not* what he appears to be, but I won't discuss a case while the investigation is going on. Believe me, though, he's not the type of man whose virtues you want to extol. When the truth comes out you'll be shocked at what you hear. Till then, you need to learn how to trust me."

Ebony was so upset from her argument with her father that she almost forgot she had a date with Malachi until less than fifteen minutes before he was to arrive. She showered in a hurry and was able to finish dressing just as he arrived. She opened the door and was surprised to see he had his niece Zoe with him.

"Zoe, you remember Miss Ebony, don't you?"

"Hi, Miss Ebony, it's nice to see you again."

"It is good to see you too, Zoe. This is a bit of a surprise, what are you doing here?"

"I owed her a treat because she got all A's on her last report card so I had her flown up here to spend a few days with me."

"Then we'll really have to make this visit extra special. Is there anything in particular you would like to do?"

"No, ma'am, whatever you want to do will be fine with me."

"How about tomorrow morning I take you shopping and then we go and get our nails and feet done and later we meet your uncle to go to dinner at a fancy restaurant and see a Broadway play. Would you like that?"

"Oh yes, ma'am, that would be great."

"Ebony, that's very nice but I can't ask you to do that," Malachi said.

"You're not asking, Mal, it would be my pleasure. After all, Zoe is a great kid, and she has earned at least that much. There's only thing that I require."

"What's that, dear?"

"That she stops calling me 'ma'am.' She's making me feel older than my mother," Ebony said with a wink. "Can you do that, Zoe?"

"Yes, ma'am, I can. Oops. I mean I sure can, Miss Ebony."

"I'll tell you what. While you're here, you're going to be my special friend so you can call me Ebony. Would you like that?"

"I would like that a whole lot."

"Okay then, Malachi, what are we doing today?"

"It's a little late to go to the Statue of Liberty so I figured we would go to the Museum of Natural History and then either to the Planetarium or to the Empire State building and let her look down on New York City at dark as the lights come on."

"May I use your bathroom?" Zoe asked.

"Sure, sweetie, it's right through there," Ebony said as she pointed the way to Zoe. After Zoe left the room, Ebony turned to Malachi and said, "Since we have plans for early tomorrow, would you like to spend the night at my place?"

"I kind of thought the first time you offered me the chance to spend the night with you would be under different circumstances but nonetheless we accept."

"It's not quite what I envisioned either but it might be fun anyway. We can get some movies and lots of Thai or Chinese food or either we can play a rousing game of Monopoly or Dominoes. It will be nice and it might be just what Zoe needs and that still leaves us with our first night together alone to look forward to."

"I still have an intimate night with you to look forward to?"

"It could be."

"I sure hope so and I hope after you hear my snoring you don't change your mind."

"Yeah, that could be a deal breaker," Ebony said with a laugh as Zoe reentered the room. "Okay, if you're ready we can go."

· · · · ·

When Ebony returned home late the following day, she was still wrapped in the glow of the most enjoyable thirty-six or so hours she had ever spent. She had thoroughly enjoyed herself with Malachi and Zoe. For the first time in many months, she imagined what it would be like to be married and have a happy family. The argument with her father, the bureaucracy of the NYPD, and the complexities of the Barnett case for a short while were all distant memories. Even several urgent messages from Ted asking that she stop by his office first thing in the morning couldn't spoil her great mood. She went to bed with memories of the magic on Zoe's face as she marveled in the *Lion King* and stirred by the warmth in her lions from an increasing desire for Malachi.

She arrived at Ted's office the next morning shortly after he arrived for work.

"Good morning, Ted. I got your message so I came right over. What's going on?"

"I called you a couple of times yesterday but you didn't answer my page."

"I went out with a couple of friends and I forgot my cell phone in the car."

"I wanted to speak with you because I have some good news for you. I must admit when you first decided to confront Barnett I thought it was a mistake. I thought you were jumping the gun and exposing our hand by needlessly alerting the suspect but your instincts were right on. That move got better results than I think even you anticipated."

"I'm glad something good came out of it because I got a reaction out of him but so far it's just been a nuisance."

"Why? What happened?"

"That creep went running like a little kid to Assemblyman Green and gave him some bullshit line that I was harassing him and trying to set him up for committing murder because he turned down my sexual advances. Green then complained to the Mayor who then complained to the Commissioner who pulled my Captain on the carpet. Mr. Green even complained to my father."

"They didn't believe that crap, did they?"

"No, but it took some serious explaining on my part to set things straight. I guess he thought he could scare me off by trying to get my superiors to intimidate me. I don't think he knows me every well."

"That's not all he did. Listen to this." Ted got up and put a tape into the tape player. Within minutes the room was filled with the recent meeting between Justice and Brandon.

"Where did you get this?"

"Remember we alerted the DEA to Permentier and his growing operation. Well, unbeknownst to him they placed him under twenty-four-hour surveillance, including wiretaps. He led them right to his meeting with Barnett that they not only taped but also filmed."

"I knew it. I knew someone had to be arranging the muscle end of the operation for Barnett. It looks like the two of them planned the murders and then Permentier got the muscle to carry it out. My question is what can we do with this? Is this admissible in court?"

"It's admissible, but it doesn't really prove what they did. Associating with a known felon is not a crime, and this doesn't prove that they committed any of the murders. Once we get some more evidence, this can be a significant piece though. It establishes their relationship and indicates that they have planned some murders. We have to prove they actually did it and didn't just talk about it. We're starting to make some progress. What do you think should be our next move?"

"We need Omar or we at least need to find him before they do. It seems he either left town or was chased out of town. I don't know what happened between him and them, but it's possible that he might be a weak link that we could use against them. If we can catch him and convince him that we have a strong case against him, he might be persuaded to testify against them as the ones who set it all up. Why don't you make a serious attempt to see if you can locate him?"

"What are you going to do?"

"I don't believe in messing with success. If turning that little bit of pressure up on Barnett got him to make one mistake, maybe if I turn up more pressure will make him commit another one or an even bigger mistake."

"Be careful, Ebony. We're talking about a murderer here. If he gets desperate, he might do something stupid."

"Don't worry about me. I can handle myself."

· · · · ·

Ebony checked the clock to see if she had time for another cup of coffee before meeting Malachi and Zoe. Ebony loved the delectable aroma of this special blend of coffee beans, and when her mind was deep in thought, coffee seemed to help her unwind and focus on what she was thinking about. For just a few moments she put aside her thoughts on Brandon Barnett and the ensuing investigation. She was always very careful not to let whatever investigation she was conducting consume and overwhelm her. She had gotten so passionate about this case, if she wasn't careful that would definitely be the case. Though it was a bit of a struggle, she would take her entire thoughts on the Barnett case and put it in a little box and tuck it away in a corner of her mind.

Ebony was also tempted to avoid thinking about her feelings for Mal. The truth of the matter is that she would be smart not to think about it and just enjoy it, but she wasn't that smart regarding matters of the heart. She told herself she couldn't have developed such strong feelings about him because: a) she hadn't known him that long and b) they hadn't even made love yet. Truthfully the reason they hadn't made love was not because she didn't desire him, because she did very badly, but deep inside she feared that intimate act would chase away the magic that they were currently enjoying. Sometimes crossing that line into intimacy made things more real, more human, and altogether too realistic. There was something about feeling like a young teenager in love that was very fresh and new and for the lack of a better word: magical. With new love there were no boundaries and anything and everything was possible and that felt incredible.

What she did know was the minute she left him she started looking forward to when she would see him again. She didn't care what they did because she knew she would enjoy it. Mal had a way of changing the simplest things into fun and making even an ordinary act, like a walk in the park seems alive and new. He always made her feel special. When she was with him, she felt that his attention, his focus, and his world for just brief moments centered on her. When she kissed him, she felt she had to hold on to something or she could lose herself in him.

As great and amazing as it felt, today she felt she had to stop and assess things before she could move on with their day. She was so excited she almost felt giddy and bubbly but one large problem had cropped up in a small package—Zoe. At first Zoe was a little withdrawn, but as she got more comfortable, she opened up and revealed what a fantastic little ten-year-old she was. She was smart, funny, witty, sensitive, and all around just about perfect. If Ebony wasn't careful she would love this child like she had come from her womb. She wanted to spoil her and pamper her and heap love on her like she had Trump's millions. *But* this girl had suffered an incredible loss.

She had lost her mother *and* her father. Even if the father was a slime ball who had contributed to the death of her mother, Zoe didn't know that, and if Ebony had any say in the matter, she would never know. She truly loved both her parents, and didn't almost all little girls worship their daddies? Wasn't that what God made daddies for? If Ebony exposed the truth about Brandon Barnett, wouldn't she also expose the truth about Larry Richardson?

Ebony's other problem was: how sincere were her feelings about Malachi? Was this just a whirlwind romance, or was Malachi destined to spend the rest of forever with her? Just that simple possibility brought a smile to her lips and a song to her heart. But what if Malachi didn't feel the same way? What if he was just lonely being so far away from home in Texas and she was just filling some of the void? Did she have the right to allow Zoe to get closer to her if she might be walking out of her life one day soon? Her parents didn't have a choice about leaving her, but Ebony did. Shouldn't she at least ask Malachi how he felt about her before she allowed Zoe to get any closer? Didn't she owe that fantastic little girl that much?

On the other hand, Malachi was the one who brought Zoe around and invited Ebony to join them on their many excursions into the beauty of New York City. Ebony had enjoyed helping the city come alive for that little girl. What had started as a chance to be nice to a little girl and show her a good time had turned into so much more. From shopping at Bloomie's to the Baby Phat boutique at Macy's to the Statue of Liberty to lunch in Chinatown to the incredible view of New York city from the top of the Empire State Building to the wonder of the *Lion King* on Broadway to the five-story movie screen at the 3D Imax, the last few days had been full of beauty and wonder. She had seen sides of New York that she hadn't seen since she was a little girl on her daddy's arm.

Malachi was nothing if he wasn't thoughtful and considerate. Malachi had done a masterful job of making her and Zoe feel like princesses of the city. He could be attentive and relaxed and fun and protective all at the same time but was he aware of the effect this week was having on them both? Surely Malachi had to have thought of all these things. Surely he had to think about the emotional impact this week could have had on her and Zoe. Surely he had to. But Malachi was a man and did they even think about such complex, emotional matters?

What was she gonna do about today? Then she realized, she didn't like Zoe because she was Malachi's niece. She liked Zoe because of Zoe, and if that was the case she could continue to be Zoe's friend regardless of how her relationship turned out with Malachi. She could still call her and write her and even have her visit her. She was going to be Zoe's friend because she was starting to love Zoe. The fact that she was starting to love Malachi as well was in this case an irrelevant factor.

Having gotten a degree of peace related to her relationship with Zoe, Ebony prepared for the day with renewed zeal and enthusiasm. She finished dressing mere moments before Mal and Zoe arrived.

"Hi, beautiful. How are you feeling this morning?" Malachi said as he gave Ebony one of those spine-tingling kisses.

"I'm feeling great. How was your night?" Ebony responded.

"It was great except I was missing you. Plus, a certain little one snuck into my bed in the middle of the night and I had to spend the rest of the night sleeping with her little feet in my face," Mal said.

"What's wrong, Zoe, couldn't you sleep?" Ebony asked.

"I was fine, but Uncle Malachi was feeling lonely so I went to keep him company," Zoe said.

"Really? What was wrong with him?"

"I think he was sad because he was missing you."

"Why do you say that?"

"Because he had this real sad look on his face and he was moaning to himself."

Laughing, Ebony asked, "Oh yeah? What did it sound like?"

"Something like 'ooowah' 'ooowah.'" The face that Zoe made to accompany the sound was so funny that Ebony could not stop laughing. Finally, Malachi had to intervene, "Okay, that's enough out of you two. I'm not gonna spend the day being the butt of your jokes." At which point Zoe started laughing hysterically. "What is so funny?"

"You said butt."

"And why that is so funny to you?"

"You said a nasty word."

"It's not that kind of butt—oh never mind."

"Miss Ebony, is Uncle Malachi your boyfriend?" Zoe asked.

Looking at the laughing Ebony, Malachi said, "Oh you are in some mood today."

"What did Malachi tell you?" Ebony asked.

"He said to ask you."

"Well, he's a very good friend and he is a boy so—"

"That's not what I mean," Zoe said.

"Well—"

"Okay, that's enough; it's time for you to get out of adult's business young lady," Malachi said. "Ebony, what would you like to do today?"

"I think it's time we went up to Harlem and visit the Schomberg Library and where Langston Hughes and James Baldwin lived."

"We're going to the library today?"

"This library is not like any library you ever been to. Don't worry, you'll like it, and as an extra treat for dinner we're gonna eat on a yacht that cruise around Manhattan. I got to get home early because I have some business that I have to get back to. It's been a lot of fun these last couple of days but I have some things I have to get to."

. . . . .

Ebony sat in her car parked in front of IMA's building, while she patiently waited for Brandon to leave his office. She wanted to confront him outside his office or comfort zone, as she was trying to make him uncomfortable and invoke a response out of him. Barnett had appeared to be a cool and calculated customer on the surface, but just the little bit of pressure she had exerted had developed a couple of cracks in his cool veneer.

While she was waiting, she mentally debated different ways to irritate and to try to make him lose control. She could turn up the pressure by letting him know some of the things they knew about him. The question was how much to let him know. She didn't want to reveal too much because there was a chance he then might try to cover his tracks.

After waiting almost an hour, Ebony saw Barnett exit the building accompanied by a very attractive Eurasian woman. As always, Barnett was impeccably dressed in a tailor-made suit, and expensive Italian loafers completed the outfit. As Ebony walked up they were deeply engaged in conversation and Ebony noticed an alluring look in the girl's eyes as she spoke to Barnett. Ebony didn't hesitate to interrupt their conversation "I can't believe they still allow you to contaminate our streets with your presence. Don't worry, Barnett, that's a situation I will be fixing for you shortly."

Annoyed, Brandon turned and, seeing Ebony, said, "Detective Delaney, I wish I could say it's good to see you but that would be a lie. What do you want?"

"What I want is to put your ass behind bars where you belong." Turning to Brandon's companion, Ebony said, "Didn't anyone ever warn you about being careful of the company you keep? If they didn't, I will tell you that this *man* is not the type of person you want to be around and he sure isn't someone you want to be seen in public with. I hate to admit it, but our society has certain dregs and low-lives that we can't seem to get rid of. It's like when you flush the toilet and there is some persistent waste that refuses to go down the drain and keeps floating to the top. That's how Barnett is, but don't worry, because we're gonna keep flushing until we can finally get rid of him once and for all. Be careful that you don't get flushed away with him."

"Detective, I've told you once and I will tell you again I am not interested in you. I am only used to dealing with *ladies* and you *damn* sure don't qualify. I know you think you're fine and you're not accustomed to men telling you 'no' but you're just not my style."

"A maggot is more your style, but you can run this bullshit all you want but you know I would rather kiss a rabid dog then have you touch me."

"Then leave me alone."

"The one thing you can count on is me not leaving you alone until you are locked away in prison the way you deserve to be."

"I understand that my complaint was registered with your superiors and they instructed you to leave me alone."

"Their instruction was to 'stop sexually harassing you or pursuing you' and if that was what I was doing I would gladly have followed their orders. But I not chasing you for romance, I'm chasing you for murder and I won't stop until you are brought to justice."

Turning to his companion, Brandon said, "Mia, this detective is intent on continuing to slander me and this is nothing you should hear. Please take my keys and meet me in the car." After the girl had left, Brandon turned to Ebony and said, "What is your problem? Why are you hassling me? I know most of you Black cops are the establishment type of *Negroes* but you're the biggest *Tom* I ever met. You are so busy trying to be White that you even married a White boy. I would have thought after he dumped you, you would have wanted to come back home and get with a Black man instead of still trying to bring us down."

"Don't you dare insult Black *men by trying to associate with them.* If you were a *man* you would have stepped to me like a man and tried to handle your business instead of running to your political patsies like the little *bitch* that you are. You try to act like you're so tough and thug, but the only ones I see you stepping to are women. If you decide you want to be a man, let me know the time and place and we'll handle this between us without the legal system even getting involved."

"Bitch, all you try to do is hide behind that fucking badge. If you wasn't a cop, I would—"

"You wouldn't do shit except do the same thing you always do which is to hire someone else to handle your business for you."

"I don't know what in the hell you're talking about. Look, I don't like you and I can see you don't like me so why don't you go your own way and leave me the hell alone?"

"I can't and I won't because some pretty important people send me after you."

"I also had some pretty important people like your mayor and commissioner instruct you to leave me alone."

"There are not as important as Larry, Zoe, and Jaleesa Richardson, who want to know why you took both of their parents from them, or Tyshawn and Tyler Burleson who have to face each day without their mother thanks to you. Do you want me to go on?"

"I don't know what you're talking about."

"Instead of standing here denying what we both know you did, if I were you I would be worrying about where Omar is and I would be worrying about how much he is telling me about you and Justice Permentier and your little side hustle. I got enough information to bring down Permentier's drug operation but I want to get both of you for the big one. Multiple murders in the first degree. You're right. You don't want to see me because maybe the next time I see you I will be slapping these cuffs on your ass. I got your punk ass just where I want you and I'm just gift wrapping you for the electric chair. Life in prison is too good for you. I will have you prosecuted in a state that has the death penalty so I can watch you fry. I will say goodbye for now but watch for me because I'll be coming for your ass soon," Ebony said as she walked off and then she said over her shoulder, "Oh yeah, don't try to leave the country because I got my eyes on you, and if you try to run I won't hesitate to put a bullet in your ass."

"Who does that bitch think she's talking to? She must not know who the hell I am or what I will do to her. No wonder she confronted me in public because if we were in private I would have smoked her my damn self. That bitch is dead, dead, dead and I don't give a damn if she's a cop or not. I ain't letting anyone talk to me like that without paying the cost. I don't care if she is a pig or not. She thinks 'cause she is five-O, she's safe? Well, she has another thing coming. Hi-yellow trick! I'm gonna piss on that bitch's grave if it the last thing I do," Brandon thought as he headed to his car. The conversation with Ebony had infuriated him to the point where he was in danger of losing control. He was heading to his car with the intention of taking the Glock he kept stashed in his Beamer and following Ebony and putting two in the back of her head.

When he got to the car he realized that he had forgotten Mia and any plans to kill Ebony would have to be put on hold but there was no way he could deal with Mia or any woman in his current state of mind.

"Yo, Hon, look here. Something came up and I'm gonna need a raincheck on our date."

"But, Brandon, I leave for a photo shoot in Europe tomorrow."

"Then we'll get together when you get back."

"But I'm hungry now and I cleared my schedule so I could see you today. I know you didn't let the foolish things that woman said upset you so much that you're cancelling our date. I know she was just saying those things because she was jealous."

"Mia, this is not about her or any woman. This is about business. My business and I have to take care of it right now. I can't even take the time to take you home. Go back up to the office and have my assistant call a limo to take you home."

Mia got out the car and stood there pouting with her arms folded across her chest "That's okay, I'll take a cab home. Will you at least call me later?"

Forcing himself to smile, Brandon said, "I sure will, baby. I will try to stop by and maybe it will still be early enough to grab a bite to eat." As he drove off, Brandon thought "What is there about women that would allow you to treat them any kind of way? Mia is one of the most beautiful women in the world and the worse I treat her the more she seems to like it. If I was a woman and a man left me standing in the street, he could never call me again. Instead, this fine-ass woman will sit and wait for my call, and if I want, I can show up later with some jive-ass flowers and spend the night fucking her. Women are so weak and stupid. Shit, my mama was probably no better. She claimed to have been out working when she was probably out getting her freak on. Bitches ain't shit! That Delaney bitch ain't no better. She's probably a butch. That would explain why she walks around trying to be all hard and shit. She probably wants to be a man. Oh shoot, if everyone at the police department knows she's gay, surely they won't believe she's harassing me because I turned down her advances. She wouldn't proposition me. She might proposition my girlfriend but not me. I'm gonna have to switch up the reason why she's giving me a hard time. What am I thinking? That chick is dead and she won't be around long enough to matter."

Brandon drove on about a half a mile before he saw a working pay phone on a corner. He parked and called Justice. "J, get free man. Get one of the special joints and call me back at this number in ten minutes. 911 baby." He immediately hung up and waited for Justice to call him back.

Justice went to the vault and opened one of the new cell phones they kept just for emergencies. As it was a new phone, it was virtually untraceable. After the call was completed Justice would destroy the phone. Justice got the cell phone's number off his cell phone's caller id and called Brandon back. "What's shaking, Pred?"

"Are you good? Are you using a new phone?"

"Of course, dude, I know the procedure. Why the 911 call?"

"We got problems."

"How so? Talk to me."

"It's that Delaney detective bitch. She ran up on me in the street with all kind of accusations."

"So how is that different? She's been running up on you for a minute now. Don't worry about her. She ain't got nuthin."

"Not this time. This wasn't a fishing expedition. She knew details on the Richardson job and the Burleson hit as well. She also dropped your name. Now how in the hell does she know your name or about your involvement with me?"

"Don't look here man. I ain't let nothing out. The leak ain't on my end"

"Then how does she know?"

"I don't know you tell me."

"Don't get me wrong Just. I know it wasn't you that would anything slip. You're my nigga for life and you've proven that over and over. I am just trying to figure out where the leak is so we can plug it. She also mentioned Omar and hinted that they have him in custody. Maybe they do have him and he the one babbling and spilling his guts."

"If she does have him, is there a way we can get to him?" Justice asked.

Brandon paused and took a deep breath before he said, "This chick has me so tight that all I want to do is choke the life out of her, but we're not thinking clearly. If she has Omar and so much information on us, why isn't she making an arrest? Is she bluffing or trying to goad me into revealing something?"

"She must know something because you said she knew about our connection and about some of the hits."

"Then why haven't we been arrested? Something's just not adding up."

"Well, we better figure it out because I'm not gonna sit around waiting for them to lower the boom," Justice said.

"When was the last time you checked with our guy downtown at Police Plaza?"

"That's strange that you would bring that up. I spoke with him yesterday. I offered him a five thousand dollar bonus if he can come up with anything on Omar as to his whereabouts or if he is picked up somewhere. The way I was thinking is that Omar is one trifling-ass nigger and he couldn't have left here with enough cash to stay out of sight for too long. So he must be working in the street somewhere making that money. *If* he was picked up by anybody he would show up in the system. If he was picked up by anybody, our guy would have been able to find out. So I think it's safe to say he's not in custody anywhere. I had him check to see if there is an investigation into either one of us and there isn't. He also called some friends at the precinct to see what Delaney is working on, and dig this, she out on personal leave."

"You mean this Delaney broad isn't even part of a legit investigation?"

"Exactly."

"That's means she is going solo or doing some renegade shit."

"Most likely."

"So if we eliminate her, this whole problem would go away."

"Whoa, partner. Do you realize what you're talking about here? You want to kill a New York City cop and a female cop at that? You bugging, man. Do you know what kind of heat will come down if we do a cop?"

"Not if we do it right. If she's working solo she probably hasn't even told anybody what she knows. So even though I want to do this bitch myself, we can hire some out of town talent to do the deed. Get those cutthroat boys from Baltimore that you were telling about to do it. Have them rape the chick. Make it look like a gang rape that got out of control. Pay them whatever they ask to do it right."

"You do realize how risky this is?"

"Not as risky as waiting until she gets enough information to tell someone or to come after us herself. Either way, waiting won't do us any good. Get them boys up here and on this thing right away. Tell them if they do some real dirty shit to her before they kill her, I'll pay extra."

"Pred, are you sure about this, man? Why don't we take a pause, cool off and see if there is another way to handle this?"

"Waiting will serve no purpose, man. I want this bitch dead, and the sooner the better."

· · · · ·

An exhausted Ebony was getting frustrated because she had been driving around for almost ten minutes while she searched for a parking spot. As this was a residential neighborhood with few driveways, parking was a premium.

She finally found a parking spot about five blocks from her house. The unfortunate part was not just that it was so far from her house but she would have had to move it by 8 A.M. the next morning because of alternate side of the street parking. She didn't know why it was necessary to have alternate side parking four days a week. They were lucky if the street cleaners that the streets had to be clear for came to their neighborhood two days a week, not to mention four. She was sure there were some weeks they didn't come down these blocks at all.

She loved living in this section of Brooklyn. The tree lined streets that provided shade in the sunlight and shadows after dark didn't seem dark and foreboding to her, they seemed quiet and intimate. After the 9/11 disaster, many of the yuppies and professionals from Manhattan had fled to this section of Brooklyn probably because it was a few minutes' train ride to lower Manhattan and midtown. The influx of new money was serving to renovate this neighborhood, and it had quickly become an upper middle-class/working family's neighborhood. There were luxury high rises sprouting up among the many two-story brownstones, though Ebony couldn't see paying the exorbitant prices they were seeking.

As Ebony headed home, she put on her iPod to kill the boredom during the long walk. As the neighborhood became more upscale and family-oriented, the police patrols became more frequent and crime greatly decreased. The music was a minor diversion, but her mind was focused on the meetings she had that morning with Ted and Gary as they brought each other up to date on developments in the case.

Though Gary was still on assignment at the precinct, he was becoming more involved in the case, and since he had gone with her to confront Barnett the first time she felt obliged to keep him abreast with whatever was going on in the case. Gary was less than thrilled with her confrontation of Barnett. He seemed to feel that putting Barnett on edge could be dangerous. Ebony didn't agree because she was convinced that Barnett was too intelligent to go after a NY police officer.

After the meetings, she spent the remainder of the day looking at thousands of photographs of suspects who came close to Omar's description who had been arrested in the past six months in NYC, Washington, Philadelphia, Charlotte, and Baltimore. Her thinking was if he left New York he probably would have gone to another big city. Ted had assigned two agents to do the same thing utilizing the federal computer system. They all felt if they could find Omar he could be the link to tie it all together. Based on what she heard on the tape between Barnett and Permentier, she was sure that facing murders charges, Omar could be convinced to testify against Barnett and Permentier in exchange for a lesser charge.

As she turned onto her block, Ebony checked behind her because she got the feeling that someone was following her. Seeing that no one was there, she accredited it to her imagination and fatigue and continued on home. She only had a few minutes to get ready for her date with Malachi. If she wasn't sure that Malachi was probably on his way to her by now, she was so tired she would have cancelled their date.

As she climbed the stairs to the entrance to her building, one of her favorite songs, Earth, Wind and Fire's "Boogie Wonderland," came on her iPod. The rhythmic bass line and syncopated horns always gave her a burst of energy. As she joined the Emotions in singing the background vocals, she cut a little step as she went through the front door. Out of the corner of her eye she saw two men rushing up the stairs trying to catch the door before it closed.

It really didn't startle her because she figured it was the teenage boy who lived on the first floor and one of his friends trying to get in. "He must have forgot his key again," she thought. As she neared the top of the first flight of stairs she noticed that the two males were coming up the stairs behind her. She turned to identify the men and ask them where they were going when she simultaneously saw a glint of metal in one man's hand and felt someone rushing at her from the landing above her. Turning too late, she felt the man from above strike her with a hard metal object, probably a gun, in the back of her head.

Fighting off unconsciousness and waves of dizziness, Ebony's survival instincts kicked in and she cleared her head.

Ebony immediately assumed a combat stance and shifted her mind into combat mode as she prepared for their attack. Her quick reaction stunned her attackers, and that may have accounted for their slow response. Their initial plan was to earn the extra money by subduing Ebony and taking her to a hidden place and molesting and raping her, thus earning the double pleasure of obtaining sexual gratification and getting paid for it. That plan was formulated when they thought that Ebony was a regular female police officer and not a trained martial arts expert. Now they had reason to rethink that plan.

The lead attacker from below raised his pistol as he prepared to get off a shot just as the attacker from above reached Ebony. Ebony planted her sharp elbow in the attacker's sternum, and as the oxygen was forced out of his body, he doubled over. Ebony grabbed him by the shoulders and using his weight and momentum flipped him over her shoulder into the two attackers approaching from below. He crashed into the other attackers just as one's gun was going off, deflecting his arm and causing the shot to go into the ceiling. The three men ended in a heap at the bottom of the stairs.

Years of martial arts training had taught Ebony that the difference between life and death often lay within making instant decisions when in combat. Ebony had to decide whether she had the time to draw her gun or to run up to her apartment and open the door before her attackers recovered. Deciding it was too close to chance, Ebony launched herself in the midst of her attackers. Seeing that the situation was getting far more dangerous than she anticipated, as all three attackers were struggling to their feet as they pulled out their guns, Ebony's mindset shifted from disarming and disabling her attackers into a deadly mode. Converting her hands into deadly weapons, she sprang inside one man's guards and threw a lighting fast fist into one man's throat, crushing his larynx, and he dropped to his knees as he suffocated to death.

Seeing that they were up against an experienced and deadly fighter, the other two killers showed that they were not strangers to the murder game. They separated to two different sides of the room, thus giving themselves angles where they could fire their weapons without hitting each other or getting in each other's way.

Ebony dove, hit the floor, and rolled into the legs of one shooter, who was in a wide-leg stance, and her leg shot up, placing a well-aimed kick into the man's groin. She sprang to her feet with her back flush against the shooter. She grabbed the arm with the gun around the wrist and, using her shoulder as a lever, snapped the man's forearm in two pieces while she removed the gun from his prone fingers. As she aimed the gun at the other shooter, she made her first error in judgment.

She assumed the last attacker wouldn't open fire for fear of hitting his companion. She was wrong, and he opened fire with what looked to be a Glock automatic pistol. The room was filled with arid gun smoke and the man's screams of pain as his fellow attacker's gunshots ripped across his torso. Unfortunately, two bullets also caught Ebony. One shot hit her right above the left clavicle and the other in the left rib area. As she was going down, Ebony discharged her gun in a spray of gunfire in the general direction of the last shooter. Whether it was skill, luck, or the will of Providence didn't matter, but Ebony hit the other shooter two times. Once in the thigh and once in the chest, which pierced his heart and killed him instantly.

Ebony lay on the floor and struggled to get her cell phone out to call for assistance, but before she could complete the call, the approaching waves of darkness enveloped her.

Chapter Fourteen

Ebony started her deep climb out of the well of soothing darkness. Slowly she was able to recall images of her parents, Jack, Gary, Malachi, Ted, and countless others that had streamed through her consciousness. What she couldn't determine was which ones were dreams and which were real, as they all were seen through a haze. Suddenly, her darkness was interrupted by a white light that was so bright that it gave her a headache.

She struggled to open her eyes but her lids felt as if they were glued shut. She could not remember a time when opening her eyes was as difficult as lifting a hundred-pound weight. With her eyes finally open, she looked at the unfamiliar white walls and ceiling. Exhausted by the effort, she closed her eyes for what she thought would only be a second but instead drifted back into the engulfing darkness.

She awoke again several hours later and took a few minutes to look around and try to acclimate herself with her surroundings. At first she couldn't figure out where she was, and then noticing the numerous monitors realized that she was in a hospital but she had no idea how she got in the hospital or why. Her eyes had an itchy, burning feeling and she attempted to rub them but she couldn't move her arms. There had to be a mistake. Could she be so tired that she couldn't lift her arms? She redoubled her efforts and tried again and still she couldn't lift her arms. Fighting back the waves of panic, she tried to lift her legs. Nothing! She couldn't move her legs either? She was paralyzed? How could she be paralyzed? What the hell happened? Those same waves of panic that she had fought back earlier now took over her.

She struggled mightily to move her arms and legs without any measurable degree of success. She tried to call out for help but her voice was weak and barely a squeak came out. She swallowed and tried again this time a noise came out that was a little louder. Exhausted by her strenuous efforts she rested her head back on the pillow and tried to regain her composure. She tried to raise her head to look around the room and a bright, searing pain flowed through her left shoulder and down through her body. With a moan, she fell back into the pillows.

After the pain subsided she thought, "That was a good thing. If I can feel pain that means I'm not totally paralyzed at least not from the neck down. Now, let me get some help and see if I can get some answers to what is going on. By the number of monitors in this room, I must be in an extreme care room so if I wait, it shouldn't be long before someone comes in." She lay back and tried to see if she could remember what happened. She remembered the nasty meeting with Brandon Barnett and after that: nothing.

She closed her eyes while regaining her strength, and in a few minutes she heard voices, one of whom sounded like her father. Opening her eyes, she said, "Daddy?"

"Ebony, you're awake. Mal, go get the doctor," Ebony's father said as he came over and took Ebony's hand.

"Daddy, what happened?"

"Baby, we were so worried about you. You gave us a hell of a scare. I have to call your mother and tell her you're finally awake. She hadn't left your side since you came in here and I sent her home because she hadn't slept in days and hadn't really had a decent meal in that same amount of time. It was all I could do to convince her to go home. I told her if she didn't *she* would have to be hospitalized as well and we didn't know how long you would be out."

"How long have I been out?"

"This is the ninth day."

"Nine days?! I've been here nine days?! Dad, what happened?"

"Honey, you were shot two times, and you had other serious injuries as well."

Though she was scared to know the truth, she knew she had to ask the question that was plaguing her mind. "Dad, how bad off am I? Am I paralyzed?"

"The doctor will be here in a minute to answer all your questions. I sent Malachi to get him."

"You know Malachi? How?"

"We've gotten to be pretty good friends. He's been here every day. His mother has even been here and little Zoe had a fit because they wouldn't let her in to see you. She finally charmed Gertie into sneaking her in to see you. That little girl really took a liking to you. Malachi sent her home because he couldn't take care of her and be here every day too and she cried like her heart was breaking. We finally got her to agree to leave when we promised that we would have a grand big party when you came home. Malachi promised that he would fly the whole family up for the party including somebody called Lee-Lee. Judging by Malachi, this family must be pretty special."

"Dad, will I be coming home?"

"Yes, you will honey."

"In what condition? Dad, you done everything but answer my question. Am I paralyzed?"

"We don't know yet. That seems to be in the hands of the doctors and God."

"But I can't move my hands or feet."

"That's because the doctors have you belted down."

"Why do they have me belted down?"

"Because even while you were in the coma, you were tousling and moving around almost like you were still fighting someone and you have a bullet lodged near your spinal cord. The doctors were scared that you would move around and do more damage before they could take it out."

"I was in a coma?"

"Yes, until a few minutes ago."

"Why?"

"Here is the doctor now. He can explain everything a lot better than me. We'll wait outside until he finishes but don't worry I won't leave. I love you, baby."

"Ebony, I'm Dr. Navi, and it is very good to speak to you. You had quite a few people very worried about you."

"Doctor, could you please tell me what going on with me?"

"How about we do it like this? You let me examine you and then I will answer all your questions. Okay?"

"Okay."

The doctor removed the restraints and he and the nurses gave Ebony a very thorough examination including blood work and EKGs. After the exam was finally finished the doctor said, "There are a lot of people waiting to see you, so I guess we need to answer your questions. Maybe what we will do is I will tell you what has happened since you have gotten here and then I can answer any questions you still have. Will that work?"

"That would be fine because I have a lot of questions."

"You were brought in about nine days ago unconscious with trauma and in shock because of two gunshot wounds. One wound was to the left shoulder area and missed the shoulder and clavicle so it didn't pose much of a problem. The other wound was another story altogether. It entered your body at the left, lower chest area fracturing two ribs in the process. At first we thought we were lucky because the bullet missed the intestines and the kidney by a fraction of an inch. Unfortunately, the bullet lodged itself near your spine in the thoracic area and nicked your spinal cord in the process, resulting in loss of sensation and no response to pinprick in the lower extremities. Your surgical team wanted to go in right away and remove the bullet before additional complications like inflammation or infection set in, but you had lost a lot of blood and we wanted to stabilize you first.

"We got you stabilized and you were scheduled for surgery the next day when you developed difficulty breathing. It appeared that

the bullet had grazed the lower lobe of your left lung. It did not punc-
ture the lung, but the trauma led to the lung collapsing. It took a couple of days for us to restore the lung and after we did we still couldn't
perform the surgery because of problems with your head.

"You had some trauma to the head and there was some swelling
of the brain so we induced a coma to relieve the swelling so we could
determine whether you had any intracranial bleeding which would
have necessitated brain surgery. The swelling greatly subsided two days
ago and we stopped inducing the coma. Now that you're conscious,
I'm sure they'll reschedule the surgery very soon."

"Why was I restrained?"

"Before we induced the coma, you were thrashing and moving
around a lot. We couldn't take a chance that movement would shift
the bullet and allow it to cause further damage."

"Am I paralyzed or not?"

"We really don't know. You weren't awake for us to do a full examination, but there was some deficit when we did pinprick examination. What we don't know is whether that deficit is permanent or
temporary, which is why we need to remove that bullet right away."

"So even if I am paralyzed, it might be temporary or until you can
get that bullet out?"

"I'm not a surgeon so I won't be part of the team operating on
you, but from what I know of the case, there is a strong possibility that
you could regain full use of all your limbs."

"When can I expect to get out of here?"

"That's getting way ahead of things. Although we're talking about
your problems in the past tense, that doesn't mean that they aren't
very serious problems. You've been through quite a lot and at one time
our focus was just helping you to survive. It's way too early to speculate
about a possible discharge date even though you have such a strong
spirit that I'm encouraged about a full recovery."

"What happened to me?"

"You were involved in a gun battle, but I don't know many of the
details. It shouldn't be hard for you to find out though because there
are a flood of people waiting to see you. You've been a very popular

girl, with everyone from the mayor on down waiting to see you. When you were in critical condition and only immediate family was allowed in to see you, Gertie said you had more husbands, parents, and brothers and sisters than anyone she's ever seen."

"Gertie?"

"Oh, you haven't met Gertie yet? Then you're in for a treat. She's the head nurse on this ward. She's lovable but no-nonsense. Unless you have any more questions that won't hold I'm going to leave you now and let some of those people waiting in to see you. I'm restricting you to five guests, and they can only stay for five minutes each. You're still a very sick young lady, and you still need your rest. I'll see you tomorrow."

Within seconds of the doctor's leaving, her parents entered the room. Her mother literally ran to her and swept her in her arms in a hug so fierce it was as if she was scared to let her go. Watching her mother cry was scarier to Ebony than the whole conversation with the doctor.

"It's okay, Mom, I'll be all right."

"Oh, Ebony, we were so scared. I thought we had lost you."

"I thought Dad said you had gone home."

"I had but I was on my way back to the hospital when your father called me. I was only two blocks away. I guess I sensed that you were about to wake up."

"Mom, you have to take care of yourself. You can't run yourself down. After all, I might need you to take care of me for a while when I get out of here."

"You know I'll be there for you baby."

Taking his wife by the hand, Ebony's father said, "Come on, Maxine. Let's leave so we don't wear her out and so some of these other people can stick their head in for a minute. You know the doctor said she needs her rest most of all."

"Dad, what happened to me?"

"Honey, there will be plenty of time to talk about that later. Right now, I want you just to concentrate on getting better. We'll see you tomorrow."

Ebony's parents were followed by Malachi. "Hi, Ebony, I have so many things to say to you but they will hold for a minute. Right now, I just want to look in those beautiful eyes and just tell you I want you to focus on getting better. We need you in our lives, and I can't imagine living my life without you in it. If there is anything at all you need, you just tell me and I'll get it for you. I just wanted to tell you that I'm here and I will be here for the duration until we get you up and around again. I can't stay long because there is a long line of people waiting to see you and I'm just grateful that I was allowed in to see you."

"There are people waiting to see me?"

"Are you kidding me? Everyone from your lieutenant to Gary and Ted and Jack and the press and people I can't even name. Your brothers just left about an hour before you woke up. With all those people out there who mean so much to you, it's a miracle that I was able to get in at all."

"A miracle?"

"Actually, it was your father who insisted that I be allowed in to see you."

"My father?"

"Yeah, he's a pretty cool dude. We've really gotten a chance to get to know each other over the past eight days. It pays to have friends in high places. You get some rest now, *my love*, I'll see you later."

"Will you be back tomorrow?"

"Wild horses couldn't keep me away."

· · · · ·

"Hey partner."

"Gary, Ted what are you doing here?"

"Where did you expect us to be? As far as we're concerned, there is no other place I would rather be than to be here when you opened your eyes and give me that smile."

"Gary, what the hell happened?"

"We were allowed to come in only on the understanding that we wouldn't discuss anything about what happened to you yet. I gave my word. You get some rest and we'll talk about all that later."

"I didn't know you knew Ted."

"We've gotten real well acquainted over the last week. Gertie said I was the last one to see you today so I convinced her to let Ted come with me, if we promised to make it real quick."

"But the doctor said that—"

"Gertie said she doesn't care what the doctor said. She said you are shut down for the rest of the day. We're gonna leave now and let you get some rest. We don't want Gertie to come in and throw us out, and believe me, she will. She's put me out of your room so much this week, she said she will ban me from the hospital if she has to put me out again, and I believe she means it. I'll tell Melendez and the folks at the precinct you're better and will speak to them soon. You get some rest and we'll talk tomorrow."

· · · · ·

Early the next day, the doctors came and visited her and after her examination informed Ebony that she would have her surgery the next day unless she had any further complications. Ebony was equal parts eager to have the surgery and nervous about the outcome. Her feeling pretty much was: when you had something you *had* to do and there was no choice as to whether or not to do it, then to not hesitate or procrastinate but do it and get on with life.

She was all too aware that this surgery would determine the course of the rest of her life. Up to this point she still wasn't able to move her legs though the feelings had returned to her toes. That fact encouraged the doctors but it didn't change the fact that she still couldn't move her legs. *She couldn't move her legs. What if after the surgery she still couldn't move her legs?* What if this became her new reality? What if she could never again move her legs? Would she be able to live the remainder of her life in a wheelchair? Could she even deal with that? Did she have a choice?

The doctors told her that even after the surgery it might be weeks before she found after whether she would regain full use of her legs. Weeks! She would have to live for weeks with this anxiety of not knowing whether she would be a cripple or not. She made a promise to herself that under no circumstances would she be a cripple. Regardless of the outcome of the surgery and no matter how much or little use she had of her legs, she would not be a cripple. No matter how she had to redefine herself she would still be a person of value and contributor to society. The promises she had made to the victims of Brandon Barnett would be kept. She didn't know how just yet, but she was determined that justice would find Barnett and she would have a major part to play in his downfall.

Shortly after, the doctors finished their morning rounds and the nurses had finished washing and dressing her in preparation of her daily visitors. Her doctor told her they had already updated the press and they didn't think it was a good idea to meet with the press yet. The nurse told her that the doctors had established very strict guidelines as the number of visitors she would be allowed.

Her first visitors were her father and the Deputy Mayor, who met with her and offered her words of encouragement on behalf of the administration and then he met with the press. It was all in keeping with the official posture of being very concerned and sympathetic when a law officer was injured. By the time he left, he had Ebony convinced he was sincere in his concern. Her father went with the Deputy to represent the family at the news conference, and he assured Ebony he would be back to see her later that day.

Ebony was preparing for lunch, which would have been the first solid food she would have since the shooting, when she looked up and was surprised to see Gary and Ted enter the room. "When did you two start hanging together?"

"When some assholes tried to kill our partner," Gary said.

"Will you guys finally tell me what the hell happened? Everyone acted like they were scared to tell me how I ended up in here, like the knowledge of how this happened would be worse than the thought that I may never walk again."

"I can understand why your doctors preferred to be cautious. Right now, your focus should be on trying to get healthy and not on trying to figure out what happened," Ted said.

"Whether I like it or not, I'm here and in not such great condition and I would at least like to know how I got here."

Gary said, "If you're sure you want to know, I guess we should tell you. I'll tell you what we know and not what we suspect. Two units were dispatched to your address in response to reports of gunfire. The officers found you and three bodies in the foyer of your building. The other bodies were Black males between twenty-three and twenty-eight years of age. One man was killed as a result of a crushed larynx, which we attributed to you and your martial arts training. The other two men were killed by gunshot wounds. Ballistic tests have confirmed that one was killed by the gun that was recovered in your hand. The other man was killed by bullets from the same gun as the bullet that was removed from your shoulder.

"Whether there were more assailants we don't know because they could have fled after shooting you and thinking you were dead, or there might only have been three assailants to start with. After the bullet is removed from your spine, we might have a better picture because if it's not from one of the guns we recovered at the scene that means there were more assailants. As bad off as you are, it seems you gave a lot worse than you got.

"At first the officers were working under the assumption that it was a botched break-in or robbery attempt but when the identification came back it showed all three were from the Baltimore, Maryland area and have criminal records. Who comes all the way from Maryland to force their way into a police officer's house to rob them? All three have extensive criminal records with everything from assault with a deadly weapon to possession of a narcotic with intent to distribute. Ted's having some friends at the DEA see if they have a more extensive file on these guys. We need to know if they are part of a posse or gang down there or if they are independent contractors."

Ted asked, "Ebony, when you left me you were talking about going to see Barnett to see if you could rattle his cage. Did you go see him?"

"I think so. The last couple of days are vague and kind of fuzzy, but I kind of remember talking to him and him getting real pissed off."

Gary said, "I told you, Ted. I knew that punk was behind this shit. Why don't we stop messing around with the son of a bitch and let me smoke him. I can do it so it looks perfectly legit. I could get him so *it* would like a robbery too."

"Who do you think would believe that?" Ted asked.

"They may not believe it, but no one could prove anything."

"This scumbag complained that Ebony had a thing for him, then Ebony gets shot and he mysteriously gets killed in a robbery attempt and you think the powers-that-be will buy that bullshit?" Ted asked.

"They might not believe it, but all they could do would be launch an investigation and after a while they would close the investigation without any tangible evidence which they won't have," Gary argued.

"They will *not* let the investigation drop. If they knew what we know about this guy, it might be a different story. They might not make the investigation an intense investigation in a sense that justice prevailed but right now they think he's an upstanding member of society. We couldn't let them know what we know because we can't prove it. All it would do point the finger directly at us if you killed him. It ain't worth the risk," Ted countered.

"That scumbag tried to have my partner killed. You know it and so do I. And you're talking about letting him get away with it? No way! No fucking way!"

"Who said anything about letting him get away? I'm going to nail his ass if it's the last thing I do but we're not mavericks or renegades. I believe in justice. I believe in fair play *and* I also believe in the law. You do remember the law, right? I have spent my life fighting for and enforcing the law and you have too. I will not spit on our lives' work by taking the law into my own hands. No matter how bad I may want to. I won't do it and neither will you. You're a better person and a better cop than that."

"You're talking about taking a chance on him getting away with this."

"No, I'm not. First of all, no way is he smarter than me or you. He is not quick enough, slick enough, or clever enough to have done this crap and get away with it. That ain't gonna happen. I don't know if we'll get him tomorrow or the day after but we're gonna get him. He's already made some mistakes, and going after Ebony was one of them. We just have to wait for the mistake that will allow us to crucify his ass."

Finally, Ebony intervened, "How long has this been going on with you two arguing back and forth like this?"

"For about a week now. What with these guys in your life: Gary, your father, your brothers, and even some guy name *Malachi, who's a college professor* have wanted to go and pop Barnett. It was all I could do to convince them to wait and see if he even had anything to do with it. What's with this desire for personal revenge? It must be a *brother* thing," Ted said with a wink at Ebony.

"Oh really? Isn't vendetta an Italian word?" Gary countered.

"Actually, it's of Latin origin."

"Same difference. Revenge is not an African American concept but it doesn't make it less sweet."

"Did you two come here to see me or to have a political argument? I thought you were here to make me feel better?" Ebony asked.

"We're sorry, Ebony. I guess that was pretty thoughtless of us," Ted said.

"Gotcha. You two clowns better act like your normal selves. You better not come in here treating me like some kind of invalid. Watching you two carry on almost makes me feel like myself. I'm also feeling the way you two have kind of bonded."

"Yeah, it was kind of hard, but I think he's almost all right even if he is a Fed," Gary said.

"Gary, let's get serious for just a moment. Ted is right. You can't go and pull a Rambo on Barnett," Ebony said.

"Why not? Do you know how I feel to see my partner lying there in that bed?"

"How do you think I feel? Did they tell you there's a chance that I might not be able to walk again? How do you think it feels to think that Barnett thinks he can do this to me and get away with it? Well, I'll tell you. I will be able to walk again, and Gary, *you* will not be the one to get Barnett. If someone gets to pop a cap in his ass, it will be me. What I am planning is the three of us bringing him down together. Guys, it might feel good to walk up on Barnett and blast him and believe me I want to in the worse way, but we can't. If we do just shoot Barnett, that means all the husbands who participated in this with Barnett get away with murder. That would mean that the men who benefitted most from having *their* ex-wives killed would get away scot-free. We can't allow that to happen."

"You're right, Ebony. I didn't think about that."

"Barnett must think that I'm in this investigation by myself or else why would he try to have me killed if it wouldn't end the investigation. So we let him think he's right and that I am doing the investigation by myself and because I'm out of the scene and trying to recover and that could take months that the investigation's over. Meanwhile, we go real low-key and you guys continue to gather the information that will bring them all down. Maybe this will help him make the mistake we thought he would make. Let him relax his guard and then we lower the boom."

"Melendez wants to launch a formal investigation into your shooting and also into Barnett. Do you think we should?" Gary asked.

"What do you think?" Ebony asked.

"I think we should let them do whatever investigation they want to. If they come up with anything on Barnett, that can only help. If they take him off the street before we do, I can't see that as anything but a good thing. If they don't then we still will go after him. I don't see what harm it can do," Gary said.

"What if they alert him that the police are still after him?" Ebony asked.

"If they don't come up with anything on him, he might get more arrogant and less cautious if he thinks that he's once again beaten the system. It could make him more careless," Gary said.

"I don't think Ebony should make the link between Barnett and the Baltimore boys for the NYPD. If they make the connection, fine, but Ebony shouldn't do it for them because we don't want them to think that Ebony has some kind of vendetta against Barnett or see him as the culprit for anything bad that happens to her," Ted said.

"Okay, I'll help with the investigation, but I won't mention Barnett at all," Ebony said.

. . . . .

Noticing that Ebony was dozing, Malachi crept into the room careful not to wake her. He silently pulled a seat close to her bed and sat where he could look at her face. As she rested she looked so beautiful and so peaceful. Malachi had a hard time imagining that someone could want to hurt this beautiful creature. He reached over and took her hand and started to gently caress it. Malachi sat holding Ebony's hand, eyes closed deeply absorbed in thought. He wasn't sure how long he stayed like that but after a while he felt her stirring. He looked up and noticed that she was looking at him. He stood up, leaned over, and kissed her on the forehead.

"Is that the best you can do?" Ebony asked.

"What do you mean?"

"I mean I don't deserve a better kiss than that? You kissed me like I was your little sister or something."

Malachi leaned over and gave her the kind of kiss that was in his heart to give her in the first place. He placed his lips on hers tenderly and allowed it to linger while he tried to convey some of the things he was feeling.

"That's a little better, but I know you can kiss better than that," Ebony teased.

"I guess I'm just being a little careful."

"Don't worry, I won't break."

"I don't know about that. Right now, I think you're busted up pretty bad and I don't want to take a chance on making you worse."

"I'm a lot stronger than you think."

"I hope so. Ebony, I don't know what I would have done if you hadn't made it."

"Is that why you look so sad?"

"Part of the reason, but I will wait until you get better before I tell you the rest."

"Didn't anyone ever tell you 'why put off until tomorrow what you can do today'?"

"I don't want to be selfish and deal with my feelings when we should focus on you and getting you better."

"Maybe knowing what's on your mind and what you are feeling will make me feel better."

"Okay, I'll tell you everything after your surgery tomorrow."

"What if I don't make it through the surgery tomorrow?"

"Honey, don't say that. Please don't even think anything like that."

"Malachi, look at me. Stop worrying. I'll come through tomorrow's surgery in great shape. It's not that serious. My point is: to not put off until tomorrow the things you want to do or say because tomorrow is not promised to anyone. Lying here in this hospital gives you a lot of time to think and one of the things I thought about how close I came to dying. I wondered if I was at death's door would I have a lot of regrets about some of the things I meant to say and do, I put off because I would get to them later? I'm not talking about unfinished business like Brandon Barnett because I was dealing with him the best I could. I'm talking about things like personal desires and ambitions. I don't want to leave here with some things I wanted to say and do, unsaid and undone."

"Are any of those things pertaining to me?" Malachi asked.

"Don't even try it, you chicken. You are the one who had so many things on your mind. You talk to me," Ebony insisted.

Malachi paused for a minute as he collected his thoughts and summoned his courage to say the things that were in his heart. "You may not believe it, but I'm eager for the chance to talk to you. In fact, I prayed that God would grant me a chance to tell you just how I feel. I can't remember the last time I was so scared. I was scared that I would lose you and I could not imagine what my life would be like without you. The last few weeks have been such a roller coaster of emotions.

"The time we spend together with Zoe was incredible. It was so beautiful and special and I loved every minute of it. It was fun and exciting and for the first time in years. I saw how great it could be to be married and have children. I mean, I always knew, but it takes the right woman to make the situation work. Around the second or third day, I became convinced that you are that woman.

"I love you and everything about you. I love how you laugh. I love how you smile. I love how you took that broken little girl and filled up all the holes in her soul and showed her the beauty in life again. You made me see how I could never completely replace all the things she lost. You gave her love and strength and discipline and most importantly a belief in the good things in life again. You taught her that life is not just full of loss and hardship and pain but also love and happiness and *fun*.

"You are the most beautiful woman I know, inside and out. Your eyes are like mystic jewels that are gateways to a world full of mystery, beauty, and imagination and magic. You look at me and I feel like you are seeing who I really am and who I want to be and who I can be. Your lips make me want to kiss you over and over again and lose myself in you. Your smile makes me want to laugh and dream and it fills me with such joy that I can't believe it. You have the sexiest legs and when you walk it's all I can do not to watch you or I'm sure that my desire for you will overwhelm me and make me melt.

"Ebony, I love you. I want you. I need you and I will do anything to make you a part of my life in any way you want for as long as you want." Slowly Malachi became aware that the tears were flowing down Ebony's face. As he kissed her tears away, he felt so close to her he didn't even mind the saltiness of her tears. He just held her in a comfortable silence that he thought was pulling them closer together. Finally, he said, "I kind of hoped when I told you I love you, it wouldn't make you cry."

"I'm not crying because I'm sad," Ebony said.

"Then why the tears?"

"Because I'm starting to feel the same way about you."

"And that makes you cry?"

"No, but it does make me feel all full inside and that is a little scary."

"But, darling, there is nothing to be afraid of. If you feel as strongly for me as I do for you, then is really a good thing and in fact it's a blessed thing."

"I know that I will survive the surgery tomorrow, but what if it's not successful? What if after the surgery I still can't walk?"

"That won't change my feelings for you one little bit. I'll still love you and want to spend my life with you."

"You say that now, but how can you be sure how you will feel in six months or a year?"

"I say that with confidence because I know how strongly I feel for you. You have to learn to trust me. I don't love just part of you. I've learned to love all of you. Not just your body, and I will still love that body even if you have to learn to walk again, but I also love your mind and your heart and your spirit. All of you is great. Every part is special and that will sustain us both through the hard times ahead, no matter how hard they get. I'm here and I ain't going anywhere."

"But—"

"No more buts. If you truly care about me, then let us get through this together."

"Malachi. Let me ask you something. Gary and Ted said you were talking about going after Barnett? Is that true?"

"Is he the one responsible for this?"

"We don't know."

"I didn't ask you what you know. Do you *think* he's behind this?"

"There's a strong possibility. But I need you to promise me that you will let us handle this. I know Gary expressed the same sentiment and I had to convince him as well to handle this the right way. I want you to promise me that you will let the authorities handle this."

"How can you ask me to promise that? If this is the man who killed my sister and tried to kill you, how can you ask me to let someone else handle this? If I let him go, what kind of man would I be?"

"The smart kind of man. Revenge would feel good, but it would deprive a lot of people of justice. You cannot do that. We've got to nail him the legal way so those people that worked with him can be brought to justice as well. Mal, you are the smartest man I know—*think*!"

"How close are you to bringing this bastard to justice?"

"Closer than you think or else he wouldn't have tried to have me killed. You have to trust me that this is the way to go. The only way."

"Okay, I promise but in return you must do me a favor, if you're up to it."

"What's that?"

"A couple of people really want to talk to you. I know I'm not supposed to use my cell phone in here, but maybe they'll forgive this one exception. I'll bribe Gertie with some flowers and candy. Hold on a minute." Malachi paused as he waited for the phone to make the connection then he said, "Hey, Mom, how are you doing? I'm doing a lot better. She's right here. Hold the phone." Then he placed the phone under Ebony's ear while he held it. Rather meekly Ebony said, "Hello."

"Hello, Detective Delaney. How are you doing, dear?"

"Hi, Mrs. Moore, I'm doing much better."

"You've had us very worried about you. I want you to know you have very much been in our thoughts and prayers."

"Thank you, I can use all the prayers I can get."

"Malachi told us you have another major surgery tomorrow."

"Yes, ma'am."

"Ebony, I thought I asked you to call me Juanita. You be strong young lady and have faith that everything will be all right. You're a good person and God looks out for his own. Do you need anything?"

"No, ma'am."

"I told that son of mine to let me know if you need anything at all but he seems real distracted. I know he's real worried about you. He's not keeping you from getting your rest, is he? You've become very important to this family and we cannot afford to lose you. Since Zoe has been home, all she's been saying is Miss Ebony said this and Miss Ebony did that."

"Is Zoe there? I want to let her know I'm all right."

"The kids are outside playing. I'll get her for you. I know she would love to hear from you." Ebony could hear her call "Zoe. Telephone. It's Ebony." "Ebony, she's coming as fast as her legs can carry her. We are all planning on coming to the party to celebrate when you're discharged from the hospital. There's something I want you to consider. How about having the party down here? We could throw a real Texas barbeque. We'll gladly fly in all your family and friends and we'll rent out a hotel so everybody can be real comfortable. Also, we'd love for you to come stay with us while you convalesce. Zoe, if you don't stop pulling on my skirt, I won't let you speak to her. Now, wait your turn. I'm sorry, Ebony, but it's hard to talk with Zoe jumping up and down trying to get the phone. Now, as I was saying, we would love for you to stay with us while you get better."

"Thank you for the offer, but I think my mother is looking forward to me staying with her. She would probably kill me if I deprived her of the chance to make her baby better."

"You know she's welcome to come too. We have plenty of room and with the two of us together you should be back on your feet in no time."

"I'll discuss it with her. Thanks again for thinking of me."

"I'll be praying for you tomorrow honey. I better let Zoe talk to you before I have to put her on punishment. We'll talk to you after the surgery as soon as you're able. Here's Zoe."

"Hi, Miss Ebony! How are you feeling?"

Hearing someone so eager to talk to her, made Ebony feel as good as the most potent medicine. "I'm feeling much better. How are you?"

"I'm fine but I was so worried about you. What's happened to you? No one will tell me anything. They treat me like a little kid."

"You know I was investigating some bad people, right? Well, they tried to stop me from finding out enough to arrest them but it's not gonna work."

"I'm sorry that I didn't get to say bye, but Uncle Mal had my grandmother come and get me and bring me home. He said he didn't want to leave your side. I wanted to stay and help take care of you but they said I was too young. Miss Ebony, please tell them I could take good care of you."

"That's probably not what they meant, honey. I'm in the hospital and the rules say you're too young to visit."

"Well, that's a stupid rule. Just because I'm little that doesn't mean I don't want to see you."

"I think the rule is because some kids make too much noise and a lot of sick people need their rest."

"That doesn't make sense. Why don't their parents just tell them to be quiet?"

"You're right, honey, but rules are rules."

"Uncle Mal said we can come back to New York when you get out of the hospital and that we're even gonna have a party. But LJ and Lee-Lee get to come too."

"Don't you want your brother and sister to come with you?"

"They're not your friends."

"Yes, they are, I just haven't gotten to spend as much time with them as you."

"I told LJ you won't be taking him shopping because I'm your favorite."

"I won't take him shopping because I will be just getting back on my feet, but I'm sure your Uncle Mal will take you all shopping."

"I don't want to go shopping with him. He's a guy and they don't know how to shop."

"When I get better, I'll take you and Lee-Lee shopping again, just us girls."

"Okay, LJ wants to talk to you. You get better and I'll see you as soon as you get better," Zoe said as she handed LJ the phone.

"Hello, Miss Ebony, how are you feeling?" LJ asked.

"I'm a little tired right now but I'm getting better."

"I just wanted to tell you good luck with your surgery."

"Thank you."

"I told Uncle Mal I would come to New York and help him find the people who did this."

"I'll tell you the same thing I told your uncle: 'let the cops do their job.'"

"The police never catch anybody."

"Yes, they do, LJ; you just got to give them some time. I'm getting real tired so I'm gonna turn the phone over to your uncle and I will see you soon."

. . . . .

Omar sat parked in the Nissan Maxima that he had brought less than two weeks before and watched some of the street kids that he had out selling drugs for him. He didn't like the way they were sitting back and chilling while some of the other more aggressive dealers went up to the cars driving through the neighbor in search of drugs. These guys didn't know whose money they were messing with. In his desire to keep a low profile, he purposely kept the violence to a minimum, but now he was gonna have to hurt someone to show them he wasn't soft.

When Omar had fled New York just steps ahead of Brandon and Justice's boys, he had stopped in D.C. and got a package from some guys he knew who sold high quality coke. They had done him a favor and sold him a package that was of pretty high quality so when he cooked it down into crack, he could increase his profit. Once he had the coke he ditched the stolen car he had driven down from New York and bought a hoopty because he didn't want to get busted for a stolen car and have the coke discovered. He wasn't worried about the quality of the car he bought because he figured he only needed it to drive to Atlanta and for a couple of weeks thereafter while he put enough money together to get a better car.

Once in Atlanta it took him a few weeks to gather a few workers and turn over the package. In the subsequent time, he had made almost a dozen trips to D.C. to re-up his package and put together a rather sizable crew. Now the money in his stash was more than triple what he had when he left New York. He could easily have afforded a Beamer or a Benz, but he thought it smarter to keep a low profile.

It wasn't that he was worried about the police because as long as he paid off the people who controlled the cops, they wouldn't bother him too much. He was more concerned about the people in New York who he knew was after him. Normally hustlers would forget about the beef, especially after he left town, but he knew too much about Barnett's and Justice's business for them to leave him around alive. He knew the money they made on their operation made his seem paltry by comparison.

Now because of the laziness of his workers and his desire to stay low key, people was starting to treat him like he was soft. Already a couple of other dealers were moving into the area that he had carved out as his own and he had to let them know he wasn't the one to mess with. His dilemma was how to be violent enough to put everyone in the proper place and establish his rep once and for all but not garner too much unwanted attention. He was going to have to do something extremely vicious and sadistic to drive the point home.

He had almost decided who he was going to make an example of and how he was going to do it. He just had to put another couple of things in place first including a warning to the other dealers to leave his territory alone. He also had to make a decision about where he got his supply. The trips to D.C. was not only time consuming but it was too risky. The quality and quantity of the product no longer met his needs. He had met a new source in southern Florida who seemed like they might supply his needs, and he was deciding whether to give them a shot. He just had to be patient a little longer then he would put things right. They were going to find out why Justice had made him a member of his hit team. He wasn't like some in that he enjoyed the blood and the taking of human life and the sense of power it gave you but he didn't mind doing what he had to do to prosper in the line of work he chose. He could even convince himself he had no choice.

Chapter Fifteen

When Ebony opened her eyes after the surgery, the first thing she saw was Gertie. Gertie had gently prodded her awake. She finished adjusting several monitors and writing down their findings. Seeing that Ebony was awake she said, "Hi, honey, it's good to see you're awake. I know that you're still tired but your doctor instructed me to wake you up because he wanted to make sure you didn't have any adverse reaction to the anesthesia."

"How did the surgery go?" Ebony asked.

"Your doctor will be right in to see you, but I believe he said that the surgery went well. How are you feeling? Would like a little juice or something to drink? Usually patients are very thirsty coming out of surgery."

"Yes, please, a little juice would be nice."

"Okay, I'll be right back with some of my special mixture."

As Gertie was leaving the room Ebony closed her eyes and must have dozed off because when she opened her eyes again her doctor was standing over her reading her chart. "How are you feeling, Miss Delaney?"

"I think I feel all right but I would feel a lot better if you give me some good news."

"I think we have some pretty good news for you. The surgery went as well as we hoped. We were able to remove the bullet before there was any nerve involvement. There is inflammation of the nerve and the area around it but there doesn't appear to be any damage to the nerve itself."

"Then I should be able to walk again?"

"In time, yeah, but you have to remember that your body has been through quite a lot and you have to heal. You have some pretty significant atrophy of the legs because you haven't been able to use those muscles in several weeks. I am recommending that you go into long term rehab to build those muscles back up and teach your muscles again how to work. Don't forget that you had some pretty extensive internal damage and complications. You're on the road to recovery, but you still have quite a way to go."

"How long before I can go home?"

"That's up to you and how hard you want to work but it's conceivable that you might be discharged in four or five weeks."

. . . . .

"Wake up, sleepyhead," Ebony's brother Malcolm said as he kissed her on the cheek. Ebony awoke to see her mother and her brothers Malcolm and Bobby visiting her.

"It's about time you guys made it over to see me."

"Come on, baby sis, you know better than that. We've been to see you more than a half a dozen times. Either you've been down for tests or asleep"

"Then you should have woke me up!"

"And have your mother get me? I don't think so. You know how protective Mom can be, especially about her baby chick. Ebs, you may not realize it but you've been through quite a lot. It was easy to see you needed your rest. Girl, you scared the bejesus out of me. They were talking that mess about they didn't know if you were gonna make it. I knew you was gonna make it though. You are too stubborn and mule-headed to let some thugs kill you."

"If you knew I was gonna make it, why were you scared?"

"Because sometimes God doesn't answer prayers," Malcolm said.

"Oh, he answers all right, but sometimes the answer is no."

"Well, I'm grateful that the answer this time was yes because I don't know what this family would be like without you in it. Who would drive Dad crazy and then give him that 'what are you getting upset about' look that you have down to a science? Who else could get away with calling Bobby 'Ba-Ba'?"

When she was three, Ebony being unable to pronounce Bobby started calling her six-year-old brother Ba-Ba. It was a family joke that much to Bobby's chagrin persisted until he was almost twelve years of age and could punch the fifteen-year-old Malcolm every time he called him that.

"And she's the only one who better call me that," Bobby said as he nudged Malcolm out of the way and kissed Ebony on the cheek. "I understand that we got some good news from the doctor. So how long before my baby sister is up and around and driving me crazy as only she can?"

"I should be discharged in three more days and then I'm off to rehab for two weeks to a month, though I plan on getting out a lot sooner. I figure in terms of rehab if I work real hard my progress should be a lot quicker."

"Ebs, I don't want you pushing yourself too hard. I think you should take your time and really let things heal. I know your philosophy is that your body is capable of anything if you push it hard enough, but I don't think you should use that attitude this time," Bobby said.

"What's wrong, you're worried that I might break a nail or something?" Ebony asked.

"Stop joking, Ebony! I knew you were going to try and make light of this situation. You need to realize how seriously you were wounded. You almost were paralyzed, and you came damn close to dying. I can smile and laugh now but this is no laughing matter. This was something that you really should think about," Bobby said as Ebony looked at him with a very quizzical look on her face but before she could ask a question, her mother came over to give her a hug and kiss.

"Hi, baby, how are you feeling today?" Maxine asked.

"I'm pretty good today, Mom. What's wrong with Bobby?"

"Nothing, dear, he's just a little worried about you as we all are."

"What are you worried about? I told you that I was going to beat this thing and didn't you tell me you were going to pray about it? Well, it worked and I'm a lot better now and soon I'll be back to normal."

"I'm not so sure that normal is a good thing," Bobby said.

"What do you mean by that?" Ebony asked.

Malcolm intervened at this point. "We wanted to wait until you were fully recovered and we were all together at a family, but since my brilliant little brother has brought it up, we might as well discuss what's on our minds now. Mother enlisted us to talk about something that was on her mind, but honestly we all feel the same way."

"About what?"

"This incident scared all of us and I sincerely hoped it scared you too but shortly you'll recover and get back out on those streets and right back into the same situation that led to this. We think it's time you left the police force."

"I was thinking the same thing," Ebony said.

"That's great! That means we're on one accord. What are you thinking about going back to school?"

"No, I was thinking about opening my own private detective agency."

"I knew this was going too easy," Bobby muttered as he sucked his teeth.

"Now, wait a minute, Bobby, that doesn't have to necessarily be a bad thing. If Ebony moves into an executive capacity and leaves the street level alone, it might be the best of both worlds."

"Most of the crime is committed on the street and sometimes you have to get down to the street to catch the criminal, and if that's where I got to go to get them, that's where I will go," Ebony replied.

"I told you," Bobby said.

Silencing him, Malcolm interrupted "Yo, B, you ain't helping man. Ebony, you really don't understand what we're getting at. We think it's time you got out of law enforcement. It's getting so much more dangerous out there. It seems like every other punk has a gun and won't hesitate to use it. You're a highly skilled officer fully capable of defending yourself between your police training and the martial arts and they still almost killed you."

"You've just given me great reasons why I should remain as a cop. The criminals *are* armed and they will still be out there. If every cop that gets shot quits, who's going to be there to battle the bad guys?"

"But, Ebony, you are smart and skilled; there are so many other things that you could do," Maxine said.

"But, Mom, I enjoy being a cop and I just happen to be very good at it as well. There are some very dangerous and treacherous people out there, and I take pride on being one of the people who try to maintain some control and balance and keeping the wicked from taking over."

"Gary told us that you feel like this guy you're investigating may be behind this attack on you. I hope you're not staying a cop so you can get him back because that's not even necessary. You just say the word and Gary and I will get him for you," Bobby said.

"It's not okay for me to be a cop, but it's okay for you to be a vigilante? Do you hear yourself?"

"I know that sounds a little over the top, but you're my little sister and I'm not letting anyone hurt you if I can help it."

"Ba-Ba, we're not in the third grade where you can beat up the bully who messes with your little sister."

"I know, Ebony, but even though you're a royal pain in my butt, I love you to pieces and I can't imagine my life without you to make it miserable. And oh yeah, I *will* try to take out anyone who tried to hurt you or any member of my family."

"I love you too, Bobby, and all the rest of you too. I appreciate your looking out for me, but I have to remain true to who I am. Each of you, in your own way, are doing whatever you can to make things better for our people and society at large. Well, this is my way. I know how hard it is on each of you and how much you worry about me and I love you very much for it but this is something I have to do. Can you understand that and continue to support me even though you disagree with my choice?"

"Of course," they all agreed.

"Mom, I have one more thing I need to speak to you about."

"What's that, honey?"

"Malachi's mother wanted to know if I wanted to come to Texas to fully recover after I get out of the rehab. I explained that I was looking forward to spending some quality time with you while I got better and she extended the invitation to both of us. So I wanted to know what you think about going."

"She seemed like a very nice person when she came to pick up Zoe, so I guess it is possible. You know what? We planned on a big party when you got out of here. Why don't you invite his whole family and maybe we'll go back with her to spend a couple of days. How does that sound?"

"Pretty good. Thank you, Mom."

"I know I'm sounding like Dad and this is probably his territory, but who is this Malachi? Is he your boyfriend? Is he going to be a major part of your life? He seemed to care a lot about you and was very protective as well. So what's the deal?" Malcolm asked.

"It's nothing formal but I think you could call him my boyfriend and I think we're headed for even more."

"Cool. You could do a lot worse."

· · · · ·

A few days later, after her doctors had finished their morning rounds, Ebony had coerced her nurses into helping her wash and dress in a new robe. They then wheeled her to the sitting room at the end of the hall. The room was awash with brilliant sunlight which was a warm and beautiful change after being confided in her room so long. Her room was pleasant enough, especially with the multitude of flowers, stuffed animals, cards, and balloons that occupied every available free space. It was good to feel the sun on her face and it warmed her soul like no medicine ever could.

It felt good to be among people again. While she was in grave danger and later when she was healing, she was sure that the isolation and privacy was essential to her recovery but now watching the people coming and going was giving her an increased appreciation for being alive. Seeing the medical staff hurrying and bustling about their various duties somehow made her feel a part of life again. Her mind drifted to the culprits who had put her in this position and she started thinking about what she was going to do about it.

She had no doubt that Brandon Barnett was behind the attempted hit, and there was no way she was going to let him get away with it. Rather than being afraid after her brush with death, she felt encouraged. The investigation must have been creating more heat than she planned for Barnett to arrange such a desperate act as trying to have a police officer killed or could he possibly be that arrogant? Did he think that he was so clever that he could arrange the murder of a NYPD officer and no one would realize he was behind it?

He had sorely underestimated her in thinking that such amateur killers could kill her and that was a mistake that was gonna cost him dearly. She had several potential plans in mind but decided to put them off until she was more suited to bring them off. For now she would just sit back, enjoy the people, the sun, and just being alive.

While she was enjoying the sunshine and the moment of solitude, she noticed a familiar figure walking down the hall toward her room. It was still amazing to watch the effect that Stephanie had on people. As she walked past nearly every man and quite a few women stopped what they were doing to watch her. She sauntered down the hall oblivious to the disruption of the normal routine her presence was causing. Unlike many beautiful women, Stephanie was unaware or at least unimpressed by the effect her beauty had on people.

She saw Stephanie go into her room and in a few moments come out and go down to the nurse's station where the nurse pointed out where Ebony was sitting. Ebony noticed the flowers that Stephanie was carrying didn't leave the room with her and when Stephanie saw her, her face brightened more than any bouquet of flowers ever could.

She came over and gave Ebony a hug that was so warm and loving that it's sincerity couldn't be doubted.

"My God, Ebony, it's so good to see you up and around that it almost makes me want to cry."

"Hi, Steph, it's good to see you too."

"Girl, you can't imagine what I'm feeling. At one time they were saying that you might not make it and then there was talk that you might not be able to walk again. There is no way I could imagine something like that happening to you. So seeing you up and out of that bed and not even in your room is awesome. All I can say is 'thank God.'"

"I still have a way to go before I'm completely back on my feet and in the swing of things."

"That's okay because I *know* you're going to make it. I know you, Delaney, and no one or nothing is going to keep you down, but girl, you gave me such a scare. Now how are you really feeling?"

"I still hurt some but not as much as a week ago. I'm not used to my legs and body not being able to do the things I want it to, but I can deal with it because I know its temporary."

"Do you feel well enough to answer some questions about what is going on?"

"I guess. What do you want to know?"

"Do you want to share with me what the hell is going on?" Stephanie asked.

"Not really."

"I phrased that incorrectly. What I should have said is: Ebony, what in the hell is going on?"

"I don't think you really need to know."

"I'm sorry. I thought we were pretty good friends. I didn't know that I was just another officer or just another sister that you work with and just happens to hang out with from time to time."

"Come on, Stephanie, you know it's not like that."

"Then you tell me how it is."

"I consider you a pretty cool sister and a very good friend. You know I don't have any sisters, but I consider you to be pretty close to the real thing. I consider you somebody I can just sit back and relax with and be myself. When I can't figure out a case, I can talk to you, and your insight and instincts help me see it from another and sometimes the correct angle. You know I think you're as intelligent as anybody at the precinct. Your only downside is that I'm jealous of you because you're so damn pretty."

"Then how come you're not acting like it?"

"What do you mean?"

"I mean, you know how it is for Black women at the station house. Those boys act like all we're good for is a romp in the bed. It's like we're strangers in a hostile land. They keep us out of the loop. They won't let me in any case that requires some thinking or can advance my career. You know what I'm talking about and how they can be. At least when you were there I felt a part of things and that there was a chance I could move up. After all, if you could do it, so can I. But then you were gone. Nobody said anything, and you didn't even say goodbye. You were just not at the station any more. When I asked about it, they said you were on personal leave. I knew something was up because *no one* gets over a month of personal leave. So either you were being disciplined or you were on some hush-hush operation without official sanction.

"Then all these crazy rumors started about you harassing some agent because he wouldn't get with you. As if anyone who knows you would believe that crap. Then I was hearing stuff about the mayor had the commissioner suspend you. Meanwhile, I didn't hear a single word from you even though I left you a whole lot of messages. I didn't know what was going on, but I felt you were isolating me and I didn't know why. I even tried talking to Gary and even though he knows how tight we are, he wouldn't tell me anything. He only made me feel more pissed off because I feel like I was being shut out. I know he knew what was going on but he just told me to stay out of it. The next thing I knew you were shot in a shootout with three drug dealers from Baltimore. I can tell you that none of this feels good. If you said it's not like it appears why don't you tell me how it is?"

"I understand how you feel, Steph, but I think Gary is right. You should stay out of it."

"How in the world can you expect me to stay out of it when someone is trying to kill you? You know me better than that. Okay, I'll give you your way if you can look me in the eye and tell me that this is all over. Tell me that everyone who meant you harm is dead. Tell me that those three drug dealers getting killed was the end of that case. Tell me that, and I'll let the whole matter rest."

"I won't lie to you. This case is far from over. I appreciate your having my back, but I still think that you should stay out of it. I know you're upset with Gary, but he was just following my instructions about how I want to handle the case."

"I was right and this is a major case you're running?"

"Yeah."

"So why did you cut me out of the loop?"

"For the same reason I kept Gary out at first: to protect you."

"From who? I know you don't think I'm afraid of some punks with guns. If you are trying to protect me from the ones who came after you? I say bring it on and let's boogie."

"I know you're not afraid of thugs and criminals. That's not who I'm protecting you from."

"From who then?"

"I'm trying to protect your career. This case is not an official one, and the NYPD has not launched an investigation. I'm positive this guy is guilty, and I'm going to do whatever is necessary to bring him to justice. It gets more complicated in that this guy is politically connected and has quite a few folks fooled about the type of man he is. I was determined to bring this guy down before they tried to kill me, and I'm even more determined to get him now."

"I want in."

"Are you sure? This case can get real nasty before it's all said and done."

"Why don't you tell me about the case and we'll decide whether I should be brought in?"

Ebony spent the next half an hour sparing no details as she told Stephanie all about the case. She told her the things the team of Ted, Gary, and herself suspected as well as knew. After she finished, Stephanie asked, "So what is our next move?"

"*Our* next move? Are you sure you want in on this case? There will be other cases without the risk of us having to go against the authorities."

"What makes you think that you're the only one who wants to get this scumball? He's making money and building his empire on the blood of innocent women. You damn right I want in. You tell me what to do."

"I'm not sure because this is a new development but we'll come up with a plan and you'll be involved in the planning."

"Is this guy gay?"

"No, on the contrary, he's a bit of a ladies' man," Ebony replied.

"Most men find me attractive. Why don't I see if he's attracted to me and maybe I can get close to him without him knowing I'm a cop?"

"I don't like it. It's too dangerous."

"Where is the danger? Even if he finds out I'm a cop, what's the big deal? Especially if he doesn't know I'm a part of the investigation, and how can I be part of something that doesn't even exist?"

"Stephanie, this guy has already proven that he be dangerous. If we decide to go ahead with this, you're going to have to be very careful."

"Aren't I always?"

"I'll have to talk this over with Ted and Gary. Why don't we all meet tomorrow in the morning before I'm discharged?"

"I would prefer if you didn't," Stephanie said.

"Why not?"

"Because you know how protective the men in the Department have been over me and that was before you were shot. Now Gary and Ted might have a lot of objections to my going undercover. Men look at a pretty face and get caught in their stereotypes about models and pretty girls and think because we are pretty that we are weak and feeble and helpless. They don't realize that I see my looks as an advantage just like my brains and all my other skills especially if I use it right. Which I will. It's been almost impossible for me to move up in the Department partly because of my looks and that was despite your accomplishments. Now I might as well forget it. Plus it won't be dangerous. We don't even know if the gambit will work but if things go according to plan, Barnett won't even know I'm a cop until it's too late. There will be plenty of time to tell Ted and Gary if the plan starts to work and I get inside Barnett's inner circle and catch him with his defenses down. There is very little risk and it seems to be worth it to me."

"I don't like it but there is a lot of truth in what you say. Okay we will do it your way for a while."

·　·　·　·　·

Justice was startled when the cell phone that he rarely used started ringing. This phone was only used by business associates who needed a secure line when they needed to contact him without possibly being heard by anyone running a wiretap. Less than a half dozen people had this number so there were limited possibilities of who it could be.

Figuring that whoever was calling him called him because it was urgent, Justice wasted no time in answering the phone. "Yeah?"

"Mr. Palladin?" Justice was immediately alerted because that was the code name the detective at the local precinct that Justice kept on the payroll used to speak to him.

"I'm sorry, but you have the wrong number."

"That's a shame because if you were Mr. Palladin I would tell him to get out of the Bronx right away." Justice understood the encoded message right away. The headquarters of both of his main drug operations were in the Bronx. Either a hit or a bust was about to come down, and in either case he didn't want to be there.

"I would give him the message, but like I said, you have the wrong number," Justice said as he disconnected the call. Within seconds Justice, his second in command, and a bodyguard fled the apartment and jumped into his car and sped away from the Bronx. Justice had an apartment in lower Manhattan that he was sure that no one knew he had, and they headed there where he could wait and see what was going on. On the way downtown, Justice called the attorney that he kept on retainer and alerted him to get ready because shortly some members of his crew might be arrested.

About thirty minutes after Justice left, three cars of DEA agents and NYPD narcotic agents ascended on one of Justice's headquarters while at the same time other agents and police barged into the other operation. At the site that Justice had just left, two of Justice's crew were killed by the invading cops.

The site had several thousand vials of crack that were packaged and ready for distribution on the street. There was also a large amount of cocaine waiting to be processed into crack. Both of the Justice's men opened fire because they had lengthy records of drug possession and were looking at an extensive stay in prison if arrested again. As they tried to get away, it wasn't clear who opened fire first but the result remained the same.

At the second site the bust went much smoother and everyone was arrested without shots being fired. The bust was so large and such large quantities drugs were confiscated that it would prove to be a major boost to the careers of quite a few law enforcement officers. They had a great time posing in front of the various news media for pictures and interviews. The only down side was that the main man they were after, the kingpin of the operation, Justice, had escaped their clutches.

Once Justice was in his safe house, he used a prearranged series of security measures to get in touch with Brandon. "Yo, Pred, I got bad news, man."

"What's up?"

"I received a call from our boy downtown that a bust was getting ready to come down."

"Did he say when it was gonna happen?"

"He said right then so I got in the wind right away."

"Did the bust happen?"

"I'm not sure because I tried to talk to my people at the spots but I can't reach anybody."

"Then it's probably safe to assume that the Feds moved in. Where are you?"

"I'm at my joint downtown. Nobody knows about this place but you."

"Are they looking for you?"

"I'm not sure. I don't know how deep the investigation goes. I don't know if they were on to just the drug operation or how much they know about my operation. They only went after two houses as far as I could tell. I was able to reach people in the other three spots including the lab and things were pretty much business as usual. I told them to get any major weight out of there and put it in the safe houses I created. I don't know if they are on to my operations or whether this is related to our other endeavors."

"If they were on to our other endeavors, someone would have been here to pick me up too. So I don't think they are on to us but on the other hand if they are on to your operation there's probably a manhunt out for you right now."

"You're probably right, Pred."

"I think you need to lay low while I contact our people downtown to see if they are looking for you. Meanwhile, you need to prepare yourself in case you have to get in the wind. How much cash do you have on hand?" Brandon asked.

"About sixty thou."

"I'll get another fifty and get it to you as soon as I'm sure that no one is following me. I don't want to take a chance on leading them to you. If you need more you just let me know where you are and I'll get it to you. If you have to leave town do you have any idea where you might head?"

"Probably either around Tennessee or Kentucky, and if the move is permanent then I'll head for Cali."

. . . . .

Among Ebony's first visitors once she was transferred to the rehabilitation facility were Gary and Ted, who came with the intention of bringing her up to speed on the developments in the case. Ebony had just finished a strenuous workout with her physical therapist and she was technically finished for the day even though she had decided to put in another session later that evening rather than relaxing in her room watching television. After working with the therapist for two days, she was very familiar with the exercises she had her doing.

She was confident that after a short rest her body could withstand the stress of another workout. She was surprised at how quickly her body had gotten out of shape. Before her injury two of these workouts wouldn't have even made her break a sweat. Now she felt like she had run a 20-mile marathon with a 500-pound gorilla strapped to her back. She greatly underestimated the devastation her injuries had on her body but that just made her more determined to return to her former state of fitness as soon as possible.

As she was waiting for her evening meal she must have dozed off because she awoke when Gary placed a kiss on her cheek.

"Hey, Cowboy, I was only asleep and not under medication. Don't try to take any liberties with me," Ebony told Gary as she placed her cheek out to be kissed by Ted. "Well, if he can get away with it, you might as well get one too."

Gary said, "I just couldn't resist. You looked like such a little angel that no one would guess what a pain in the backside you can be. I guess I was having Sleeping Beauty flashbacks."

"Well, if I was Sleeping Beauty, you sure ain't my Prince Charming. You might be able to pass for the frog though."

"I'm crushed. How could you be so mean to me and I came here on a mission of mercy and to deliver good news?"

"Good news? Really? What's up?"

"I don't think I want to tell you after you hurt my feeling."

"Okay, I take it back. You really are my knight in shining armor."

"Nope. You're too late, I'm not talking."

"Ted, will you tell this joker to stop messing with me?" Ebony asked.

"I don't get involved in squabbles between partners," Ted said with a laugh.

"I don't care which one of you tell me but someone better give up some information very soon or I'll show y'all how much progress I made in therapy by getting out of this chair and kicking your butts."

Turning to Ted Gary said, "She's mighty feisty for someone who is in a nursing home. I guess she's doing so good she doesn't need any visitors. I guess we can leave."

"First of all, this is a rehabilitation facility and *not* a nursing home. Will you guys please stop messing with me and tell me? I know Brandon Barnett got ran over by a truck while he was crossing the street."

"You would consider that good news?" Gary asked.

"Not really, unless the truck is named Ebony Delaney. I want a piece of his ass in the worst way. When I get finished with him, he's gonna wish he got run over by a truck."

"We honored your wishes and left Barnett alone, but we can't say the same for his buddy Justice Permentier," Gary said.

"What happened?"

"Yesterday, NYPD and DEA in a joint effort raided two of Permentier's drug houses. We confiscated drugs that had a street value of over a million dollars as well as assorted guns and paraphernalia. A couple of his men were killed in the process."

"Were any of our guys hurt in the bust?" Ebony asked.

"Not a scratch. Things went pretty well except for one thing."

"What's that, Gary?"

"Permentier got away. Intel placed him in one of the spots but something or someone must have tipped him off that we were getting ready to bust him because he got out right before we came in."

"Do we know where he is?"

"Not yet, but it's only a matter of time before we catch him. We have an APB out on him, and we're pretty sure he hasn't left the city yet,"

"Did Barnett flee too?"

"No. Indications are that things at his business are pretty much business as usual."

"I thought we agreed that we wouldn't make a move on either of them until we had an airtight case on both of them?" Ebony asked.

Ted replied, 'That would have been ideal, but DEA and the powers that be saw it different. If Permentier had gotten strong enough that he felt comfortable moving against us and trying to kill a cop, we needed to bring him down. He had gotten too big and powerful to allow him to continue to operate with impunity. Plus, DEA had built up a damn strong drug case against him and they had run up a pretty hefty bill. They needed some arrests to justify the sizable budget they were working with."

"So they could justify spending the money on *their* investigation, they took the risk of putting our investigation at jeopardy by alerting Barnett that we are on to him and coming for him?"

"Not really. I don't see it that way. You had already put Barnett on alert by confronting him and telling him that we were on to him. He already knew an investigation was forthcoming. That's why he tried to kill you. The way the DEA ran the bust it looked like a straight drug bust. No implications of anything else. Not the hit on you and not the hits on the wives. True, Barnett's antennas are up, but they were probably up anyway."

"I don't know if it's worth the risk, Ted. I don't want this guy getting in the wind or going so far underground that we can't dig up enough information to convict him."

"I don't see how this changes anything. He would not dare arrange another client's wife's death because he didn't know who you had talked to, and if the authorities believed you, a hit might alert them that you were telling the truth. He knew we didn't have enough to arrest him, but he wouldn't be so bold as to try to pull another one off. That would be plain stupid, and the one thing this guy has proven is that he is far from stupid. Plus, I had other reasons for not trying to stop the DEA from running their operation."

"Which were?"

"One, I wanted to isolate this chump. He hasn't made many mistakes up to this point, but that might be because of the way they worked together. If we make him have to operate by himself, he might slip up and make the mistake that will finish him off. And there is one more thing. We surmised that Permentier handled the street level of the business and that he was the one who got the heavy hitters to run the hits that Barnett planned. I didn't want Permentier around in case Barnett decided to take another shot at trying to get you."

Gary interjected, "Ted spoke with me about it and I agreed with him completely. You're a pain in the butt, Delaney, but you are *our* pain in the butt and I won't take a chance on someone taking you out if I can prevent it."

"Hey, Ebony, if I didn't know better I would think this big galoot cares about you," Ted teased.

"This ain't about love, it's about being partners. That's what I keep telling you, that's what you Feds don't get. Partners are family. They are like another part of you and an extension of your body. They are like another leg or another arm. Good partners function as one. I start the sentence and my partner finishes it. You cover your partner's back. You don't betray your partner and you don't let anything happen to your partner."

Trying to lighten the atmosphere, Ebony interjected, "I don't know, Gary. You and Ted seem to have gotten pretty tight. You two seem thick as thieves to me. Maybe you want him to be your new partner."

"Hell no. Ted is cool and everything but he's still a tight-assed Fed and trying to go by the book and everything. No, girl, you're my partner. Now get up off your ass and stop playing around and get out of this place so we can finish off this Barnett character and move on to other bad guys."

· · · · ·

Stephanie was getting unforeseen benefits from implementing the elaborate plan that she and Ebony had devised. She had joined a charitable organization that was the sister organization to the foundation that Brandon had instituted. They figured what they needed to do was put Stephanie into one of his spheres of influence where he would have reason to come into contact with her other than at a party where she could be mistaken for a party girl. They were confident that once he noticed her he couldn't resist getting to know her.

Stephanie was not only very sexy and beautiful, but she also had an aura about her that men were mysteriously drawn to, almost like the Sirens of Greek mythology. Stephanie had never analyzed it and or tried to understand it, rather years ago she had learned to just accept it and now she was gonna find a way to use it.

She had joined the organization as a volunteer and she worked two nights a week as an organizer and as a mentor to a ten-year-old girl named Starr. Starr's mother was a reformed crack addict who had given birth to Starr when she was barely fifteen. Starr's mother loved her daughter and son and for their sakes struggled mightily to beat her drug addiction and keep it at bay. She attended Narcotic Anonymous religiously three times a week, and she tried her best to be a good mother, but there were just so much about being a mother that she didn't know.

Stephanie loved being a mentor, which was a pleasure she didn't anticipate. Starr was an intelligent and attractive young girl though she was a touch of the shy side. She wanted to be liked, and she made an effort to please her mother and in short time Stephanie as well. It was obvious that she looked up to Stephanie and Stephanie went out of her way to keep their relationship away from hero worship and move it toward an older sister/friend relationship. Stephanie felt it was important that we all have heroes, but how many people really felt like they could become their heroes? You could become very much like your sister or best friend though.

Stephanie didn't want Starr to emulate her. She wanted her to see there were certain aspects of her personality that Starr could adapt and make work for her. Starr liked going out to restaurants, something her mother rarely did because she had never been exposed to it or because she couldn't afford it. Stephanie took her and used that as an opportunity to gently work on her table manners. Stephanie took pleasure from watching the little girl, who last week had eaten her salad with her fingers, work with a salad fork. She struggled with it, but the fact that she tried made Stephanie proud and she didn't hesitate to compliment Starr and watch her beam at the compliment.

As they ate their baked chicken with an apricot glaze, Stephanie noticed how Starr watched how she cut her chicken into little pieces and eat them slowly and then tried her best to do the same without drawing attention to herself. Stephanie made a mental note to take her uptown to a soul food restaurant where they could eat fried chicken with their fingers and just relax and have fun like giggling little girls. She wanted to show Starr how to be comfortable in any environment. She realized that this was a special girl when Starr asked if her little brother Darren could accompany them sometimes. It was touching that despite her circumstances she would still look out for her little brother. She knew that regardless of what happened with Barnett, this was a relationship that she wanted to foster and nurture.

Two days earlier one of her fellow volunteers had told her that Barnett had been asking questions about her. She felt encouraged because now phase I of their plan was underway and she felt confident in how she should proceed. Barnett was used to women coming on to him so she decided she would remain aloof and disinterested. She would make him come out of his element and have to be the pursuer.

The next time she went to the office, Barnett came in shortly before it was her time to leave. He went into the office of the director for what seemed to be a meeting, but Stephanie noticed that he looked at her every time he didn't think anyone was watching. Stephanie wondered how much time would pass before he spoke to her. She didn't have to wonder long because he excused himself from the meeting to go to the restroom and on his way back stopped by her desk.

"Excuse me, miss, but I've never seen you here before. Are you new?"

"I just started spending some time here, if that is what you mean."

"What do you here?"

"I'm a mentor and has also do some volunteer office work. You're asking a lot of questions. May I ask you who you are?"

"I'm sorry, but I thought you knew who I am."

"Why should I know who you are?"

"Because I'm Brandon Barnett, the founder of A Better Tomorrow. And you are?"

"Not interested."

"I just wanted to know your name."

"Amber."

"Are you a rock star like Prince or Sting, or is there a last name?"

"I can't see how it's pertinent that you should know my last name."

"We don't let just anybody work with our kids. After all, we are responsible for them."

"Don't worry, I passed a very thorough background check. I'm here to help the kids not to hurt them."

"I'm sorry, I was just trying to be friendly."

"Then I would suggest that you don't question my character before you even know me."

"Look, I'm sorry we got off on the wrong foot. I'm sure not here to try to insult you. We are all supposed to be on the same team. We're just trying to make life a little better for our young brothers and sisters."

"I'm sorry too. I guess I was being a little defensive. It just seems I have assholes hitting on me wherever I turn. I'm sorry if I misinterpreted your intentions."

"Hopefully after you get to know me better you'll realize I'm one of the good guys."

"Are there any good guys left?"

"I'd like to think so and I'd like to restore your faith in the goodness of man."

"I'll tell you what. I'll keep my eye on you and see for myself what kind of person you are."

"Can't we spend a few minutes now talking so I can start to get to know you better?"

"I'm really not interested in getting to know you like that and I have a very special little girl waiting for me and I don't want to keep her waiting."

· · · · ·

"Now, this is my shit right here. That other crap like running shit is cool for other cats but that really ain't me. This is what's happening. Having your hammer in your hand and being able to walk up to muthafuckas, look him eye to eye, and just blast him. No bullshit. No pretense. Just mano to mano. Now that's what's up," Omar thought as he caressed the smooth coldness of his Glock. There was an air about the way he caressed his gun that was almost sexual, almost perverted. It reminded you of an old lecherous man caressing the thigh or breast of a young teenage lover. It was almost as if that touch could convey something mean, sinister, or evil.

Omar had decided to go up against the young dealers who were moving into the territory that he had so violently claimed a few months ago. He had come up with a plan that was so daring it bordered on brazen and reckless. It wasn't going to be no drive-by nonsense, which was safer for him but the odds of hitting his targets were greatly reduced. There was a trio of these young men who were up and coming and wanted to impress the rest of the dealers with how cold-blooded and cutthroat they were. He was going to walk up to all three of them together and when he got close enough to almost kiss them, he was gonna open fire.

"Enough of this playing around and trying to be low-key and discreet crap. I'm tired of having to act like a sucka because I'm scared of some niggas back in New York. I'm through hiding. If they want to tussle, let the niggas come on. It's time to show these bitch-ass country boys who they're fucking with," Omar thought as he snorted another hit of coke in each nostril. Omar usually didn't get high, but he liked the icy coldness the coke gave him right before he had to put in some blood work.

Finished with his preliminaries, Omar parked his car about half a block from where the trio stood. He took the time to lock his car and activate the alarm. In order for his plan to have the maximum effect on all the other dealers, Omar had to show them how cool and heartless and totally without fear he could be. He wanted everyone to see he wasn't scared of no one or nothing. He was pleased to see maybe a half dozen other dealers scattered around talking and waiting for customers. "Good, I need an audience for this show," Omar thought.

In plain sight of everyone, he took his Glock and tucked it in the waist band at the small of his back and pulled his Coggi sweater down to cover it. He put on his shades and stooped to the side mirror of his car and checked his appearance. Anyone watching him would have thought he was getting ready to go on a Saturday night date. He licked his fingertips, not sure if this was a nervous habit he picked up somewhere or if it was something he got from a gangster movie or a Clint Eastwood Western, but he thought it was cool as hell. Then he started walking toward the trio.

He walked slowly almost causally, almost as if he was out for a Sunday afternoon stroll in the park. When he got about fifteen feet away the trio realized he was coming toward them and they turned to face him. Whether they recognized him was questionable as they had only met him once. Omar usually sent his underlings to deal with the street dealers. It was clear that they didn't know his intentions and fear was not something that often ran among them. They weren't afraid of Omar or in fact of anyone else because they had already buried a few people while trying to build their reputation. They were the young lions in the street tough, fierce, fearless, and arrogant and not to be trifled with unless you wanted to die. They turned to face Omar and pushed their shirts back to reveal the handguns tucked in their pants.

"What's up, Nigger?" One asked.

Omar didn't reply he just continued to slowly walk toward them.

"Can we help you with something, partner?" Another said as he removed his gun and held it causally at his side. He didn't know it, but that movement marked him for death first. Omar didn't say anything, just continued on toward them. As he got alarmingly into their personal space, their radar sent the first signals of possible danger and their hands went to their guns, though the last two didn't pull them out.

Once Omar was close enough that he could have touched them if he wanted, he in as non-threatening a gesture that anyone could imagine, folded his hands behind his back and tilted his head to the side.

In a soft, firm, unemotional voice, Omar said, "Didn't my people tell you this corner belonged to me?"

It was then that the young leader of the trio made a fatal mistake. Kingpins or leaders of drug crews didn't handle business in the street. Their job was to run shit and make sure the product and the money ran smooth. He recognized Omar but did not recognize his intentions. He assumed that Omar was there to warn, threaten, or maybe even negotiate about the corner. The Georgia police didn't play, and violence in the middle of the day and in the middle of the street was not tolerated. He assumed Omar was there to talk a good game but he wasn't impressed. Plus, his partner already had his gun pulled out so he was ready if things got heavy. So he said, "Yo, son, who are your people?"

In a movement he had done so many times, it was as much second nature to him as brushing his teeth, Omar pulled out his gun and in one fluid motion wheeled and shot the boy holding the gun square in the face. Within seconds he turned on his heel and fired two shots into the chest of the man standing next to him. Omar's action was so swift and sudden that it stunned the trio's leader and he fumbled as he tried to pull his gun. This second mistake sealed his fate.

Omar turned and fired two more shots, one catching him in the chest and the other in the throat. Then, in no rush whatsoever, Omar walked over to each fallen man and leaned over took the money and drugs out of their pockets and shot the leader once again in the head. He was sorry that he had brought his Glock instead of his .44. The other two men were seriously wounded but not yet dead. The .44 packed such a punch that a shot placed where he shot the two men would probably have killed them. The Glock was great for rapid automatic gunfire and almost ideal for a firefight, but it was not quite as good for close-quarter fighting. He debated going over to shoot each of them in the head as well but decided it wasn't necessary. If they were lucky enough to survive, it shouldn't have mattered because he had already made his point.

Then as cool as when he came, he returned his gun to its holster, straightened his sweater, and starting strolling back down the street. As he passed two other dealers who were cowering behind a car, he threw them the drugs and money he took off the dealers and snarled, "All you bitch-ass niggers better get off my corners. This is your last warning." And he continued on to his car, stopping once again to check his appearance in the mirror before getting in the car and driving off.

· · · · ·

Brandon could not have anticipated the effect that Stephanie was having on his life. They weren't lovers, but there was nothing in this world that Brandon wanted more. It was just that everything he tried to get things to the next level didn't work. They hung out two or three times a week, but it was usually at his initiative. Stephanie acted like she could care less whether they spent time together or not. He had to believe that she enjoyed being with him while they were together or else why would she agree to continue to go out with him. Most of the time she didn't seem to be too impressed with him and sometimes Brandon wished he could say the same about her but of course that wouldn't be the truth.

Brandon had never met anyone like Stephanie and the feelings he had for her were unlike anything that he had ever felt. Brandon was used to dating beautiful women and Stephanie was among the most beautiful woman he had ever dated. A woman's beauty did not impress him, as he had been around beautiful women since college. Unlike every other attractive woman he knew, Stephanie seemed oblivious to the fact that she was beautiful. She didn't expect favors or special treatment because of the way she looked. She was unassuming in a way that made her a delight to be around. Her personality could best be described as open and outgoing with a touch of humility.

Brandon knew that Stephanie was smart but he had no idea how overwhelmingly intelligent she was until one day she was visiting his agency and he had a problem with his computer. He and the resident computer expert had a problem with a program that wouldn't respond despite their best efforts. Finally frustrated with watching the two of them stumble around, she had sat at the computer and within fifteen minutes had the program running without a hitch. On several occasions Stephanie had demonstrated just how intelligent she was but had downplayed it, which he assumed was typical of her nature. It was extremely unusual to meet a woman who was so smart and good looking but remained low key about it.

In many ways Brandon considered Stephanie the perfect woman. She had looks, brains, personality and class. She was so sexy that once or twice Brandon almost had an incident with guys in the street who openly stared at her or said inappropriate things to Stephanie that bordered on being disrespectful. Brandon was not accustomed to men disrespecting him by making passes at someone he was with. The only reason he didn't confront a couple of those guys was because Stephanie would not let him. He could almost understand because Stephanie was so flat out gorgeous and he didn't miss the constant attention she got when walking down the street. Sometimes even he couldn't resist stealing furtive glances at her.

Stephanie was near perfect in all ways but one: she refused to have sex with Brandon. This was a puzzle that confused him to no end. Brandon knew he was a good-looking man, and he assumed that Stephanie was attracted to him because she was spending more and more time with him. Lately she had even taken to returning to his luxurious brownstone with him and once even spent the night there when they returned late from a night of dancing and drinking. Brandon incorrectly surmised that once she got back to his place that intimacy would occur. Such was not the case. She insisted on remaining in one of his guest bedrooms, and when he tried sneaking in during the wee hours of the morning, she obliterated his pretense that he was just checking on her by insisting that she was fine. Only on rare occasions would she even allow him to kiss her and even less times did she return the kiss and never with the amount of passion that he felt.

Brandon was spending increasing amounts of time trying to unravel the enigma that was Stephanie. He thought that maybe she had gone through some trauma in her life that kept her from indulging in intimacy. Brandon was starting a daily ritual of telling himself that he was going to forget about Stephanie and put her out of his life. The next thing he knew he was picking up the phone to call her. Brandon couldn't understand why he continued to be bothered with her since he had numerous beautiful women at his beck and call. He had no doubt that she was worth the trouble. He just couldn't believe he was the one putting forth this degree of effort.

Brandon also didn't understand what was going on with him. If another man had behaved in this manner, he would have laughed at him as being pussy-whipped. It was not possible that he was in love with her. Love for a woman was not an emotion that he thought he was capable of. In fact, there was no such thing as love. People just used love as an excuse to act out their lust or other physical needs like desire for companionship. There was loyalty and brotherhood, and it was cool to have someone cover your back, but that wasn't love. Even if you wanted to describe that feeling as a type of love, it was between friends or brothers.

Women were not deserving of love. Women were good for helping him make his money as objects that he could use to entice clients or kill for profit. It was hard for him to conceive of a woman as a prospective life partner. But then again there was Stephanie. Beautiful, charming, enticing, bewitching, intelligent, classy, elegant Stephanie. So much unlike any woman he had ever met. He had hated women so long and held them in such low regard that seeing things differently was nearly impossible.

He did not see women as beings worthy of respect, affection, or admiration. He saw his mother as a miserable person and a horrible example of a mother. Why had she so greatly neglected her responsibility to him? They say you are supposed to love the person who gave you life but why give him life if she was going to subject him to the things he had to go through? He hated his mother almost as much as he hated the uncle who had abused him. His mother had repeatedly left him with his uncle even though he begged and pleaded with her not to do so. She had to know what type of person her brother was. After all, she had raised him. Did anyone expect him to believe that she didn't know that her brother sexually abused little boys?

His mother left him with that horrible, despicable man under the pretense that she had to go to work. He knew the reality was she didn't want the responsibility of raising the child she had gave birth to. Did she also *have* to go out with her friends after work, or was that something she wanted to do? If the money she got from working was so important, why didn't she use some it to get him a decent babysitter? A sitter who wouldn't do things to him that he could never forget.

He could still smell the funky, rancid, stale alcohol smell of his uncle's breath when he forced him to kiss him. He could still feel the throbbing hardness of his manhood through his uncle's underwear when he would pull him unto his lap. Years later he still almost gagged by the memory of his uncle forcing himself into his mouth and forcing him to keep him there until he ejaculated. He still felt like it just happened yesterday, the repulsion and self-hatred he felt at the memory of his uncle throwing him down and forcing his member into his rectum. He still felt weak and helpless at not being able to defend himself and fight his uncle off.

These memories haunted him for years and still seemed too vivid and real today. He thought he would have exorcised these demons when he finally got the chance to kill his uncle but it didn't work. He was almost thirteen years old when he finally got the chance to get his revenge. He and his highly intoxicated uncle were going to 42nd street to see a movie. As the train pulled into the station, Brandon saw a golden opportunity to bump his uncle, who fell into the path of the on-coming train.

The final split with his mother may have come when he had to watch her grieve instead of rejoicing at the funeral. To him that meant that she knew what her brother had been doing and she not only forgave him but condoned what he did. He couldn't remember the last time he had seen his mother and hadn't spoken to her in several months. His secretaries and receptionist had gotten very proficient as screening her calls and making a suitable excuse. About a year ago, he had taken to sending his mother a monthly stipend. It wasn't that he felt she deserved it, but it kept her from hassling him and it upheld the image he was trying to maintain. He couldn't appear to be one of the city's most successful and up-and-coming businessmen and have his mother living on welfare. So he would tolerate her as long as it fit his purposes. On more than one occasion, he had fantasized about killing his mother.

One could only guess why Brandon didn't blame his father as well. He hadn't seen his father in so many years that he couldn't even remember what he looked like. Instead of hating his father, Brandon had found a way to blame that on his mother as well. In his mind, he convinced himself that his mother was such a whore that she probably wasn't even sure who his real father was and that why the father on his birth certificate didn't come around. That man probably saw the same thing that he did that his mother was such a disgusting person who would want to be around her if he had a choice.

He still had to figure out what to do about Stephanie. He kept telling himself that it was only a matter of time before he got to make love with her and once he did, he could then forget her and move on. Though there was a part of him that wasn't convinced this was the truth.

· · · · ·

There were days in life when it was worth the journey. This was one of those days. Today not only was she leaving the rehab facility, she was walking out on her own. She was very close to 100 percent recovered exceeding the expectations of her doctors and almost everyone else besides herself. It had been more than three months since she was shot and she felt her life had been put on hold and she was eager to resume. Before she got back into the business of bringing Barnett to justice, she was going to take a little time to enjoy herself and celebrate life.

Mal was waiting outside to pick her up. He wanted to pick her up from her room but she insisted on walking out of the facility and not wheeled out in a wheelchair, which was the facility's normal procedure. She needed to walk out for a sense of accomplishment and to prove to herself that this was all behind her.

She refused to admit it to anyone, including herself, how badly this had frightened her. A possibility of a life without walking scared her worse than she ever thought it would. She was sure that she would be able to redefine her life if that was the case and she prayed that she would have the courage to do so. Now she thanked God that she didn't have to do so. Her resolve to keep Barnett and anyone like him from hurting people had not lessened one iota but one thing the past few months had taught her was patience. They were going to get Barnett but they were going to take their time and do it right.

Tonight she wasn't going to even think about Barnett, Omar, or dealing with the criminals that plagued the streets. Tonight she and Mal were going to a new Spanish restaurant that Mal had discovered and from time to time he brought her a treat from the restaurant. Now they were going to enjoy the entire restaurant experience complete with Flamenco dancers and red, white, and peach sangria. They made a fabulous skirt steak, stuffed sausage, broiled lobster, and exquisite paella. If she couldn't make up her mind which dish she wanted, she might sample each of them.

After bidding the nursing and medical staff goodbye and thanking them for their great care, she went outside and got a pleasant surprise. Ebony expected the new Saab that Malachi was leasing while he was here in New York but instead Mal had hired a limousine for the occasion.

"Mal, what's this? Where's your car?"

"Tonight you deserve to be swept away on the wings of chariots, but since I couldn't hire one, this was the next best thing. Tonight we celebrate, my love, and I have every intention of joining you and I don't want to have to worry about driving while under the influence."

"You know you didn't have to do this."

"I know I didn't have to, I wanted to, but if you don't want it I can always send it back."

"No, since you went to so much trouble, let the party begin."

They entered the limo, and Malachi opened a bottle of champagne that he had on ice. They sipped and enjoyed the champagne as they went to the restaurant. Halfway through the first pitcher of sangria and the appetizer of garlic shrimp in a savory tomato sauce, Ebony realized this was going to be a special evening. Throughout the entrée and dessert, the music, entertainment, and conversation were all delightful. They finished the meal with a strong coffee that was laced with brandy, when the conversation took a more serious note.

"Ebony, there are a few things on my mind that I want to discuss with you."

"Is everything okay?"

"More or less. Ebony, do you know how much I care about you?"

"I think I have a pretty good idea. You've made your feelings pretty plain throughout the past few weeks. I want to let you know how much I appreciate your support through this past ordeal."

"I didn't do that much."

"I don't know if I agree, but you being there really meant a lot to me."

"It was a lot less than I wanted to do. Ebony, I would like to know how you feel about me."

"Mal, I care about you very deeply. You've come to mean a lot to me."

"What does that mean? Are we in a relationship? Are we working toward a relationship?"

"I didn't know we had to define our relationship. I was just enjoying getting to know you and the more I got to know you, the more I care about you. You're a very special man. You once said you can't imagine your life without me in it, well, I think I can say the same. You've come to mean that much to me."

"You have quite a lot of people who seem to care about you very deeply. I understand your father's and brother's reservations toward me and maybe even Gary's, but Ted seems to have a lot of animosity toward me. Did you have a relationship that was deeper than a business relationship?"

"We are just friends as well as business associates. We have never had an intimate relationship or even gone out on a date. The only man I have had a relationship with in the past four years was my ex-husband, Jack."

"If I'm not prying too much, could you tell me about your marriage? What went wrong? Delaney is not a popular name among African Americans. What is the story there?"

"Jack is not an African American, he's Irish. He's an assistant district attorney, and we met in college. He's a fine man, but the cultural differences were so profound and I guess there just wasn't enough love there to make it work. We might have even gotten married for the wrong reasons. We got divorced more than a year ago, but we are still friends."

"What kind of friends? Friends with benefits?"

"Do I seem like that kind of woman?"

"That wasn't meant as a judgment. I know what kind of moral integrity you have, but you are a healthy, vibrant woman and you have needs. I just needed to know where things stood so I knew where I fit in."

"Where do you want to fit in?"

"I want to be your man. I want to be the person you know you can rely on, that you can trust because you know that I will be there for you. I want you to feel comfortable enough around me that one day you will let me share your world and you will become my wife. I want you to feel about me the way I feel about you. I'm falling so deeply in love with you that I have a hard time controlling my feelings. I know I'm ready for this and it is hard to wait for you to get to that same place."

"I admit that I have very strong feelings for you, but I made one mistake by getting married before I was ready and that's a mistake I don't want to make again."

"I'm not trying to rush you. Take as long as you need to be as sure as I am that this is the right thing for both of us. I just want to make sure that we're headed in the same direction. You could be looking for just a friend while my feelings run a lot deeper."

"Like you said, I am a young, healthy woman with normal needs. Plus, I already have enough friends. I would be lying if I said I think of you just as a friend. In fact, some of the thoughts I had about you while I was in rehab even make me blush."

"Those are the thoughts I want you to share with me."

"I just might if you play your cards right."

"Just show me those cards and I'll play them as well as I can."

"You're doing pretty well so far, but we'll talk about that later. For now, why don't you pour me some more of that sangria?"

"This one is almost gone. I'll get another pitcher."

They drank and enjoyed the rest of the sangria, which Mal had the waiter enhance with a couple of shots of tequila, while they enjoyed the music and floorshow. The dancers finished their performance with a steamy Tango.

Malachi and Ebony returned to the limo in a very relaxed and intimate mood boosted by the copious amount of alcohol they had drunk. Maybe the stress of the past three months or the relief from having come through such a close brush with death or maybe it was the natural progression of the attraction she had felt when they first met, but Ebony had never been closer to another person as she felt now. Maybe it might have been that Ebony was feeling desires brought on by the months of abstinence, but she had already made up her mind how this evening would end.

They got in the limo, and Malachi must have sensed what Ebony was feeling because they just sat very close together and didn't feel the need for conversation, rather just enjoyed being close to each other. They sat so close together that it wasn't necessary to have rented a stretch limousine. They could have sat in the backseat of a Volkswagen Beetle with room to spare. Malachi looked Ebony in her eyes so intently it was as if he was trying to peer into the depths of her soul. He pulled her into his arms and leaned over and covered her lips with his. He breathed in the heady aroma of the sangria on her breath and savored the velvety softness of her tongue. That first kiss led to a dozen more, each special and different in their own way. They started out as exploratory and as a valid attempt to get to know each other again and they slowly became more and more passionate. Almost as if they had a mind of their own, Malachi's hands started caressing her body and they explored the lush ripeness and hidden pleasures of Ebony's body. When his hand found the treasure of her womanhood and he gently caressed it, a moan escaped her lips.

Just as they reached the point of having to break the intense heat of the moment or making love for the first time in the back seat of a car, the car arrived at Ebony's apartment. After thanking the driver and giving him a hefty tip, they walked up to Ebony's apartment. Within seconds of entering the apartment and closing the door, they were in each other's arms, engrossed in a kiss.

It didn't take many kisses to regenerate the heat they were feeling in the car. Without breaking off the kiss, they simultaneously got undressed while Ebony led Mal to the bedroom. They stumbled into the bed still locked in an embrace. Ebony rolled onto her back and opened her legs to allow Malachi complete access. As Malachi entered Ebony, he felt more complete than he had felt in many years. Slowly they started making love and gradually the tempo and intensity increased until both lost themselves in an explosive orgasm. They barely had enough time to catch their breath before they started to make love again, this time more tenderly and intimacy was as much the goal as satisfying their urgent needs and passions. They made love until the rest of the world outside that bedroom ceased to exist.

· · · · ·

Isn't the morning after you make love to a new partner for the first time supposed to be awkward or uncomfortable? Such wasn't the case for Ebony. Aside from being a bit sore in muscles that hadn't received this type of workout for a while and the warm, fuzzy tenderness in certain special places, she felt remarkably relaxed and fulfilled. There was none of the second-guessing and doubt that often accompany such a liaison. She didn't think it was love that she was feeling yet, but it was something akin or very close to it.

There were feelings awakening in her that she hadn't felt in quite a long time. Instead of being scared or intimated by those feelings, she wanted to do anything she could to heighten and nurture those feelings. Maybe she realized that it was time to have the type of relationship that she had been denying herself for far too long.

The way that Malachi felt wasn't much different from Ebony. There was something about Ebony's persona that led him to believe that Ebony was a passionate, considerate and adventurous lover and he was not disappointed. If anything, their lovemaking had exceeded his expectations. They had connected in ways that he had never experienced before. He could tell from her movements and sounds of passions just what she needed and he was more than willing to comply. She seemed to sense all those secret things that would give him the most pleasure and do those things before he even knew he wanted them done.

He had taken Ebony's keys while she was sleep and gone out and got them croissants and bagels with cream cheese and lox for breakfast. After brewing some coffee and tea, he located a tray and after arranging the food and flowers. He placed the tray by the side of the bed and awakened her with a kiss. "Good morning, sleepyhead."

Struggling against getting up just yet, Ebony rolled over and pulled the blanket up over her head. Malachi gently removed the blanket and gave her a kiss of the neck. Ebony rolled toward Mal and wrapped her arms around his neck in a hug as she said, "Good morning, handsome. How do you feel this morning?"

"I'm feeling pretty good. How are you? Are you hungry?"

"I don't know. I guess I can eat. Mmmm something smells good. Don't tell me you got up and cooked?"

"Actually, I went out and got something for breakfast."

"Since you went to so much trouble, I guess I will have to eat something."

"Don't give me any ideas."

"Oh, you're real cute. If that's what on your mind, that's not the way to make it happen."

"Oh really, then what is the way?"

"You can always lead by example. If you show me what you want, I'm sure that I will reciprocate."

"I think I know just what you mean. I will file that away for future use. Speaking of the future, what would you like to do today?"

"Right away, more loving like last night comes to mind but I know I should take it easy. I have this urge to try to go out and do everything at once. Wisdom tells me I have plenty of time and that I should take it slow rather than chance a setback."

"Why don't we do a combination of both? You'll rest most of the day and tonight we'll go out and do whatever you miss doing most. What would you most like to do?"

"I would love to go dance the night away but that may be a little much too soon. Why don't we go to the Rose Theatre and have a bit to eat at Dizzy's and maybe catch a little jazz or either we can go to the City Center and see if there is an interesting ballet in town?"

"Okay, either of those choices will work, but I need us to get back in relatively early."

"Why? Are you that eager to get me back in bed? If so, it's not necessary because we can make love before we go out."

"That we can, but that's not why I want to get you back in early."

"Then why?"

"Because I am taking you out of town for a few days and I want you rested up for the trip."

"Where are we going?"

"That's a surprise."

"What if I don't want to go?"

"I can't force you to go, but I know it's something that you will enjoy. Do you trust me?"

"Yeah, I do."

"Then relax and pack a bag."

Early the next morning Ebony and Mal took a cab to the airport where after going through security they were approaching their gate when Ebony noticed they were on their way to Texas.

"Mal, I can't go home with you to Texas."

"Why not?"

"Not even thinking about the Barnett case, which I left kind of hanging, but I have family that was counting on taking care of me. As much as I appreciate your mother's offer, my mother and father would never stand for someone else taking care of me. Even if they didn't mind her pitching in and helping care for me, they would never tolerate me being so far away where they couldn't at least check on me. I think they would see that as an insult."

"I thought that we agreed for you to put the investigation on hold until you were almost at full strength? Come on, Ebony. Don't jump right into the case. Give yourself a chance to be ready to go after this guy full time."

"What about my parents?"

"What if I told you that I had discussed it with your parents and they agreed with you going to Texas for a few days as maybe the best thing?"

"Then I would say that I don't know who you spoke to but that sure doesn't sound like the parents that I grew up with."

"Didn't I ask you to trust me?"

"Yeah, and I said I would."

"Then trust me. Look, if when you get to Texas and you still feel the same way, I'll send you back the next day."

"Okay." Even though Ebony agreed, it seemed like a foolish waste to her. She was flying all the way to Texas to probably turn around and fly back the next day, but she had told Malachi she would trust him. She didn't want to start a new relationship on the basis of not at least giving Malachi the benefit of a doubt.

Against her better judgment, they boarded the plane. Mal had surprised her with first class tickets. When they touched down, Malachi had made arrangements with one of the ranch hands to pick them up at the airport. Since she was already in Texas, she decided to relax and enjoy the trip. She was starting to look forward to seeing Juanita and the kids.

As they pulled up to the ranch, Ebony was surprised by a colorful array of dozens of balloons and banners. She also noticed a large crowd of people milling around the side and back of the house. As the car pulled up to the house Ebony asked, "What's going on?"

Malachi's response was interrupted by Zoe who sprang from the stairs and catapulted down the stairs and ran to the car calling Ebony at the top of her lungs. In close pursuit were LJ and Jaleesa, who was also calling Ebony as well as laughing. As Ebony got out of the car, Zoe jumped into her arms and wrapped her arms around Ebony's neck in a hug that might have hurt her if she was bigger.

"Zoe, get off of her. She just got out of the hospital," Malachi scolded.

"Let her be, Mal, this love is just what I needed," Ebony said as she put Zoe back on the ground. "How are you doing, sweetheart?"

"How are *you* doing? I was so worried about you."

"I'm doing fine. Don't you worry about me. Hi, LJ. Hi, Lee-Lee. How are you both doing?"

LJ said, "Hi, Miss Ebony. I'm glad to see you're doing much better."

"Hi, Ebbny, we didn't think you were evah gonna get here. Everybody is waiting for you," Jaleesa said.

"Everybody?" Ebony asked.

"Come on before my big mouth nieces finish letting the cat out the bag," Malachi said as he took Ebony by the hand and led her around the side of the house.

"Hey, I didn't say anything," Zoe said with a pout as she took Ebony's other hand.

As they rounded the house, a stunned Ebony saw that most of the banners said, "Get well soon" or "Welcome" and she saw several familiar figures coming to greet her. She turned to Malachi and asked, "What's going on?"

"We wanted to give you a welcome home party but pulling it together in New York was just too difficult so I came up with the idea of having the party down here. Your parents agreed so we flew your family and friends down and put them up in a hotel. Today we're having a barbeque that most of the town is invited to and tomorrow we're having an intimate dinner for thirty at the best Mexican restaurant in town."

"Why did you go through all this trouble?"

"Because there are a lot of people who love you and we want to celebrate with you. Plus, you know how much we Texans love a good barbeque. Come on and stop stalling, a lot of people are waiting to speak to you." Ebony turned and started greeting the long line of people waiting to hug and speak to her. First in line were her mother and father, followed by her brothers, and her brother's kids were playing with Zoe, LJ, and Lee-Lee. There were also numerous officers from New York there as well, among whom were Gary, Melendez, Ted, and Stephanie, plus a bunch of officers who had worked with her on different cases over the years.

She met Juanita's sister Samantha and marveled how well the two of them got along with her mother. Her father and brothers greeted her and Malachi with hugs, and she had impressions of what it would be like if they were one big family. Her brothers seemed to legitimately like Malachi, and she had to wonder whether it was because he was an African American, unlike her ex-husband, or whether they had gotten to really know each other while spending time at the hospital. She hoped it was the latter because she wouldn't want to think that her brothers developed their affections solely on the basis of race. There also was the possibility that they liked Malachi because he wasn't sleeping with their sister at the time she was in the hospital. Her brothers had repeatedly demonstrated their overprotective natures.

Her father and Juanita's husband Jasper also seemed to be getting along as they stood in a cluster of other men sipping beer and engaging in conversation. She wondered what the men from New York City could be discussing so ardently with these men from the country. Maybe it was something as benign as football or baseball, but if the conversation shifted to the Dallas Cowboys and the New York Giants, World War III could break out.

She noticed there were a lot of people there that she didn't know, but they seemed to be having a great time and were contributing to the festive atmosphere of the occasion. If they were there because they were friends of Juanita, Jasper, or Malachi, she had to assume they were there to wish her well as well as to enjoy a fabulous meal.

She had heard about Texas barbeques, but the amount of food present was more than enough to feed a small city. There were two open pits over which a whole pig seemed to be roasting and over the other what looked like half a steer was being slowly cooked. Adjacent to them was a row of barrel grills which were filled by countless chickens, hot dogs, sausage, burgers, and ribs. A short distance behind them were tables full of baked beans, coleslaw, potato salad, ears of corn, and baskets of fresh fruit and slices of watermelon. There were over a dozen tables adorned with red and white checkered tablecloths where you could sit and eat at your leisure. There were kegs of beer, gallons of lemonade, and trash cans full of ice with bottles of water and soda.

There were maybe a dozen cooks and attendants scrambling around cooking and preparing the food. Though it looked like the food was ready, no one was eating yet. Ebony assumed it was because everyone was waiting for her, the guest of honor, to arrive. She felt flattered and blessed that so many people had gone to so much trouble

351

and travelled so far to wish her well. There was a seven-piece band that was playing a mixture of jazz, R&B, and country hits. They helped to keep the atmosphere lively and festive. She was starting to develop a little appetite so she decided to greet as many people as she could as quickly as she could so everyone could enjoy the food while it still was hot. She went up to Ted and Gary who were engrossed in conversation with several attractive young ladies. They separated themselves from the crowd and came up and gave her a hug.

"Hey, Delaney, you look a whole lot better than the last time we saw you," Gary said.

"What are you two doing down here? This seems like a long way to come to chase some booty," Ebony teased.

"Come on, Ebony, why do you always think the worst of us? Malachi asked us to come down to celebrate your full recovery and to wish you well," Ted said.

"Speak for yourself, Ted. "Gary said. "Malachi said we were gonna have a great time, with great food, plenty of booze, and fine women. And after he threw in free plane tickets and hotel accommodations, it was an offer I couldn't refuse. That's why I'm here."

"So you're here for the free food and a chance of some out-of-town. You don't care about me?" Ebony said.

"Hey, partner, you know how I feel about you, but seriously I never had a doubt that you were gonna come through this in flying colors and I didn't have to come all the way to Texas to show you how I feel."

Giving her partner a fist bump, Ebony said, "I hear that, partner. Well, enjoy yourself and get your party on because when we return to New York there's a certain ass we got to get into."

"Malachi made us agree that we wouldn't discuss any business on this trip."

"Well, that's a promise you can keep and let's enjoy ourselves today. This party is long overdue," Ebony said as she turned and looked for Stephanie and some of her other friends who had come down from New York. She spied Stephanie and was not even slightly surprised at the attention that Stephanie was getting.

There were several men who seemed bent on catering to her every wish. As she saw Ebony coming up she excused herself and went up to her with her arms outstretched and seeking a hug which Ebony warmly gave.

"Did you come all this way for the free food and a good time too?" Ebony asked with a smile.

"Heck no. I came to give my favorite girl some love and to let her know I got her back no matter where on this planet. I didn't even want Malachi to buy my ticket but I gave in when Ted told me what kind of money he's rocking with. You seem to have a serious winner there and he worships the ground you walk on. I think I might be jealous."

"That's strange to hear coming from you with the kind of attention you constantly get from men," Ebony countered.

"They're caught up in what they see. Very few are into or care about the real me. They just want to get with me because they think I'm attractive. They don't want to get to know the real me like Malachi seems to want to with you," Stephanie said with a slight pout.

"Speaking of men who are caught up with how you look, how are things progressing with Barnett?"

"You know the rules. Malachi insisted that we don't discuss that case or any other business today."

"Since when does Malachi or anyone else set rules for us?" Ebony asked.

"I hear you girl, but in this case I'm gonna give him that respect. Anyone who went to all the changes he went through to pull this off and spend all that money deserves that courtesy. All I will say is things are going surprisingly well and we'll talk about it at length when we get back to New York," Stephanie said.

"Malachi seems to have made a big impression on you," Ebony said.

"Yeah, he did. He seems like a real special guy, Eb. Appreciate him," Stephanie advised.

"I do. I'll talk to you more in a little bit. Let me let you get back to your adoring public," Ebony said as she headed toward Melendez and her lieutenant. Before she could get there, she saw Malachi, her parents, and Malachi's parents signaling to her. She walked over and joined them, and her father said in his loud, booming, public speaking voice "Could I have everyone's attention please. On behalf of my wife and sons and our new friends Jasper, Juanita, Malachi, and family, we want to thank you all for coming. We feel blessed and grateful that they have opened their home and their hearts to help us wish our daughter good health, a speedy recovery, and success in her future endeavors. It means a lot that so many of you have come out today and especially that some of you have come such a great distance. Most of you know that some evil beings tried unsuccessfully to take our Ebony from us. Instead, she sent them to deal with Judgment Day ahead of all of us. Today, we want to celebrate life, new friends and family, and the promise of better days. We want you all to relax and have a fabulous time and enjoy yourselves as we welcome Ebony back into our midst. So please eat, drink, dance, laugh, and love. If there is someone here you don't know, please introduce yourself because we are all here for the same purpose. To rejoice in the return of Ebony James." As he was finishing the band launched into a funky version of the JB's "Doin' It to Death" and the party took off in full swing into a party that few of them would ever forget.

Ebony met so many people she couldn't help but feel like a celebrity. She met the mayor and the town's aldermen but she took particular pleasure in meeting Malachi's best friend, Roscoe "Boobie" Franklin. Roscoe was a former high school and college football star, and he showed tremendous interest in Ebony, not just because she was Malachi's new girlfriend but because she was also Stephanie's best friend. He was enraptured with Stephanie and was desperate to get an inside track with her. Ebony found his puppy dog crush a little funny and kind of cute. It also gave her an opportunity to talk at length with Stephanie without appearing to be discussing the case.

"So bring me up to speed on what's going on with Barnett."

"Why don't we wait until we get back to New York?"

"Because you'll be going back a few days before me, and I want to be up to speed on the case so when I get back to the city, I can begin working right away. Come on, what's the big deal? Tell me what the heck is going on."

"Okay, if you promise not to tell Malachi or your parents. Things are going pretty good. Barnett seems to be more than a little taken with me. Keeping him at bay and playing hard to get has set him on his ear. He is such an obnoxious and arrogant bastard that anybody not giving him his way drives him batshit. He has tried everything he can to get me to sleep with him, and since he has been so unsuccessful, he has shown lapses of judgment and is operating out of his normal comfort zone. He keeps pulling me closer in the hope that he can slip inside my guard. I'm sure that at some point he will make a mistake that will contribute to his demise. Don't worry, Ebony, we will get this chump. He ain't so smart, cunning, or slick that he will get away with the crap he pulled. We'll get him."

"I know we will, but I'm not so sure about how. This guy seems to have done a helluva job of covering his tracks."

"I think you were on to something by suggesting that we get someone close to him. I didn't plan on being that someone, but since its happening we should go with it. I got to tell you I had a little problem at first with being so deceitful. It's seemed to be kind of low getting close to someone under false pretenses."

"You have to keep in mind who we're talking about. Don't forget that this guy has been responsible for killing at least four women for money as well as trying to have me killed. You can get out if it bothers you too much, but remember: When you're dealing with such a snake there is no such thing as being straight forward or upright. As long as you don't surrender your personal integrity, there nothing we can do that's out of bounds."

"No, I'm in until we finish the case. Don't worry, I'll do what has to be done to catch this guy."

· · · · ·

Too late to fix it, Omar realized the error of how he had executed his recent assassination. It was so foolishly reckless that if he didn't know better he would have thought that someone else must have planned it. He forgot the basic principles of what made street assassination so successful: you either had to be anonymous or have set such a barrier of intimation that anyone would have been scared to say a single word. In his desire to be daring and bold, he had made some fundamental mistakes that could cost him his freedom and maybe his life.

You had to have a network of partners and friends that was so vicious and loyal that even if you were locked up, any informants would know that there was somebody who would murder them to keep them from testifying. Here in Georgia, Omar had few partners and no friends. His partners were with him solely for financial gain and not because of any particular affinity for him. If he was arrested, they might even be eager to have him off the scene because they could then take over his operation. It was extremely doubtful that they would kill anyone to keep him out of jail.

He feared that soon that would be a reality. A member of his crew told him that they saw some members of a rival posse talking to the cops. The word on the street was that the police were looking for Philly Red (the alias he had assumed once he got to Georgia). He thought if people believed he was from Philadelphia it would make it harder for Justice to find him. He had laid low for more than a week, but he knew that at some point he was going to have to resurface. He considered leaving Georgia but he was reluctant to do so because he didn't think the cops could have that strong a case against him. Basically, it would come down to his word against the word of some rival dealers.

He also didn't feel like starting over again in another city, especially with a warrant for his arrest pending. He didn't have enough money to retire so he would have to start and set up another operation which would be a royal pain in the butt. He was finally getting established here in Georgia, and he wasn't eager to give that up. He thought about putting a bounty on the heads of anyone who would testify against him, but who could he trust to pay the bounty once he was in jail? If he gave the money to his partners, they would probably just keep the money and be glad that the witnesses got him out of the way.

One thing he had done after asking questions around town was hire himself a top quality attorney and putting him on retainer. If he was arrested, he didn't want some half-ass public defender responsible for his freedom. Having prepared himself as well as he could, he decided that today would be the day that he came out of hiding. He made a rather public display of going by a couple of his runners and picking up the cash they had made that day. He then went by a very popular diner on the strip where the dealers worked and had an elaborate lunch. He then got in his car and headed back home.

As he was exiting the car and heading up the stairs to his house, he whirled around because he could feel some one's presence behind him. As he was reaching for his gun, he froze because he saw four police officers behind him with their guns trained on him. The one closest to him barked, "Freeze. Police. You're under arrest." Omar momentarily debated about going down in a blaze of glory. He quickly dismissed that idea and raised he hands. The police handcuffed him and putting him in this car, drove him to the precinct.

· · · · ·

"What is with you anyway?" Barnett asked.

"What do you mean?" Amber/Stephanie asked.

"I mean, I can't figure you out. Most of the time, you act like you don't even want to be bothered. Then when I think I should forget about you, you volunteer to come over and cook dinner for me."

"I thought it would be a nice thing to do. You take me out a lot and try to buy me things all the time, so I figured this would be a nice way to return the favor. If you rather I didn't, I can go," Amber/Stephanie replied.

"That's not what I saying."

"Well, what are you saying?"

"Never mind, forget it."

"No, Brandon, if you have something on your mind, say it. We're both adults here. If you have something to say or something you feel, you should speak on it."

Brandon paused as he debated how much he should say before replying, "How do you feel about me?"

"Why do you ask?"

"Don't answer my question with another question. Can't you tell me where I stand with you?"

With a daunting smile, Stephanie said, "You stand on your feet like everyone else. Don't you?"

"Come on now, you said to speak on what's on my mind. Now that I have, you avoid the question."

"Maybe I don't understand the question."

"What's so hard to understand? Don't you know how you feel about me?"

"I don't know what you want me to say," Stephanie said as she purposely avoided a direct answer.

"I *want* you to tell me the truth. What is *this*? What are we doing here? Is there even a *we*? I'm feeling you. I'm checking for you. What's up? I want you and I want you to want me. I want to take this relationship to another level, but I can't do this by myself. I'm feeling all these things, and I don't have a fucking clue as to how you feel about me."

"Do you really need to know how I feel? If your feelings are real, does it matter how I feel?"

"That's bullshit and you know it. What kind of fool do you think I am? Do you think I want to catch feelings for someone who doesn't feel the same way about me? That would be just plain stupid."

"I didn't tell you to develop any feelings toward me, and if you did that's on you. It's not my responsibility."

"I'm not trying to put it on you, and I'm not asking for your permission to develop my feelings for you. I just want to know if you feel the same."

"I don't know how I feel. I told you from the beginning that I wasn't looking for a relationship, but if you wanted to hang out sometimes, that would be cool. You said you were cool with that, and now you're putting all this other stuff in the game. I don't get it. I thought you were looking for a friend, but if you wanted more you should let me know. I don't appreciate your painting me as the bad guy when we both knew where I was coming from right from the start. I'm not the one who switched up. You did."

"I thought I only wanted a friend in the beginning, but now that I've gotten to know you, I want more. Am I wrong?"

"Not wrong, but you're not exactly being fair. Look, Brandon, you're a very attractive man and you have a lot of style and honestly there are a lot of things about you that a person could love, but I'm not there yet. I told you, before I let a man in my pants he has to get in my heart. Before I let a man in my heart, I have to really get to know him. I have to know I can trust him and he has to trust me. I have to know that we can build something together that is special and monumental. I'm trying to get to that place but frankly we're not at that place yet. Are we ever gonna get to that place? I don't know but I *do* know I don't appreciate your putting all this pressure on me just because you want some pussy."

"Did I say that's all I wanted? Have I ever pressured you to sleep with me? I have a dozen women who would gladly sleep with me if that was what I wanted."

"So why don't you go get them and leave me alone?"

"Because that's not what this is all about. This is not about sex or you sleeping with me. This is about trying to develop a relationship. I can't remember the last time I had a 'woman' and I have never had anyone that I feel about the way I feel about you."

"Do you want me to go?"

"No, no, no. Pretty lady. I want you to stay. I want you to stay today, tomorrow and maybe forever."

"Careful. You sound like you're talking marriage or some other kind of stuff."

"I never thought of it like that, but I guess things are kind of headed that way."

"Brandon, have you been smoking or something? We've never been intimate and yet you're talking in those terms. You can't be serious?"

"I'm just trying to show you how serious I am about you."

"I think it must be your hormones talking and not you heart or your brain. You're still as much a mystery to me as you ever was. I don't know anything about you. I don't even know where you were born. I never met your mother. I don't know anything about your business. I know you own a sports agency, but you keep all the inner workings of your business a secret. That's not a problem, and I respect your privacy. I know a man's business is his domain and I don't want or need to be up in the middle of that, but you can't feel like that and on the other hand talk all that stuff about how strongly you feel for me.

"Marriage is a partnership. Equal partners. Before you lie to yourself any further about how you feel about me, I think you need to learn to be honest with yourself about whether you are capable of having the type of relationship you are talking about. Do you really think you trust me? I have never been in your home if you weren't here. That's cool but if you don't trust me, can you really think you might love me or are you just being a hypocrite? That is some weird love, but I can tell you it's not one I want to share. So let's not have this conversation until you are sure you are ready to take the kind of steps that are necessary to build a relationship."

· · · · ·

Omar sat calmly at the table smoking a cigarette. He was in one of the interrogation rooms in the bowels of the precinct. After the police had arrested him, they rushed him into the cell where he vied with more than a dozen men for sitting space. After about four hours they removed him from that room and put him in a solitary cell. Within an hour, they finally allowed him his phone call and he promptly called his attorney.

The detectives were doing everything within their power both legal and illegal to get Omar to confess to the crime they had arrested him for. They tried coercing, cajoling, deception, threats, and every other type of intimidation short of violence they could think of. They even tried the standard good cop/bad cop routine, but nothing garnered any success.

Omar sat as silent as a sphinx. He steeled his mind to say absolutely nothing at all rather than chance saying anything that might give them encouragement or something that might implicate him. He was very aware of the seriousness of the charges facing him, and though he put up a brave front, inside he was very nervous. He didn't see how they could have much substantial evidence against him, but countless people had seen the execution and no telling how many had agreed to testify against him. This was a matter he had to leave in the hands of his attorney, and at this point he didn't want to say or do anything that would make his job harder.

When Omar's lawyer, Ashton Morse, finally arrived at the station he immediately went to see Omar and told him he had done the correct thing in not saying anything to the police. He only knew Omar by his alias, Walter Redfern, known around town as Philly Red.

"Good evening, Mr. Redfern. How have they been treating you?"

"I guess all right. They were trying to fake me out by treating me all nice and shit."

"Did you say anything to them?"

"No way. I know better than to say a single word. I didn't even give them my name, rank, or serial number."

"Okay, let me go find out what they have on you."

Mr. Morse was gone for more than an hour, which surprised Omar and gave him more reason to be worried. He figured they must have some pretty substantial evidence if it had taken them so long to discuss his case. When his attorney returned, he could tell by the look on his face that the news wasn't good.

"Okay, Mr. Morse, what's the deal?"

"It's not good, Mr. Redfern. They claim to have several eyewitnesses to you shooting and killing a man in broad daylight. Is that possible?"

"The people they have are probably my rivals in the street, and since I'm been coming up so large, they probably are getting together to get me off the streets. We probably could make a case for conspiracy."

"We could only make a case like that if you admit to being in the drug game."

"That an easy trade-off for a murder charge."

"That's good because they got a search warrant after your arrest and the search of your house turned up numerous guns, a small quantity of drugs, and paraphernalia of materials for the manufacture and sale of drugs."

"Did they find the gun used in the so-called murder?"

"They didn't mention it, but I'm pretty sure they don't have it because they would have brought it up, though they might be holding it till we get to discovery."

"It seems like they have a stronger case for drug peddling than for murder."

"Should I take that to mean that you want to fight the charges and don't want me to try for a plea bargain?"

"Hell no. Why in the fuck would I pay you all that money if I just want to go after a plea bargain?"

"In that case, there is something else we need to discuss. Are you familiar with an Omar Douglas?"

"Excuse me?"

"They said your fingerprints came back with the identity of a Mister Omar Douglas and there is a federal warrant out for his arrest for murder. Is there any truth to their allegations?"

Omar didn't say anything as he thought about these new developments. After waiting a few minutes, Mr. Morse said, "Mr. Redfern, if you want me to help you, you have to be straight with me. I'm on your side, but I have to know the deal if I'm gonna help you."

"Give me a few minutes to think about all this."

"What is there to think about? Look, when I accepted your retainer I knew what line of work you are in. But if you don't think you can trust me, there's nothing I can do for you. I can give you your money back so you can get someone you feel you can trust because I think you're really gonna need a good attorney."

"I heard you're the best."

"I'm very good at what I do, but what I can do is limited if you're not telling me the whole truth and the police keep getting a chance to blindside me. Keep in mind, everything you tell me is in complete confidence."

"Okay, I guess I have to tell you everything. Get comfortable because there's a lot you don't know."

· · · · ·

Ted and Gary picked up Ebony at the Atlanta airport. Though they had returned to New York, she had remained in Texas for a few more days of rest and relaxation until they called her and told her to meet them in Atlanta right away. As she retrieved her overnight bag from baggage claim, her partners greeted her with a smile and a hug. Ted asked, "How was your flight?"

"There was a little turbulence but nothing significant."

"How are you feeling, Ebony?"

"I'm feeling pretty good."

"I think what Ted means is: are you well enough to get back to work?" Gary asked.

"I'm fine and ready to get things up and popping. What's going on?" Ebony replied.

"No, seriously, Delaney. Things are getting ready to go down and we're getting ready to kick ass and we need to know that you're well enough to rock and roll."

"Stop BS'ing, Gary. You know I'm well enough to be a part of whatever is going on or you wouldn't have called me in from Texas to be part of this. So stop playing and tell me what is going on."

"It seems our hard work is finally starting to pay off. Guess who has set up shop here in Atlanta and has been arrested for murder?" Ted asked.

"Justice Permentier?"

"That reminds me, I think we have a serious lead on Permentier's whereabouts. We'll deal with him when we get back to New York. No, even better. Omar Douglas."

"What has Omar been up to?" Ebony asked.

"It seems that Mr. Douglas has come to Atlanta and set up a drug operation of his own. He was operating under the alias of Philly Red and was therefore able to stay under our radar until he got in a dispute over some drug territory. In his normal reckless and cut-throat style, he killed one man and severely wounded two others.

Once he was arrested and printed, he popped up in our database and I understand that he is interested in trying to cut a deal with us."

"He doesn't seem to have a lot to bargain with." Ebony said.

"Actually, he has a lot to give us. If he can give us a multi-million-dollar murder for pay ring, then I will consider that a lot. What we don't have is a lot to offer in exchange. This guy has killed at least two people that we are sure of, including a celebrity wife. There is no way that he is gonna walk." Ted said.

"Then why did we come all this way? What makes you think he will talk to us if there is nothing we can offer him?" Gary asked.

"I didn't say we don't have anything to offer him. I said that there's no way he will walk. We have a little bit of luck on our side. Georgia is a state that has the death penalty. We could offer to take the death penalty off the table if he testifies for us."

"Will the Atlanta police go for that? They seem to have a righteous bust. They're not just gonna give that up," Gary countered.

"Technically, he committed our murder first and therefore we can claim jurisdiction. If he'll confess and give up the ringleaders, I think we can convince the Georgia authorities to go for it. When this goes down it should be a national, high-profile case. We can give them equal credit. It could be a tremendous feather in their cap," Ted said.

"Same old system and it stinks to high hell. It becomes about who can get the most credit and notoriety and not about justice. Don't you ever get sick of it?" Ebony asked.

"Hell yeah, I get sick of it but if that's the game we have to play to get some of these sleazeballs off the streets, I'll keep on playing it. Ain't that the most important thing?"

"I guess it is but it still sticks in my craw."

The conversation died down as they arrived at the county jail and presented their credentials. They were shown into a conference room where they had to wait a while for Omar's attorney to arrive. When he finally arrived, he and Omar were shown into the room where they sat at a table facing Ebony and her partners as introductions were made all around. Ted took the lead "Okay, Mr. Morse, your client said he wanted to speak to us. We're listening."

"It would appear that my client has extensive information about a network that was arranging the deaths of wealthy ex-wives."

"And how would he know about that?"

"That's information that he would rather not discuss at this time."

"Look, we didn't come all this way to waste time. If you want to play games, we can call this meeting to an end right now. Why don't we tell you what we know and you can tell us how you can help us. We know all about the operation being run by Brandon Barnett and Justice Permentier. We know that they have been arranging the deaths of wives who were awarded large divorce settlements in exchange for clients signing with them. We also know that your client was responsible for the death of Tanya Richardson. Now, what can your client do for me?"

"Agent Delaphine, let's be honest with each other. I had an associate within the legal system assess your data bank to obtain the status on these two alleged suspects. Neither Justice Permentier nor Brandon Barnett is in your custody. Mr. Permentier has a warrant out for his arrest for drug possession and marketing, not for murder or conspiracy to commit murder. Mr. Barnett hasn't been charged with anything and is going about his business as usual. Which gives me reason to wonder if you know so much about what is going on, why haven't any arrests been made? Could it be that you know a lot but have no witnesses or substantial evidence? If that is the case, my client can provide both. He knows where the bodies are hidden, and he can provide enough evidence to lock your case down and he can testify against them. So now, the question isn't what can my client do for you, but rather what can you do for my client?"

"What does he want?"

"He wants the murder charges dropped on the Richardson case and changed to conspiracy or assault."

"I guess we're through here because that is not going to happen," Ted said as he got up and prepared to leave. Following his lead, Ebony and Gary started assembling their papers as they were getting ready to leave too. Ebony went to the door and signaled the bailiff to open the door because the interview was over.

Seeing that the officers were serious and they were really getting ready to leave, Mr. Morse knew he had to soften his position so he asked, "Okay, what are you offering?"

"Let's get one thing straight. Just because murder charges haven't been filed, that doesn't mean that we don't have a strong enough case to get a conviction. This was such a heinous crime that we don't want to leave any stone unturned. We don't want to take a chance on any of them walking from this case. I personally think we have enough but my partners want just a little more. That's why we are after Permentier on the drug charges. Once we have him in custody, we are going to see if we can turn him against Barnett."

"You must also believe in the tooth fairy if you think that Justice will ever give anybody up especially his boy," Omar said. Morse shot him a look that clearly reprimanded him for breaking their arrangement and speaking. Omar immediately realized his error and fell silent again.

Ted responded, "Yeah, I have a tendency to believe in improbable things, but clearly so do you too, Mr. Douglas, if you think that charges will be dropped. We have you cold on at least two murders and attempted murder on at least two more. Freedom is not an option."

"What is an option?" Mr. Morse asked.

"This is Georgia, as you know, and there are some prosecutors that are going to push hard for the death penalty. We can make arrangements so that the death penalty will not be considered."

"So what are we looking at?"

"We can get his charge reduced to Murder 2 and several other lesser charges."

"So we're looking at twenty-five to life on two different charges? That's not good enough."

"I'm gonna be straight with you. With the case your client has built up against him, there is no way that he will see daylight before he's a very, very old man. But at least with us he has a chance at parole. If he doesn't testify against Permentier and Barnett, he will be charged with Murder One in both cases and we will allow Georgia to have jurisdiction and I promise you they will seek the death

366

penalty and probably get it. I think that's a pretty good deal, especially for someone who committed murder and whose testimony is not essential to the case."

Turning to his attorney, Omar said, "I think it's time I spoke with them. Maybe after I prove my value to them, they might give up a better deal. Now, what do you want to know?"

"Tell me what part you played in the plan. Tell us what you know about the operation."

"Permentier hired me to romance Tanya Richardson. I was to entice her into a relationship, which was quite easy because she was still reeling from the breakup with her husband. She was vulnerable because her self-esteem and confidence were badly shaken by all that had come down. All I had to do was give her back a portion of what she had lost. After she had caught feelings for me and developed a measure of trust, I was to take her on a cruise and I was to arrange an accident. It was strongly suggested that I made sure she fell overboard. I was then to leave and return to New York alone."

"How much did you get paid?" Gary asked.

"He promised me a hundred large but they reneged on the balance so they only paid me fifty thousand. If I knew they was gonna rip me off, I never would have agreed to do the job. She was a nice lady and didn't deserve what happened to her."

"Then why did you do it? Didn't it dawn on you that this lady was a mother to three kids?" Ebony barked at Omar.

"Hey, it wasn't personal. This was business. They paid me to do the job, so I did the job."

"You keep referring to 'they.' Who is this 'they'?"

"Justice and his partner."

"What's his partner's name?" Ebony asked.

"I don't know his real name, but Justice kept referring to him as 'Pred" or 'Predator.'"

"Predator? Like in the movies?" Gary asked.

"Yeah. I got the feeling that he was the one who was running shit though."

"Why do you say that?" Ebony asked.

"Because I had a beef with him and instead of paying me my money they tried to kill me."

"Why did you have a beef with them?" Ebony asked.

"They had this real elaborate plan, and Justice's boy got real upset because I didn't follow it to the letter. It had something to do with an alibi. That's why I think he did all the planning because Justice didn't mind the slight deviation from the plan but his boy sure did."

As Gary slid Omar a picture of Brandon Barnett, he asked, "Is this Omar's partner, Pred?"

"Yeah, that's him," Omar said.

"Did they try to kill you because of the beef or because they didn't want to pay you your money?" Ebony asked.

"I'm sure it was because of the beef because a couple of my boys did work for them and they all got paid without any problems."

"So you know about other women that they had killed?" Gary asked.

"A couple of my boys told me about blood work they had done for them, but I'm not testifying against them."

"Why not?

"Because I don't have beef with them. They didn't do anything to me."

"So you're testifying against Permentier because you have a grudge with him?" Gary asked.

"Can you think of a better reason? It's not like you guys are giving me my freedom. So if I'm going down, he might as well go too."

"What about his partner?" Ted asked.

"That punk-ass nigger? I would love to drop dime on him but he didn't give me any orders directly," Omar said.

"But wasn't he the one who had a problem with you for not following the plan exactly?" Gary asked.

"Yeah."

"Did he ever call the plan 'my plan' or indicate that the plan was his? "Ebony asked.

"Yeah, he did."

"Are you sure?" Ebony asked.

"Positive."

"And you will testify to that?" Ted asked.

"You damn right I will."

• • • • •

An ecstatic Ted, Gary and Ebony went out for dinner that night to celebrate finally having a major breakthrough in the case against Brandon Barnett. Though they disagreed on how significant Omar's testimony would be, they were still in a great mood. After enjoying a delicious surf and turf dinner, they discussed the case while they enjoyed their cognac and coffee.

"I don't know, Gary. I agree with Ebony. I don't think the confession gives us an ironclad case." Ted said.

"What are you two thinking? This makes the case as close to a slam dunk as they get."

"I agree that it makes the case a lot stronger but a good attorney could shoot holes in Douglas' testimony and you *know* that Barnett is going to have the best attorney that money can buy. I just wish we had a little more on him." Ted countered.

"So while we wait for some more evidence that we may or may not get, we let this scumbag continue to walk around free?" Gary asked.

"I think it's less a risk than bringing him to trial and he somehow gets off. With double jeopardy, we only get one shot at this guy and I don't want to take any chances. Barnett is pretty toothless now that we've taken Permentier out of the picture. That reminds me, Alan from the DEA called a few minutes ago and they think they have a lead on Permentier. They're planning to move on him tomorrow afternoon. They're waiting in case we want to be there for the operation meanwhile they have the place staked out and if they see him or he tries to run they will move in. I think at least one of us should be there. I need to stay here and finish all the arrangements with the Atlanta DA and the police."

"I think the NYPD should be represented in case DEA wants to push the drug charges first to boost their numbers and since Ebony is still out on sick leave: that leaves me. Ask them to wait for me; I'll get a flight first thing in the morning," Gary said. "Hey, Delaney, you're awfully quiet. What are you thinking?"

Ebony replied, "I agree with you that someone should be there to take Permentier into custody. We don't want him getting charged with just drug charges so someone can justify their budget. He needs to be charged with Barnett for Murder One. As for Barnett, I think we need to wait a few more days before we bring him in."

"Why wait?" Gary asked.

"I have an ace up my sleeve."

"Really? You want to tell us about it?" Gary asked.

"Not really," Ebony said.

"Why not?

"Because there's a strong possibility that you might get pissed," Ebony said.

"Oh, Ebony, I think that now you have to tell what going on. We are on the same team, right?" Ted said.

"I have someone inside the Barnett camp getting close to him."

Both Ted and Gary looked at each other with incredulous looks on their faces. Finally, Ted asked, "Now, how did you manage that? You have been out of commission for months now!"

Gary touched Ted on the arm as he said, "Hold up a minute, Ted. Ebony, who do you have working undercover?"

"That's what might piss you off."

"Delaney, stop playing. This isn't a joke. You need to tell us who is working with you so we can protect her," Gary said.

"What if it's a him?" Ebony asked.

"That's highly unlikely, but it doesn't make any difference. This is not a woman's liberation or equality issue. It's about providing a safe haven or backup for a fellow officer. Who the hell is it?" Gary said in a voice loud enough to get the attention of the other diners.

"Calm down, Gary. Ebony, what were you thinking? You know that Barnett is a murderer. You sent a fellow officer undercover without telling anyone. Do you know how dangerous that was?"

"Yeah, but it was her plan not mine and she would have carried it out with or without my consent."

"So it was a woman? Who are we talking about? We can still get her some coverage and protection before things get more dangerous," Ted said.

"It's Stephanie."

"Stephanie?! Are you crazy? She's not even a detective, and she's never done undercover!" Gary almost screamed.

"Ebony. Ebony. Ebony. I can see why you have so many problems within your department. You pay rules and protocol no attention at all. Isn't Stephanie that very pretty officer from your precinct?" Ted asked.

"Hell yeah, and if something happens to her, half the men at the precinct will have our heads on a stick," Gary said.

"Hold up, Gary. It makes sense in an unorthodox and risky way. Stephanie is truly enchanting, and she has a way of wrapping men around her finger like nothing I've ever seen. She wasn't even trying and I would have done anything she wanted if she had looked my way."

"That's just because we know what a horn dog you are De-laphine," Ebony teased.

"I can't believe you two are joking about this. This ain't a laughing matter," Gary said.

"I'm not taking it lightly either, Gary. I'm well aware how dangerous and risky this is. If something goes wrong and something happens to my girl, I couldn't live with myself. But I think you're underestimating Stephanie. She's not as weak and helpless as you think. You're getting swayed by her looks. I've seen her on the shooting range and I've been in the gym with her. My girl can take care of herself. Plus, you forget that Barnett hasn't hurt anyone himself. He hires someone else to do his killing," Ebony asserted.

"No one that we know of," Gary weakly argued.

"Now that the damage is done, why don't we play it out and see where it goes. Gary, when you get to New York tomorrow, why don't you contact Stephanie and bring her up to date on the developments in the case. Tell her that we might have enough to arrest Barnett so not to take any additional chances. If things get dicey, she is to come in and leave Barnett alone. Make sure she understands that she's not to take any chances, regardless how small. Tell her we'll give her a few more days to see if she can come up with anything. How long do you think we should give her, Ebony?" Ted said as the voice of reason.

"She's been under this assignment for a while now, why don't we give her another week? Then we'll bring in Barnett with whatever we have," Ebony said.

"Do you agree with that, Gary?" Ted asked.

"I don't like it but I can live with it," Gary said.

"Well, that will be the plan then," Ted said.

Chapter Sixteen

Justice was hiding out in the loft he kept in Harlem just below 110th Street. He allowed one of his girlfriends, Janae, to stay there and the loft was technically listed in her name in preparation of a situation like this. In case he was ever on the run from the police and he needed a place that would be hard for them to trace back to him, this was it. Though he didn't do any business out of this spot, he had his girl-friend, hired a couple of boys in the neighborhood to be on the look-out for the police, and Justice had prepared a couple of emergency contingencies just in case.

He had just finished eating and was playing a game of NCAA foot-ball on the PlayStation 3 that he kept in the house to keep him from getting totally bored. Janae was in the kitchen doing the dishes when the downstairs buzzer went off in the preplanned pattern. Janae rushed to the intercom to hear the teenage lookout scream: five-O, five-O. Justice sprang up and dashed to the bedroom followed by Janae.

Using an idea Justice had gotten from the Spike Lee movie *The Inside Man,* Justice hurried behind the duplicate wall he had built al-most six feet from the original wall thus creating a wall that was nearly invisible to the unsuspecting eye. Inside the room were a chair, a cot, food, bottled water, and several pistols in case he had to shoot his way out. Janae closed the hidden door which, because of the design on the wallpaper, was very close to invisible. She then moved the full-length floor mirror in front of the door as that would further help hide the seams.

She ran back to the kitchen and returned to her dishes mere seconds before the police used a battering ram and forced the door open. They hit the door with such force that the door frame splintered and shattered. Justice had often thought about having a metal door installed but he didn't want the place to seem to be too secure, like they had something to hide.

As the half dozen officers burst through the door with guns drawn, Gary shouted, "NYPD! Get on the floor facedown and put your hands behind your head."

Janae slowly did as Gary instructed while she protested, "What do you want? Why did you bust into my house? I didn't do anything wrong."

As the other officers spread out throughout the apartment, Gary came over and forcefully pushed Janae the rest of the way to the floor. Then he grabbed her hands and cuffed her hands behind her back.

Janae complained, "Ow, you're hurting me. What do you want?"

"We're looking for Justice Permentier."

"I'm the one who needs justice. Which I will get as soon as I get me a lawyer. I don't know anybody named Permentier."

"Stop lying. We know he was living here with you. We have photos of you two together. Where is he?"

"I don't know who you talking about."

"We both know you're lying. If you cooperate, things could go easier for you."

"What are you talking about? Why should I worry about how things are for me? I haven't done anything."

"Miss, do yourself a favor. If you're not going to help us, lay there and shut your mouth."

"Don't tell me to shut up. This is my house and I will say what I want. When I get through with you Gestapo bastards, you'll be real sorry."

The other officers after searching the apartment came back to Gary in the living room. "We searched the place but he's not here."

"Are you sure? All indications are that he should still be here. Did you search thoroughly?"

"Of course. He was here, but now he's seems to have gotten away. Should we leave?"

"Hell no. Search it again. Look for hidden compartments or drop spaces in the ceiling."

After searching for several more minutes the officers returned "He's not here. Did she tell you anything?"

"She didn't say anything worth listening to," Gary said. "I guess we better leave. Don't worry we'll get him soon."

"What do you want to do with her?"

"We could take her in." Gary suggested.

"Under what charges?" Janae asked.

"We could start with harboring a fugitive," Gary told her.

"What fugitive? I'd like to see you make that stick in court. In fact, go ahead in arrest me. By the time I get finished suing your ass in court, you'll be sorry you ever set eyes on me," Janae snarled.

"Oh, it wouldn't be hard hitting you with charges that would stick. If we stop looking for Permentier and start looking for other things, like drugs, I'm sure we'll find enough to lock you away until Permentier has long forgotten about you. But we usually don't go after such small fish. People like you we throw back because you ain't worth the time or the paperwork but if you don't shut that piehole of yours, I'll take you in just for the hell of it," Gary said as he removed Janae' handcuffs and then turned to the other officers and said, "We wasting time here. Let's go."

Janae said to their backs as they were leaving, "What about my door? Who's gonna pay to fix my door?"

"Send the city a bill," Gary hollered over his shoulder.

As soon as they got back to the car, Ken the DEA agent said to Gary, "Do you think this was where Permentier was hiding?"

"Oh, he was there. I don't know how we missed him. He was definitely there. If she was doing the dishes, who was playing the video games?"

"The bathroom showed two towels and she was washing a lot more dishes than one person would use. He must have got away right before we came in. Someone must have told him we were coming. What's our next move?" Ken asked.

"We'll leave a man here in case he decides to come back. "

· · · · ·

Brandon had been highly anticipating this evening for quite some time. He had concocted a plan that he thought would finally make some headway with Amber. She had spoken on several occasions about the things she required to take their relationship to the next level and he wasn't sure he could do those things but for the first time he wanted to try. Trust was not something that came to him naturally because of all the betrayals in his past but also because of his sideline hustle. He could never trust anyone completely because he could never reveal everything about himself. After all, "loose lips sank ships" was his motto and he would never tell anybody about the deaths he had arranged and committed because that meant life in prison for him and his clients.

Aside from that great secret, he was willing to allow Amber access to much more of his life than anyone had ever had before, but he could not tell her that because she would doubt his sincerity. He would just have to show her. He was prepared to show her his willingness to head toward a commitment. He had bought her a ring. It wasn't an engagement ring, because after all he had only known her weeks, but the ring was stunning. It was made of platinum with a large purple sapphire that was surrounded by diamonds. The salesperson at Tiffany's had assured him that Amber would love it and if she didn't he could bring it back. "I guess when you spent more than $12,000 on a girlfriend's ring, you got that kind of treatment," Brandon thought as he looked at the ring before he put it away as he expected Amber any time now.

She had been coming over at least once a week and preparing him some of the most delicious meals. Her culinary skills were surprising and they were almost as great as he imagined her skills in the bedroom to be. He wanted her so bad it was all he could not to force his desires upon her. He had even gotten some Rohypnol, known as the date rape drug, to slip in her drink and then have his way with her. It wasn't a moral issue that kept him from using the drug, because he had used it in the past, but experience had taught him that the drug could only work for a one-night stand. The victim would know that someone had sex with her, and though she couldn't prove anything, it was highly unlikely that she would have anything to do with him after that. He didn't want a one-night affair with Amber, he wanted a long-term relationship. He would do what he had to do to make her his for as long as he wanted her to be.

He headed to the kitchen to join Amber because judging from the smells coming from the kitchen dinner must be close to complete. He came up behind Stephanie and was deciding whether to wrap his arms around her waist when his Blackberry buzzed. He looked and saw he had a text message in code from Justice signifying an emergency. He went into his office, and using a new cell phone, he called Justice back at the pre-arranged number. He was so preoccupied with his call that he didn't notice that the door was partially ajar and Stephanie was perched out of sight listening to his conversation.

"Yo, Justice, what's up?"

"Problems, Pred, I got to go. I got to get in the wind. The pigs busted into my secret place and I barely got in my hole before they came in."

"What do you need?"

"As much cash as I can get my hands on and I need a clean car that won't be traced."

"I got over a hundred large in the safe in the office and another twenty-five here in the house. You're welcome to all of it. One of the secretaries has a used car for sale that's in pretty good shape. How far are you going?"

"I think it would be best if I left the country. I'll head for Mexico or Central America. Will the car make it that far?"

"It should, and if it doesn't you can always buy another one close to the border. Where do you want to meet?"

"The bar on 118th street. When can you make it?"

"I got to go down to the office and then over to pick up the car. Are you safe for about two and a half hours?"

"Yeah, I should be good. I'm sure I can slip out the basement and come out through another building. I'll see you in a couple of hours."

As Brandon went to his safe, Stephanie slipped back down to the kitchen. After he had retrieved the money, he returned to the kitchen. "Amber, an emergency came up and I have to run and take care of some business."

Stephanie went to the sink to wash her hands and start preparing to leave. "Are you gonna be gone long?"

"A couple of hours."

"That's a damn shame because dinner is almost ready and to try to put it on hold will mess it up. I'll tell you how to finish it and you still may be able to eat it."

Brandon thought about his plans for the evening and the crossroads he felt their relationship was at. That he had to go and be there for Justice was indisputable, but was it necessary for Amber to leave? Wasn't it time for him to have something more than just money? If he was ever gonna have a real relationship, wouldn't he have to cross this threshold at some point? And if he did leave her alone in the house what harm could it do? He knew she wasn't going to steal from him, so what was he worried about?

"Why don't you stay and finish cooking?" Brandon asked.

"I thought you had to leave right away? It's gonna take me maybe a half an hour to finish. Can you wait till I finish?"

"No, I have to leave right away, but there's no reason why you should have to. You can finish cooking and wait for me to get back and then we can finish our evening."

"How long are you going to be gone?"

"Maybe as much as two to three hours."

"I don't know if I want to be here by myself that long."

"Come on, you've went to so much trouble. It would be a shame to waste it, and I have a really special evening planned. Please stay."

"What would I do until you get back? It will only take a minute to finish cooking, what will I do with the rest of the time?"

"Watch TV, listen to music, or do whatever you want. You said I don't trust you in the house alone and that's why we can't get close. Now I'm asking you to stay in the house and you're backing down. Do you want to build a relationship, or was that just talk?"

"Okay, I guess I'll stick around."

"Good, you know how to work everything. Make yourself at home. If you have any problems, just hit me up on my cell. I gotta dash."

After Brandon left, an anxious Stephanie finished cooking because she wanted to wait some time in case Brandon came back. Approximately thirty minutes later she went into Barnett's office and started working on his computer. It took her more than fifteen minutes before she was able to discover his password. She was extremely proficient with the computer, and it took all her expertise to fight her way through the numerous firewalls that Barnett had set up but she was finally successful. She didn't know who had installed his system, but she had to admire their mastery.

As she went through his files, she was amazed at how much of his personal information she was able to obtain. Realizing that she was running out of time, she took a zip drive apparatus from her pocketbook and started copying files. After she had copied all of the pertinent files, she returned the zip drive to her pocketbook, turned off the computer, and left Barnett's house, she hoped, for the last time.

· · · · ·

Brandon drove up to the bar where he agreed to meet Justice and parked the car down the block from the entrance. He got out of the 2004 Pontiac Grand Am and stood by the passenger's door until he figured that Justice must have seen him. He got back into the car and waited for Justice. A few minutes later, Justice walked up to the car and got in on the driver's side. "Thanks for coming, Pred."

"Was there any doubt that I would?"

"No, but thanks for being there anyway. This car ain't half bad."

"It should be pretty much what the doctor ordered. The engine is in pretty good shape and should be able to make it as far as South America if you want to go that far. It's nondescript enough that it should blend in with the other cars on the road. Justice, what happened that you are in this situation?"

"I knew five-O was still on the hunt. I just didn't know how bad they wanted to get me. They busted into that crib I kept under Janae's name and I still can't figure out how they knew about that spot because only a few of my men knew about her."

"Somebody must have dimed you out."

"Yeah and whoever it was better hope I never find out."

"I thought you were going to leave town weeks ago."

"I wasn't sure if they were after me, so I decided to lie up and keep a low profile until I could get a sense of how things were. Now this shit is too hot so I'm getting out of town while I can. I'm gonna put some distance between me and New York before they plaster my picture all over the wire."

"What route are you taking?"

"I was gonna jump on 95."

"Naw, don't do that. That will take you through too many cities and they might be on the lookout in the urban centers. Plus, the state police are on 95 real heavy. Take the West Side Highway down to the Holland Tunnel to route 78. Take that to around Harrisburg and pick up route 81 South. That's a pretty obscure way, and if you hold close to the speed limit you won't get pulled over by the troopers. Eighty-one should take you through Virginia to Tennessee and you can pick your route to Mexico from there.

"You shouldn't run into any major cops until you try to cross over into Mexico. Get you some shades and grow you a beard and they shouldn't look at you twice even if your picture is put out on the wire. See that panel under the speaker? It pops off and I put a .38 in there in case they pull you over and you can get away if you pop one, but the best way would be to try to slip under the radar.

"Here's 15 hundred for your pocket for gas and food and shit. The 125 large is hid in the trunk in a panel on the right side above the spot that holds the jack. When you get to a safe location, you holler at your boy and I'll wire whatever you need to a bank once you let me know which one and the account numbers. I'm still holding over two mill for you and I know you have another two in your own accounts, but I don't know how long it will be before you can get to your shit. But don't worry, I'll hold you down until you do. I think you should be able to live like a king down there. You deserve it."

"What about you, partner?"

"Don't worry about me. I'm good."

"We've been through a lot of shit together, Pred, and we've had each other's back for a lot of years. Are you gonna be okay without me covering your ass?"

"Yeah, it's been a great run, but I think it's time to go completely legit. The agency is turning a pretty lucrative profit on its own and maybe it's time I really became a businessman."

"What about the crap with that detective who was after your ass?"

"I think that whole issue is dead. She still isn't well enough to return to being a cop, and I'm not sure if she ever will. I don't think that ever was an official investigation, at least that's what our people downtown said. With her incapacitated, the whole thing could just go away."

"So you figure there's nothing from stopping you from turning legitimate?"

"I think it's time."

"If you're not worried about getting caught, why are you going legit? There is easy money to be made in the street."

"I met someone who made me want more. She makes me want a different life. All of a sudden I want the house in the country with the white picket fence type of life. Maybe some kids and see if I can be a better parent then my old man was, which won't be hard because he disappeared before I was old enough to remember him."

"She must be one hell of a woman."

"She is. You would dig her if you ever met her. Let me know where you end up and maybe we'll come down to visit you on vacation. You know we've been through so much that we're partners for life."

"You know, Pred, that you're my Nigga for life through thick and thin. I'll always be there for you."

"You know I feel the same but right now we got to get you out of Dodge. Why don't I drive you through the tunnel? You get down on the back seat and act like you're sleep if they pull you over."

"That ain't even necessary, man."

"Please let me do this for you. It might be the last time I see you for a while."

· · · · ·

There are things in life that give our lives a sense of meaning and purpose. It can stimulate, motivate and sometimes define our lives and everything we do. For Ebony among the things that had become very important to her including family and love, two things were starting to become more of a main focus. One was getting her body back in the same shape and condition it was before the shooting and the other was to bring Brandon Barnett to justice and satisfactorily conclude that aspect of her life.

Finally, she was starting to get her body back; at least that's how Ebony felt. She felt invigorated after running at a very brisk clip the three miles to the park where she put in a strenuous workout of pull-ups, leg raisers and push-ups before running the three miles back home. As she stepped into the shower that was a few degrees short of scalding, she felt the familiar stiffness and aching that came from muscles being pushed to their limits and it felt great. After her shower, she would enjoy the salad she had prepared earlier that had a Mexican twist with avocadoes, black beans, and salsa instead of dressing.

This was the third day since returning from Atlanta that she had put her body through this grueling workout, and she was really starting to enjoy its effects. She was a firm believer in the positive results of hard work, and she found it to be true once again. Her mind was clear, and she had a renewed sense of purpose. Despite how much better she had gotten, she couldn't deceive herself into believing that physically she was near the condition she was before she got shot. She was still weak and easily fatigued and less than half of where she was physically, but slowly and steadily, she was getting better.

She was looking forward to going back to work and the subsequent arrest of Brandon Barnett, and she wanted him to see her walking tall and strong as she put the handcuffs on him. She wanted to see his face when he realized that his greatest efforts to destroy her had failed so miserably.

After she finished dressing, her intercom rang and she checked the security camera to see who was trying to get admission into the building, a practice that she started doing after she was attacked. After she buzzed Stephanie in, she went to the door to greet her friend.

"I'm glad to see you. I didn't know if you had gotten my message," Ebony said as she gave her a hug.

"I'm sorry about that, but I've running so hard doing a double shift and everything that a couple of days got past me. I figured it must be important because Gary left me a couple of messages too. What's up?"

"Don't worry. You're here now. We'll talk about it. Would you like some lunch?"

"What are you having?"

"Does it matter?" Ebony asked.

"Heck yeah. You look like a health and fitness nut. I'm not really ready for tofu or bean sprouts or something like that."

"I'm having a salad, but I could grill you a piece of salmon or something else if you would like."

"No, I'll have some salad with you if you have enough."

"I have plenty."

"What did you need to speak to me about? It seemed kind of important," Stephanie asked.

"We've decided that in a couple of days that we're gonna pull you in off the Barnett investigation."

"Who are we? And why wasn't I brought in on that discussion since it was me you were discussing?"

"It was Ted, Gary, and me, and we had the discussion in Atlanta or you sure would have been part of the discussion."

"I thought we didn't want them to know that I was involved."

"I thought it best to let them know for your protection. I never did like you going undercover on such a dangerous assignment without backup."

"Don't worry I was never in any danger and if I was I can take care of myself."

"Well, I hope we don't find out because I think you should terminate the undercover by the end of the week. There have been some developments in the case and I think we're getting ready to arrest Barnett. We just wanted to give you a last chance to see what you could come up with."

"Your patience has been rewarded."

"What do you mean?"

"I mean that last night I was able to get everything we need. He had to run out to help a friend and while he was gone I cracked his computer system and, *voila*, I got enough here to put him behind bars for a very long time." Stephanie reached into her briefcase and pulled out a dossier of computer printouts about four inches thick. After briefly looking through it, Ebony said, "This is amazing. You've got copies of everything he's done in his life in the last couple of years. You've done a fantastic job. I told the guys to give you some time and that you would come up with something to help the case but I never dreamed you with come up with this much. It's gonna take us some time to go through all this stuff and see what can help us with our investigation."

"I guess we'll be working through lunch," Stephanie said.

"I'm gonna call the guys and bring them up to date on what you were able to pull on Barnett. Why don't you get comfortable?" Ebony said as she took out her cell phone and called Gary and Ted and briefly brought them up to date on this latest development. She told them she would call them back when she finished going through the paperwork then she and Stephanie got busy sorting and dissecting papers and documents. They were at it for hours only taking a short break to eat their lunch, before they were able to make some sense of order of the papers. The hardest thing was deciding which papers were appropriate for their purposes.

They divided the papers into several different piles, the largest of which was the pile of information they didn't think was relevant. The other piles contained information that was so incriminating that it made the work easy-going and lighthearted because it was the final nail in the coffin that would put Barnett behind bars for the rest of not only this life but three more besides.

"I'm still shocked that someone as devious and crafty as Barnett had all this information where someone could get to it."

"Not just someone but me. Brandon made the—"

"Brandon?" Ebony interrupted. "You two are on a first name basis?"

"How do you think I got close enough to him to expose his weaknesses? How do you think we got all this information?" Stephanie replied.

"I hope you didn't do anything to jeopardize your integrity."

"You know me better than that. I can play a role with the best of them, but that's what that was: a role. I wouldn't do anything in my role of Amber that Stephanie couldn't live with. I wanted to bust that snake as bad as any of you, but I wouldn't sleep with him or anyone else to make a bust. So if that's what you're thinking, get it out your mind."

"I'm sorry. You're right, I should have known better. It's just that Barnett doesn't seem like the type to let anyone get that close to him."

"You just had to find the right bait to dangle in front of him. He's like most womanizers, the right—or in this case, wrong—woman would bring him to his knees. I just threatened his ego. I made him feel like he wasn't good enough to get with me. The rest was like taking candy from a baby."

"That explains the why but I'm not clear on the how."

"As I was saying: Brandon made the same mistake that so many people make in this new electronic age. No information is safe and can't be kept secret if the right person tries to infiltrate your system. Brandon made the first mistake of looking at me and seeing a pretty face and underestimating my intelligence. When I got a Master's in computer programming and engineering, I didn't think I would be using it for this but it sure came in handy. What do we do next?"

"Let's take a close look at his financial records." After half an hour of close scrutiny, the picture that revealed itself surprised them both. Ebony marveled at the revelations "I didn't realize the murder game was so lucrative. Close as I can tell, Barnett has nearly seven *million* dollars scattered across banks in the Caribbean as well as banks in Panama. He's got several accounts in three banks in Curacao and two in the Cayman Islands. There are reputable banks like the RBC Royal bank in Cayman and the Mauro & Curiel's bank in Curacao as well as banks whose reputation is not quite so sterling. I don't know if this guy is more intelligent or sinister," Ebony pondered.

"He's like so many criminals, in that it makes you wonder how far they could go if they put the same amount of brain power into going for good instead of taking the fast way out. You said he's got more than seven million there? I didn't know he was worth that much. Why did he scatter it across so many accounts and so many different banks?"

"I would guess that it would make it harder to detect how much he had and avoid the question of where did he get so much money."

"How do we use it?" Stephanie asked.

"Ted has some connections at the Treasury Department that we could use to seize the account and if nothing else we can hang him on income tax evasion, but putting this together with the testimony of Omar Douglas is pretty damaging."

"Who?"

Ebony filled Stephanie in on Omar's confession and what had occurred in Atlanta. "Let's look at the rest of these papers and see what else we can find out."

The next hour was spent going through more papers. Ebony rejoiced when she saw the receipts for the cruise and the flights to Miami for the cruise, thus establishing a link between Barnett and Tanya's death. They found numerous other pieces of evidence that was incriminating but would be considered circumstantial at best if it was brought to court. Things like plane tickets including one to San Francisco three weeks before Kayla Battle died in a "car accident" or two tickets to Baltimore three days before the Burleson kidnapping.

There are a lot of things that indicated that Barnett had his hands in quite a few nefarious deeds but not much that would stand up in court. Ebony didn't see that as a major issue because the evidence on the cruise and the bank records, including ledgers that showed withdrawals from clients' accounts all of whom wives mysteriously had an untimely death and subsequent deposits in Barnett's accounts. That alone was a serious indication to Ebony of which deaths Barnett had his hand in.

"I believe you're right, Stephanie. The evidence from these files pretty much seals Barnett's fate. I'm trying to decide our next move."

"What did Gary and Ted suggest?" Stephanie asked.

"They wanted us to wait for them to get here."

"And what do you think we should do?"

"I'm ready to go arrest Barnett right now."

"What's the rush? Can't it wait until they get here and then we all go together?"

"It might, but Permentier already seems to have slipped out of the net and I don't want to take the chance that Barnett gets spooked and takes flight as well. Barnett might sense the noose tightening around his neck and try to get out of town before it does."

"So why don't we just go and arrest him then?"

"There are a couple of reasons not to. Though Gary and Ted weren't involved at the beginning, they have put in too much time and effort to not be there at the end. The other reason is I'm not technically a police officer right now, or at least I am still out on medical leave. I really don't have the authority to make an arrest unless the crime is committed in my presence. I don't know if that's an argument we can make in this case."

"That might not be necessary. I think you're overlooking a very obvious solution to both issues. Do you think Gary and Ted will agree with your conclusions of the evidence and agree to arrest Brandon?"

"Of course."

"Then why have them come here? Have them meet you at Brandon's office, where he probably is right now, and arrest him. You can fill them in on the evidence later. Second, you forget that I am a peace officer in good standing. I can make the arrest and that would not be in violation of any regulations."

"You're right, that makes sense. Let me finish dressing and you call Ted and Gary and tell them to meet us outside Barnett's office."

. . . . .

"Ebony, what is the rush?" Ted asked.

"I don't want to chance Barnett trying to get away."

"But Gary and I are almost at your house."

"Then turn around and head to Manhattan because we are on our way to his office."

"Who is with you? Are you going after him without backup?"

"Stephanie is with me, and she's more than enough. Anyway, he's not gonna start any shit in his office. He's slick enough to go meekly to jail and try to beat the charge in court."

"Is there any chance of that happening?"

"Absolutely none. You haven't seen the stuff that Stephanie brought. We got more than enough to bury him. She's got his financial records and evidence that ties him in with at least four murders. Any assistant DA straight out of college could get an easy conviction with this stuff."

"Okay, we'll on our way there. Will you at least wait for us before you make the arrest? Don't forget, this guy is still pretty damn dangerous. He's killed quite a few women and he's tried to kill you once already."

"Well, hurry the hell up because we're in Manhattan already."

As Stephanie was listening to Ebony's side of the conversation, she wasn't sure if she agreed with Ebony, not about her conclusions but the chance of Brandon's flight. She didn't see any need for urgency, especially not to a degree where they couldn't wait for Ted and Gary. Even if there was a chance of flight, couldn't Ted have the Feds shut down the airports? More importantly, Stephanie couldn't understand what was going on with Ebony.

Behavior like this was very much unlike Ebony. To act so impulsively, almost rashly, was very much unlike the Ebony she knew and totally unlike how the investigation had been conducted. She thought that Ebony was the epitome of good police work: she researched, obtained leads and recreated the possible scenario before drawing any conclusions and then looking at those conclusions from many different perspectives, thereby building an ironclad case.

On the other hand, Ebony was her best friend and if she was acting a bit hasty, that didn't matter because she would still have her back. If she didn't go with her there was a real possibility that Ebony would have gone without her, and that wasn't a chance she was ready to take. As long as she went with Ebony, she could not only support her but also try to control the situation.

Ebony was only vaguely aware that she wasn't her normal, calm, and in-control self. Ebony had spent countless hours working on controlling her inner anger and learning how to stay centered with the universe, but now all that training went out the window. She didn't know if she was unable to control her anger or if she was just didn't want to. "We finally got him," she thought over and over as her fear that Brandon would get away with his crimes dissipated. She remembered the men he had dispatched to kill her. She remembered her recent battle with death and her angst over whether she would be able to walk again. She remembered Jasper and Juanita and their grief over the loss of their daughter. She remembered Zoe and LJ grieving over the loss of their parents and little Jaleesa and the mother she would never really know and the anger in her started simmering hotter and hotter till it was almost ready to boil over.

Twenty minutes later Ebony and Stephanie arrived at Barnett's office. As Ebony started to get out of the car Stephanie said, "I thought we were gonna wait for Gary and Ted?"

"We will wait, but I want to wait upstairs. I don't want to wait here in the car and Barnett slips out the back."

"Why would Brandon try to slip away? He doesn't even know we're coming."

"You can wait here if you want, but I'm going upstairs now. We don't even know if he is in his office. We need to find out at least that much."

"Okay, I'm with you, let's go," Stephanie replied. "Are you okay, Ebony? You're not acting like yourself."

"I'm okay. I just want to get this done."

"Relax, we got him where we want him. We're in charge, not him," Stephanie said in an effort to calm Ebony down. She wondered whether Ebony even heard her because her last words were said to Ebony' back as she headed into the building.

As they arrived upstairs at IMA's office, the sheer opulence and elegance of the office infuriated Ebony when she remembered that this office was built upon the blood of innocent women who fell victims to the greed of Barnett and men who had once promised to love them forever.

As Ebony approached the office, she thought, "How dare this man think he could get away with this? How could he be so heartless that he didn't care if kids lost their mothers and women lost their futures and lives, just so he could have more millions to put in those offshore accounts? How could this pig think he could kill them and get away with it? How could this arrogant son of a bitch think he could outfox the entire legal system of New York and indeed the entire United States?"

Ebony intention was to wait outside IMA's office but she was in such an agitated state that before she knew it she had burst into the office's foyer and asked Barnett's obnoxious eye candy, "Is Barnett in his office?"

The secretary asked, "Do you have an appointment?"

"I asked you if Barnett is in his office. You answer is a simple yes or no."

"*Mr.* Barnett is in his office but he is only available if you have an appointment. Since I see that you don't have an appointment, would you like to make one?"

Ignoring the secretary, Ebony burst into Barnett's office with the secretary in hot pursuit. Brandon was sitting at his enormous desk peering over some papers while he talked on the phone. He looked startled to see Ebony in his office but maintained his composure enough to gesture to the secretary to stop and return to her desk.

Speaking into the phone he said, "Let me call you back. I have someone in my office and she seems to have an urgent need to speak with me. Okay?"

After hanging up the phone he said, "Detective Delaney, or should I say Miss Delaney, I wish I could say it is a pleasure to see you but it very clearly is not. What do you want?"

"Your life. Like you tried to take mine."

"I assure you I have no idea what you are talking about."

"I'm talking about you having your punk-ass friends try to kill me. It didn't work, did it? And now it's time to pay for your sins."

"You are one paranoid bitch and I think it's time for you to go before I call security and have you removed."

"Call security because I will be leaving soon, but when I do, I will be leaving with you in handcuffs."

"I knew your ass was crazy. You are going to arrest me? On what charges? In fact, are you even a cop anymore because I heard your ass got fired?"

"Oh, don't worry, I'm still a cop and the charges are first degree murder and conspiracy to commit murder for starters, though I'm sure that other charges will be following imminently."

"Bitch, you are crazy. Get your ass out my office before I call the cops."

"That didn't work the first time and it sure won't work this time. Those politicians that you have in your pocket won't protect you this time. Get up and put your hands on your head."

"There is no way that you can arrest me. Who do you think I murdered?"

"How about Larry Richardson and Tanya Richardson for starters?"

"What are you talking about? Larry Richardson died due to a drug overdose, and is Tanya even dead?"

"Oh, she is very dead thanks to you, at least according to Omar Douglas."

A look of confusion passed across Brandon's face as at first he couldn't place the name and then it dawned on him who it was. For the first time it occurred to Brandon that he might be in trouble and a look of panic crossed his face. The look of panic changed to a look of total confusion as Stephanie entered the room. She looked so beautiful to him that it was amazing and temporarily he forgot that Ebony was even there and why she was there.

"Amber, what are you doing here?"

"Amber? You think her name is Amber?" Ebony asked with a snicker. "Please meet Officer Stephanie Givens of the NYPD. It's so good watching the player get played."

"Amber, you're a cop? You're a fucking cop?"

"Yes, I am, and you are under arrest. Please stand up and put your hands on your head."

"You're a cop and you're arresting me? You pig bitch. You cold-hearted low-life slut. I trusted you. I believed in you. I fucking loved you and you were betraying me all the time. I let you in my house and you were trying to get information for the cops all the time."

Ebony said, "This is your last warning. Stand up and put your hands on your head. You are going down, sucker. We know all about the banks in Curacao and the Caymans. We know about the cruise line. We know about California. We know enough to put you away for the rest of your life."

"You stupid bitch, you don't know nothing. You ever hear of encroachment? You ever hear of entrapment? I'll be walking with the city's money with all the cash I will receive from my law suit. And you Amber. You ain't nothing but a cunt, a whore. You prostituted yourself for the NYPD. You're just proof that women ain't shit. I took a chance on you and you fucked me." As Brandon was ranting, Ebony saw that he was reaching into a drawer in his desk.

"*Freeze, Barnett*! Right now. *Freeze*," Ebony said as she started to draw her gun.

The cunning survivor in Barnett instinctively knew his best chance of escaping this trap was to try to catch Ebony and Amber off guard. Based on the evidence they hinted that they had on him, he knew if he left there is custody he probably would not be offered bail and his chances on acquittal at trial were slim to nonexistent. He had to do or say something that would make them relax their vigilance and allow him to get the drop on them. He knew his secretary couldn't hear what was going on in his office, as his office was soundproof, but did the cops know that? If he could make them think that he was trying to give his secretary the impression that they were trying to assassinate him, that might back them off a bit and thereby give him a chance. "Oh now, you sneaky bitches want to shoot me. You're just looking for an excuse so you can murder me. You and I both know you'll never make them bogus charges stick and so you're setting me up to never make it to trial."

Falling for the gambit, Ebony took her hand off her gun as she said, "No, Barnett, we don't want to shoot you. We need you to go to trial so we can get those guys that were in this vicious plan with you. Just put your hands where we can see them."

Continuing the ruse, Barnett placed his hands on his desk as if he needed the leverage to help him stand up. Then he quickly shoved his hands into the drawer where he kept his pistol. Just as quickly and as fiercely as a tiger fighting for survival against the pursuing hunters, Brandon pulled a gun and in one fluid motion he sprang across the desk at Stephanie, who was caught with her gun half out of the hostler and at an awkward angle. Fueled by the duel demons of deception and betrayal, Brandon moved with quickness and ferocity that under other circumstances would have surprised even Justice, who had seen Brandon operate under violent environments before. Though over the past few years Brandon had sat behind a desk plotting and scheming, he was so enraged that the evil assassin known as Predator was back from his long sojourn.

Brandon's quick reaction caught Stephanie completely off guard. Like Ebony, she believed that when the actual arrest came down, Brandon would go to jail and trust his money and attorney to get him off. She underestimated how deeply Brandon felt for her and therefore how deep his anger ran. It burned in him like hot lava or magma, and at the moment he wanted nothing more than to destroy the woman who had confirmed the worse of what he thought about mankind and especially women. Somewhere in the dark recesses of his mind, he felt if he could destroy this woman he could keep the things he feared most from being true.

Brandon either forgot he had his gun in his hand or didn't want to take the time to aim and fire, because instead of shooting Stephanie, he struck her a glancing blow with the pistol in the area right above the temple. The blow, while not fatal, did make Stephanie reel on the borders of consciousness. She stumbled as the waves of dizziness almost made her fall. Brandon uttered a guttural scream that was either from rage or pain as he continued to pummel Stephanie about the head and torso.

Ebony was momentarily stunned by the ferocity of the attack. She was unable to venture a shot for fear of hitting Stephanie, but she wasn't just going to stand there and allow Stephanie to endure such a beating. She sprang across the room and with a sweeping kick at Barnett's ankles she knocked him off his feet. Barnett jumped up and launched a vicious attack on Ebony. The next few seconds both parties launched a barrage of thrusts, parries, and kicks. And for a few seconds they were evenly matched.

Ebony had skills and expertise on her side, while Barnett had desperation and emotions, and he fought like an enraged bull. A few months ago this would have been no contest and Ebony would have had a decisive advantage, but the weakened and recuperating Ebony was a shadow of her former self. Suddenly it appeared like Barnett had gained a slight advantage and he said, "I'm gonna kill you, bitch," as he tried to aim his gun at Ebony. Realizing she had to disarm Barnett or the consequences might be dire, she summoned strength from her rapidly declining reservoir of energy. Ebony stepped inside Barnett guard and grabbed his gun arm with both hands. She simultaneously twisted his wrist inducing stress that would quickly break the wrist if he didn't change position and she then placed a vicious elbow to his solar plexus area.

With a grunt of pain, Barnett dropped his gun, but Ebony would not give up her advantage. She realized that her back was to Barnett and he could use his superior size and strength to try to turn the advantage. Before he could seize the opportunity, she pushed up and smashed the back of her head into Barnett's nose, shattering it and sending a spray of blood across the room. She took secret pleasure from the knowledge that the pretty boy that was Brandon Barnett would cease to exist without extensive plastic surgery. Not giving Barnett a second to recover, she rained a series of blows on his face and head and then kicked him directly in the stomach with her knee. The force of the blow knocked the air out of Barnett, and he dropped to his knees.

As luck would have it, Barnett fell a few short feet from his gun. Spying his weapon, in a last desperate act of rage and frustration he sprang toward the gun and picked it up. For subsequent years in moments of reflection, Ebony would always wonder whether she had the time to prevent him from getting to his gun and surely a few hard kicks to the ribs would have rendered him incapable of grabbing his weapon but she hesitated. Was it to catch her breath or did she want to inflict more punishment on him? Did she want to stop him from getting his weapon? Did she in that moment want to arrest him or enact her own revenge for the things he had done to her?

She paused and then she pulled her own gun. She shouted, "Stop, Barnett. Freeze! Drop your gun!" She was in worse condition than she realized and her gun wavered under the stress of maintaining her stance. She hesitated as she realized she couldn't kill him, as she needed to bring him to trial so the whole operation could be exposed. Barnett had no such compunction. He squeezed off two shots in Ebony' general direction but didn't come close to hitting her.

Barnett' focus on Ebony had given Stephanie vital seconds to recover her equilibrium and reenter the scuffle. She drew her pistol, and rather than issue a warning, she fired at Barnett. She had seen Ebony warn him and saw that all she got for her trouble was Barnett firing at her. Stephanie was a marksman of high quality, but like Ebony she didn't want to fire a kill shot at Barnett. Rather she wanted to put him on the defensive and minimize him as a threat.

Barnett dove behind that expensive, exotic desk, and it became one of the world's most expensive shields. Barnett was still enraged but through the haze of his anger better judgment started to clear some of the cloudiness away and he saw where he might be able to escape. Brandon must have been akin to a cat because it seemed he had nine lives, most of which he hadn't used yet.

He replaced the clip in his pistol, which gave him more than twenty shots. He placed the pistol on the top of the desk and laced a steady stream of gunfire. He got in crouching position as he prepared to run. Before the clip emptied and Ebony and Stephanie could return fire, he jumped to his feet and headed to a door that wasn't obvious to the casual observer, maybe eight feet from where he was hiding.

Seeing that Barnett was going to make a run for it, Ebony took quick aim and fired two shots at his back. One missed him as he ducked under the sound of gunfire but the other caught him in the left shoulder. He dove/stumbled/fell through the door and slammed it behind him. Quickly as he could he locked it and pushed a desk to block the door reopening, hoping that it would give him crucial moments to execute his escape.

Knowledge of the building was going to give him an essential advantage and probably his only chance to get away. He dashed through the three adjacent meeting rooms that were part of his office and out into the hall around the corner from the main entrance to IMA. He headed toward the staircase that led up to a vacant office three floors above. The realtor had shown him the office the week before when he was considering expanding to the larger office. Though the office was vacant, the agent had given him the security code to the door in case he wanted to look around the office on his own.

Barnett entered the office and silently locked the door behind him. He slid to the floor and tried to regain his breath. He was delighted to see that his good fortune was holding firm. Though the wound hurt like hell, it didn't leave a trail of blood. As close as he could tell there was no blood to tell anyone looking where he went. He sat as he tried to decide whether to try to flee the building right away or wait out the police search that was sure to come.

Chapter Seventeen

At first Ebony sprang to her feet and dashed to the door in mad pursuit of Barnett. Finding the door was locked and hearing Barnett's fading footsteps served to drain the emotions from her body. She had functioned on anger, hatred, and adrenaline and maybe just a touch of fear. Suddenly she was so empty she felt she would have collapsed if Stephanie hadn't been there to catch her. She wanted to tell Stephanie to ignore her and go after Barnett but she was too weak to get her mouth to operate properly.

This probably was a good thing because if she thought about it she would have been hesitant to send Stephanie after a wounded and desperate Barnett by herself. She looked down and noticed that Stephanie's hand was covered in blood. Ebony wondered whether she was wounded. Was that why she felt so tired and weak? She checked herself but couldn't find a wound. If she wasn't bleeding than it had to be Stephanie.

"Stephanie, did one of those shots hit you?"

"Yeah, in the side, but I don't think it's serious."

"Let me see." Ebony's previous desire to pursue Barnett was replaced by her need to make sure that Stephanie was all right. Barnett might have gotten away, but he wouldn't get far. She looked at Stephanie's left side and saw that her shirt was blood-soaked. Tenderly she removed the shirt and saw a bullet wound about four inches from her navel. The puckered outer rims of the wound weren't gushing blood but it was pulsing out at a steady rate.

"Oh shit," Ebony said. "This isn't good. We need to get you to a doctor. Lay down and I'll call it in." Ebony pulled off her shirt and wadded it into a bunch and put it on the wound. "Here, put some pressure on this," she instructed Stephanie as she took her cell phone and called 911 and reported an officer down and in distress. Less than two minutes later, fighting their way through the chaos that the outer offices had become, Gary and Ted burst into Barnett's office.

Ted asked, "Ebony, what in the hell happened? Where's Barnett?"

"We tried to arrest him but he attacked us and as we tried to subdue him he pulled a gun and opened fire. Stephanie caught a round and I called it in."

"Is Stephanie okay?" Gary asked.

"She needs an ambulance. Hopefully one should get here soon."

"Where did Barnett go?" Ted asked.

"Through there," Ebony pointed.

"Gary, you stay here with Ebony. I'm going after Barnett," Ted said as he drew his gun and headed through the door.

Stephanie told Gary, "I'll be okay. You go with Ted."

Gary stood there like a statue frozen with indecision. He wanted to stay and make sure Stephanie was okay but he didn't want Ted to go after an armed assailant alone. His stalemate was broken by the shrill blare of sirens as they drew closer. "Take care of Stephanie. We'll be right back," Gary said as he headed after Ted.

EMS and four police officers arrived and EMS started stabilizing Stephanie as Ebony started to brief the officers on what happened. Within moments Gary and Ted returned, and after presenting his credentials, Gary took control of the situation. "Ted, you go with Stephanie to the hospital. Ebony and I will join you as soon as we can. NYPD is gonna have jurisdiction over the scene so Ebony needs to stay here with me. Officers, I need y'all to prevent any African American males from leaving the building without talking to me first. The man who shot this officer is also a suspect in numerous murders. He might still be in the building. So no one comes or goes without proper identification. The man we are after is Brandon Barnett. We will get you a photo of him shortly. When more officers arrive, send them up here and we will dispatch them to canvas the neighborhood."

"I'm sure I caught him with at least one shot as he was trying to get away," Ebony added.

"Okay, Sergeant Delaney said that he's wounded, so keep a close eye out. She and I will interview the staff and then we will come down to coordinate things from downstairs. Let's move, people."

After the room was cleared, Gary turned to Ebony and said, "Delaney, what the hell is wrong with you? Why didn't you wait for Ted and me? This is going to be one major shitstorm. You know there's going to be hell to pay for this."

"I know, but let's try to find Barnett if we can. I'll deal with the fallout later," Ebony said.

· · · · ·

Two hours later at the hospital, they were waiting on word about Stephanie, who was still undergoing tests. So far, they hadn't found Barnett, and he seemed to have slipped through their dragnet. Ted turned to Ebony and said, "In about an hour, all hell is going to break loose. Internal Affairs, the Mayor's office, and your Captain are all going to want to speak to you. The press is lining up to meet with you. Ebony, there is one hell of a firestorm brewing. I know you want to be here for Stephanie, but she is out of danger and you could do more harm than good if you have to talk to anyone before we can get together. I want you to come with me to my office. Gary can stay here, and as soon as Stephanie's status is clear, he will join us."

"But we didn't do anything wrong."

"You didn't?! You may see it that way, but I'm not sure everyone is going to share that view. At any rate, you need to be inaccessible until we have briefed you and brought you up to speed on a few things.

Though I am not happy with you right now, believe me this is the way to go. Trust me."

Gary interjected "Ted, I will agree to that if you promise that *all* discussions will hold until I get there."

"Agreed," Ted said.

"Who do you two think you are debating and deciding what I should do and what can be said and when? Are you kidding me?" an irritated Ebony asked.

"Ebony, you know I love you, right? And that you're my partner, so anything I do will be looking out for your best interest, right? So for once, don't argue, don't debate, and don't contemplate. Just do what we're asking you to do. In fact, I'm not asking. I'm telling you. Stop making our lives any harder than it has to be and go with Ted. *Now*!"

• • • • •

Gary sat at Ted's desk going over the dossier of information that Stephanie had pulled from Brandon's computer. Earlier Ted had spent almost an hour going over the same files. Every so often Gary would look up from the files, exchange a look with Ted, and continue reading. The more he read, the stormier the look on his face became. Finally unable to control himself any longer, he jumped up from the desk cursing and with a sweep of his arm scattered the papers around the room as he shouted "Months of blasted work down the drain just like that."

Ted grabbed his arms and said, "Come on, calm the hell down. What's done is done. We still can get this guy. I don't think he had a chance to leave the city yet."

"Do you believe this shit? Delaney, you are a great partner and a fantastic cop but sometimes I would love to wring your humping neck. Just answer me one question: Why? Why?" Gary asked.

"Why what?" Ebony asked.

"Don't you sit there and make believe you don't know why I'm pissed with you. You are a lot of things but stupid sure isn't one of them. You know *just* what time it is. Don't you—"

Ted interrupted "Gary, you have got to calm down man. This isn't helping anyone and is solving nothing. It's time we put our game faces on and move forward. Ebony, I think that Gary is overreacting a touch but he does have a valid question. Why didn't you just wait for us?"

"Like I told you, I was afraid that Barnett would get in the wind."

"Were you afraid that Barnett would run or did you want to be the one to bring him down?" Gary asked.

"That's an unfair question," Ebony argued.

"Is it? Can you honestly tell me that you were unaware that there was a possibility that the situation could turn violent?"

"I honestly thought that Barnett would go peacefully thinking that he could beat the system especially after he thought he had out-foxed the authorities for so long. He didn't know about all the evidence we had built up on him. What I think happened is that he must have really fallen for Stephanie because when he saw her and realized how she had played him, he kind of snapped."

"Need I point out that you were the one who brought Stephanie in?" Gary asked.

"And look how well that worked out. Look at all the information she got. Nobody else would have been able to get inside his guard and get so much access," Ebony argued.

Ted wanted to mediate and be the voice of reason between the two partners because a prolonged fight would benefit no one. "There were certain aspects of her involvement that did work very well, but that doesn't change the fact that you should have waited for us before going after Barnett. If it didn't accomplish anything else, I doubt that Barnett would have reacted violently if there were four of us there with our guns drawn on him. We would have been able to bring him in and our case wouldn't be ripped to shreds."

"The case isn't ripped to shreds. If anything, it's stronger than before. All we have to do is find Barnett."

"Which is going to be harder than it sounds."

"Damn it, Delaney, that's months of work down the drain."

"Do you think you have more time or energy invested in this case than me? I was working on this case for weeks before I brought either one of you in. Do you really think I wanted things to turn out this way?"

"Let's not panic yet. I don't believe our whole case has disappeared yet. With all our resources, it's only a matter of time before we catch him. Already the airports are closed to him," Ted said.

As Gary's anger abated a bit, he tried to put things in perspective and formulate a game plan. "But Ted, what happens to the case is only part of the problem. The first thing we're going to have to deal with is the NYPD. Let's look at it the way the officials and IAD are going to look at it. Ebony, you know how the Department works. They are going to say it is debatable whether Barnett was a flight risk, and since a crime wasn't being committed in your presence, where was the urgency to arrest him? Why didn't you get a warrant for his arrest before you went to arrest him? They could nail you to the cross if you arrested him under these circumstances and everything went smoothly. That is far from the case here. Now you are looking at a questionable arrest that resulted in an officer being shot and a suspect being at large, so you know the firestorm that could come out of this mess. What you don't know is that the reason we were so late getting to Barnett's office was that Ted called in a major favor to get a judge downtown to give him a warrant for Barnett's arrest.

"The way we're gonna play this is: our story is that you and Stephanie went to IMA to secure things while we went to pick up the warrant. Seeing that the authorities were closing in and that escape wasn't possible, Barnett tried to shoot his way out, shot Stephanie and escaped. I don't know if they will believe you, but they sure won't be able to prove it's not the truth. It's a weak case but it's not far from the truth.

"The reason why I'm so angry with you Ebony is: you cannot keep thumbing your nose at NYPD procedures and protocols. This time you put not only your career in jeopardy but Stephanie's as well. Ebony, we've talked about this before. You can't keep going on being a gunslinger and thinking there won't be consequences."

"Gary, the *only* reason I'm accepting this chastisement is because I'm as angry with myself as you are. I can understand your being angry but we're angry for two totally different reasons. You seem angry because I might have made the department upset with me. The hell with them. Until they start worrying as much about the rights of the women who were murdered as they worry about the right of the criminal who murdered them, I don't care about their getting mad. If Barnett's rights mean more to them than Tanya's or Kayla's or Heather's, then I say later for them. That's not a department I want to be part of and they can have my gun and shield right now.

"I don't feel good about Stephanie getting hurt, but thank God she's going to be all right. I am pissed because I may have hurt the investigation. Now Barnett is in hiding, and I'm sure he's trying to figure out how to get away. It's going to take some time to catch him, and until we do we can't go after his accomplices.

"I'm upset because he didn't do this alone. What happens to the husbands who reaped the benefits from these evil deeds? All those rich athletes who got their money back and, in some cases, custody of their kids, what happens to them? Do they just get away with this shit?"

"You're right, Ebony, and that's the main reason I'm so upset with you. I don't know how this affects the case but it can't help," Gary said.

"This does complicate things, but I don't think the case is dead. The case we were building up was against Barnett and we could have made the logical conclusion that if he was hired to kill the ex-wives, someone must have hired them. The only tangible evidence we have linking the husbands to the murders is the withdrawals from their accounts and the subsequent deposit in Barnett's account. The time frame between the deposits and the murders help some but I don't know if that's going to be enough," Ted said.

"But even if Barnett was caught and brought to trial, it would still be an enormous leap to include the husbands," Ebony said.

"I just got off the phone with the Federal Prosecutor and let me explain it to you the way he explained it to me. When we bring Barnett to trial, we will also try the husbands who we had the strongest cases against as well. We can charge them with conspiracy to commit murder and therefore used the same evidence that indicted Barnett against them. Now it's up to the discretion of the judge to determine whether he will even allow it. We can hope for a judge that sees things our way, but it's pretty much a crapshoot."

"Is the prosecutor even going to be willing to charge such celebrities?" Ebony asked.

"I don't know. He wants to meet with us and see the evidence himself before he decides who if anyone they are going to charge. He doesn't doubt that they did what we suspect them of but the issue is: does he think he can get a conviction. The strongest case would probably be against Larry Richardson, but he is already dead."

"So what are we doing to catch Barnett?" Ebony asked.

"We have an All Points Bulletin out with his picture plastered on the internet and television. We've closed down the airports and train stations. His picture is at border crossing to Canada and Mexico, so he can't get out the country. We have the homes of his employees staked out. Though he doesn't have a steady girlfriend, we have someone keeping an eye on the last three women he kept company with. He's keeping a low profile right now, but sooner or later he's gonna stick his head up and when he does, we got him," Ted said.

"I appreciate you guys having my back so tough. I know you guys are having a hard time believing me, but if I knew things would turn out this way, I would have done a lot of things different," Ebony said.

Ted said, "Things may get quite hectic and you might be put under a lot of pressure over the next few days until we catch Barnett. Even though we sound like we're pissed at you and have problems with the way you do things, there's one thing you must remember. You are one hell of a cop. You started this investigation alone and without any help and you brought down one of the most treacherous criminals I have ever encountered. Just in case I don't get a chance to tell you with all that going on, know that you did a great job and I would work with you anytime. I still think you are the best that the NYPD has to offer."

"I appreciate your saying that, but I don't think the NYPD will agree right now," Ebony said.

"When are they meeting with you?" Gary asked.

"In the morning."

"Do you want me to come with you?" Gary asked.

"No, I think this is one I better do by myself."

"Then I'll go to the hospital and spend some time with Stephanie. Why don't you come by when you're done," Gary suggested.

"I don't know how long they'll keep me but I'll swing by as soon as we finish."

· · · · ·

While dozens of police officers and Federal agents were scrounging the city searching for him, Barnett was still in the building where IMA was located. He figured that the NYPD would leave his office after a couple of hours, so he waited four hours then sneaked into his office and took food from their hospitality suite and a new cell phone then returned to his hideout. He didn't know how closely the police was following him so he figured he couldn't go to anyplace the authorities might be familiar with. He knew he couldn't go around any of his employees because the authorities would probably have someone watching their homes.

The best place to lay low for a couple of days until he could get out of the city would probably be at one of his sexual liaisons, of which he had numerous. Because he had so many, he didn't see any of them on a consistent basic and therefore there was little likelihood that the authorities knew of their existence. The best person would probably be Mia because she traveled so extensively doing her modeling thing that even he didn't know when she would be in New York. She usually called him when she was in New York City to see if he was available to get together. He called Mia and to his relief she was in New York so he made arrangements to come visit in ten hours. He wanted to wait a while to make sure any police in the vicinity of IMA gave up and cleared out.

· · · · ·

At 9:00 the next morning Ebony as per instructions arrived at One Police Plaza. She had to account for her actions in the Barnett arrest and shooting. She thought she was meeting with the Commissioner but he was replaced by his top assistant Ken Wiggins. "Thanks for being so prompt, Detective Delaney. We can begin, but Captain Riley and Lieutenant Melendez wanted to be present, so if it's all right with you we'll wait a few minutes for them?"

"That would be fine," Ebony replied.

"They must think a lot of you for both of them to want to add their input into the hearing."

"Or they want to make sure my goose is cooked," Ebony thought.

"We'll give them another fifteen minutes and then we'll start with or without them."

The fifteen minutes proved unnecessary, as the Captain and Melendez arrived in five minutes. They all went into a conference room where they were seated around an eight-foot circular table. Commissioner Wiggins placed a large file in front of him. "We're here looking into the matter of the attempted arrest of Brandon Barnett, his subsequent escape and the shooting of Stephanie Givens. I have read your personal file and your account and Detective Dansby' report of the incident, but I wanted to hear your account on the matter in person."

"I don't know what I have to add that's not in the report. Things pretty much went as it says," Ebony says.

"What I am trying to understand why you went in the first place," Wiggins said. "You were out on medical leave but you not only went with Detective Dansby and Special Agent Delaphine but you and Givens got there ahead of them."

"Detective Dansby and Agent Delaphine knew I had initiated the investigation into Barnett and they felt that after all my hard work I had a right to be in on the arrest. As to my getting there ahead of them, it took a little longer for them to get there from the judge's office as they got caught in traffic."

"And how did Officer Givens get involved? Was she visiting you and just went along for the ride?" Wiggins asked with more than touch of sarcasm.

"She was doing some undercover work against Barnett and had uncovered some vital information that was the final touches in the case against Barnett."

Turning to Captain Riley, Wiggins asked, "Is it your usual policy to allow regular officers to work undercover? I know that's not the procedure outlined by the Department."

Melendez responded, "Except in the case of special conditions. Officer Givens brought some physical attributes to play that made her a perfect undercover officer in this case. I decided to make an exception for her because of that. Plus, she is a very promising officer who I am sure will be promoted after the next promotional exam."

Wiggins was silent for a few moments while he contemplated the situation. Then he said, "Y'all seemed to have covered your tracks pretty well, but I must tell you that this whole story stinks to high hell. It feels like a bunch of renegade officers not following the rules and trying to get their own sense of justice."

"Detective Delaney can be a bit unorthodox, but she is no renegade or vigilante. She has been one of the most productive and efficient officers in the Department. It can be difficult dealing with her sometimes but there is no question that she is one fine detective."

"Didn't Brandon Barnett file a complaint against Detective Delaney on the grounds of sexual harassment?"

"He filed a complaint, but he did it as a smokescreen to try to divert attention away from his operation," Ebony said in her defense.

"Look at things from the perspective of the Department. We had two officers go to conduct an arrest without an arrest warrant: one who was on leave and the other who had no business involved in the investigation in the first place. This resulted in one of the officers being shot. There was no backup present at the time, which helped the suspect get away. Too many rules and procedures were broken to list them all. The press and the media are asking questions that we don't have reasonable answers to. Detective Delaney, I read you file and it is exemplary. I also see that your commanding officers hold you in high regards and believe me that speaks volumes. That is why we are not terminating you outright. But we can*not* have officers doing their *own* thing. The rules are in place for a reason, and we can't have officers choosing when to follow them. I can't put you on modified duty because you are already on leave so I am going to have to ask for your gun and shield. You are suspended for ten days pending my investigation into the case you have built against Barnett. If after reading the file more thoroughly I see that your actions were reasonable, maybe not well thought out but reasonable, I will rescind the order."

· · · · ·

In the early morning hours, about forty-five minutes before dawn, Barnett escaped from his refuge in the IMA building. He walked the silent, dark, deserted streets trying to draw as little attention as possible until he was about four blocks away and he could hail a cab. He had planned on taking the subway hoping that he could blend in with early morning work crowd but decided that his disheveled appearance might draw unwanted attention. Plus, his jacket had blood stains and maybe a bullet hole where he was shot in the shoulder. Due to the lateness of the hours he assumed that the cab driver might not be as attentive as in the daylight hours.

His good luck must have been holding up because he made it to Mia' without incident. She greeted him at the door dressed in a sexy, red lingerie but one look at Brandon's appearance and any plans she had for a night of intimacy went out the window. Every time she had seen Brandon he was impeccably dressed and groomed. This man who hadn't showered or shaved in two days was a new beast. When she saw the bruises on his face and the bullet wound, she fought down waves of panic and tried to get him to go to the hospital. When Brandon refused, she continued asking questions and Brandon knew he was going to have to provide some answers.

"Brandon, what happened to you? Who shot you? Did someone try to rob you or something?"

"Do you remember that female cop that ran up on us in the street? Well, she showed up at my office with more accusations and she set me up for a murder that she's trying to frame me with. When I tried to get her out of my office, things got violent and then she shot me."

"We've got to get you to the hospital and then tell her bosses what she's trying to do."

"Not just yet. I need some time to think and get my thoughts together. Then I will call my attorney."

"I think you need to call the police and report her to the police."

"Not yet. I have to see what lies she telling everyone first."

"Well, I think you need to at least go to the hospital."

Brandon knew that if he went to the hospital they would have to report the gunshot wound to the authorities so he said. "Let's clean out the wound first and then I can see how bad it is."

"But, Brandon, I think—"

"Damn it, Mia, will you stop telling me what you think and just do what the fuck I say," Barnett yelled. He was not accustomed to Mia offering her opinion and now wasn't the time to start. Mia went in the bathroom and returned with some antiseptic and bandages. Barnett noticed that she was pouting and he correctly assumed he had hurt her feelings. Normally Barnett didn't care about her feelings, but right now he needed a place to hideout and it wouldn't do to have her upset with him. That might make her even more unpredictable than she usually was. "I'm sorry I yelled at you. It's just that I'm tired and in a little pain."

"You cursed at me too." She was pouting so profusely she reminded Barnett of a twelve-year-old but he knew he needed to pacify her.

"I said I'm sorry, baby. Give me a chance to take care of this wound and get something to eat then I will make it up to you. Can you fix me something to eat?"

"Would you like a sandwich or I can order some Chinese food?"

"Whichever you prefer, both sound good to me."

A few hours later after he had eaten and taken some pain killers, Brandon tried to make love to Mia. Though he wasn't in the mood for sex, he figured that was the easiest way to get her to go to sleep and therefore leave him alone. Though he was physically and mentally exhausted, he was unable to fall asleep. All that had occurred over the last couple of days continued to torture him.

He intended to spend his down hours planning on how to escape from New York but despite his intentions all he could think about was

Amber and Delaney and how they had set him up. Everything negative that he had thought about women, these women had proven to him that he was right. As beautiful and classy as he thought Amber was, she had turned out to be nothing but a whore. Even though she never slept with him, she faked like she wanted to. She made him think she was into him, when all she wanted was to get close enough to him to get inside his defenses.

As to that Delaney bitch, she was sneaky and conniving and though he hadn't done anything to her, she had done everything she could to get him. She had many opportunities to go about her business and leave him to his but that wasn't what she did. She continued to harass and pursue him relentless like the ugly ass bulldog that she was. Even after she got away from those D.C. cats that he sent after her, it was the perfect opportunity to get out of his business but she still didn't get the message and leave him alone.

The hatred he felt for these two creatures, he didn't want to disgrace women further by calling them women, burned in him like a white-hot ember in a dying fire. Getting out of New York wouldn't be hard. He could buy Mia' car or have her buy one for him and he could drive down to South or Central America to some Third World country where he could live like a king. If he was honest with himself, he had to acknowledge that no amount of fine clothes, fine women or palatial estates would give him peace of mind as long as Amber and Delaney were alive. The only recourse for him was to kill them both and then get out of town.

He knew this was going to be no easy task because he didn't have the time or resources to thoroughly plan out the hits. He also didn't have Justice to back him up or kill one while he killed the other, but that was okay. This was one time he wanted the pleasure of killing them both himself. Slowly he started to plan how he would kill them. Mia had a straight razor that she used to shave him when he stayed over. He would use that to slit Amber's throat while she slept in a hospital bed. He would love to cut up Delaney, and he would take special pleasure from slashing her face repeatedly before killing her so she would need a closed casket funeral.

He had to be very careful with Delaney because she had already proved that she was pretty proficient with the martial arts. He had made the mistake of underestimating her once and that wasn't a mistake he would repeat. He decided that since dead was dead, he would shoot her first and then disfigure her face and body. There was no point in taking unnecessary chances.

Having decided on his course of action he started calling the hospitals to find out where Amber—actually, her name was Stephanie—was recovering. He already had Delaney's address from when he had sent the D.C. cats after her. Then he would force himself to get some sleep because it was still early morning and the work he had planned would work better as darkness was falling.

· · · · ·

For once, Ebony had decided to follow the instructions of her bosses, the hierarchy of the NYPD. Usually despite whatever they said she proceeded doing exactly what she planned to do. She had planned on devoting today and the next couple of days locating Barnett but since she was on suspension she was going stay away from the precinct and let them deal with the active cases on their own. She had always acted in a manner that many could accurately call a rebel because she felt that too many officers let the rules and protocol restrict how many crimes they could solve. But this was a case where her failure to follow rules and procedures had resulted in Stephanie getting shot and no telling how much damage she had done to their careers.

Stephanie was on the fast track toward detective and beyond, and now whenever the hierarchy looked at her chart this incident would glare at them. Ebony was full of remorse and regret over her poor judgment regarding Barnett. She had totally screwed the entire arrest up, and there was no way she could hide that truth from herself. She knew she was a better cop than that. She thought she had enough control over her emotions that she wouldn't let her desire for revenge keep her from doing her job. This time her lapse in judgment could have cost her friend her life. Maybe it was time for her to assess herself and the way she handled personal crises. Maybe the rules weren't always a bad thing. Protocols and procedures were formulated by people with experience and pretty good judgment. Maybe she needed to take a step back and look at the bigger picture and how she fit in that picture.

One of the strangest developments from her suspension was her waking up the morning after the meeting with the Commissioner and she had nothing planned and nothing to do. In case she thought about calling or visiting the precinct, she remembered what Lieutenant Melendez said when she went up to him after the meeting to thank him for his support and he said, "Delaney, right now I am totally pissed with you. I am so sick and tired of getting my ass chewed out because of you. Don't thank me because I didn't stand up for you in there because I thought you were right but because I defend all my people. I'm not gonna let the Commish or anyone else rake my people over the coals, but this time, Delaney, truthfully you deserved it. I'm not even gonna ask you what you were thinking with that stunt you and Givens pulled because if you gave me the wrong answer I might take out my gun and shoot you myself. You know I love you Delaney and you are one of my favorite cops but I do not want to see, talk to you or hear from you for *at least two weeks* or so help me God…"

"Okay, Lieu, I hear you."

"No, Delaney, I'm not playing with you. This was serious and we're gonna have a looooooonnnnng talk about your willingness to follow regulations and procedures. Seriously you need to do some serious soul searching about whether you want to continue being a cop and whether you want your legacy to be considered a renegade or rebel or the great cop that we both know you can be."

"Lieutenant, Mel—"

"No, I'm serious, Ebony. Don't talk now. I want you to spend some time thinking about what I said. I will speak to you in a couple of weeks." To further illustrate his point, he walked off without another word before she could respond.

That conversation after the comments of Deputy Commissioner Wiggins had a lot to do with her starting her day out a little depressed and with a multitude of things for her to think about. She was on suspension from the NYPD but that wouldn't stop her from going by Ted's and giving the Feds a hand in trying to locate Barnett. Maybe in a couple of days if he still hadn't been caught she would see if her expertise about Barnett could help expedite the chase.

Just a she was deciding between a long, luxurious bubble bath and a couple of hours at the dojo followed by that long, luxurious bubble bath, her phone rang and Mal invited her to brunch at her favorite bistro. Afterwards he said he would drop her off at the hospital. He had to come into the city to do some research at Columbia University's library but could spend a few hours with her before getting down to work. Last night he had picked her up at the hospital and then stayed at her house until after midnight as they talked about all that had happened and her opinion on how she mishandled things. Mal had done a great balancing act on not judging her on what she had done and still not letting her feel sorry for herself or beat herself up. After he left she went to bed again feeling lucky that he came into her life.

She accepted Mal's invitation because she felt that time spend with him was better than anything she could plan. She was still in that magical period with Mal where time stood still and no matter what was wrong in her world it didn't seem quite as bad when she was with him. Was she romantic or just enjoying the springtime of love? That was one of those questions she didn't want the answer to for fear she might lose whatever it was. Maybe the way to go would be: not to analyze things and just enjoy them.

When Mal found out about her suspension he decided he would use her time away from work to spend more time with her. Just the idea that she would get the opportunity to spend significant time with Malachi was the few reasons that Ebony thought that she might be able to deal with her suspension. One thing was becoming increasingly obvious to Ebony was that the more time she spent with Malachi, the more time she wanted to spend with him. For right now she was going to spend a couple of days just trying to relax and enjoy herself. In order to do that, she was going to have to put Barnett on the back burner and trying to block him from her thoughts.

After a delicious lunch, Malachi went with Ebony to visit Stephanie. The steady stream of visitors had slowed significantly during the early afternoon hours. When they came into the room she looked like an angel with the afternoon sun peeking in on her room, and she was propped up in bed with her dark brown hair fanned out across the white pillow. Someone must have brushed her hair because it wasn't gnarled or tangled like someone who had been in bed for several days. Either she was feeling a lot better, because her complexion had a rosy glow, or she was wearing makeup. She was gently drowsing so Ebony and Malachi was very quiet so they didn't wake her. After a couple of minutes Stephanie must have sensed their presence because she woke up.

"Hey you two, how are you doing?" Stephanie asked.

"We're doing fine. How are you feeling?" Ebony said.

"A little better. They had me up walking earlier and it kind of tired me out but other than being weak, I'm getting there. They said I can go home in a couple of days. They're just concerned that there was a little blood in my urine."

"Well, that can't be a good thing," Ebony said.

"It's such a small amount my doctor said it's nothing to be worried about. They're just being extra careful."

Malachi walked over and kissed Steph on the forehead as he said, "You're looking pretty good, Gorgeous. Do you need anything?"

"I have pretty much everything I need, but I would kill for some fried chicken, collard greens, and some yams."

"You must be feeling better to want normal food," Ebony noted.

"Stephanie, I would love to bring you whatever you wanted but if the nurses find out we brought you that stuff in, we would be put on the restrictive visiting lists," Malachi said.

"Yeah some friends you are. I bet you just came from getting something to eat?"

With a chuckle, Ebony confirmed "You're right we did."

"A sister has to survive on this horrible hospital food and you two are enjoying fine cuisine at one of New York's finer restaurant. There just ain't no justice in this world," Stephanie complained with a smile. Teasing her best friend always gave her serious pleasure. This gave her further proof that she was getting better and no measly gunshot wound was going to keep her down. "If you really loved me you wouldn't leave me to starve in here."

"First of all, I'm not leaving you in here. I'm spending the day with you. So you better get ready for a day of girl-talk and I might just take all your disability check playing gin rummy."

"That sounds good, and I welcome the challenge, but that still doesn't address my dining situation."

"Only because I like you and not because you deserve it but maybe I can convince Mal to go downstairs and sneak you in some food," Ebony said.

"Oh, so I get to be the bad guy huh? You two are going to get me banned from this hospital," Malachi joked.

"Not if you're careful," Ebony said.

"You two are so beautiful that no man in his right mind can tell both of you no. One of you is bad enough, but the two of you together is irresistible. Okay, what do you want?"

"I want a full soul food dinner but I'll take what I can get," Stephanie said.

"It might be real tricky trying to smuggle in a full dinner. Why don't you try to bring in a sandwich?" Ebony suggested.

"Okay, here's a plan. If I'm gonna break the rules, I'm not doing it by myself. Since you are my co-conspirators, you're going to do more than come up with the plan and leave it to me to do the dirty work. I'm gonna go down to Katz's Deli on Houston Street and bring you whatever kind of sandwich you want. Then I'll call Miss Ebony from downstairs and she can come and bring the sandwich up to you and I'll head on up to Columbia to finish my work. Now what kind of sandwich do you want?"

"Katz makes the bomb-diggity pastrami sandwiches, so I'll take one of those with extra pickles."

"Don't you think that may be a little too spicy for someone on a restricted diet?" Mal asked.

"Maybe you're right. How about a brisket of beef with extra gravy on wheat bread?" Stephanie said.

"Okay, now you're talking. We can do that," Mal said as he gave Stephanie a kiss on the forehead and gave Ebony a quick but warm kiss on the lips. "Okay, pretty one, I should be back inside an hour. Be on the lookout for my call."

After Malachi left, Steph turned to Ebony and said, "Okay, now that we're alone, tell me the real deal."

"About what? Me and Mal?"

"No, it's clear where things are headed with y'all. No, I mean what going on with the Department. Gary won't tell me. He just grimaces and shakes his head."

"Two weeks' suspension and maybe restricted duty when I get back."

"Ouch."

"Don't I know it. I guess I should consider myself lucky because it could have been worse. I think that if Melendez hadn't gone to bat for me they might have tried to terminate me."

"No, they wouldn't fire you because of this. You are too fine a cop for them to let you go over this."

"You're probably right, but they sure wouldn't hesitate to demote me."

"Now you might be right about that."

"And if they did, I'm not sure I could accept that. It wasn't like Barnett was innocent. I'm not letting them punish me but so much over their rules and regulations."

"So what are you going to do?"

"That depends on what they do. Right now the ball is in their court. If things pick up where they left off before the suspension, then I'll be the best cop I can. After all Barnett is still out there and I'm not gonna let him get away with shooting my girl. So you know I'm gonna get his ass. If they come with more disciplinary measures, then I'll decide what to do. Have they said anything to you?"

"Not yet, but Melendez told me there would be an investigation when I am discharged. He didn't go into details but it was clear they are upset about me doing unsanctioned undercover work. I think they don't want the bad PR of disciplining a wounded officer. We'll have to see what they have in mind when the other shoe drops."

"I think you should just worry about getting better. The ball's in their court. Neither one of us can do anything until we see what they do," Ebony advised.

"Yeah, you're right. There will be time enough to worry about that later. Hey, Ebony, what's the story with Gary?"

"What do you mean?"

"What's his deal?"

"If you mean as a cop, he's a damn good officer. He's as good as any officer on the force. If I was in a dogfight, he's one of the few officers I would want to have my back. I trust him completely. Why do you ask?"

"I was just curious."

"There has to be more to it than just that. What are you not saying?"

"No, it's not a big deal. It's just that he's been coming by almost every day and we've had a chance to really talk. He's seems pretty together."

"You know he's married with kids, right?"

"It's not like that. He just seems like a really nice guy."

"He is. He's not my type even if he wasn't married, but I love the hell out of him as a person."

"It's no big deal, but I think we are becoming good friends."

"That's probably a good thing."

As the afternoon sun faded into the beginning dusk the two friends sat, chatted and enjoyed each other's companionship. Close friends drew closer and they started to find one of the things that was missing from both their lives: a sister. Shortly after dinner, two officers from the precinct stopped by to visit followed by Gary and a few more officers. Seeing that Stephanie's regular stream of visitors had begun, Ebony gave her a hug and a kiss and headed home. Malachi had told her he would pick her up at the hospital but rather than stay with Stephanie while so many were trying to see her, she called Mal and told him she would meet him at her house and she headed home.

· · · · ·

417

Brandon was a smart if not brilliant man. He was smart enough to know that when you were planning actions emotions had no place in logical thoughts. He was trying unsuccessfully to control his emotions but right now it seemed his emotions were controlling him. He knew the smart thing to do would be to get out of the United States because there had to be a dragnet after him and it was only a matter of time before it started to close in around him. He had devised a plan where he would drive to Florida and then he would hire a private plane that Justice used to fly drugs into the country, to fly him to Brazil. Brazil seemed to have such a large and powerful underworld that he could probably disappear and wait a couple of months and then rebuild his life. He had enough money that even if he couldn't live like a king, he could probably have a pretty good life anyway.

This plan was possible and probably easy to implement. He could drive at night and stay in hotels during the day and if he used cash he wouldn't leave a trail the police could follow. It would take him two or three days to drive to Florida and he didn't have to worry about the pilot betraying him because they had too much dirt on the pilot. All he had to do was buy Mia's car off her and go. She was more than willing because he had promised her he would send for her when he got to Brazil.

What he could do was go to Brazil, liquidate his accounts in the Islands, and send for Justice. He and Justice had set up a way to contact each other through mistresses that no one knew they had, in case either of them or both had to flee New York. Most likely Justice was in a secret getaway he had bought years ago in Costa Rica, but Brandon wasn't worried because he knew he could locate Justice when he needed to. The way their operation worked, it probably wouldn't take them long to become major players in the Brazilian underworld.

There was only one problem: them two bitches. The hatred he had them was unlike anything he had ever known. It gnawed at him like an impacted tooth. He couldn't put them out of his mind. The betrayal, the manipulation, the deception and everything else they did made him feel like a complete fool. The smart thing would be to disappear rebuild his empire and then take out a contract to have both of them killed. Unfortunately, that would deny him the chance to look in their eyes as their lives are snuffed out. He has fantasized for hours of the many things he could do to them.

He would like to kidnap Amber and put her in a dungeon or prison for weeks where he could rape and mutilate her repeatedly, and when she was a shell of what she once was, he would douse her with gasoline and burn her until she no longer resembled a human being. He hated Delaney but not as much as Amber. She was clearly the mastermind behind their scheme, but Amber was the one who deceived him. Amber made him develop feelings for her so she could put him in a cage. What kind of person would do something like that? There was no doubt in his mind that they both deserved to die, and he had to be the person who made that happen. He had to regain his manhood and the only way he could achieve that was by killing them both.

As the day was ebbing and darkness approaching, he decided that he was not going to wait another minute but go out right now and kill at least one of them if not both. The police probably weren't looking for him in New York City because the logical thing would have been for him to flee the city right away. He had to alter his appearance and take advantage of the coming darkness. The police were looking for a slick businessman or a trained professional. He decided to go for a young, youthful look because they were looking for a man not a teenager.

He took out the clothes he had sent Mia after in case he needed to change his look. He put on some crumbled jeans and some retro Jordan Nikes. It would look more convincing if he didn't tie the sneakers but he tied them because he had to ready to run after he shot Amber. He put on a hoodie and put a baseball cap on his head to further obscure his face. He pulled the hood up to make his face even less visible. He put a Glock in his waistband and a .32 in the pocket of the hoodie next to the straight razor he took just in case he got a chance to get his revenge. Without any hesitation, he headed toward the hospital where Amber was being treated.

Chapter Eighteen

Barnett had used the telephone to find out which hospital Amber or Stephanie was an inpatient simply by calling patient information and surprisingly they even told him what room she was in. He knew it was important to be seen as little as possible so he avoided the elevator. He took the stairs up to Amber's floor and looked around. The floor was occupied and busy with people visiting patients and nurses and doctors going about their duties. He wedged the door partially open so that it didn't close and lock behind him.

He casually walked past Amber's room, as he knew where he was going but had no urgency in getting there. He glanced in Amber's room and saw her sitting up in bed but the room was full of visitors. There was no way he could get Amber right now. He returned to the staircase, where he decided to wait until her visitors went home. He might have to wait until visiting hours were over, but that would be all right if it helped him accomplish his goals.

After about an hour past, the cop who had come with Delaney to his office walked down the corridor with two other cops. The cop stopped outside the room and spoke with Delaney, who gave him a hug and headed to the elevator. The one he really wanted to destroy was Amber, but Delaney was a good consolation prize. He hurried to the lobby, but Delaney had already left.

He made up his mind that he would get both of them tonight. What he had to decide was whether to go upstairs and wait for Amber's guests to leave, kill her, and then go to Delaney's house and do her. The issue was how was going to get into Delaney's house. The best move would be to beat Delaney to her house and get her before she got in her house, then hurry back to the hospital and kill Amber before the cops realized his plan.

He tried to hail a cab, and it took three tries before he got one willing to go to Brooklyn. Now all he had to do was hope he arrived at Delaney's house before she got there.

· · · · ·

Ebony spent most of the afternoon with Stephanie and they had a great time. They talked, they joked and Ebony sat back and enjoyed watching Stephanie devour the sandwich Mal had brought her. After a couple of hours Stephanie slipped into a gentle slumber. Ebony started to leave so Stephanie could get her rest but she didn't want to leave without saying goodbye so she spent her time organizing her thoughts on where she thought Barnett might be. If she could use her knowledge about Barnett to give her insight into his whereabouts she could then trade that knowledge to regain some of the favor she had lost in the Department.

Coincidentally when she got up to stretch her legs she saw Gary and a couple of brother officers coming down the hall. She went and kissed Stephanie goodbye which woke her up. She was leaving as the other officers were coming and she hugged Gary and gently pulled him to the side.

"What's up, Delaney?" Gary asked.

"How are things going, partner?"

"They're going but we still haven't been able to find Barnett. We're pulling out all the stops so it's just a matter of time before we catch him. How are you holding up with your suspension and everything?"

"I'm dealing with it so far. I was out on sick leave so there's not a lot of difference."

"Ebony, you really pissed off a lot of people downtown. They might let you go with just the suspension but don't do anything further to upset them."

"I accepted the punishment even though you know it's nonsense. We had Barnett dead to rights."

"And it was some fine police work too, but you have to ask yourself one thing: Did you doing things the way you did cause Stephanie to be in this hospital?"

"I didn't put her here, Barnett did."

"Come on, Ebony, you know what I'm saying."

"I do, and I think about it every day. You know I have a lot of regrets, but I can't do anything about that now."

"You might want to think about doing things differently next time."

"I have thought about it, and I'm going to make some changes. I'm not so arrogant that I won't consider that there might be a better way to do things."

"And a safer way?"

"That too. Speaking of safer: what's the deal with you and Stephanie?"

"What do you mean?"

"I understand that you've been here every day."

"Yeah. I guess I feel a little responsible. If we had gotten there sooner, Stephanie probably wouldn't have gotten hurt."

"Are you sure that's all there is to it?"

Gary didn't respond he stood there with a strange look on his face that Ebony couldn't tell if it was guilt or embarrassment or what he was feeling. She realized she might have been in a sensitive area and it really wasn't her business. She said, "Just be careful. We don't want anyone getting hurt. You have a lot to lose."

"Don't worry, I have a handle on it. I'll keep things where they belong."

"Sorry if I was out of line, partner, but I care a lot about both of you. I'll go now and let y'all have your visit. I'll talk to you later."

After calling Malachi and telling him to meet her at the house, Ebony went downstairs and hailed a cab. She decided to surprise Mal and stop by Grimaldi's, and get some of his favorite brick oven pizza. She still should be able to beat him home and if she didn't, he wouldn't have to wait outside too long for her.

· · · · ·

They call Paris the "City of Lights" but a look at the twenty-first Century New York City makes one wonder if the proper city received the title. The brilliant, dazzling, and colorful array of the neon and electric lights of NYC especially Manhattan is amazing. Under the tutelage of Mayor Bloomberg, the transformation of the Broadway Times Square area from one of sleaze and porn shops to a tourist attraction that could rival any city in the world was completed.

Manhattan wasn't the only borough or section of New York that was well lit. Every borough had multiple business and entertainment sections, and the residential streets were well lit as well.

One of the things that drew Ebony to her block was the numerous trees that lined both sides of the block obscuring the light from the street lights and casting the sidewalks and entrances into shadows. To Ebony it was secretive and intimate and when she walked down the street late at night she felt wrapped in her own world. To Malachi, who was used to the broad and wide open spaces of Texas it was mysterious and foreboding if not downright dangerous. After reading and hearing about New York's criminal element, Malachi could imagine a mugger or rapist in every shadow. It wasn't that Malachi was scared. He was just cautious.

Remembering that criminals in New York frequently broke into cars in search of valuables and things they could pawn, Malachi made a mental note to make sure he brought Ebony's pistol with him upstairs. Like most good detectives, Ebony carried not just her service revolver but also a backup pistol. Knowing she had made numerous enemies, many of whom were still walking the streets, Ebony rarely left the house without being armed. Figuring it wasn't a good idea to bring a weapon into the hospital with all the security and equipment there, she left her gun in the car figuring she would retrieve it when Mal picked her up.

Malachi was able to find a parking space about a hundred feet from Ebony's apartment on the same side of the street. While he was waiting for Ebony, Malachi found himself dowsing off. He didn't know if it was a dream, his imagination or paranoia but he thought he saw a tall, dark figure lurking in the shadows about two houses from Ebony's place. He couldn't see well enough to determine whether the figure was really there.

Malachi hoped that Ebony got home soon because it had been a long day and he was tired. He still had to drive back to his place in New Jersey. His relationship with Ebony had not evolved to the point where he was a sleepover guest. He didn't think it was a good idea to drive such a long distance when he was this tired. He was strongly considering leaving but he was hesitant to do so because Ebony told him she was bringing a surprise and he didn't want to disappoint her. When he was just about ready to give up he saw a taxi turning onto her block and decided to wait to see if that was her.

· · · · ·

When Brandon arrived at Delaney' apartment, he wasn't sure whether he had beat her there. Her building looked dark and empty but he had never been to her apartment so he didn't know whether her windows faced the street or the rear of the building. Though the apartment on the street side looked dark and whoever lived inside either wasn't home or asleep, he might have been looking at someone else's apartment all together. He decided to wait a few minutes to see if she arrived and then he would try to get entrance into her building. Truthfully, he didn't even know if Delaney was coming home when she left the hospital, but he had come too far to give up without exhausting his options.

His instincts told him she was coming home and he had arrived before her. This feeling wasn't based on any facts and might have just been wishful thinking but his instincts had rarely failed him so he was gonna trust them one more time. There was a three-story brownstone two buildings away that seemed dark and empty as well, so he went and stood in the deep shadows by the street level or lower entrance. From this vantage point he not only couldn't be easily seen but he had a full view of the street and the entrance to Delaney's building.

He removed the gun from his waistband because he wanted to be ready if she did pull up to the building. He didn't intend to give her a chance to say anything or do anything. He was just going to walk up to her like a stranger passing her by on the street, and before she realized it was him, he was going to empty a full clip in her face. He stroked the pistol in a sensuous, almost sexual way as he visualized how he would kill her. He had never wanted to kill anyone as badly as he wanted to destroy Delaney. In fact, he rarely wanted to kill anyone before this incident. Usually when he had killed before or planned someone demise it wasn't because he took any pleasure from the act, it was just a mean to an end. Killing was a way to escape or to get paid. Of course, he killed his uncle but that beast deserved to die just like Amber and Delaney.

Amber was that even her name. Didn't Delaney call her Stephanie or something like that? Amber was probably a phony name just like everything else about her was fake, phony, and a lie. Did it really matter? She had to die no matter what her name was. He would wait an hour for Delaney so he could finish his business with her, but whether he met up with Delaney or not, as soon as visiting hours were over and the hospital quieted, he was going back to visit Amber one last, final time. The mere thought of what he was going to do to Delaney and Amber was exciting him in ways he didn't imagine and he felt his loins stirring. Subconsciously he started to rub and stroke his semi-erect member.

He was so absorbed with his ruminations about Amber and Delaney that he almost didn't notice the taxi pull up to Delaney's. He felt a surge of wicked glee as he noticed her getting out of the cab. It seemed as if fate was deciding it was his destiny to kill her. Her arms were full so she would have no chance to defend herself before it was far too late. He stepped out of the shadows and purposely started walking toward her.

Ebony sensed him coming toward her and looked up as she tried to identify the foreboding figure walking toward her. She was a little tired because her recovering body wasn't accustomed to the amount of activity that she had engaged in today. Maybe because she was looking for and thinking about Malachi or maybe because of the fatigue but her street and battle tested danger sensors hadn't chimed in yet. There was something hauntingly familiar about the figure, and she was trying to place where she knew him from.

When the figure was less than ten feet away, he raised his head and Ebony looked him directly in the eyes. She was shocked to realize it was Brandon Barnett. The brazenness that he not only hadn't fled the city, but he was actually here on her block, stunned her. Her instinctive reaction was to drop her packages and beat him to the draw. Then she remembered that she had turned in her service revolver and had left her back-up in Malachi' car. Her mind was working at a thousand beats a second but still she couldn't come up with an alternate plan.

He was too far away to disable him with a kick, and at this distance even the most incompetence marksman couldn't miss. Refusing to give in to this despised nemesis she continued to try to find a way even as Barnett raised the pistol and took aim at her. Suddenly she heard a familiar voice yell, "Ebony, Get Down!" With no other recourse than to obey, she dropped the wine, threw the pizzas at Barnett and dropped to the ground.

· · · · ·

As Malachi saw Ebony get out of the cab, he was relieved that he didn't have to make the decision of leaving to go home or waiting for Ebony. Seeing that her hands were full and she was struggling with her packages, he got of his car to help her. Out of nowhere he saw that figure that he thought was standing in the shadows of that brownstone come out and head toward Ebony. There was something about his presence that was ominous and threatening. Mal started to jog to intervene what he thought might be a mugger. Suddenly the figure raised what looked like a gun and pointed it at Ebony.

Malachi was a Texas boy and had been shooting rifles and guns before he was old enough to ride a horse by himself. He raised Ebony's pistol and simultaneously clicked off the safety as he shouted a warning to Ebony. He figured the mugger was some teenage kid who had gotten in over his head and was in for more trouble than he realized. He couldn't shoot him without a warning so he screamed, "Yo, man, put the gun down!"

· · · · ·

Barnett was as an experienced street warrior as you could find in the hardened jungle of New York City, but so much happened so fast that for a second even he didn't know to do. Suddenly there was a man shouting, running toward him and pointing a gun at him. Then Delaney was on the ground and there was a crash and white boxes headed toward his face. The smart thing to do would be to kill the new protagonist first and then shoot Delaney. But this was Delaney! The bitch who had ruined his life. The bitch who had him and Justice running for their lives. The bitch who had sent that other tramp to set him up. Rage welled up in him and mixed with bile as if he had eaten rancid pork and he felt nauseated at the thought that she might get away.

Predator was so effective because he remained cool and collected even in the most stressful situation. That man was gone. Barnett's emotions allowed him only to kill, kill, kill that wretched bitch in front of him. He raised his gun and fired a shot at Ebony. Maybe because of his anguish, maybe because of the darkness on the street or maybe because of all that was happening but he missed. He took a deep breath to compose himself and took aim as he prepared to shoot again. He heard a bang and felt a white-hot fire start in the center of his chest. He dropped his gun as he struggled for the breath that was avoiding him. He needed his gun if he was going to finish his task but the heat was merging with oncoming waves of blackness. And he collapsed.

· · · · ·

Malachi saw that not only wasn't the mugger following his commands but he took a shot at Ebony. He had never killed anyone before and it was something that he never thought he would do but he had no other choice. He couldn't allow some punk to take the precious Ebony from him. Their love was just beginning. He wouldn't let it end. Not this way. Not now. Without a moment's hesitation, he remembered Jasper's instructions and squeezed off two shots. Both of which caught the man in the center of his torso.

The man dropped his gun, grabbed his chest, and collapsed into a heap on the pavement. Malachi sprang to Ebony's side intending to check if she was okay and cover her should the mugger or anyone with him tried to pose an additional threat. As he swept Ebony up in his arms, he looked at the mugger. He could tell from the way his body laid that he was never getting up again. He looked around but didn't see any other threat.

"Ebony, are you okay?"

"Yeah, I'm fine. Help me up."

As he gently pulled her to her feet he asked, "Are you sure you're okay?"

"Yeah, he missed." She felt a little queasy to her stomach when she realized how close to death she had come and that Malachi had saved her life. Then the gravity of the situation dawned on her, and she said, "Malachi, give me the gun and go home."

In disbelief, Mal asked, "What?"

"I need you to give me the gun and go home now."

"What are you talking about? I'm not leaving you."

"That was Brandon Barnett, and the cops are gonna be here soon. They are gonna ask a lot of questions I don't like the answers to. They might arrest you, but I *am* a police officer who was attacked. Nothing will happen to me."

"I don't care. Let them arrest me, but I ain't leaving you."

"Mal, please. Can't you see I love you and I'm looking out for you? I can't risk you going to jail even if they find you innocent later. I need you to go. Now."

"Ebony, I love you, and I'm not leaving you."

"Well, then at least give me the gun and wait in your car until after the police come. Can you do that?"

"As long as I can see you, I'll wait in the car."

"Well, go quickly. I think we got my neighbor's attention. Call Gary on his cell and tell him I need him and to get here as soon as he can."

Reluctantly Malachi returned to his car though his gaze stayed upon Ebony. Less than ninety seconds past before neighbors from across the street came out of their house. "Are you okay?" they called.

Ebony replied. "Yeah, there's been a shooting. Call 911."

CPSIA information can be obtained
at www.ICGtesting.com
Printed in the USA
BVHW03s2240220518
517093BV00008B/66/P